MW00773415

BLOOD MOON

Novels by Sandra Brown

Out of Nowhere
Overkill
Blind Tiger
Thick as Thieves
Outfox
Tailspin
Seeing Red
Sting
Friction
Mean Streak
Deadline
Low Pressure
Lethal
Mirror Image
Where There's Smoke
Charade
Exclusive
Envy
The Switch
The Crush
Fat Tuesday
Unspeakable
The Witness
The Alibi
Standoff
Best Kept Secrets
Breath of Scandal
French Silk
Slow Heat in Heaven

BLOOD MOON

SANDRA BROWN

NEW YORK BOSTON

This book is a work of fiction. Names, characters, places, and incidents are the product of the author's imagination or are used fictitiously. Any resemblance to actual events, locales, or persons, living or dead, is coincidental.

Grand Central Publishing
Hachette Book Group
1290 Avenue of the Americas, New York, NY 10104
grandcentralpublishing.com
@grandcentralpub

First Edition: March 2025

Grand Central Publishing is a division of Hachette Book Group, Inc. The Grand Central Publishing name and logo is a registered trademark of Hachette Book Group, Inc.

Library of Congress Cataloging-in-Publication Data

Names: Brown, Sandra, 1948- author.
Title: Blood moon / Sandra Brown.
Description: New York ; Boston : Grand Central Publishing, 2025.
Identifiers: LCCN 2024033429 | ISBN 9781538742983 (hardcover) | ISBN 9781538743010 (ebook) | ISBN 9781538768778 (large print hardcover)
Subjects: LCSH: Louisiana—Fiction. | LCGFT: Thrillers (Fiction) | Detective and mystery fiction. | Romance fiction. | Novels.
Classification: LCC PS3552.R718 B56 2025 | DDC 813/.54—dc23/eng/20240724
LC record available at https://lccn.loc.gov/2024033429

ISBNs: 9781538742983 (hardcover), 9781538743010 (ebook), 9781538768778 (large print pbk.)

Printed in the United States of America

LSC-C

Printing 1, 2024

BLOOD MOON

Chapter 1

Saturday, March 8

The poignant lyrics of "Desperado" filtered through the cobwebs crocheted across the scratchy speaker in the ceiling.

The ballad seemed a fitting soundtrack for his entrance.

Two steps inside, he stopped and stood silhouetted in the wedge of midday sunlight that shrank as the tufted leather door swished closed behind him and returned the barroom to the simulated nighttime in seedy watering holes on every continent.

This one hunkered near the line that separated Larouche Parish from Terrebonne. Neither parish would be proud to claim it, but the liability fell to Terrebonne. There wasn't a town close enough to have any significant attachment to the place, but it shared a zip code with Auclair.

He took off his sunglasses, folded the stems, and hooked one of them into the placket of his chambray shirt above the third pearl snap.

The bartender stopped thumbing through a magazine that appeared to have been thumbed through frequently, took his customer's measure, then said, "Is it raining yet?"

"Not yet, but I wouldn't bet against it by nightfall." He walked over to the bar and mounted a stool.

"Cold beer?"

"Coke, please. Lots of ice."

"Coming up."

Then, from the outer reaches of the room: "Dude comes into a bar and orders a Coke. Ain't that what Dairy Queens are for?" The remark elicited a round of guffaws.

The newcomer at the bar looked over his shoulder toward the row of billiard tables. The only one currently in use was lighted by a fixture suspended from the ceiling. It hung low above the felt and shed light on a grungy foursome.

The one who'd scoffed at him was propped against the wall, arms crossed over his chest, knee raised, left foot flat against the concrete blocks. He was grinding a matchstick between his teeth. Another was idly chalking a pool cue. The other two were leaning against the table, slurping from their bottles of beer.

All were eyeing the "dude" with insolent challenge.

But after being on the receiving end of a prolonged and unflinching stare, the spokesman of the four anchored the matchstick in the corner of his mouth beneath a droopy mustache, let his foot slide to the floor, pushed himself away from the wall, and said to the one preparing the cue, "You gonna shoot, or what?" Still muttering with amusement among themselves, they resumed their game.

The bartender, having watched the exchange with

interest, opened a can of Coca-Cola and poured it over a glassful of ice. "Here you go."

"Thanks."

"Bartender, add that to my tab, please."

She was seated in a dim corner booth, chosen because it had an unobstructed view of the entrance, allowing her to see him when he arrived, which she'd wished to do. She'd been early; he'd been right on time.

She'd observed everything that had transpired without having been observed herself. The bit he'd done with his sunglasses had looked casual enough, something one would naturally do when coming from daylight into a darker interior. But she deduced that it had also given him time to let his eyes adjust, take in the scene, and get an idea of the bar's layout and what he was walking into. She'd escaped his notice only because her booth was in a section of the bar where only meager light relieved the gloom.

As he'd walked from the entrance over to the bar, his tread had been loose-limbed, his demeanor nonchalant. His exchange with the bartender, although not effusive, had been friendly enough. But it had taken nothing more than a look from him to squelch the derision of the men playing billiards.

At the time, he'd been facing away from her. But she knew that he must have fixed on them the calculating gaze that now zeroed in on her as he picked up his drink and walked over.

When he reached the booth, he tipped his head toward the vacant bench. "This seat taken?"

She shook her head.

He slid in across from her. They appraised each other with undisguised interest but without comment until he said, "Thanks for the Coke."

"You're welcome."

Dunking the drinking straw in and out of her glass of club soda, she continued her assessment of him. He'd gone to no trouble whatsoever to impress her. He was unshaven and had bed head. His shirt was wrinkled and worn tail out.

His jeans were clean but faded, worn to near white at the knees. They had a hole in the left front pocket and stringy hems. They seemed to be one with him, fitting his form and sauntering tread too well to have been purchased that way, already fashionably distressed. The aging had come from actual wear. Years of it.

"You're not what I expected," she said.

"No? Except for the getup, you're exactly what I expected."

"Based on what?"

"Your voice over the phone."

"What about it?"

"Butter wouldn't melt in your mouth."

She stopped fiddling with the drinking straw and let it sink into the glass. Sitting back against the booth and crossing her arms, she subjected him to a lengthier and even more disapproving once-over that terminated on his implacable stare, from which she didn't back down. "What did you mean by 'except for the getup'?"

"The LSU ball cap? You've never worn it before. It doesn't fit your head, it's way too new, and it doesn't go with your bespoke purse." He glanced down at it lying beside her on the bench. "Between those two accessories, I'm betting the LV is more you."

She didn't acknowledge that he was right. "You're not wearing a badge."

He didn't comment on what was obvious.

"Do you *have* a badge?" she asked.

"In a wallet."

"Photo ID?"

"In a wallet."

"On your person?"

"Yes."

"Would you show them to me, please?"

"No."

"*No?*"

"No."

"Why?"

"Well..." He folded his arms on the table and leaned in, lowering his voice. "First off, you asked me—no, *instructed* me—not to show up here looking like a cop. Wearing a badge sort of gives that away. And anyhow, I never wear my badge to be seen.

"Secondly, the pack of hyenas shooting stick? I know that the DEA is on their tail. Now, if they saw me flashing you a badge and ID, they'd peg me as some brand of law officer, and that would likely result in an outbreak of trouble. I know damn well they're armed; I just don't know what kind of firepower they're carrying, and finding out could lead to bloodshed.

"Thirdly, the bartender has given up his *MotorTrend* to polish a shot glass. In a joint like this, that level of cleanliness is uncommon if not downright nonexistent. He's pretending not to watch us, but he hasn't missed a thing. I don't know whose side he would be on if a gunfight erupted. If one did—and I can almost guarantee it—you could get hurt, and I would hate that."

"Your conscience would never recover?"

"No, my career. For a while now, my superior has been looking for an excuse to fire me. If you, an innocent bystander, got injured or killed during a shootout initiated by me, it would be more excuse than he needed to give me the boot.

"All that to say that I'm going to keep my ID wallet in my pocket, my weapon under my shirttail, play it cool, and after we conclude this—whatever this is—I'll be sure to get the license number of that redneck pickup parked out front, which I'm almost certain belongs to those fentanyl pushers and not to you, then notify the DEA where they're hanging out.

"So, for everyone's safety and well-being, let's just go on pretending that this meeting is random, that you're a neglected housewife who's slumming in Auclair, Loooziana. You came in here trolling for an afternoon rodeo. I happened in, you looked me over, and figured I'd do."

By the time he'd finished, she was seething, but she tried to appear as unfazed as possible. "Your back is to the bartender. How do you know what he's doing?"

"He's reflected in the blacked-out window behind your right shoulder. No, don't turn to look. Trust me." He picked up his glass and took a long drink, then barely smothered a burp.

She tamped down mounting irritation, which would get her nowhere with him. But she couldn't resist saying, "I came here with an open mind, willing to give you the benefit of the doubt, but you actually are an arrogant prick, aren't you?"

"Hey," he said, looking affronted, "if you're angling for a rodeo—"

"I most certainly am not."

"Well, who invited who? For reasons still unknown, by the way." His eyes skittered over her. "I do have the right woman, don't I? If your name isn't Beth Collins, then—"

"It is."

"Whew. I was about to get embarrassed." With no attempt to suppress a grin, he slouched against the back of the booth.

To hell with irritation getting her nowhere. She let it show. "You're enjoying yourself?"

"A little, yeah."

"I assure you that this isn't fun and games."

"No?" He shrugged. "Okay. When are we going to get around to why you wanted to talk to me? I'll admit to being curious. Especially now that I've seen you."

She didn't dare rise to *that* bait. "You came here out of curiosity alone, then?"

"Honestly? No. I figured I owed you the courtesy of showing up because you pronounced my name right. Not Bow-ie like the rock star. Boo-ie like the knife."

"Well, Mr. Bowie like the knife, in all seriousness, thank you for agreeing to see me without an explanation and on short notice. Let's start over, shall we?" She paused. He gestured for her to continue. "The matter is important, and I'm on a deadline."

He lost the smirk and studied her for a moment. The intensity with which she'd spoken seemed to have penetrated and captured his interest. At least he no longer looked like it was putting a strain on him not to laugh at her.

"All right, Ms. Collins, I'm here. I came at your request like I told you I would. What's this about?"

She forced her shoulders to relax, mostly because the bartender, who was in her line of sight, *was* observing them as he polished a shot glass. She forced herself to smile at the disheveled man sitting across from her, then coyly lowered her eyes, as though flirting. Under her breath, she said, "Yesterday, did you tell anyone in the police department that you'd spoken to me?"

"No."

"Or that we were meeting today?"

"No."

"When you left the police station to come here—"

"It's my day off. I came straight from home." After a beat, "Straight from bed."

She knew he'd added that to see how she would react, so she didn't react at all. "Did you tell *anyone* you were meeting with me? Your wife?"

"Don't have one."

"Oh." Her surprised reaction to that was involuntary. "You did."

"Not anymore." His brows drew together to form a deep cleft between them. "How the hell—"

"I was given some background information on you."

"By who?"

Whom, she thought. But she didn't correct him or give him a direct answer. "I also did some research of my own."

His stare practically pinned her to the back of the booth. Without looking away, he reached for his drink and took a swallow. When he set down his glass, he said, "What are you up to?

We're a mediocre department in a modest city. And that's a generous description. If you've got trouble, why call us?"

"You. I called *you*."

"What makes me special?"

She dampened her lips and lowered her voice. "The case of that young woman who vanished in November of 2022."

He clenched his jaw. His gray eyes turned flinty. He assumed the menacing aspect of a cobra about to strike.

Even though she'd anticipated hostility, his reaction was acute and intimidating and caused her to lose her footing. "Her name—"

"I know her name."

She glanced at the bartender, who was still polishing that damn glass. When she came back to John Bowie, she spoke sweetly through a phony smile. "Our observer may not be able to hear what you're saying, but he'll pick up on your angry tone as well as your body language, which is less than convincing that you're hoping for a hookup."

He blinked as though to reboot the law officer in himself. "The playacting is important?"

"Yes. For now."

Taking her at her word, he relaxed his posture and leaned forward again. "Then I'd better up my game." He reached across the table, took her hand, and stroked the palm of it with his thumb. "How's this? Better?"

She curbed the impulse to jerk her hand away from his, resisted the implication of the stroking, and denied the flutter it caused beneath her navel. Instead, she gave him a demure smile and reclaimed her hand with feigned reluctance.

He drained his Coke and shook a pebble-size ice cube

into his mouth. He crunched it while watching her with mistrustful intensity. "What does the Crissy Mellin case have to do with you?"

"It became a national news story."

He snorted with bitterness. "Tell me something I don't know."

"You were deeply involved in the investigation."

"I already know that."

"Your name was frequently mentioned in the news coverage."

"Again, something I know."

"But you declined to be interviewed."

"Not for the bloodsuckers' lack of trying."

She hesitated and took a breath. "Although you were never on camera, you were referenced and often quoted. A snippet here, a phrase there, and it soon became obvious that you were dissatisfied with your department's handling of the investigation." She paused, then asked, "Was your outspokenness the reason your superior has wanted to fire you?"

"That's one reason."

"There's another?"

"My dick is bigger than his, and that galls him something terrible. Not that we've ever actually compared them, but, you know."

She kept her expression droll. "Ah, intentional vulgarity. Used in the hope that I'll be offended, will snatch up my bespoke handbag, and storm out."

"Don't let me keep you, Ms. Collins."

"Sorry, Mr. Bowie. You'll have to do better than that."

Brow still furrowed and stern, he leaned in farther and

lowered his voice to a near growl. "I'm tired of this back-and-forth. Why did you invite me to this out-of-the-way, low-rent dive? In the middle of the afternoon. On my day off. Like I don't have anything better to do than reminisce about something I'd rather eradicate from memory?"

His eyes narrowed and took a leisurely visual tour of her. When their eyes reconnected, he gave her a lazy smile. "Unless you really are hankering for a rodeo. Maybe with a man who has handcuffs, a badge, and a pistol? Is that it? That's a big turn-on for some women. You'd be surprised by how many."

"I wouldn't be in the least surprised."

"Then if that's the case," he drawled, "let's move it along."

Her cheeks went hot. She bit back an angry retort, reached for her glass, and took a sip from the straw. She returned the glass to the table with a thump. "I called because *Crisis Point*, the true crime network show for which I work as a producer, is soon to air an episode covering the Crissy Mellin case."

His eyes took on that fearsome glint again as he hissed, "Son of a bitch. When the crew was down here filming, it created a big stir. But it's been a while back. I hoped it had been deep-sixed."

"No."

"And you're one of them?"

She hesitated, then nodded.

"Bye-bye."

Before he could scoot to the edge of the booth, her hand shot out and grabbed his forearm, anchoring it to the tabletop. "You were the only key player on that case who refused to cooperate with our production team. You took no one's call, and when someone did get through, you hung up on them the moment they identified themselves.

"You were unshakable against our senior host, renowned for his persistence and powers of persuasion. You wouldn't grant him an interview or even a private conversation. He's the one who told me that you were an arrogant prick." Her heart was thumping. She took another breath. "I reached out in the desperate hope that you would talk to me."

He looked down at her hand, which was clutching his arm just below the rolled cuff of his sleeve. "I don't want to arm-wrestle you. Especially with an audience. Let go."

"Hear me out."

"Let. Go."

"Please, Mr. Bowie. It would be a terrible mistake for you not to discuss—"

"My terrible mistake was being lured by an urgent and sexy female voice on the phone. Gotta hand it to you. You laid an enticing trap."

"Give me two minutes."

"Thanks again for the Coke."

He moved to leave. She gripped his arm tighter. "Two minutes."

A hard shake of his head. "I'm out of here."

"Thirty seconds. Please. Thirty seconds and you won't have wasted the trip out here." When she sensed his hesitation, she squeezed his arm. "Half a minute. Please."

He chewed on the inside of his cheek as he thought on it, then said, "Tell me something I *don't* know."

She exhaled and whispered, "It's going to happen again."

Chapter 2

Another?"

As the bartender came out from behind the bar and made his way over to them, John had seen his reflection in the blackened window. But Beth Collins, entirely caught up in their conversation, seemed to have been unaware of his approach until he spoke, and then she flinched.

John leaned away from her, smiled up at the bartender, and reached for the fresh drink. "Thanks, man. How'd you guess?"

"Well, from the look of things, one wasn't gettin' it done." A chuckle rumbled from his barrel chest. "What about you, sweetheart? Something stronger this round?"

She tensed in reaction to being addressed as "sweetheart" but responded with a smile and a cool, "No thank you." Like butter wouldn't melt in her mouth.

"In fact..." She opened her pricey purse and took out a twenty-dollar bill, as though she'd planned to have it at the ready rather than pay with a credit card. "This should cover our drinks. Keep the change."

"'ppreciate it." The bartender took the bill from her, and, as he lumbered away, socked John on the shoulder, saying under his breath, "Good luck, buddy."

When he was out of earshot, she asked, "Do you think he'll remember me?"

Was she kidding? If she'd been wearing a diamond tiara in place of the baseball cap, she couldn't have looked more conspicuous in this setting. Despite the cap and plain white t-shirt, everything about her screamed *class*.

True, he'd only seen her from the waist up, but the t-shirt was made of stretchy stuff, and if the bottom half of her came even close to being as shapely as the top, he was thinking that an hour or two rodeo in a hasty-tasty motel wouldn't be a bad way to play out the rest of the afternoon.

So long as they didn't converse.

In answer to her question, he said, "Yeah, I think he'll remember you. Why is that a problem? Does it throw a wrench into your sabotage scheme?"

"It's not a scheme."

He gave her a look.

She set both hands flat on the table and leaned across it. "Didn't you understand what I said?"

"I understood perfectly. I also understand that this was an ambush. I hate myself for falling for it, but now I'm leaving."

He glanced behind him toward the four at the billiard table and saw right through their seeming disregard of them. Of her in particular. He muttered a curse under his breath and sighed as he came back around. "Tuck that damn purse under your arm. Tight. Don't make eye contact. Got it? Not with anybody. And don't even think of arguing with me about this."

He scooted out of the booth, reached down and took her by the elbow, and, when she was standing, steered her toward the exit. The bartender sent him a wink and a thumbs-up.

As they walked past the grungy group, the mustachioed one with the attitude and a matchstick in his mouth flipped him the bird. John ignored it, pulled open the heavy door, and guided the woman outside.

Rain clouds were gathering, so, although the temperature was seasonally cool, the atmosphere was damp with the promise of precipitation.

She worked her elbow free of his grasp and pointed toward a black sedan. "Figured," he said.

Besides his SUV and the sedan, the only other vehicle on the gravel lot was a pickup truck with a bashed-in grill and two bullet holes in its rusty rear fender. He walked Beth Collins over to the sedan.

After she unlocked it with a fob, he reached around and opened the driver's door for her. "Nice wheels. All the extra options."

"I don't know what half of them are for. It's a rental I picked up at the airport."

"When?"

"Yesterday."

"You flew in from New York?" That was an easy deduction. The show she worked for broadcast from there.

"Yes."

"You don't sound like New York."

"I grew up in this area. Straight out of LSU I moved up there."

"Where you trained to trick people into clandestine meetings. Or did you need training for that? Did the television network teach you how to do it effectively, or did it come naturally to you?"

Looking perturbed, she turned her head aside to watch an eighteen-wheeler on the highway blow past. Coming back to him, she said, "Mr. Bowie—or should I call you Detective Bowie?"

"How about John?"

Without calling him anything, she said, "I came down here specifically to talk to you."

"Well, that's too bad. Because I'm not talking. Tell your slick host that calling me an arrogant prick gives pricks a bad name. Tell your bosses that I was rude, lewd, misogynistic. Tack on whatever unflattering adjectives you want. I don't give a damn about their opinion of me. In fact, the lower it is, the better I like it."

To her credit, she kept her cool. "Aren't you the least bit curious to hear why I think that what happened to Crissy Mellin will happen again, that there'll be another victim?"

"Of course it'll happen. A hundred times. A thousand times. Regrettable. Sad. Tragic. Violence against women is a malignancy eating away at the fabric of most so-called civilized cultures. But those crimes will be somebody else's problem. Not mine."

"But it will be your problem. That's what I'm trying to tell you."

If the bartender hadn't interrupted, he might have asked her to elaborate, or at least asked, *What the hell?* But he'd lost the opportunity, and he was now glad he had, because he wasn't stupid.

He'd spent the past three and a half years since the Mellin case walking a razor's edge, trying to avoid embroilment of any kind. If he gave an ounce of credence to what Beth Collins had said and pursued it by even one baby step, it could easily tip the scales of the balancing act he had going with Thomas P. Barker, his boss and nemesis. Their antagonistic relationship was none of her business, and filling her in on it could stimulate further conversation, which he would avoid as fervently as he would avoid leprosy. But despite what he'd said about his disregard for the opinion of others, he didn't want her to leave remembering John Bowie as a complete and utter asshole.

He shifted his weight, crunching the gravel beneath his boots. "Listen, Ms. Collins—"

Rather than listen, she interrupted. "The upcoming episode establishes that Crissy Mellin's abductor is dead."

"He fucking *is*. I cut his body down."

"What if that young man wasn't the culprit?"

"Oh. I see where you're going. We got the wrong guy." He scoffed. "The one we found hanging in his jail cell."

"Yes, that one."

"And the real bogeyman is still out there?"

"It's possible."

"Uh-huh."

Agitated, she said, "How can you do that?"

"Do what?"

"Be so blasé. I just told you something that should rattle you. You've dismissed it out of hand. Like this isn't extraordinary. Like it happens to you on a daily basis."

"It does. We and every law enforcement agency in the world get dozens of crank calls every day. Crazies call with conspiracy theories or to report—"

"Never mind." She turned her back to him and climbed into the car. "I began with you because you were quoted in one article as saying that the investigation was handled 'hastily.' Apparently, during the years since, you've had a change of heart. I'm sorry to have bothered you." She reached out to pull the door closed.

"Wait a minute, wait a minute." Knowing that he would probably kick himself later for what he was about to do, he grabbed the door above the window and held on. They played tug-of-war with it. He outlasted her and continued to hold the door open while she glared up at him from the driver's seat.

She placed the heel of her hand over the horn icon on the steering wheel. "Let go of the door or I'll lay down on this."

He hitched his head toward the building behind him. "The scumbags come to your rescue, and after they vanquish me, what then? You're left alone with them to have their wicked way with you? I don't think so."

She expelled a breath. "Please let go."

"Why the subterfuge?" Asked out of context, the question got her attention. She stopped trying to close the door.

"What?"

"When you called yesterday, why didn't you tell me straight off you were from that show?"

"You would have hung up on me."

Correct answer. But as she'd said it, her gaze had shifted from looking directly at him to the third snap of his shirt. He spotted a lie. At least a half lie. "And?"

She didn't say anything.

He lowered his pitch and volume. "And?"

She opened her mouth to speak, but then closed it. Her shoulders slumped, her head dropped forward. The baseball cap fell off, and handfuls of streaky blond hair tumbled down around her head. With irritation, she tossed the cap onto the passenger seat and raked her hair back off her face using all ten fingers.

"I'm not representing the network or the show," she said. "I came of my own accord and at my own expense." She gave a soft laugh of chagrin as she looked up at him. "Please forgive me for wasting your time. Enjoy what's left of your day off." She tugged on the car door again.

He was about to release it, walk away, go home, turn on ESPN, crack a beer, and do exactly as she had suggested: enjoy what was left of his day off.

But in a split second of remarkably messed-up judgment, he changed his mind and held on to the door. "What makes you think he's out there waiting to strike again?"

Now looking him straight in the eye, she said, "The blood moon."

She held his gaze for a beat or two, then succeeded in pulling the door shut.

Mystified and annoyed, John watched her back the sedan out and jounce over the rutted parking lot to the two-lane highway. Several vehicles went past before she was able to turn left into the eastbound lane. While she'd waited for a clearing, he'd been able to get to his phone and take a picture of the rear license plate.

His impulse was to follow her. Common sense blared, *Have you lost your freakin' mind?*

He watched until her car disappeared around a bend, then walked slowly over to his SUV. He opened the driver's door but remained standing in the wedge, taking a moment to process everything that had happened since he'd walked into the bar.

No, even before that. Yesterday's phone conversation with her had felt covert from the start, like she needed to speak in a half whisper, like she had something to hide. Or was…apprehensive. Scared? Guilty? Hell if he knew. But he'd wondered.

It had nagged him enough that he'd kept their appointment this afternoon. He'd arrived at this most unlikely of places curious, but also with a jaundiced eye. For the first five minutes, he had been amused, just as she'd called him on.

But now, he couldn't shake the feeling that even if she was wrong, she believed it: *"It's going to happen again."*

Irritably, he swatted at mosquitoes that dared to light on him when he was this pissed off. First of all, he was angry at her for the intrusion. He didn't need anything upsetting the rickety apple cart that was his present and future life.

Then he was mad at himself for being such a chump, driving all the way out here to meet the woman with the sexy phone voice and now standing here trying to keep mosquitoes from sucking him dry, mulling over her certainty that all was not right with how the Crissy Mellin case had been resolved.

He'd wanted like hell to accept the official sign-off of that investigation. He'd wanted to embrace it, then bury it deep, expunge it from his mind, rule it forever over and done with. *Finis.*

More than three years' distance from it, he'd been this close to coming to terms with it. Now…*her.* Her of the just-got-laid hair. She'd refreshed his memory, resurrected doubts, awakened an obsession that had the potential to wreck every aspect of his life all over again, turning lousy into lousier.

No way in hell, lady. No matter how delectable your lips.

All the while his anger had been mounting toward Beth Collins, he'd been staring hard at the entrance to the beer joint. "Screw it," he said, and underscored that by slamming the door of his SUV. He stalked over to the padded door, pulled it open, and went inside.

The barkeeper looked up from his magazine and gave him a lupine smile. "Struck out, huh?"

Without replying or breaking stride, John walked up to the matchstick guy who'd given him the finger and socked him in the gut.

"She must've been speaking metaphorically."

John was lying on his sofa, his head on the armrest, fully clothed except for his cowboy boots, which were on the floor. In his right hand was a bottle of beer, held upright on his stomach. In his left was a makeshift ice pack he was holding against the side of his face.

"'Blood moon' could be a metaphor for lots of things, right? Doomsday. A reckoning. Armageddon. Spells, and prophesies of end times, and spooky shit like that. I don't think she meant it in a literal sense."

He'd turned the ceiling light off because it had been an irritant to his swollen, discolored eye. The TV was on, but he wasn't paying any attention to the programming, and he'd muted the audio because it was contributing to his headache. A handful of ibuprofen tablets had blunted neither it nor the additional aches and pains that kept him trying to find a more comfortable position on his lumpy couch.

The beer—his second—had gone down real good, but he'd eaten only half of his carry-out burger. The remains of it lay on its foil wrapper on the coffee table. He gestured toward it with the beer bottle. "Help yourself."

He called the dog Mutt, because the animal defined the word. One morning as he'd been about to leave for work, he'd noticed something underneath his car that looked like an unraveling burlap tow sack that had been wadded up and discarded. Upon further inspection, he'd discovered that it was a flea-bitten hide wrapped around a skeleton that whimpered.

He'd made the mistake of getting a slice of leftover pizza from his kitchen trash can and tossing it to the bag of bones before driving away. When he'd returned home that evening, the mutt had been curled up on his front porch. Another slice of dry pizza had sealed the deal. He became John's dog.

He'd broken the neglected animal of his habit of scarfing food, convincing him that it was no longer necessary to snatch at it and swallow it whole. But now, having been given permission, Mutt made short work of the burger, then lay down in the narrow space between the coffee table and sofa. Yawning hugely, he laid his head on one of John's boots.

"You're welcome." John eased himself up, swung his legs off the sofa, stepped over the dog, and scooped the trash off the coffee table. On his way into the galley kitchen, he downed the remainder of his beer, then disposed of the empty bottle and trash, and pitched the plastic bag of melting ice into the sink.

As he reentered the living room, he said, "Looks can be deceiving, you know." Mutt didn't raise his head, but he opened his eyes and looked at his owner. "She was hot, all right. That hair. Brown eyes, but not dark like chocolate. Lighter. Like really good whiskey.

"Nice rack. Not overly endowed, just…nice." He got lost in the thought of the allure of a plain white t-shirt, then pulled himself away from the remembered image.

"As I was saying, she looked normal, but she had to be a certified kook. It's as simple as that. Or maybe not a kook, maybe just bored. Needing attention. Turning a dull afternoon into an adventure. Except that coming all the way from New York to seek adventure here makes no sense."

He rubbed the back of his neck. "She remembered my name from years back, but that would be easy enough. Bowie like the knife. So she…she…"

Mutt raised his eyebrows inquisitively.

John cursed and made a slicing gesture. "Never mind. Let's just scrub this whole damn day from memory. Don't bring it up again. Okay?" Mutt closed his eyes. "All right then."

He went down the short hallway into the bathroom and switched on the light fixture above the sink. He braced his hands on its rim as he leaned in and regarded his battered face in the mirror.

No permanent damage had been inflicted, but he wondered how he was going to explain to Barker the obvious drubbing he'd taken.

I got mugged. Can you believe it? Coming out of a 7-Eleven with a six-pack and a bag of chips.

Damn dog tripped me up. I stumbled into the edge of the closet door. About broke my neck, and it hurt like hell.

Or maybe he would avoid the encounter altogether and just call in sick. *I feel like shit,* hammered *shit, so I took a Covid test. Guess what?*

Barker would smell those lies from a mile off. He decided to sleep on it, see how he looked in the morning, and decide then how he was going to explain.

He showered. The hot water eased his aches and pains, but he stayed in the stall until it ran cool. He dried, pulled on a loose pair of gym shorts, and was making his way back down the hall toward the living room when someone stepped into the connecting doorway, filling it with a menacing silhouette that said, "Hey, asshole!"

It was the matchstick guy.

Chapter 3

"You dickhead," John said. "Good thing my gun is in the bedroom. I could have shot you."

The other man grinned through his scraggly mustache. "I knocked."

"I was in the shower."

"No lights on. Your front door unlocked. Useless dog. Anybody could've waltzed in here."

"When I got home, I had other things on my mind, like getting painkillers into my bloodstream."

"Hey, you started the fight." He gave John's face a closer look and grimaced. "Looks ugly. How's it feel?"

"Throbs like a mofo."

"I had to make the fight look authentic."

"You made it look authentic enough," John grumbled. "What's with the matchstick?"

"I need to look like a creep with an attitude."

John snorted, giving the other man a disparaging

once-over. "Well, you succeeded. In fact, you may have overshot it. How's your belly?"

The guy raised the hem on his dirty t-shirt. Beneath his rib cage was a bruise the size of John's fist. John whistled. "Landed it right where I was aiming. I feel better." He smiled beatifically. Then they laughed, high-fived, and man-hugged, slapping each other on the back.

Mitch Haskell and John had been partner detectives before Mitch was recruited by the DEA to work undercover. He was a former Marine with a service record that included one deployment to Iraq and three to Afghanistan. He was whipcord lean and as tough as boot leather—a guy you didn't mess with. But at heart, he was *all* heart. John had seen him unashamedly cry over fallen service members and law officers of every stripe.

John looked down at Mitch's raggedy jeans. They were wet up to his knees, his boots caked with mud. "You're tracking up my floor."

"Your fault. You live on the edge of a swamp. Muddied floors are the price you pay to have visitors."

"You weren't invited."

Mitch only grinned. "I'm just glad I made it here without having a run-in with a gator or getting bit by a water moccasin."

"You came by boat?"

"Less likelihood of being followed. Wouldn't do to be seen making a house call on a cop, although it seems to get darker out here every time I come."

"Which is why I like it." The living room was still lighted only by the muted television, and John kept it that way. He gestured toward the kitchen. "There's beer in the fridge."

"Bring you one?"

"No, thanks. I've had my limit for the day."

Mitch gave him a knowing look, but John didn't need a reminder of the period of time when his limit had been dangerously high. "Make sure the fridge door closes all the way. You have to push on it." He stepped over Mutt and plopped down on the center cushion of the sofa.

From the kitchen Mitch said, "I'm over my quota, too. Had to pretend to guzzle longnecks all day." He returned with a bottle of water, uncapped it, and almost emptied it with one long drink. Then he sprawled in an easy chair. "God, this feels good. Played pool till I wanted to impale myself on the cue. High point of my day was when you sauntered in. Couldn't believe my eyes."

"You could've knocked me over with a feather when I turned around and saw that you were the smart-ass. Not that you aren't one. You're just not the smart-ass I expected."

His friend toasted John with his water bottle. "You played it well. No reaction except that steely-eyed glare of yours. Ten seconds of it had me shivering in my shoes. I was thinking, 'Shit, I hope he recognizes me.' Nearly peed myself when you stormed back in and belted me in the gut."

John laughed. "Well, you'd flipped me the bird. I took it as an invitation."

"It was, but I wasn't sure you'd pick up on it. Sorry about the black eye, the jaw, but laying into you won me points with those guys."

"Only one pitched in to help you."

"My new partner. He didn't know you, bought our act, too."

"Did you tell him later?"

"No. I thought we needed to show the dirtbags how we'd do in a fight."

"You did all right," John said, working his jaw from side to side.

"So, mission accomplished. Thanks for the sacrifice. I owe you a favor."

"Thanks for not pulling your knife on me." John knew Mitch carried one in an ankle holster. "How close are you to nailing them?"

"Close, I think."

"Be sharp, Mitch."

"Always." He downed the rest of the water, then set the bottle on the floor. "What the hell were you doing in that place?"

"Having a Coke."

John knew the quip wouldn't satisfy his intuitive friend, and he was right. Mitch squinted one eye and stared him down.

John leaned against the back of the sofa and linked his fingers over the crown of his head, trying to look casual and indifferent. "Just killing a Saturday afternoon. Went for a drive through the boonies. Thought about fishing but was too lazy to get the gear out. Got thirsty and stopped at the next place I came to, which happened to be that bar." He shrugged.

"Uh-huh." Mitch continued to look at him through his squint.

John rolled his eyes. "She was just a woman."

"I noticed that right off. I'm smart that way."

John thought of dropping it there, but curiosity wouldn't let him. "How long had she been there ahead of me?"

"Fifteen minutes. Thereabouts."

"Did she talk to anybody?"

"Except to order her drink, no. Sat over there all by her lonesome until you showed up. Is she someone special?"

"*Special?* Mitch. I never laid eyes on her until today. It was totally random. You saw. She paid for my Coke. I went over to thank her. We chatted. She said she had to go. I saw her safely past you reprobates and to her car."

"A perfect gentleman."

"On this particular occasion."

Mitch grinned. "You didn't score. Either that or it was a record-breaking quickie."

"She bailed. No loss." He gave another uncaring shrug. "How's Angela? What does she think of the Fu Manchu?"

Mitch stroked the mustache, which extended a couple of inches below his chin. "Hates it." He sat forward, elbows on his knees, and stared down at the floor. "The mustache will be the first thing to go as soon as I get enough on these guys to win an indictment." He raised his head and looked across at John. "I'm getting out."

John lowered his hands from the top of his head. "You're leaving the agency?"

"Yep."

"You're serious?"

"Angela's pregnant."

John sputtered a soft laugh. "Congratulations, man."

His friend smiled sheepishly. "Thanks. It's a boy," he added with obvious pride.

"How far along?"

"Five months."

"Why didn't you tell me sooner?"

"Angela and I wanted to make sure everything was okay, find out the sex. And, sorta, you know, savor our secret."

"You're still sappy over that woman."

Mitch placed his hands over his heart. "I confess." But after a moment, he resumed looking down at the floor and turned serious. "You uh...you know how you felt after the Mellin girl's case? Fed up? Disillusioned?"

The pleasure John had felt over Mitch's happy news drained from him. He went as still as stone and said nothing.

"Shortly after the book was closed on that, I took you out in my bass boat. Remember? You were in pretty bad shape. About as low as you ever got. I thought a day on the water might help. I'd brought along a six-pack. You brought a bottle of Patrón.

"The bottle was almost empty when you asked me—I doubt you recall, you were so drunk—but you asked me, 'Why do we do it, Mitch? What's the point?'

"You said that we were spinning our wheels, fighting a war that'll never end because the bad guys just keep getting badder. You said the justice system was a joke and that seeking justice was an exercise in futility."

"I was shit-faced on straight tequila. Blubbering. Nothing I said was worth listening to."

Mitch shook his head. "Drunken ramblings, maybe, but when Angela told me about the baby, I thought over everything you'd said. I want to see my son grow up. I want to grow old with my wife. I don't want to take a forty-five-caliber bullet in the back of my head and have my body dumped in a swamp by some punk doper who got wise to me."

"No explanation necessary. I get it," John said quietly. "What do you plan to do?"

"I've got some irons in the fire. A position in Florida is looking good. Generous benefits, regular hours. Angela wouldn't have to eat dinner alone every night."

"You're an adrenaline junkie," John said. "You'll miss the rush."

"I've thought of that, sure. I'll take up motocross, white water rafting, hang gliding. Something that keeps my battery charged. Do you miss it?"

"The rush? Naw."

"Liar. What's Butthole Barker got you doing these days?"

"Let's see. Follow-up on a home burglary. The thief got away with a lawn chair. Last week I was sent to check out a report of rabid skunks under someone's house."

"Jesus. What a waste. Who're you partnered with?"

"Nobody. I don't need a partner to investigate the dirty words spray-painted on Walmart's restroom walls."

"John," his friend sighed.

"No, no. It was an interesting case of vandalism. All the obscenities were misspelled."

Mitch didn't look amused. "You should have left when I did."

"I didn't get an offer from the DEA."

"Would you have taken it?"

John said nothing.

Mitch sighed. "John, why do you stay? What's keeping you from telling Barker to go fuck himself and leaving?"

"The paycheck." He glanced around his living room. It had been shabby in the 1950s. Today it bordered on derelict. "I'd have to give up living in the lap of luxury."

"Yeah, this house is swell, the bayou in your backyard is a petri dish for creatures that bite and sting and poison." Mitch gave him a sympathetic smile and shook his head remorsefully. "You gotta get over that case, John. Move back into town. Move *on*."

"One day, maybe."

Mitch held his gaze a moment longer, then indicated Mutt. "When did he move in?"

"A few months back."

"As a watchdog, he's useless."

John regarded Mutt fondly. "Yeah, but at least he's got pedigree and good looks."

Mitch chuckled, then slapped his knees and stood up. "I gotta get home and explain to Angela how I got the bruise on my abs."

"Give her a hug for me."

"Like hell I will." He headed toward the door. "You gonna see her again?"

John knew he was no longer referring to Angela, but he played dumb. "Who?"

Mitch looked back at him and laughed. "She was cute."

"She was. Just not my type."

Mitch laughed harder.

"Anyhow, she was too young for me."

"You doth protest too much, my friend. Did you at least get her digits?"

"I didn't even get her name. If I did, I don't remember it," he lied. "I told you, the encounter was—"

"Totally random. Right, right," Mitch said, still grinning. "Don't turn any lights on till I'm long gone. I can't be seen sneaking out of a cop's house. Take care of you."

"Same."

They fist bumped, then Mitch slipped through the door and melded into the misty darkness so easily he didn't even disturb the wispy Spanish moss hanging from the lower tree branches. John locked the door and made certain that it was also bolted. He let Mutt out the back door in the kitchen. "You've got two minutes. But no pressure."

John walked back into the living room to turn off the TV but was brought up short by what was on the screen. It was a photograph of a full orange moon that shone like a gold coin in a deep purple sky. The weatherman appeared to be waxing eloquent about it. At the bottom of the screen was superimposed: *A blood moon.*

Beth's phone call was answered with a grunt of displeasure. "It's an hour later here, you know."

"Oh, sorry, Max. I didn't think."

"It's okay. I don't sleep much anyway." There was more grunting, what sounded like the rustle of bed linens, and the unmistakable snick of a cigarette lighter.

"You're *smoking*? You promised, Max."

"With my fingers crossed."

Arguing wouldn't make a dent with him, so she moved past his unhealthy habit to address his mood, which was more irascible than usual. "Bad day?"

"They're throwing me a retirement party."

"They? The network?"

He muttered several curses. "Black tie affair. Waldorf Astoria. They're inviting every living president, a British royal or two, and A-list movie stars."

Knowing how he would feel about that, she winced, but said, "Wow. How nice."

"*Nice?* No. Gratuitous. I'd rather die than be there." After a puff of breath, no doubt creating a cloud of smoke, he said, "It's late there, too. Why are you still up?"

"I've been putting off calling you."

"Why?"

"I didn't want to hear 'I told you so.'"

"Ah. You've met with Bowie and struck out."

Max Longren, who was four decades her senior, was her boss. Also, in truth, her best friend. Until recently he'd been executive producer of *Crisis Point.*

But since last year when the network had been bought by an international media conglomerate, the corporate shift had been seismic, and the infrastructure of *Crisis Point* hadn't been immune to changes in management. Max had been replaced by a much younger corporate animal named Winston Brady.

Max wasn't taking his forced exit well. His career had been his lifeblood. He was a living legend, known throughout the industry for his talent, grit, caginess, and often tyrannical tactics.

Beth had been with the show for only two years when, to her dismay and delight, Max had handpicked her to be his personal assistant producer. Under his tutelage, she'd received the best education she could have wished for. She'd been taught by the headmaster himself, the developer of techniques that told true stories in a manner that made them as exciting and compelling as fiction. His innovations had been replicated by just about every other successful documentary series.

Through all the years they'd worked together, naturally they'd had disagreements, but nothing compared to the explosive quarrel they'd had when she'd approached him with her reservations about the accuracy of the soon-to-air Crissy Mellin episode. He'd frowned and reminded her that it was a done deal, that Brady had signed off on it.

"I know that, Max. But recently something's come to my attention. We might have missed a vital element of that story. The impact could be major, and we'd be derelict to leave it out."

"Are you saying we'd go back in and change it?"

"Let me explain and then you decide."

So he'd listened, but by the time she'd finished, he was bristling.

"A blood moon?" he asked with incredulity. "That's your vital element? What the hell is that, anyway? Have you gone loopy? Are you eating those funny gummy bears?"

"Max, please don't dismiss—"

"Around here, you and I are considered a unit, Beth. Everyone regards me as your Merlin. If you start spouting this moon cycle crap, they'll think it originated with me, that I thought up something outlandish just to get under Brady's skin."

"Don't you think it warrants deeper digging?"

"It no longer matters what I think. Professionally, I've

been castrated. I'm surprised they haven't confiscated my executive men's room key. Now, forget about it, and let that episode air as is."

She'd dropped the matter that day, but, on the next, she'd informed him of her intention to take a few vacation days. He'd eyed her with the daunting shrewdness that a *New York Times* columnist had accurately described as "withering."

"Let me guess," he said. "Destination Louisiana."

"Even you don't have authority over my vacation plans, Max."

"Vacation, my ass. When do you leave?"

"Tomorrow morning. There's no time for delay."

He'd shot up from his massive chair and stabbed his desktop with his index finger. "You have no authority to go nosing around the police department down there. It's Louisiana, for crissake! They feed people they don't like to the alligators. They'll have a voodoo doll of you in no time. But never mind the danger to yourself."

Here, he'd gotten really wound up. "I created *Crisis Point.* I nursed it through infancy, whipped it through puberty, and eventually placed it in the top five of ratings, where it has remained for years. Your amateur sleuthing will put the show, my baby, at risk.

"In addition to the smudge on my hard-won reputation, the egomaniac who's taken my place will shit bricks if you go behind his back. This obsession of yours could get your butt fired."

Quietly, she'd said, "Not if I return with an Emmy-winning story for us to work on together before your retirement."

Despite his lauded career, that most coveted award had eluded him. She knew the disappointment he suffered for being forced into retirement without having received it.

"Emmy-winning story," he scoffed. "Based on this crazy notion of yours? Ha! What I think is that you'll make a fool of yourself and be drummed out of the business."

"Very possibly. But it's a chance worth taking."

"Then go," he'd shouted, waving her toward his office door. "But if you're sunk in a swamp down there, expect an 'I told you so.'"

His rejection had cut deeply, but she'd left without his sanction. She hadn't consulted Winston Brady at all, a move that very well could get her butt fired, especially if Detective John Bowie complained to him about being ambushed and harassed by one of his producers.

Now, as though Max been following her thoughts, he said, "Just how much of a prick was Bowie?"

"As reputed."

"Wasn't happy to see you, huh?"

"Hostile, actually. He wasn't at all interested or open to discussing Crissy Mellin's case. He was completely unmoved by my attempts to persuade him otherwise. Why don't you just say 'I told you so' and get it over with?"

"Hell, no. I'm not letting you off that lightly. I want details."

She gave him a bullet-point account of her unorthodox meeting with the detective. Max listened without interruption except for his wheezing inhales and exhales of forbidden tobacco smoke.

When she finished, he said, "Did he take it like a kick in the nuts?"

"Take what?"

"Mention of the blood moon. How'd he react?"

"He didn't. He gave me a blank stare."

"Meant nothing to him, then?"

"No. I'm almost positive."

Finally he said, "I told you so."

"I concede, but not happily." After a moment, she made one final pitch. "You know, it's not like I dreamed up this mysticism surrounding blood moons. For millennia, mankind has regarded them as omens, both good and bad."

"Silly superstitions. You're reading too much into it."

"Possibly." She rubbed her forehead, no longer feeling defensive but defeated. "Maybe I should leave it alone. You were certainly right about the detective. It was a contentious meeting from the start. We got off on the wrong foot, and it never got better."

"What kind of wrong foot? Why a wrong foot?"

She wasn't going to tell him about the sexual undercurrents of those first few minutes. "Doesn't matter. As soon as I said the girl's name, he shut down. How did you know he would?"

"Fifty years of reporting news and current affairs. The code of honor among law officers is sacrosanct. Band of brothers. Blue wall of silence. You know."

"But during the investigation, he mouthed off," she argued. "He was quoted as saying that it had been sloppily conducted. Rushed. You read what he'd said."

"Yeah, yeah. People bitch and moan off the cuff. But it's different when backed against a wall and asked to go on record."

"I don't think he was speaking off the cuff then. I think

he wanted people to hear, to know, that the investigation was being streamlined. I also think he was right."

"Take off your rose-colored glasses, Beth. Nobody gives a damn about what's right or wrong anymore. Or accurate. Even if Bowie was right back then, it no longer matters now. Obviously not even to him. Especially not to him. He was your golden key. If he blew you off and wouldn't listen to you—"

"Then no one will," she said.

"Which I told you before you went down there. So, when are you coming back?"

"Tomorrow. I'm booked on a four o'clock flight."

"That late in the day?"

"There's a morning flight. I could stand by for it, I suppose."

"Do that. The sooner you drop this, the better. Start thinking about how you're going to impress your new executive producer, not alienate him."

"I can't stomach Brady."

"Then he should excel." He gave a phlegmy laugh. "Nobody could stand me either. Nobody even liked me a little."

She would have told him that she liked him a lot, but he would have rebuffed it, even knowing that it was true. More than a mentor, he was a father figure and plain-speaking friend she depended on for sound advice, even if she didn't welcome it.

"Sorry to have disturbed you. Try to get some sleep. I'll call you when I land." Before he could disconnect, she said, "One more thing, Max."

"I know, I know, don't smoke."

"You mispronounced his name."

"Huh?"

"It's Bowie. Like the knife."

Chapter 4

Sunday, March 9

After a virtually sleepless night, Beth decided not to be deterred by her blustery conversation with Max. He was viewing the situation from the perspective of one who'd already lost his standing.

But Winston Brady hadn't asked for her resignation. He hadn't insisted that the Mellin story was ready for airing and for her to leave it alone. Of course he was unaware of her renewed interest in it, but still. Until he specifically forbade her to back off or risk losing her job, she would persist…at least until the afternoon flight to New York.

Having determined that, she brewed a cup of coffee using the sputtering machine in her hotel room and braced herself with a few swallows before calling the Auclair PD.

"Detective Bowie, please."

A woman with a soft drawl and pleasant manner told her that he hadn't come in yet. "Can someone else help you?"

"No. I really need to speak with him." She asked for his cell phone number, but wasn't surprised when told that it was department policy not to give out personal contact information on personnel.

"But I can have him call you back," the woman said. "What's your name, please?"

The first time she'd called two days ago, she had been put through to his desk without supplying her name. She was reluctant to do so now. "That's all right. I'll try later."

Having struck out there, she moved to Plan B, which was to contact Crissy Mellin's mother, Carla. Although she'd been integral to the story, she'd been loath to appear on *Crisis Point.* She had argued with the dogged producer that she'd lived the ugly story. Why go on TV and rehash it when it wouldn't change the ending?

Eventually she had capitulated, but the interview hadn't gone well. The interviewer's suavity had had no softening effect on her. She'd been surly, answering every question with as few words as possible. Her bitterness and antipathy toward the police department had come across on camera.

Beth intended not to be as pushy as her cohort had been. She would ask Carla Mellin for only five minutes, during which she hoped empathy would make the woman more agreeable to talking openly about what had happened to her daughter. Beth had nothing to lose by trying.

She checked out of the hotel and went in search of Ms. Mellin. Her address turned out to be a lot in a mobile home park located in a less than desirable part of town. Beth glanced around cautiously as she got out of her car and approached the door.

Her knock was answered by an elderly man dressed only in his undershorts. He seemed as surprised by her as she was by him. He was also perturbed. "Where's Tuck? Why'd they send you? I want Tuck back."

After several stops and starts, she learned that a physical therapist came twice a week to strengthen his "gimp knee." Once she assured him that she wasn't Tuck's replacement, she asked how long he'd been living there.

"Goin' on two years."

"Did you know the previous resident, Ms. Mellin?"

"No. Place was empty when I rented it."

He had no idea who Beth might ask about the former tenant or where she'd relocated. "I ain't got to know none of the neighbors, and I want to keep it that way," he said. "Now shoo. I gotta get ready for Tuck." He slammed the door in her face.

With diminishing optimism, she went from door to door. Most of the neighbors either weren't at home or pretended not to be. Those she did speak to claimed not to know Carla Mellin personally, only by the notoriety her daughter's disappearance had created. "I felt sorry for her," one woman said. "Hounded day and night. I don't blame her a bit for moving away without telling anybody."

Disheartened, Beth returned to her car but didn't start it. She sat mulling over what to do next while watching a little girl two lots down, riding a tricycle with wobbly wheels. She went round and round in a never-ending circle, getting nowhere.

She was going in circles and getting nowhere, too. The wasted effort to reach John Bowie. The failed attempt to talk to Carla Mellin. These weren't omens, they were blatant strikeouts.

Her dejection bone deep, she started the car and asked the navigation system to guide her to the New Orleans airport.

"Bowie!"

John looked up from his computer screen to see Tom Barker threading his way through the Crimes Against Persons unit. When he reached John's desk, he placed his hands on his hips and regarded John's battered face with displeasure. "Somebody told me you looked like you'd gone fifteen rounds. What happened?"

"I was carrying an armload of dirty clothes to the washing machine. Didn't see my dog, stumbled over him, and broke my fall with my face on the edge of the closet door."

He stopped there. Elaboration could ruin a semi-plausible lie. He knew by the way Barker was rocking back on his heels that he wasn't buying it, but he went along and asked if John had seen a doctor.

"No need. Looks like hell, but I'm fine. Thanks for your concern, Tom."

"Yesterday was your day off."

"Yeah. And?"

"You do laundry on your day off?"

"When my clothes need washing."

"That's what wives are for. Maybe you should get you one."

"Had one. I'd rather do my own laundry." Enough of

this bullshit do-si-do. "Something special you needed me for? Because..." He tilted his head toward his computer screen. "Things got backed up yesterday."

"No, nothing special." He gestured toward John's face. "Try some bruise cream." He turned away, then came back around in a slow pivot that looked like a choreographed move. "Actually, there was something I wanted to talk to you about."

"I'm all ears."

"*Crisis Point* has scheduled the episode on the Mellin case. Not this week's program, but next week's."

Beth Collins hadn't specified when it was scheduled, but he pretended that this was news to him. He brightened. "Oh, yeah? Be sure you're all set to record it. You don't want to miss seeing yourself on TV."

"Before it airs, I'm sure the media around here will play it up big. You know, recap the story to refresh everyone's memory."

John wanted say that his memory didn't need refreshing, but he merely nodded.

Tom went on. "I'm already scheduled to do two interviews."

"Maybe you need a talent agent, Tom, to handle all that scheduling for you."

John's nonstop sarcasm hadn't escaped the other man. His lips had tightened into a thin, straight line. "The point is, you may be approached with a request for an interview. In fact, the officer working the switchboard this morning informed me that before you came in a woman had called asking for you."

John struggled not to act too interested, but he couldn't help but wonder if the caller had been Beth Collins. "Did she leave a message, say what she was calling about?"

"No. Declined to talk to anyone else. Didn't leave her name."

"Huh." John shrugged. "No clue."

"She asked for your cell number."

John reacted with a start. "Well, I hope to God that whoever took the call didn't—"

"Of course not. Department policy."

"And we all know how strict you are about adhering to department policy." John relaxed back into his chair.

By contrast, Barker hiked up his trousers and assumed a combatant stance. "Now, on the outside chance that you're being sought for comment about this upcoming program, or about any aspect of that Mellin case, you'd do well to decline. Graciously but firmly." He lowered his pugnacious chin and looked at John from beneath his eyebrows. "It would be a really bad idea for you to go before a camera."

John chuckled. "No shit. Looking like this?" He pointed at his face. "There's not enough makeup in the world to—"

"Cut the crap, Bowie. You know what I'm leading to."

"Actually, I think I lost the thread."

The other man's expression turned even meaner. "Don't dredge up all that stuff you were mouthing before."

"Before? By before, do you mean before you closed the case when the body was still missing? That *stuff*?"

Tom's face turned red. "I should have convinced the chief to fire you then."

"For what?"

"Dereliction of duty."

"I wasn't the one who was derelict, Tom. But you're right. You should have convinced him to fire me. I wonder why you didn't. Oh!" He snapped his fingers, then pointed his index finger at Barker. "It would have looked bad on you.

"One of the senior detectives on the case," he said, pointing to his own chest, "started raising questions." John spread his arms at his sides. "Isn't raising questions in our job description? Isn't that what detectives are supposed to do in order to detect? Aren't we meant to be on the lookout for inconsistences, do some meddling, poke and probe when called for?" He paused, but Barker didn't say anything.

"Obviously that's not standard operating procedure when you're leading an investigation," John said, scoffing. "The truth now, Tom. You wanted me to stay employed *only* because you didn't want me out of here and at liberty to talk about the goings-on inside these walls. Am I warm?

"If I'd been free to speak my mind, the public, the attorney general, just about every-damn-body might have wanted to take a closer look at just how hastily and irresponsibly you investigated that girl's disappearance."

Barker's face had become congested with rage, but his voice remained controlled. "You're a head case, Bowie. An undeclared alcoholic. Your wife had the good sense to leave you and is getting happily fucked by her new boyfriend every night and most daytimes, too.

"Your kid has run off to God knows where. You've got nothing to recommend you. And the funny part? Despite all that, you're a delusional smart-ass who thinks he's got it all figured out."

John stood up and lifted his sport coat off the back of his chair. "I've got one thing figured out. I don't have to take this shit."

"Then *quit*," Tom bellowed.

John bore down on him and got right in his face. "Not. On. Your. Life."

He held the man's furious stare for several seconds, then turned and walked out, becoming aware that he and Barker had attracted an attentive audience. Other detectives, uniformed patrol officers, a janitor emptying the wastebaskets had all stopped what they'd been doing to watch. John didn't care. He wouldn't take back a single word he'd said.

He jogged down the stairs to the ground floor. A minute later, he was in his car, booting up his laptop.

On every thoroughfare between the mobile home park in Auclair and the New Orleans airport, traffic was heavy and belligerent, adding an extra fifteen minutes to the hour and a half drive. Beth was frazzled by the time she had returned the rental car and made her way to the ticket counter.

She'd fibbed to Max in a text, telling him that she'd stood by for the morning flight but had been unable to get a seat. She was confirmed on the four o'clock. He hadn't bothered sending a return text, but he'd viewed her trip as a fool's errand and would be happy that she was on her way back.

But she wasn't happy, damn it. She decided to give it one last try. She moved out of the flow of the airport foot traffic and called the police station again. She was relieved that this time a male voice answered, reducing the chance that her repeat calls would be noted. She asked for John Bowie and was put on hold.

When the officer came back on the line, he informed her that Bowie had been there, but had left. "Couple of hours ago, they said. Maybe longer." Nobody knew if or when he'd be back before the day was out. Did she want to leave him a message?

"No, thank you," she said into her phone. Disconnecting, she thought, *Take it as a sign. It wasn't meant to be.*

She got in the security check line, listlessly tugging her roll-aboard behind her and staring absently at all the cities in which U2 had performed on their world tour. The itinerary was printed on the back of the t-shirt the young woman in line ahead of her was wearing.

"That's her."

As did most of the people around her, Beth turned in the direction of the authoritative voice. Her stomach dropped.

John Bowie, looking grim and intimidating, was pointing her out to a TSA agent. "The one in the blue jacket."

Had he been in an accident? What had happened to his face?

The TSA agent asked those in line to move aside as she made her way forward. When she reached Beth, she said, "Beth Collins?"

Beth dragged her astonished gaze from John Bowie's unflinching stare to the uniformed woman. "Yes."

"Would you come with us, please?"

"What for?"

"A police matter. " Bowie opened the right side of his sport coat so that everyone nearby could see the badge clipped to his belt.

"Ms. Collins, if you'll follow me, please." The TSA agent motioned for Beth to step out of line.

But she stayed where she was, too appalled to move. By now, everyone was gawking at them. Those in line ahead and behind her were craning their necks to get a better view. She shot John Bowie a murderous look. "Why are you doing this?"

He sighed as though put out. "Thank you, Agent Gorman. You've been very helpful. I'll take it from here."

He reached behind the agent and closed his hand around Beth's elbow. "This way." He gave her arm a tug, which she resisted. In a silent threat, he arched an eyebrow and wrestled the handle of her roll-aboard from her grasp.

Damn him! She couldn't defy him without making a scene. *More* of a scene. If it should get back to Winston Brady that she'd been apprehended...It didn't bear thinking about.

Resentful and fuming, she went along as the TSA agent opened up narrow avenues in the queue for them to squeeze through. When they were clear of it, Bowie propelled her forward and again thanked Agent Gorman for her assistance.

"You're welcome, but, if you don't mind me asking, what did she do?"

Over his shoulder, Bowie replied, "She cut in line."

Chapter 5

He herded Beth through the exit and toward an SUV she recognized from the beer joint's parking lot. It was parked at the curb, an airport police officer guarding it.

Bowie opened the passenger door and practically heaved her inside. He shut the door, shook hands with the guard, and thanked him. In back, he opened the hatch and put her roll-aboard inside, then came around and climbed in.

As he started the car, she launched. "You had better have a damn good reason—"

He interrupted. "There was a blood moon the night Crissy Mellin disappeared."

The sudden statement took her aback, but after a few seconds she bobbed her chin.

"And you think that's significant?"

Again she gave a curt nod.

He didn't immediately look away from her. She held his gaze. Then, after a quick glance over his left shoulder, he gave the steering wheel a sharp turn, entering the stream of traffic to the chorus of a dozen protesting horns. "Buckle your seat belt," he said, and wrestled with his until it clicked.

Nothing more was said until he turned into the drive-through lane of a fast food chain no more than a mile from the airport. "I'm starving. You want something?"

He pulled up to the backlit, multicolored menu and lowered his window. Her head was still spinning over the rapid series of events. All the brightly colored pictures of high-calorie meals blurred. She couldn't isolate a single item. "Diet Coke."

"That's it?"

"Yes, thanks."

By the time they reached the pickup window, the order was ready. He set the sack in his lap, their drinks in the cup holders, then steered into a parking spot in front of the building. It faced the runway across the boulevard where a jet was landing.

He switched off the car engine, dug into the sack, and took out a cardboard tray piled with French fries and breaded chicken tenders. He extended it toward her.

"No thank you."

"You sure?"

"Yes. What happened to you?"

"What do you mean? Oh, this?" He looked in the rear-view mirror and gingerly touched the bruise on his cheek-bone beneath a vivid black eye. "After you drove off, I went back into the bar and got into a scuffle with those rednecks." He picked up a piece of chicken and took a bite.

"More than a scuffle, I think. What provoked it?"

"You."

"Me?"

He picked up a couple of fries and, as he bit into them, looked over at her. "You left without me. That brought my manhood into question. I took exception to their observations about it."

She didn't believe him, but she wasn't about to challenge his truthfulness. Not on that subject. "Why did you pull that stunt at the airport?"

"To stop you from leaving before I could ask you some questions."

"How did you know I was leaving?"

"I called the car rental company and asked for your contact info."

"And they gave it to you?"

"I identified myself, told them you were a material witness who'd skipped out on the prosecutor, and the trial starts tomorrow. Words to that effect. They'd recently rented you a car, and the contract was bound to have your contact info on it. At least a cell phone number. The agent was still reluctant. The manager was sent for."

He scarfed the rest of the tender before continuing. "I told him, look, I could get a court order, but the judge is already pissed off because we lost track of our witness, and I'd hate to rile him further. Eventually, though, he'd grant me the order because he wants the trial to proceed as scheduled. In the long run, I would get the info from you anyway. So why not save us both the hassle?"

He raised his shoulder. "He gave me your number. He also volunteered that you'd already turned the car in." He stopped eating and gave her a baleful look. "You were clearing out awfully quick, weren't you?"

When she didn't offer an explanation, he continued. "Anyway, I thanked him, checked the flight schedule, and had to beat it up here to catch you before you got on that four o'clock."

"If you had my phone number, why did you create that mortifying scene? Why accost me at all? Why didn't you simply call me?"

"Because you might have simply hung up on me." He continued to eat, took another drink, all the while watching her. "Did you call for me at the station this morning?"

"Twice."

"Why?"

"I thought I'd try again."

"To get me to talk about the Mellin case?"

"To get you to be civil."

He grinned. "Try me. Being civil shouldn't be too hard."

"Apparently it is, Mr. Bowie. You just made a public spectacle of me."

"Wait. You're angry? What right have you got to be mad?" He dropped the fries he'd been about to eat back into the container. "Remember, you lured me into that meeting in the bar."

"Which you adjourned."

"Because I wanted no part of your agenda. But you baited me, and I was left believing that you would welcome reopening the discussion. Guess I read you wrong. You were winging it. That speaks volumes."

"I tried to reach you."

"It's just as well you didn't."

He checked his wristwatch. "With luck you can still make the flight. Want me to take you back to the airport? Believe me, I'd love nothing better than to wave you off. Because, see? I don't want to get caught up in another shitstorm, and that's what you represent to me."

"This isn't all about you," she exclaimed. "My purpose in coming down here wasn't to disrupt your life, Mr. Bowie."

"Oh, for pity's sake, I'm John, okay. *Okay?*"

After their raised voices, the abrupt silence was even more noticeable. They exchanged hostile looks; then he did some swearing under his breath as he turned his head away from her and stared out the windshield. He remained in that pensive pose for what seemed to her a long time. Instinct cautioned her not to intrude on it.

Then, speaking softly as though talking to himself, he said, "Maybe my life needed disrupting." He turned back to her and held out the half-empty tray of food. "Last chance."

"I'm good."

He dumped everything into the sack and got out of the car to carry it to a nearby trash can, giving her an opportunity to look at him without his knowing. He was broad-shouldered, tall, lean, almost lanky. But she'd felt his forearm yesterday when she'd detained him at the table in the bar. There was no doubt of its strength.

Wind sweeping across the road from the runway lifted his hair, which was dark blond with an occasional gray strand threaded in. She'd noticed a dusting of gray in his scruff and eyebrows, too.

Had the premature gray been genetically programmed?

She didn't think so. The lines at the corners of his eyes and that dent that frequently appeared between his eyebrows indicated that it had been earned.

Today he was wearing trousers, an ironed shirt, sport jacket, and necktie, although it had been loosened. However, the dressier clothing didn't alter his blue-jeans saunter. Innate confidence was in every step.

But another quality also characterized that stride. Disregard? Indifference? She had described him to Max as being "unmoved." This man would be moved by little, she thought now. He was audacious and seemed beyond embarrassment, like he didn't give a damn about opinions of him or consequences of his actions.

That was it. She'd hit the nail on the head. John Bowie didn't give a damn.

He took off his jacket and tossed it into the back seat as he slid behind the steering wheel. He made himself comfortable in the seat and said, "About the moon."

"Are we officially reopening the discussion?"

"Not officially. No promises. Off the record. Understood?"

"Understood."

"Okay. Why do you think the moon that night was significant?"

"Did no one ever consider that it might be?"

He gave her a grim smile. "No. Including me. But I researched it last night. The last blood moon straddled the night of November seventh and eighth of 2022. Here in southern North America, Central time zone, the eclipse occurred during the wee hours of the morning of the eighth. Are we in sync on those points?"

"Yes," Beth replied. "Please continue."

"Before going to bed that night, Crissy's mother, Carla, noticed they were out of milk, low on bread. Crissy offered to go to the nearest convenience store. It's just outside the mobile home park where they lived, a five-minute walk at most."

Beth didn't interrupt to tell him that she'd made note of the store today when she was there.

"Carla gave Crissy a twenty-dollar bill, which she clearly remembered her slipping into the pocket of her hoodie. The hood was up. It wasn't raining hard, but it was drizzling. Crissy left. Carla went to bed. She didn't know that was the last time she would see her daughter.

"Because of an office staff meeting, Carla left for work early the next morning, assuming that Crissy was safely asleep in her room. Crissy was usually home from school by the time Carla came in from work. She wasn't there. Carla called Crissy's cell to see what was up. She heard the phone ringing inside the house and located it in Crissy's bedroom.

"Apparently, the night before, Crissy had left her phone behind. But why hadn't she taken it to school with her that morning? Feeling some alarm, Carla checked the kitchen. No new loaf of bread in the bread box, no carton of milk in the fridge.

"She called the boy next door, Billy Oliver. Crissy was eighteen and would have graduated high school the following May. He was two years younger and didn't go to public school, but they were friends. He told Carla he'd seen Crissy leaving their house on foot and had gone outside to ask where she was off to. She told him she was running a quick errand and invited him along. Because of the weather, he declined and went back indoors. That was the last he'd seen or heard from her. She hadn't been at school that day. That's when Carla called the police."

"And was given the run-around," Beth said. "That's a quote from her *Crisis Point* interview."

He nodded somberly. "She was put through the normal drill. Had the two of them had a fight? Had she left the house angry, threatened to run away? Could she be with a boyfriend, or on a jaunt with girlfriends?

"Carla was adamant that an unexplained vanishing act would be out of character for her daughter. She was convincing. And as of then, it was the evening of the eighth. My partner and I were assigned to begin investigating it as a missing person's case. We usually wait twenty-four hours before making it official, but Crissy had already been missing for almost that long."

She noticed that his forehead furrowed, creating that dent between his eyebrows, as though it pained him to think about that even now.

"We were the first to question Billy Oliver. Then Tom Barker turned him over to another detective. He was questioned relentlessly and two days later was taken into custody."

He said nothing more for a time, then turned to her. "When I began thinking about all this last night, I couldn't remember what kind of weather we'd had the night of November seventh and into the wee hours of the eighth, so I looked it up. It was lousy. Overcast, foggy, heavy rain off and on. Typical coastal Louisiana weather.

"You asked why I didn't consider the moon as being

significant. Why anybody didn't. According to what I read last night, the eclipse here began at two A.M. and lasted until six-thirty. Because of the cloud cover, nobody would have seen it, even if they were awake at that time.

"We'd had heavy rains that entire week, causing local flooding and necessitating evacuations. Two people down in Chauvin drowned when their car was swept away. Every law officer and first responder in the southern half of the state was stretched thin. In the midst of all that, Crissy went missing. No one was paying attention to a moon we hadn't seen for a week and couldn't see that night, either."

He repositioned himself in his seat, stretching his legs out beneath the dashboard as far as they would go. "I didn't even know for sure what a blood moon was. I'd heard the term, but I was thinking voodoo, end of the world predictions, folklore legends and rituals, werewolves. But it's a real thing, right? An astronomical phenomenon?"

"Yes. Some lunar eclipses are referred to as blood moons when they're actually not."

"I got sleepy before I learned what defines one."

"It's a total lunar eclipse, not partial. Earth gets between the sun and a *full* moon. That's the distinction. It's a specific alignment. Earth is perfectly positioned to cast an encompassing shadow onto a full moon.

"With Earth in the way, so to speak, sunlight isn't projecting directly onto the moon. It's being filtered through Earth's atmosphere. That filtration is what causes the moon to appear orange or reddish in color. Thus the name."

He took it all in, then said, "Son of a gun. Who knew?"

She smiled. "Well, ancient civilizations knew. They may

not have known what caused the phenomenon, but they attached spiritual or supernatural significance to a red moon. They were recorded and anticipated. They figured out that they occur every three and a half years and that there are two blood moons during the years they occur."

"Interesting. The one in November of 2022 when Crissy disappeared was the second that year."

"Right. The first was the night of May fifteenth–sixteenth, depending where on the globe you were."

He nodded absently, thought on it a little longer, then said, "Okay, I now have a basic understanding of the astronomical properties. What I don't get is how all that intersects with Crissy's disappearance. Let's recap. You don't think Billy Oliver was the guilty party."

"Do you?"

The question seemed to upset him. In any case, he didn't answer. "Still recapping. You believe the actual perp is out there and will strike again during the next blood moon."

"I have reason to believe that it's a possibility."

"How good a reason?"

"Good enough that you shouldn't rule it out."

"I'm not ruling it out."

"Not yet," she said, "but skepticism is written all over your face."

"Look, this is all new to me, and, fair to say, it's a little off the wall. Give me a minute here, all right?"

"We don't have a minute."

"Yeah, last night I caught the tail end of the weatherman talking about a blood moon. He said we'll have two sometime this year."

"Not 'sometime,' John. The first one will occur on the night of March thirteenth–fourteenth."

"The thirteenth and..." She saw when realization struck him. He ran his hand over his mouth "Holy shit."

"That's right. Four days from now."

Chapter 6

Tom Barker came around so quickly, he sloshed freshly brewed coffee over the back of his hand. "He did what?"

The rookie officer who'd had the misfortune of delivering the message gestured toward a nearby desk where one of the lines on the phone was blinking. "The TSA guy is still on the phone if you want to hear it for yourself. I'll just go..." He took a few steps backward, then turned and quickly retreated.

Tom went over to the desk, shook the hot spill off his hand, picked up the receiver, and pressed the blinking button on the panel. "This is Lieutenant Barker."

The man identified himself by name and explained that he was the TSA's supervising agent of the morning shift. For the next several minutes he talked, giving an account of an incident at the New Orleans airport involving John Bowie. Tom listened without comment because his teeth were clenched too tightly to speak. The agent wound down by saying, "To Agent Gorman, he seemed legit at first. But after the crack he made as he was escorting the woman out, Gorman became concerned and reported it to me.

"I spoke with the airport police officer who'd watched his car while he was inside the terminal. Bowie had showed him his ID and explained that he was trying to intercept a material witness who was hotfooting it despite a subpoena. I thought I should call and get your verification."

Tom wished he had John Bowie in a chokehold. He wished he had Bowie on a rack. He was about to assure the TSA agent that his detective would be harshly dealt with for misrepresenting their department.

But in an instant of lucidity, he realized he shouldn't react out of anger. He needed to think this through, give himself time to plan how best to work Bowie's shenanigan to his advantage.

Rather than expressing his outrage, he chuckled. "I tell John all the time, 'That mouth of yours is going to be your undoing.' He's a smart aleck, but what can I say? He's an asset to my division." Tom tasted bile when he said that.

"Agent Gorman will be relieved to hear it. She said Mr. Bowie was polite but had an…an edge. He was also sporting a black eye."

Tom forced another light laugh. "He had a run-in with his closet door. Maybe one margarita too many. We've all been there."

There was a smile behind the agent's voice. "A time or two. I'm sorry to have bothered you, Lieutenant."

"No, no. I'm the one to apologize for troubling you and your agent. Thank you for telling me. I'll speak to John, warn him against crossing a line. Sometimes even the best officers do. You're a supervisor, you know what I mean."

The agent agreed on that point. Tom was about to say goodbye when he had another sudden thought. "Did the woman he apprehended go along quietly? Ms. uh…? Oh, gosh, her name has slipped me."

"Beth Collins."

"Right, right, Beth Collins. John had told me he was afraid she would get skittish when it came down to testifying in court. Going against an abusive ex-boyfriend. Something like that."

"That was another thing that struck Agent Gorman. She said Ms. Collins didn't look like someone the police would be chasing down."

"She's a witness, not a suspect. At least not yet."

They said their goodbyes. Tom went into his private office and sat down at his desk. Using the office phone, he punched in an extension. It rang twice, then, "Hey, boss."

"Get in here."

"Sure, soon as I finish up—"

"Now." Tom hung up.

Less than a minute later, Frank Gray came into the office and pulled the door closed. One of Tom's most loyal facilitators, Gray could be relied on to do what he was told and to keep his mouth shut about it.

Without being invited to sit down, he wedged himself into the chair facing Tom's desk. "What's up?"

"Bowie."

"No surprise there. Heard y'all had quite a showdown this morning. Hate I missed it. What was it about?"

"Same ol'."

"The Mellin thing?" Frank ran his palm over a greasy comb-over that did nothing to conceal his shiny, pink bowling ball of a head. He had jug ears that were equally pink. "The boy is stubborn, I'll give him that."

"*The boy* deserves to be horsewhipped." Tom related what had happened at the New Orleans airport.

"A woman, huh?" Frank guffawed as he smacked his chewing gum. He was never without a wad of it in his mouth, which he never closed while chomping. "Maybe he's just trying to get laid."

"He doesn't have any trouble getting laid, and this isn't funny, Frank. I want to know what he's up to."

"Who was the gal?"

"Her name is Beth Collins."

"Who's she?"

"That's the first thing I want you to find out. The TSA agent said she was booked on a flight to New York. Whoever she is, she's important to Bowie, or he wouldn't have jerked her out of the security line and made off with her."

"Okay. So? She and Bowie had a ring-a-ding. He wasn't done with her yet. It's kinda romantic. Like a movie. Outsmarting security, racing down the concourse. Will he make it? Can he stop her? Big tongue swap at the end."

He leered again and, even though Tom was used to that gaping grin, it still turned his stomach. Unfortunately it was part and parcel with Frank Gray, and he needed this enforcer.

"Bowie may well be in rut," Tom said, "but he's not a romantic. And there's something else that's worrisome. A woman's been calling here for him, and only him. The first time was the day before yesterday, twice this morning."

Gray stopped grinning. "That shoots my theory all to hell. A new bedmate would call his cell phone."

Tom nodded. "Bowie played dumb when I mentioned the calls, but if they're traced back to this Collins woman, I want to know what her connection is to him and why he went to extremes to keep her from leaving." Tom flapped his hand in the direction of the door. "Get on it."

"Right now?"

"Drop everything."

Gray worked his considerable bulk out of the chair. "If it does turn out to be something unromantic, how far do you want me to take things?"

"Bowie's been a pain in my ass for too long. *Far* too long." Tom gave him a look that didn't require explanation.

Gray popped his chewing gum and flashed another misshapen smile. "I've been itching for some fun."

"Don't expect too much."

John unlocked his back door and pushed it open, then stood aside and motioned Beth across the threshold into his kitchen. He didn't like mess, he kept a clean house, but for the first time since he'd moved in, he was embarrassed by his rental, quaintly misnamed a "bungalow."

It was at the end of a shadowy, potholed cul-de-sac, where similarly run-down dwellings were tucked between moss-laden live oaks, shaggy cypresses, and unidentified brambles. It was the perfect setting for a depressing

Tennessee Williams drama in which every character was miserable and nothing went right.

As Beth was taking in the unattractive kitchen, Mutt wandered in from the living room. "Who's this?" she asked.

"He answers to Mutt. His gene pool is murky, but he's harmless."

Proving him right, Mutt padded over and sniffed her hand, then gave it a lick. She didn't jerk her hand back as John would have expected of her. Instead she addressed Mutt by name and introduced herself.

When she bent down to rub his bony head, her slender black slacks that hugged and delineated her shapely bottom were pulled even tighter across the curves, causing John to tell himself for the thousandth time what a bad idea it was to have brought her here. Because when she'd begun explaining the geometry of a blood moon, using phrases like "specific alignment" and being "perfectly positioned," his mind had drifted away from the relationship between heavenly bodies and had instead entertained the thought of a relationship with her body. Which was also heavenly.

Made uncomfortable by his prurient thoughts, he said crossly, "Come on, Mutt. Out you go."

Mutt seemed reluctant to leave her stroking hand, and who could blame him? But he ambled over to the door John was holding open. Before going outside, the dog looked up at him with a *Did I miss something?* expression.

He wanted to tell Mutt that there was a logical explanation for this notably attractive stranger being in their kitchen. Which was that, while still parked in front of the fast food restaurant, Beth and he had agreed that they needed someplace to talk in more depth about the relationship between the Mellin case and a blood moon.

"I checked out of my hotel," she'd told him. "Where do you suggest we go to compare notes?"

His spontaneous reply had been, "My place." She'd been about to shake her head no, when he jumped in ahead of her. "Look. You're safe from me, all right? I'm not going to hit on you. But the subject matter we'll be discussing is likely to get intense, and it would be easier to concentrate without the distractions of a public place like in the bar yesterday." Having said that, he'd been reminded to ask her how she'd known about that dive.

"I grew up in Thibodaux," she said. "When I was in high school, that bar was widely known to have relaxed rules about selling alcohol to minors so long as they didn't drink it on the premises."

"Encouraging kids to drink and drive."

"Which is why it was shut down for a while. It's changed hands since then, but I didn't know how seedy it had become until I walked in yesterday. By then it was too late for a change of venue."

"I can't help but wonder, why the subterfuge? Why didn't you just come to the station and ask for me?"

"Because you were the detractor. I didn't want to rattle anyone until I'd had a chance to talk to you first."

"Well, they are rattled."

"Already?"

"Yes. Word is out that a woman keeps calling the department, asking for me and only me, and won't leave her name."

"Oh."

"Right. We have to assume we're on borrowed time before someone discovers you're from *Crisis Point.* When they learn that, they'll presume, correctly, why you want to talk to me. So, until we know the extent and outcome of this conversation, and I determine how disruptive it might be to my life—"

"To mine as well."

"—it would be better if we're not seen together looking like collaborators."

Even though she'd been sitting in the passenger seat of his car, she'd propped her hand on her hip. "Then maybe you should have thought twice about creating that scene at the airport."

"Maybe I should have, but I didn't want you to get on that plane, forcing me to follow you to New York."

He could tell she'd been surprised by that. "Would you have done that?"

"After yesterday's parting? No. I was glad to see the last of you. But as of nine-thirty this morning, yes. I would've gone to New York if necessary to continue this."

"What happened at nine-thirty?"

"A confrontation with the jerk who shut me down when I tried to extend the Mellin investigation."

"The boss who's looking for an excuse to fire you?"

"That's the one. Lieutenant Tom Barker."

"Why did he do that? I mean, why did he shut down the investigation?"

"He had a promotion pending. Solving the Mellin case would put him on the fast track toward getting it. Solving the case *swiftly* would make it a shoo-in."

She'd lowered her hand from her hip. "He used the Mellin case to gain a promotion?"

"That's the kind of person he is, and he relishes being boss. Believe me, Tom Barker wouldn't welcome an examination of how he conducted that investigation. He wants the Mellin case to remain *solved.* So you were right to exercise caution. This morning the set-to we had began with him warning me against giving any interviews about the *Crisis Point* episode or the case itself."

"That sounds like a giveaway as to how nervous he is."

"I thought so. Which is why I came after you and caused a scene."

Her gaze had shifted to an airliner that was taking off from the runway across the busy boulevard. She'd glanced at the dashboard clock. "I think that must be my flight." Turning back to him, she'd said, "We could go back to the bar."

"Oh, like we'd go unnoticed there." He paused, then said, "Listen, by the time we drive around looking for a place, we could be at mine. No one will bother us there, or even see us there, because nobody but my best friend knows where I live. After we talk, I'll drive you anywhere you want to go. Okay? Daylight's burning."

She was still hesitant, but she had agreed.

And now here they were in his kitchen, which was so narrow there was barely enough room for one person, much less for two who'd somehow come to be standing face-to-face in the confining space.

She looked at a loss.

He looked at her.

Neither moved until Mutt scratched on the back door.

John stepped aside and pointed. "Living room is through there." She turned and made her way in that direction.

He went to the back door and let Mutt in. He snatched his reward kibble from John's fingers, then headed straight for the living room in a frisky trot that John had never seen him exercise before.

"He must've noticed her ass, too," he muttered as he took two bottles of water from the fridge and kneed the contrary door shut.

In the living room, Mutt was lying on the floor at Beth's feet where she was seated in the easy chair. He wondered what she'd think if she knew that one of the grungy guys from the bar had been sitting there last night. Still looking ill at ease, she thanked John for the bottle of water he handed down to her.

He went over to the sofa, detached the holster from his belt at the small of his back, and set it on the coffee table. She must not have noticed him wearing it before now, because he caught her looking at the pistol with misgiving. However, she didn't remark on it, so he didn't acknowledge it, either.

He pulled his tie from beneath his collar, unbuttoned his cuffs, and rolled up his shirtsleeves. Made more comfortable, he settled back against the sofa cushions. "Before we start, I want to ask you a question, but don't get your back up, all right?"

"Ask."

"You seem convinced that another woman will go missing on the night of the blood moon come Thursday. Are you psychic? Do you read tarot cards? You're a fortune teller?"

"My back is up."

"Okay then, tell me what qualifies you to make a prediction like that?"

"Fair enough." She took a deep breath. "For seven years, I've worked on *Crisis Point*, which, as you know, is a program that documents criminal cases."

"I'm a faithful fan of *Law & Order.* But to become a detective, I had to earn a degree and then go to the police academy."

She frowned over his sarcasm. "Do you want to hear this or not?"

"You have the floor."

She took another deep breath, which he really wished she would stop doing. Each time she did, he couldn't help but notice the rise and fall of those more than just "nice," actually oh-so-sweet breasts. They challenged his effort to stay focused.

She was saying, "I was hired by the network to work on *Crisis Point.* My first position was that of gofer. Within a year, I was promoted to fact checker. Everyone involved in the production process relies on fact checkers. The title defines the job."

"You made sure everything was correct."

"Yes. It could be something as minor as the spelling of someone's name, or a major discrepancy that required further investigation. I wasn't the only one, of course. At any given time, several are working on a project."

"You were the best, though. Right? You advanced."

"Well—"

"Come on now. No false modesty. Who is Mr. Max Longren and just what all do you do for him?"

Chapter 7

How did you…" Then her eyes turned glaring. "You checked me out, didn't you?" His shrug of admission ignited her further. "You talked to Max? About me?"

He raised his eyebrows. "It's not Mr. Longren? It's *Max*?"

Emphasizing each word, she said, "Did you talk to him?"

He'd expected a reaction from her, but not one this extreme. "No, I didn't. All right? Can we move on?"

"No, no," she said, wagging her finger at him. "I want to know why you went behind my back to—"

"I didn't go behind—"

"You absolutely did. You didn't trust me, so you had me validated."

"Okay, I did."

"*Why* did you?"

Now, angry in his own right, he shot to his feet. "Self-preservation."

He rounded the end of the sofa and braced his hands on the back of it. "Yes, I checked you out, because *you* met me yesterday looking like a coed that I'd have liked to get on when I was in college. Then I learn that *you* are someone who can fuck up my life more than it already is.

"And since *your* appearance on the scene, life has already turned rocky. Even if it wasn't your intention, *your* repeat calls to the police station sent up Tom Barker's antennas. When he discovers—and he will—who *you* represent, he'll implode.

"This morning when he warned me off giving interviews regarding the Mellin case, I confronted him about his handling of it. He became incensed, red-in-the-face livid. Which is a clear indication of just how badly he fears it will be reexamined.

"His tirade didn't squelch my interest; it spiked it. I came away from our shouting match with one goal in mind, and that was to hear what *you* had to say about the Mellin story, even if your source *is* a crystal ball."

She didn't say anything, but he could tell by her demeanor that her anger had cooled. He relaxed his stance and moderated his tone. "Self-preservation, Beth. As much as it sucks, I need the job. Before I got myself into an unholy fix with Barker, I damn well needed to vet you first. If you're offended, try putting yourself in my place. I think you would have done the same. In fact, you had. You admitted to researching me before setting up our tête-à-tête."

"You've made your point. I overreacted."

"Thank you." He returned to his seat on the sofa and took a drink from his bottle of water.

She said, "Who did you talk to?"

"At the network? I went through an endless menu but finally reached a man named Richard."

"My assistant."

"So he said. He also told me that you were out of town. I asked to speak to Longren. Richard informed me that Mr. Longren had just left for his lunch date with the mayor. Acting like a hayseed, I said, 'Wow. The mayor of NYC? Are you kidding?'

"Unable to resist an opening like that, Richard boasted that it's not unusual for Mr. Longren to lunch with the honorable mayor but he'd almost missed this luncheon date because his right hand, Ms. Collins—who, Richard confided in an undertone, is essentially Mr. Longren's keeper—wasn't there to remind him."

"That was terribly indiscreet of him."

"He must have realized it, because after that he clammed up. He wouldn't give me your cell number or tell me where you were staying while on vacation. No amount of wheedling worked."

"You could have told him you were a police officer."

"No, I didn't want to play the cop card because…well, because I didn't know what I was dealing with yet."

"You played the cop card with the car rental company."

"Because they don't know you, they don't work with you every day."

She gave a light laugh. "Let me get this straight. You didn't trust my integrity, you thought I might be a little wacko, but you wanted to safeguard my reputation among my coworkers?"

The irony had merit, but he didn't pursue it. "Who's Longren?"

"The retiring executive producer of—"

"I already know. I just wanted to see if you would admit it. You're the boss's right hand."

"He recently became the former boss," she said ruefully. "Max is a living legend in the network news industry. After I'd been with *Crisis Point* for a couple of years, he took me under his wing as an apprentice. I was thrilled because I knew I would be trained by a master. Writing, editing, all aspects of production. We've been working side by side for the past five years."

"Why's he stepping down?"

"It isn't by choice. A year ago, the network was acquired by an international media conglomerate. The expected corporate shake-up ensued, but because *Crisis Point* is so highly rated and one of the network's cash cows, Max maintained his position as executive producer.

"Then he began experiencing some health issues, minor at first, then one serious health scare. He recovered, but the medical setback was the opportunity that his detractors, led by a smarmy shark named Winston Brady, had been waiting for."

"He's been elbowed out?"

"Internally. Publicly, a fanfare has been made of his impending 'retirement.' His official departure date isn't for another three months, but Brady, who was appointed the new EP, is already making all the decisions on *Crisis Point* content."

"How does this baton passing affect you?"

"My situation is tenuous. Ruffling Brady's feathers is one reason Max discouraged me from coming down here. He warned that my 'obsession' with the Mellin case could be unhealthy for my career path."

"It's certainly been toxic to mine," he muttered.

"But you haven't been fired. Max thinks that I'm at risk and that if I want to keep my job, I should leave well enough alone."

"So you didn't ask Brady's permission to take another look at the episode that covered the Mellin case because you were afraid he'd say no."

"Correct."

"Hmm. Beyond Brady's reaction, what were Max's other reasons for discouraging you from coming down here and poking around?"

She lowered her gaze. "He thinks it's hooey."

"The blood moon angle?"

"He called it 'moon cycle crap.' In other words, he agrees with you." She raised her head and looked at him. "Satisfied?"

She was still miffed, and, for some nameless reason, that was a colossal turn-on. He wanted to get up and go to her, lift her face to his, and kiss her. Without timidity or finesse. Kiss her until those lips, now unsmiling and compressed, softened and opened to him. And then take it from there.

He put the brakes on that runaway-train fantasy and came back to the subject at hand. "It's a long way up the corporate ladder from gofer and fact checker to where you are now."

"Not all that far. I still do research and fact checking,

only now it's exclusively for Max. I also serve as his personal assistant. I order chocolates for staffers at Christmas and forge his name on the enclosure cards." She raised a shoulder in a slight shrug. "I'm his go-to person."

"For what else besides chocolates and fact checking?"

"Like foot rubs and sex?"

"You give him foot rubs?"

"No. And I don't have sex with him, either."

"I didn't ask."

"You didn't have to. The implication was loud and clear. Let's get this out of the way so we can move past it, all right?" She didn't wait for him to answer. "Max isn't my sugar daddy. He's eighty-two years old. He's been married and divorced four times, and none of his exes has a good word to say about him.

"His son by wife number two is his only progeny, but they haven't spoken to each other in twenty years, even though he also works in the television industry and they often attend the same functions.

"Max isn't a warm fuzzy. In fact, he's rather horrible. On a good day, he's merely irascible. Ordinarily, he's hot-tempered, mule-headed, dictatorial, rude, often crude, and he views all those traits as assets. Despite all that, he's my mentor and friend."

"How does he feel about you?"

She smiled wistfully. "I'd like to think he has a soft spot for me, but he would never acknowledge it, and, if he did, it would feel patronizing. Given the choice, I would far rather have his respect. It's not easily earned. He would regard that as the greatest honor he could bestow on me."

John processed everything she'd told him, then asked, "When did your obsession with the Mellin case start?"

"Initially, I took special interest because it happened here, my old stomping grounds. My familiarity with the area made me useful to the production crew while they were down here. I got twenty calls a day, asking for background info on this or that. And then Max and I oversaw the post-production process, as we did for every episode."

"What does post-production entail?"

"A lot of work," she said with a light laugh. "As a piece was being constructed, he and I would watch the edited segments and give the producer our notes."

"Like what?"

"Well, like 'This interview runs too long. Trim it, but don't cut the last sentence because it's a cliffhanger. Go from it straight into a commercial break.' Things like that. We'd nitpick and suggest edits that could make a big difference, give the story more oomph."

"No wonder the show is so highly rated."

"Thanks." She shot him a smile, but it didn't last long. "Shortly after Max and I had watched what was to become the broadcast version of the Mellin episode, he had a heart attack that kept him out for six weeks.

"When he returned, it was obvious to everyone that it had taken a toll. He was still a dragon, but he had little fire left in him. It wasn't long before he was asked to resign. Brady took over. It was he who gave the Mellin episode final approval and put it into the schedule."

"But that episode didn't get your approval. If it had, you wouldn't be down here secretly meeting me in a beer joint."

"The episode is good, but no, it didn't win my wholehearted approval."

"Why not?"

"I felt there was more to that story than we had. We'd skimmed the surface well enough but hadn't gotten to the bottom of it." She sat forward, clasped her hands on her knees, and looked directly at him. "I believe you think the same about the investigation. Don't you?"

The question sank into him like the claws of a lion, holding him inescapably captive like newly caught prey.

He looked away from Beth's inquiring eyes and noticed how dim the room had become. Today was the start of daylight saving time. Even so, when the sun slipped behind the trees that surrounded his bungalow and formed a thick canopy above its low roof, darkness fell earlier than it did most places.

The encroaching dusk contributed to his feeling of entrapment.

He was about to reach for the lamp on the end table and switch it on. But lamplight would make Beth's incisiveness all the more evident, all the more compelling, so he left the lamp alone.

"Don't you?" she repeated.

She wouldn't spare him from answering, so he gave her the straightforward answer he felt she deserved. "To me, a homicide investigation remains open until the body is found."

"Crissy's isn't shut. It's classified as a cold case."

He scoffed. "If her remains are ever discovered, it won't be by anyone inside the Auclair PD. It's understood that the lid is on that case and that it's to be left as is. Dormant."

"For all the criticizing attributed to you, you've never come right out and said that."

"Only in private."

"Have I won your trust, then?"

"Working on it. Keep talking."

She gave a small smile. "Thanks." After a beat, she said, "Without Max's knowledge, I continued to probe that story like a sore tooth, looking for the elusive element I felt was missing. I surfed the internet, searching for any articles or YouTube segments that I might have missed. On one of those explorations, I came across an article referring to another missing persons case in Galveston, Texas."

John held up his hand. "I know all about it. Since it took place only a few months ahead of our case, we looked into it to see if there was a connection. Larissa Whitmore, a sixteen-year-old from Houston, was playing hooky with a group of girlfriends in Galveston.

"They went out clubbing. Larissa got stoned on marijuana and tequila shots and started making out with twenty-two-year-old Patrick Dobbs, whom she'd met on the beach earlier that day. He and Larissa left the nightclub together and went off in his cabin cruiser."

"That was the last time she was seen."

"Right. The following morning, the Coast Guard discovered Dobbs's boat adrift. It had run out of gas. Dobbs was found in the cabin, naked and sleeping like a baby. There was no sign of the girl except for her discarded clothing and her purse, with nothing noticeably missing from it.

"Dobbs swore he'd passed out and didn't remember what had happened after they'd had sex. Lots of sex, lots of pot and tequila. He theorized that she woke up, went up on deck, and, still wasted, fell overboard."

Beth picked up there. "Dobbs came from a venerable Galveston family with money and privilege. Larissa's parents typified him as a spoiled rich kid with a sense of entitlement. They were convinced that Larissa had denied him a sexual favor, that he threw a tantrum, turned violent, and their daughter ended up in the Gulf."

"That's what they alleged," John said, "but there was no forensic evidence to support any allegation of violence. Dobbs didn't have a scratch or bruise on him. The boat was a mess, but it looked like the scene of an orgy, not an assault or homicide. There were used condoms to support his claims that he'd practiced safe sex."

"With an underage girl."

"Yeah. That definitely didn't help him. While the search was still on for her body, he was held on charges of kidnapping, statutory rape, and a laundry list of other crimes associated with her being a minor."

"Her body was never found."

"No. They searched the Gulf for weeks. If there's an update on that, I haven't heard about it. Anyway, as it related to the Mellin case, Dobbs was ruled out. He'd been denied bail and was in jail when Crissy Mellin went missing. No connection whatsoever between that case and ours."

Beth appeared to stop breathing for a moment, then said quietly, "Except that on the night of May fifteenth and sixteenth when Larissa Whitmore went missing, there was a blood moon."

It took every ounce of willpower John possessed not to

recoil. That single tidbit of information had the effect of a wrecking ball. It hit him much harder than Mitch's slug had yesterday. He'd been braced for that retaliating punch. He hadn't been prepared for this at all.

Beth was watching him closely with an earnest, almost sympathetic expression, while he was trying his damnedest not to give her any indication of the tumult going on inside him.

Speaking softly, she said, "Earlier, when we were discussing the two blood moons that had occurred in 2022, it didn't ring a bell that the first one was in May, coinciding with the Whitmore girl's disappearance?"

"I, uh…I remembered that she'd been abducted sometime that spring. I had no cause to remember the exact date. So, no. It didn't ring a bell."

She inched forward in her chair until she was virtually perched on the edge of the seat. "In the article I read about Larissa's disappearance, it was speculated that the eclipse was one of the lures Dobbs used to get her to go out on the water with him.

"The article writer digressed to explain to his readers what a blood moon was and, as a footnote, said that the next one would occur over the seventh and eighth of November. When I read that, a chill went down my spine, because I knew from working on the Mellin episode that that was the night Crissy had disappeared. That's when my obsession began, John.

"My immediate thought was in regards to the show. *Why hadn't we mentioned the blood moon in our episode?* It would have had terrific production value. We could have edited in graphics that would have made great visuals, set the mood, added drama and eeriness.

"Then I realized that we hadn't included it because no one involved had ever referred to the moon on that night, not in any of the interviews, nowhere. If someone had, I wouldn't have missed it."

"Wasn't Crissy's fate eerie enough for production value without the goddamn moon?"

She was about to speak, but his testiness must have changed her mind. She let the conversation die there and reached down to scratch Mutt beneath his chin. After a few seconds of that, he rolled onto his back. She scratched his belly. His dog had become completely addlepated over her.

He said, "Thanks a lot."

She looked over at him. "For what?"

"From now on, he's going to expect me to do that."

She smiled, gave Mutt one last pat, then sat up straight. After a hesitation, she asked, "What do you think?"

"I think I'll never start scratching his belly."

She frowned. "You know what I meant."

He sighed. "I know what you meant, but there's no correlation there, Beth. Dobbs couldn't have taken Crissy. The moon thing is a bizarre coincidence."

She looked at him with annoyance. "When you're investigating a crime, and you come across a link to a similar crime, no matter how bizarre that link seems, don't tell me that you dismiss it out of hand as a coincidence. I know you don't."

"Okay, no, I don't. So let's say the orange moon was a lure, that Larissa and Dobbs screwed beneath it on the deck of his boat. But bloody or otherwise, the moon had nothing to do with Crissy's disappearance."

"How do you know?" she said in a raised voice. "You

didn't even realize there had been a blood moon. You told me that no one was paying attention to it, that no one could even see it. You said—"

"I know what I fucking said!"

Then he drew a breath and tried to stop the rapid unraveling of his conviction that she was wrong. He wanted desperately for her to be wrong. Even as he tried to convince himself, he tried to convince her.

"Look, Beth, you work for a TV show that's all about drama. You look for elements in a story that have production value. You make edits that add oomph. It's what you do, and obviously you're good at it. But now you've cooked up this…this…" Failing to find the word he sought, he raked his fingers through his hair. "*Shit!*"

"John, everything you just said, I've told myself. Dozens of times I tried to talk myself into forgetting about it. Max tried to talk me into forgetting about it, and I respect his opinion more than anyone's. I would have dismissed it as a wild and crazy coincidence except for—"

Suddenly two things happened at once. Mutt shot up as though the floor plank had launched him. And John, in one conditioned motion, reached for his holster, slid the pistol out, and hurdled the coffee table.

Beth jumped up from her chair. John planted his left hand in the center of her chest and pushed her back into it. "Stay down." He extended his gun hand toward the front door.

She gasped, "My God, what's happened?"

"Mutt growled."

Chapter 8

Beth's heart was in her throat.

Mutt had practically gone airborne and was now standing rigid, staring at the front door as though he could see through it, his growl low but menacing.

Apparently John had excellent night vision. Without a misstep, he went to the window nearest to him and peered out. He stood unmoving. Mutt remained in his sentinel stance.

Not knowing the source of the threat, Beth was afraid even to breathe.

John came over to her chair and reached for her hand. "Hurry. Not a word," he whispered as he pulled her up. "Mutt."

Instantly obeying, the dog trailed them into the kitchen. John looked out the window above the sink, then went to the back door, and, as soundlessly as possible, unlocked it.

He waited, straining to listen for any sound coming from

the other side of the door. Hearing nothing, he gradually opened it several inches. He looked through the narrow crack, turning his head from side to side in order to have a view from different angles.

From Beth's vantage point behind him, all she could see through the opening was darkness. No light, no motion, nothing to indicate a lurking danger. John turned to her, leaned in close, and whispered, "Try not to make a sound."

Before she could question him or protest, he opened the door wider and guided her outside, waited for Mutt to clear the door, then closed it. The air was chilly but heavy with moisture. There was no wind. Thick cloud cover blocked out any light the waxing moon would have provided.

Both man and dog seemed not to need light as they made their way down a path invisible to her, but obviously well known to them. They walked quickly but quietly until they reached an outbuilding that appeared to Beth to be listing. The door was held shut by an old-fashioned padlock, but it hung from the latch unfastened.

John opened the door. Mutt went inside. Since the structure appeared to be on the verge of collapse, Beth hesitated. John put his hand on the small of her back and urged her forward. The enclosure smelled of damp earth and, faintly, of onions. After John pulled the door closed, the darkness inside was impenetrable. He said, "Mutt, be still."

He'd spoken in a whisper, but it had sounded like a command given to a well-trained dog. Beth couldn't see Mutt, but she sensed that he'd laid down and then remained motionless. He wasn't even panting.

In the darkness, John somehow found her, specifically

her ear. He placed his lips against it. "If a shot is fired, drop to the ground. Don't think about it, just do it."

The instruction stunned her. But why should it when he still gripped a pistol in his right hand? He gave her no time to ask who might be shooting at them before slipping away from her. She curbed a cowardly impulse to reach out for him and then to cling.

She approximated the shed to be only a few yards square, like a tool or gardening shed. It had a dirt floor that absorbed any sounds John would have made as he moved from one side of it to another, pausing periodically. She could tell where he was in juxtaposition to her only by the subtle shifts in the air as he patrolled.

Then he stopped and became perfectly still. She sensed that there wasn't much distance between them, but she couldn't even hear his breathing, only her own heartbeat pulsing against her eardrums.

It seemed they remained like that for an eternity. Then, a car engine grumbled to life. The distinctive sound came from quite a distance, and it was further muffled by the dense atmosphere, but she sensed an immediate lessening of John's tension. Mutt must have, too. He stood and brushed against her hand. She patted him on the head as he went past her.

John came up from behind her and placed his hand on her shoulder. "You good?"

She nodded, then, realizing that he might be unable to see that, she said, "Fine. Scared out of my wits and wondering what the hell is going on. But fine."

Maybe she imagined the light squeeze he gave her shoulder before he took his hand away. "Let's go."

Compared to the mustiness inside the shed, the humid outside air seemed almost brisk. She breathed deeply of it as she turned to John, who was shoving the pistol into his waistband. "What in heaven's name was that all about?"

"Nothing good."

"I would appreciate an explanation." She started walking in the direction of the house.

But behind her, he said, "This way."

She turned and looked past him in the direction he indicated and saw only a meshwork of trees and unrelieved darkness.

"This way," he said again, tipping his head with impatience. Mutt had already disappeared into the woods, obviously expecting them to come along after him.

"We're not going back to your house?"

"Not tonight. Come on. He may come back."

"Who?"

"Come on." He covered the distance between them, clasped her hand, and tugged.

She pulled her hand free and stayed where she was. "Where are we going?"

"I'll tell you when we get there."

"I'm not going anywhere except back to your house. I need my purse, my phone, my suitcase. If you don't want to drive me to a hotel, I'll call Uber."

He muttered something unintelligible but undoubtedly profane. "Okay. Go back. Get your purse. Your suitcase is in the car. Call Uber. Have a nice return flight to New York."

"I—"

"One more thing. If you don't come with me now, don't ever contact me again."

"Wait. If—"

"No, not waiting."

"You're being unreasonable. If you would just tell me why we're... *fleeing*."

"I will, but not now. If you're coming with me, it's gotta be right now." He placed his hands on his hips.

She wanted to stand her ground, but one glance back toward his house changed her mind. Everything was cloaked in a darkness that was more than simply an absence of light. It was ominous in character.

Coming back around, she said, "When we get wherever we're going, I demand a full explanation."

He dropped his hands from his hips, reached for her hand, and struck off in the direction Mutt had taken. She either had to fall into step behind his long strides or be dragged.

They walked on for another five minutes before he stopped. "Wait here." Mutt started after him. In a soft but imperative voice, John told him to stay. Mutt sat and looked back at Beth as though to say, *That means you, too.* She watched John's retreating figure for as long as she could see it.

Since moving to Manhattan, she had walked the sidewalks of the city alone and after dark, always cautious but without fear. Now she looked back in the direction from which they'd come with uneasiness.

She couldn't see John's house, the shed, or any other structure. Interspersed with tall pines, the live oak trees appeared as solid as monoliths, ancient and mystical. Their drapery of Spanish moss looked like shredding winding cloths. She strained to see or hear any indication that they were being pursued, but nothing moved until John reappeared from out of the deep shadows. "Over here," he said.

She followed him and Mutt through tall weeds and over ground that became increasingly spongy, but she didn't see the channel of water until they were steps away from it. The bayou was wide. In the darkness, she could barely make out the opposite shore. She didn't detect a current. The water seemed not to be moving at all.

Mutt was already standing in a boat, tongue out, panting happily, as though declaring that this was the most fun he'd ever had. The craft was small—very small—and looked as though it would tip over if someone nudged the shallow hull with a feather.

John stepped into it, and, as she'd predicted, it rocked violently. He balanced with seemingly no effort, and extended her his hand. "Easy does it." She just looked at him. "Beth."

"Why are we leaving, John? What are we running from? We are running, aren't we? Give me an inkling, at least."

He hesitated, cut a glance past her in the direction of his house, then looked at her directly. "I don't want anything bad to happen to you because of me."

"Bad like what?"

"Like the Mellin girl."

Surprised by that, she expelled a short breath. "What are you talking about? You didn't cause that."

"I didn't prevent it, either. She was disposed of God knows where. Now get in the damn boat." As an afterthought, he said, "Please."

It was a nameless bayou, but to Beth it felt like the Rubicon as she reached out and took his hand.

She'd grown up near swamps, had gone into them on school field trips, had even ventured into them on a date or two. But those excursions had always been in the daytime. With sunlight filtering through the cypresses, the swamps were beautiful and, so long as one was careful, benign.

It was a different story at night when the swamp was wrapped in darkness.

Of the three in the boat, she appeared to be the only one bothered by the skeletal silhouettes of the trees, the sudden screech of a small animal captured by a nocturnal predator, the startling flap of great wings when an owl took flight.

Curled up in the bow of the boat, Mutt had gone to sleep. After his oblique statements in reference to Crissy Mellin's sad end, John had said nothing more. Sensing that he wouldn't welcome her asking what more he could have done to prevent Crissy's fate, she hadn't engaged him in further conversation—which was awkward since they sat facing each other in a vessel smaller than an average size sofa.

He'd helped her into the boat and made sure she was seated as securely as possible on the wood bench that spanned the hull. He'd then moved to the stern and used one of the oars to shove them off into the channel. He rowed without vigor, but with sure and steady hands.

If he had a destination, Beth couldn't fathom how he would be able to locate it. The bayou was one of a countless number of identical waterways that formed an aquatic labyrinth studded with islands of various sizes. Some could be crossed with one giant step. Others were much more sizable.

John navigated around all of them smoothly, somehow avoiding collisions with the knotty knees of cypress trees that jutted out of the water. It was obviously an acquired skill that he'd practiced often.

After being on the water for half an hour, she broke the silence. "How can you tell where you're going? It all looks the same."

"Not if you know where you're going."

"And you do?"

"Um-huh."

She tried to read her wristwatch, but it was too dark to see the hands. "What time is it?"

"Does it matter?"

"If I'd been on that flight this afternoon, I'd have been home long before now. If Max doesn't hear from me, he'll be worried sick."

"You can call him when we get there."

"When will we get there, and where is *there*?" Her patience at an end, she said forcefully, "John, I'm entitled to know what happened back there and why we left the way we did. It felt like an escape."

"It was."

"From what? Something Mutt heard outside? That's what dogs do. They react to noises."

"Not Mutt. He's never growled. Not once. Not since I've had him. Just last night, a friend dropped by. He walked in unannounced. I wasn't even in the room. Mutt never made a sound."

"Well, he wouldn't have growled at a friend."

"He'd never met that friend. But Mutt sensed that he wasn't a threat. I don't know any of my neighbors. They're strangers. They come and go without ever rousing him. Up till tonight, I thought he was useless as a watchdog. I'm glad I was wrong." Appearing lost in thought, he pulled on the oars a few times before adding, "Mutt sensed a threat, and his instinct was right."

"You saw someone?"

"From the shed. I have peepholes in all four walls, and I have the shed for just the purpose it served tonight. To watch someone who came there to watch me."

"Is that what he was doing?"

"He walked around the house, looked through the windows."

"Did he go inside?"

"No."

"Any idea who it might have been?"

"I don't have to speculate. I know." He stopped rowing and rested the oars against his thighs. "When Mutt alerted us, you were in the middle of saying something. Was it important?"

She heard a rustle of motion on a nearby island and looked toward the sound. Whatever was there remained camouflaged, but she continued looking that way as she murmured, "You tell me whether or not you think it's important."

Turning back to him, she said, "The blood moons prior to the two in 2022 were in 2018. January thirty-first and July twenty-seventh. On each of those dates, young women were reported missing. One in Jackson, Mississippi, the other in Shreveport, Louisiana. As of yet, their fates remain unknown, the cases unsolved."

He stared at her as though willing her to revise what she'd said; then his head dropped forward until his chin was almost touching his chest. Before either of them spoke again, Mutt woke up, stood, and shook himself energetically.

John picked up the oars, murmuring, "That means we're here."

Deftly he maneuvered the boat to the tip of a peninsula and pushed them through the shallows using one of the oars against the muddy bottom. When the hull scraped against the shore, Mutt jumped out onto the marshy ground.

Beth got out unassisted. When John joined her, he surprised her by dragging the boat out of the water and into a grove of trees. He covered it with brambles that had obviously been cut for that purpose.

By the time John had concealed the boat, Mutt had watered several trees and seemed to be waiting for them to follow him. "Go on," John said, and the dog took off. "I'll take the lead," he said to Beth. "Stay close and watch your step. It's an uneven trail."

"To where?"

"Have you ever been to a Cajun fishing camp?"

"No."

"Well then, you're in for a real treat."

His ironic tone suggested the opposite of what he'd said, but she had no choice except to fall into step behind him. They wound their way through the trees, ducking beneath low limbs and sidestepping depressions where scummy water had collected. Carefully placing her feet in John's footprints, watching for obstacles like ropy tree roots and anything that slithered, Beth kept her head down, eyes on the ground.

She didn't see the clump of Spanish moss dangling from a branch until its tendrils creepily grazed her cheek. Her breath caught as she drew up short and reflexively made a swatting motion.

John turned quickly. Seeing what had startled her, he brushed the strands of moss off her face. His touch was lighter than a waft of breath, and even after breaking contact, he didn't withdraw his hand, but left it raised, close to but not quite touching her cheek.

Then he folded his fingers to form a loose fist and lowered it. "I know you're not used to shit like this. You're sure not used to me. I've put you through a lot today." One corner of his mouth tilted up in a quasi-smile. "Just want you to know, you've done okay."

He didn't turn away immediately. In fact, he didn't turn away for seconds that numbered in double digits. When he finally did, Beth realized that she'd been holding her breath in achy anticipation.

John removed the pistol from the waistband of his pants and set it on the middle shelf of an open cupboard that held a collection of mismatched dishes and serving bowls. Glancing at Beth, he said, "There's a bullet in the chamber, so be careful if you pick it up."

As if, she thought.

He took a bag of dog food from an upper cabinet and filled a bowl for Mutt. As he knelt to set it on the floor, he cupped his hands around Mutt's head and scratched him behind the ears. "I'm on to you now. Playing dumb and useless is an act you perform to get me to feel sorry for you. When, in fact, you're a genius." Mutt tilted his head back, leaning into the massaging fingers, then nudged aside John's hands in order to get to his dinner.

John patted him on the rump and stood up to find Beth watching him from where she seemed to have taken root in the center of the large but overcrowded and cluttered room. Again, she looked lost. A lot lost.

Extending her hands at her sides, she said, "This is quite a place. It's got…" She took a look around, stopping on the stuffed head of a snarling razorback that hung on the wall above the sideboard. Coming back to him she said, "Character."

He gave a humorless chuckle. "Very diplomatic."

He looked around as she had at all the memorabilia affixed to the walls, which included rusty license plates from decades past, yellowed posters announcing boxing matches and parish Easter egg hunts, school pennants, words of wisdom embroidered on framed squares of muslin, shellacked prize-winning fish mounted on wood plaques, a stuffed baby alligator, and numerous hunting trophies whose antlers were cobwebbed. One of them had a glass eye missing.

"This place has belonged to my maternal grandpa's family for generations," he said. "He and my great-uncles would come out here at least once a month to escape their wives, kids, responsibilities. Fish all day, get drunk at night, repeat stories they'd repeated a thousand times, cuss freely, and tell dirty jokes without censure."

He smiled wryly. "They used any excuse to throw a party, so a few times each year the whole clan would gather. Some of the happiest times of my life were spent out here, making mischief with my boy cousins, spooking the girls just to hear them scream, drinking beers we'd swiped from the coolers when the grown-ups weren't looking."

As he'd been talking, she'd sat down on the arm of an upholstered chair that had been in that spot for as far back as John could remember. She asked, "Does the clan still gather?"

"No, my grandparents, aunts, and uncles are all gone."

"Your parents?"

"Alive and well. After Dad retired, they moved to Natchitoches and opened a gift shop."

"Really?"

"It was a dream of my mom's. They've made a slew of friends. Dad has fishing buddies. They're happy. They worry about me," he added wryly.

"You're lucky to have someone who does."

Her tone was telling, but her bearing and facial expression advised him not to go down that path. "Anyhow," he said, "the cousins scattered. You know how it goes. I regret the years that I skipped those family gatherings."

"Why did you skip them?"

"Roslyn, my ex, had ruined it for me. She didn't take to the culture the way my dad did when he met and married my mom. Dad fit right in. Roslyn didn't, and didn't want to. Said it was all too rowdy, too redneck, too Cajun." He took another look around and reached up to jangle the multiple strands of Mardi Gras beads hanging from a wall sconce. "It was that. I wouldn't trade for the memories."

Having cleaned his bowl, Mutt wandered over to John. "Need out?" John opened the door for him. "Don't go far."

When he turned back into the room, he asked Beth if she was hungry.

"Considering the scare I've had, I can't believe it, but I'm actually starving."

"Do you like gumbo?"

"I love it."

"I made some the last time I was here."

"You?"

"Using Grandma's recipe." He took a container of gumbo from the freezer section of the refrigerator and set it on the drainboard. "Let's give it a little time to thaw before heating it up. We need to talk."

He got two beers from the fridge and, without even asking her, uncapped both. He passed one to her and motioned her into a chair at the dining table. He sat down across from her.

Then, her eyes on the bottle label, she scraped it with her thumbnail. "Are you ready to tell me who you saw at your house and why he was there?"

"His name's Frank Gray, but everybody calls him the ogre. Big, lumbering guy. Shoulders like an ox. Large round head. Ugly as sin, knows it, and uses it to frighten people."

"How do you know him?"

He took a sip of beer and wiped his mouth with the back of his hand. "He's a detective. But he's one of Tom Barker's henchmen."

She gave a start. "Surely you don't mean that literally."

He steadied a look on her. "Listen carefully, Beth. I wasn't kidding when I told you that nobody knows where I live except for the one friend I mentioned earlier. He's my former partner, and he wouldn't betray me under pain of death."

"How is it possible that no one knows where you live?"

"I've never given out my address or even an indication of the general area. As far as the department knows, I live in a PO box."

"Driver's license?"

"The pre-divorce address. I never had it changed. What this means is, the ogre went to a hell of a lot of trouble to find me tonight."

"Why was he looking for you?"

"Us. He was looking for *us*. Under orders from Barker, I'm certain."

"How did the ogre know where to look?"

"Best I can figure, he tracked your cell phone."

"*My* phone? No one had the number."

"It would have been easy enough to get. I did."

"True," she said thoughtfully. "But why track mine? It would have been easier to track yours."

"Oh, I'm sure they tried that first. They would have found it in the bottom drawer of my desk where it's kept on perpetual charge. That's the number they have. But that phone routes my calls to this one," he said, fishing one from his pants pocket. "It's a burner, they don't have this number, and I get a replacement for it every few weeks."

"You go to a lot of trouble not to be located."

"I do, yeah."

"Any particular reason why?"

He rested his forearms on the edge of the table and leaned toward her. "This is going to sound paranoid, but it's the part you must understand. The ogre wasn't paying us a social call."

Chapter 9

"Well?"

Tom's voice was strained, but he kept his volume down as he answered the call he'd been expecting. His wife was in the kitchen, humming as she set the table. He'd stayed late at the office, she'd fed the kids and had sent them upstairs for baths and homework. She was happy over the prospect of having a quiet supper, just the two of them.

By contrast, Tom was seething. After having been dispatched hours earlier, Frank Gray was only now reporting in. "What's taken so long?"

"Driving all the way out there, for one thing. Jesus. I got lost twice even with GPS. Thought I was never gonna find it."

"Okay, okay. And?"

"They weren't there."

Tom felt like he'd been hit by a two-by-four. "Say again."

"What part didn't you get? They weren't there. Another

reason I delayed calling you was because there was nothing to tell."

"How could she not be there?" Tom asked, his voice rising an octave. "Her phone is there."

"Well, it might be, but she wasn't, and neither was he. Which was weird because his car was in front. That's how I knew which house was his. There are several tucked into a cul-de-sac. His is at the end of it, kinda sitting off by itself. Not a sign of life anywhere near it."

"Christ, Frank, if his car is there, they—"

"Honey?" The whiny voice came from the kitchen.

"Shit. Hold on." Tom held the phone against his chest. "Yeah?"

"Dinner's ready."

"I'm on the phone."

"Don't let it get cold."

"I'm about to wind up." He put the phone back to his ear. "They've gotta be there."

"I'm telling you, they weren't."

"Just by driving past, how could you tell?"

Frank gave a long-suffering sigh. "I overshot the turnoff. Pulled over and found a spot to leave my car where it wouldn't be too conspicuous, went back to the cul-de-sac on foot. But which house was his?

"I had to walk the length of the street before I saw his car. A few of the neighbors had lights on, but none were on inside his house, and it's dark as freaking pitch out there. I looked in the rear window of his car and saw a suitcase in the hatch. Maybe her phone's in it."

"You could've called it to find out."

"Bad idea, Tom. If Bowie and the woman were in there with the lights out, doing what I suspect this is about, he could've heard her phone ringing, come out to check, seen me sneaking around his car, and shot me for trespassing. Palace doctrine or whatever it's called."

"Castle doctrine. And it's not a defense unless there's been forcible entry."

"Well, I wasn't going to test it on Bowie and his Glock."

Tom pulled on his lower lip, wishing his wife would stop with the damn humming. It was a stupid song, and she was off key. It was distracting, and he was trying to work through this puzzle. "He's mentioned a dog. Doesn't he have a dog?"

"Don't know, but none barked."

"This makes no sense," Tom hissed. "His car was there."

"Maybe he had another means of transportation."

"The TSA guy told me she turned in her rental. The DMV has only one vehicle registered to John Preston Bowie." Supremely frustrated, Tom ran his hand over his thinning hair. "If you didn't think they were in there, why were you afraid of getting shot? You should've searched the place."

Again, Frank sighed heavily. "I waited there by his car for several minutes. Didn't hear a sound from inside, so I dutifully made a three-sixty around the house and looked in every window. The house is small. Not many rooms or places to hide. In the bedroom was a bed. Nobody fucking on it." He snorted. "Which I would've paid to watch."

Tom was beside himself. "I wanted to nip this in the bud, scare him into humility and compliance, *today*, before he had time to think about defying me. I wanted to have this done with before all the hubbub over that damn show begins. Uppermost, I didn't want him talking to that woman."

Calls to the network offices in New York had confirmed that Beth Collins was a senior-level producer. But she hadn't made the trip from the Big Apple to interview *him*. No, she'd come to talk specifically to Detective Bowie. And Bowie had gone to extremes this morning to keep her in town.

Regardless of the ogre's belief that they were only hooking up for sex, Tom's conclusion was that whatever they were doing together had the potential for being calamitous to him. Where the hell could they be? "People don't just disappear."

He didn't realize he'd spoken his thought aloud until Frank laughed in that nasty way he had and smacked his chewing gum. "Isn't that what Bowie kept telling you? Over and over like a broken record. 'People don't disappear. Bodies don't disappear. That girl is somewhere, Tom.' That's when you started hating him."

"I'd started hating him long before that," Tom mumbled.

"Hon-ey." He turned to see his wife standing in the open doorway holding a glass of wine and pouting.

He made himself look regretful. "Sorry, babe. One minute."

She huffed, held up her index finger and mouthed *one*, and left.

He went back to Frank. "Was his backyard fenced?"

"Yeah, completely ringed in. By a *wilderness*. On the back side of the house I could barely see my hand in front of my face, but I didn't want to announce my presence with a flashlight. Neighbors aren't that close, but someone might've seen me and told Bowie."

"We don't want him alerted."

"What I thought."

"All right," Tom said. "Go back out there and—"

"Look, boss. I don't like him, either, and I had just as soon have popped him tonight and used my charm on the woman till she cooperated. But I'm not driving all the way back out there tonight. I'm late for a poker game. French dip sandwiches and high stakes night. Let's give it a rest and pick back up in the morning. Bowie will turn up. Okay?"

Without waiting for Tom's consent, the ogre hung up on him. Tom disconnected and addressed his phone. "I hope your fat ass loses a wad."

Chapter 10

Beth pushed away her empty bowl and linked her fingers across her midriff. "That was delicious. You did your grandma proud."

"I'm glad you liked it."

"What's your secret?"

"The roux."

"Would you give me the recipe?"

"Then it wouldn't be a secret."

"You'd have to kill me."

"I'm afraid so." He paused, then, low and suggestively, said, "Or I would consider a swap."

"A swap? One friendlier than killing me?"

"A lot friendlier." His gaze lowered to her mouth, then moved down to her breasts. God, did they entice. All but begging for the gentle squeeze of a man's hands.

It took every ounce of willpower he had to look up from them into her eyes, which were wide and unblinking. He saw in them that she understood without his having to spell it out: He wanted her. Bad.

Of course, under the circumstances, his licentious thoughts were inappropriate. He got up and carried his bowl and utensils to the sink. Beth did the same, although the implication of the nature of his "swap" and the way he'd looked at her had left her uncharacteristically aflutter.

He turned on the faucets. "I'll manage this."

"Let me wash. It's the least I can do by way of thanks."

"I would have heated up the gumbo for myself anyway."

"I need to thank you not only for the meal, but also for getting me to safety tonight. I shudder at the thought of someone nicknamed the ogre."

He turned off the water and faced her. "I meant it when I said you held up well."

"You said I'd done okay."

"I understated." He gave her one of his brief, crooked smiles, but it was half-hearted, and he seemed reluctant to continue. But he did. "You should never have come down here and meddled in this. You're out of your element. I don't mean to be condescending. I hope it didn't sound like it."

"It didn't. It sounded like Max. Exactly like Max."

"Smart guy."

"Smart and, by now, I'm sure he's frantic because I haven't called him."

John went over to the cupboard and opened a drawer beneath the shelving. Inside it were several cell phones. He chose one and checked the signal and battery capacity, then handed it to her. "Never been used. You can break it in for me. Go call your boss before he has a fatal coronary."

He showed her into a bedroom, which was directly off the main room. It was furnished with an iron bed whose white paint was chipped in spots. The patchwork quilt was no doubt handmade. The room was spotlessly clean, but as cluttered as the rest of the cabin with memorabilia that represented generations of family history.

"Does this place belong to you now?"

"By default," he said. "None of the cousins who are still in the area wanted to maintain it. It was deeded to me by a round of handshakes, nothing official. It's still on the tax rolls in my grandpa's name, which was Lamont, not Bowie. No one will find us here."

"I couldn't find my way back to the boat."

"Which is the point and why I keep the place. Take your time." As he left the room, he pulled the door closed.

She toed off her shoes and sat down on the bed with her bare feet tucked beneath her hips. After taking a bolstering breath, she tapped in Max's number.

It rang only once before a growled, "Who's this?"

"Me."

"Whose phone?"

"John Bowie's."

"Says 'Caller Unknown.'"

"It's a spare."

"Huh. If you're using his phone, I guess you missed your flight."

"I didn't take the flight, Max. I changed my mind."

He cursed. "I was afraid you were going to say that. Where the hell are you?"

He hadn't asked for details about her current location,

so she didn't volunteer that she was in a bedroom at John Bowie's fishing camp in a swamp she couldn't name or find her way out of.

Without embellishment and as chronologically as possible, she summarized her day, leaving out segments of it that she feared would indeed cause a cardiac episode, such as their perilous escape from a henchman called the ogre. She finished by saying, "It's been a long and eventful day, but I'm all right."

"Just so I understand, you hadn't changed your mind about returning to New York until Bowie hustled you out of the airport with what sounds to me like an unacceptable he-man tactic?"

"I'm glad he stopped me, Max. It gave us an opportunity to have an in-depth conversation. I talked him through that case in Galveston that I'd discovered. He knew a lot about it except for the fact that it had occurred on the night of a blood moon."

"What did he make of that?"

"It got his attention, but he concluded that it was a bizarre coincidence. However, I think he was trying to convince himself, not me. I get the sense that he would love to reopen the Mellin investigation, but he's reluctant to. I'm not sure why."

"That's easy. He knows that if he starts picking at a scab involving the integrity and competence of the police department that employs him, there could be harsh repercussions."

"More than professional ones, I think. The Mellin case affected other aspects of his life as well." Before Max could pounce on that, she said, "That's only conjecture, of course, but I sense that whatever backlash he was subjected to then, he's still grappling with now. He's…troubled."

After a short pause, he said, "Tell me again why you're on that phone. What's wrong with yours?"

She'd hoped to gloss over that, but she should have known Max had been ruminating on it. "Mine was out of juice." She told herself the fib was to prevent him from suffering a medical emergency. "I didn't want to wait for it to charge before calling you. Detective Bowie lent me one of his spares."

"Spares? Plural? Charged and ready?"

Tired of the third degree, she snapped, "Yes, Max. So what?"

"This troubled man accosts you at the airport. He keeps spare burner phones handy. Are you sure he's on the right side of the law?"

"It all sounds a lot worse than it is." Lord, if he only knew.

He harrumphed, then asked, "This in-depth conversation you two had, where'd you leave it?"

"Unfinished. There's a lot more I need to tell him."

"And after you do?"

"I hope he'll be more forthcoming about the Mellin case."

Max exhaled, his chest rattling. "Beth. My advice?"

"I've already heard your advice."

"All right then, I'll give you a heads-up that may make you think twice. I returned from my lunch with the mayor to find Winston Brady waiting on me. Impatiently. He asked if I could explain why the production office had received two calls this morning from people asking about you. The first caller declined to leave his name. Brady didn't think much about it. But a little while later, he got a call from Tom Barker."

She swallowed but said nothing.

"That call concerned our new EP because A: He's accountable to network executives and show sponsors. B: All of them are persnickety and uptight. And C: Brady is an ass-kisser whose main objective is to keep his own ass well covered.

"Sooo," he continued, dragging out the word, "because he couldn't reach you by phone, he wanted to know from me why Barker of the Auclair, Louisiana, PD was calling to verify your association with *Crisis Point* and to ask what you were doing in their fair city attempting to contact one of his detectives, who's a troublemaking malcontent."

"Oh."

"Yes. Oh."

"What did you tell him?"

"That you hailed from Louisiana, that you'd taken some vacation time to go see old friends, and that your trip had nothing at all to do with your work on the show or the upcoming episode. It was nothing more than fluky timing."

"Did he buy that?"

"In his shoes, would you?"

She imagined Max glowering at her from beneath his eyebrows, which sprouted from his forehead like a shaggy shelf. "I'm sorry, Max. I realize that your relationship with Brady is thorny, and I hate that I placed you in the position of having to lie for me."

"I'm still in that position, Beth. As long as you're down there, I'll be in this position."

"I realize that, too." She massaged her forehead while she considered what her next step should be. "I'll see what happens tomorrow. If Detective Bowie shuts down completely, I'll have lost my one and only source. In which case, I had just as well come home."

"Book your flight tonight. Get your tush back here and make nice with Brady."

"That holds no appeal whatsoever."

"It has more appeal than unemployment." He paused to take a breath that trailed off in a gurgle. "As your mentor, I'm duty bound to tell you that it's time to punt. You're not going to wear Bowie down. You said so yourself that a hammer and chisel wouldn't crack that guy.

"And even if he was singing like a canary about in-house corruption and ineptitude in that police department, Brady won't forget that you pursued that angle without his authorization. You're already out of his favor, and he doesn't even know that you're risking the show's reputation on a wild hare about red moons."

That stung. Did Max really have so little confidence in her? She straightened her spine and, in as crisp a voice as she could muster, said, "I'm not ready to punt. I may stay here through the blood moon. If nothing evil happens, and God willing it won't, then I'll acknowledge that my hypothesis was a wild hare, and you can say you told me so. You'll relish that, I'm sure. Right now, I'm exhausted. I'm going to bed. Good night."

The bedroom and bathroom John used whenever he stayed at the cabin was on the opposite side of the broad living area from the bedroom in which he'd deposited Beth. He'd used the time she was on her call to shower and change into a pair of jeans and an old t-shirt.

When Beth emerged from the bedroom, he was sprawled in his favorite chair. "Coffee's fresh. Want a cup?"

"Yes, thanks, but I'll pour."

As he made to get up, she motioned him back into the chair and went into the kitchen area. She returned with a mug of strong coffee, which she'd liberally doctored with the powdered creamer and sugar he'd set out.

He'd draped a multicolored throw over the upholstered chair nearest his. As she sat down in it, she looked warily at his pistol now lying on the table between their chairs. He said, "I wanted it within reach."

"You said nobody would find us here."

"I've been wrong before." He sipped from his coffee mug. "How'd it go with your boss?"

"He's peeved. He wants me back in New York. Yesterday. Your tactics seem to make him nervous."

"They make me nervous."

She laughed softly, then became serious. "There's been a development."

When she finished her rundown of their conversation, he said, "Add another reason for me to despise Tom Barker. Not only did he sic the ogre on us, he also put you on the new top dog's shit list."

"Well, if my visit here results in a jaw-dropping twist ending to the Mellin story, all will be forgiven."

"What if it doesn't result in that?"

"I'll have to get back to you on that." Smiling ruefully, she rubbed the fringe of the throw between her thumb and fingers. "Hand knitted?"

"By one of the aunts, who must've been color-blind. It's ugly as all get-out, but not as ugly as the chair's upholstery."

"It's cozy." She draped the tail of the throw over her feet.

"Are they cold? I can help with that." He got up and fetched a pair of thick white socks from his bedroom. "They're clean," he said as he handed them to her. "They'll be too big for you, but warm."

Setting aside her mug of coffee, she slipped off her shoes and pulled on the socks, then wiggled her toes and sighed. "Much better. Thanks."

"You're welcome."

She dipped her head and snuffled a laugh. "Yesterday when you came over to the booth and thanked me for the Coke, never in my wildest dreams would I have imagined that soon I'd be thanking you for a pair of borrowed socks." She tilted her head and regarded him with perplexity. "You didn't strike me as the type."

"What type?"

"A man who would keep his grandmother's gumbo recipe, much less make it. Who would share socks." She looked over at Mutt, who was curled up asleep on a folded blanket on the floor. "Who would be so fond of his dog. You looked too…um…"

"Mean?"

Her head came back around to him. "I wouldn't go so far as to say that."

"It's okay. I was trying to look mean."

"Why?"

"To make the impression I apparently did."

"On me?"

"Definitely on you. But also on the bartender and the guys shooting stick. I could've been walking into a trap." He cocked an eyebrow. "One laid by someone other than you, that is."

"Someone like the ogre? Tom Barker?"

Exactly like that, he thought, although he didn't say so. Restless and agitated, he spread his fingers wide and ran his hands up and down his thighs, dreading like hell the course this conversation was about to take. Since their arrival, neither of them had acknowledged what had brought them here. The meal had delayed addressing the subject. Then her phone call. They'd put off talking about it long enough.

He looked over at her, where she was curled up in the oversize chair. "Tell me about the two abductions that happened in 2018."

She stopped winding strands of the fringe around her fingers and let them fall into her lap. "In January of that year, a nineteen-year-old woman in Jackson disappeared while riding her bicycle home from her shift at a Waffle House.

"In July, in Shreveport, a woman in her early twenties was seen for the last time walking her dog around the playground of her apartment complex. The dog was found roaming, still on his leash, unharmed. She'd vanished."

He glanced over at the long folding table where he permanently kept a laptop. He was tempted to boot it up and research those cases, but he was also afraid of being drawn farther in. The less he knew, the easier it was to remain detached.

"They're regional," Beth said.

"That's a stretch." But not that much of one. He ran a rough calculation in his head. You could drive the distances between those points in one day or less.

She said, "I think 2018 was when he started."

John came out of his chair, picked up his empty mug, and headed for the kitchen. When he got there, he realized he didn't want a refill of coffee. Instead, he took a bottle of bourbon from the cabinet. The lip of the bottle clinked against the drinking glass as he poured a shot. He hesitated, then poured a bit more. "Want one?"

"No thank you."

He took a swallow, then another, loving the burn, the bite, the rush of relief that was too damned temporary. He returned to the living area but prowled around the room, swirling the liquor in his glass.

"What makes you think that's when he started?" he asked. "What about three and a half years earlier and those two blood moons?"

"I didn't find any accounts of missing women that coincided with those dates. And—"

"Jesus, there's an and?"

"And the two 2018 eclipses were particularly significant."

"I can hardly wait. Why were they particularly significant?"

He could tell she didn't approve of his sarcasm, but she let it pass. "The one on January thirty-first was also a blue moon."

"I forgot what that means."

"The second full moon within a month."

"Right," he mumbled into his glass as he took a drink from it.

"They called that January thirty-first eclipse a super blue moon blood moon. Super moon for short."

He whistled as though impressed.

Then, with annoyance, "Are you getting drunk?"

"Maybe. What of it?"

She thumped her coffee mug down on the end table and placed her hands on the arms of the chair as though to pull herself up.

Instantly, he said, "Stay where you are. We've got to talk this out."

"Not if you're going to be obnoxious."

"I apologize."

She settled back into her chair. He walked over to the dining table and set down his glass of whiskey, which was still half full. Then he covered his face with both hands and whispered into his palms. "Fuck, fuck, fuck."

"Why are you so upset, John?"

"Because I don't want to hear this. Not any of it." He took a moment to get a grip, then lowered his hands, turned back to her, and, in spite of his denial, asked, "Why was the one in July of that year special?"

Observing him closely, she spoke softly, almost warily. "The total eclipse lasted for one hundred and three minutes. It will be the longest lasting blood moon of the twenty-first century."

"How do you know all that?"

"The internet. Anybody could know it. When you researched blood moons, you had to have seen how much information is available."

"Then our unidentified suspect doesn't have to be an astronomer, an astronaut, a physicist. Just some whack job who went out to howl at the super blue whatever moon on January thirty-first of 2018, grabbed a girl, and liked it, and celebrated the next blood moon in the same way. Poor sucker had to wait till '22 for his next fix."

"You're being obnoxious."

"I'm not running for Mister Congeniality." He plopped into the chair, laid his head back, and closed his eyes.

Beth broke a drawn-out silence. "Do you think the theory of serial abductions is so far-fetched? Do you think I'm fanciful? Crazy?"

"No."

"Then—"

He opened his eyes and held up his hand, stopping her. "My aversion to this topic has nothing to do with you and everything to do with me. I won't go through it again. As compelling as your observations are—and they *are*, Beth. Everything you've told me rouses my interest, but I don't want to hear any more. I can't help you."

"Can't or won't?"

"Won't."

"Because of the Mellin case?"

"Which had the effect of an H-bomb on my life."

"Your marriage?"

"No, the marriage had already been leveled, but my obsession over the balled-up investigation, my drunken nights after, gave Roslyn the excuse she needed to blame the failed marriage on me, instead of on the affair she'd been having."

"For how long?"

"A year or more."

"You knew about it?"

"Knew and didn't care." He met her gaze head-on. "I wasn't living like a saint, either."

"I see." She looked down and picked up a strand of fringe again. "Why did you stay married?"

"That's not open to discussion."

"All right." She wetted her lips, then said, "What specifically happened between you and Tom Barker?"

He was about to hedge on that, too, when she said, "I deserve to know why my life was endangered tonight. Unless you were exaggerating about that."

"I wasn't." He sat up, rolled his shoulders, shifted positions in the chair. "When I cut Billy Oliver down from the ceiling in his jail cell, he had a suicide note tucked inside his shirt. Barker's take on that? 'Crissy is dead and gone, but at least the perp saves us the trouble of executing him. That's cause for celebration.' That kid's body was still warm."

"That's obscene."

"I thought so."

"You didn't think Billy Oliver was the culprit, did you?"

"No."

"And you still don't."

"No." He came out of his chair again and ran his hand around the back of his neck. "But, as I said, I've been wrong before."

Beth got up and followed him over to the dining table, where he retrieved his glass of whiskey and shot the remainder of it. "I don't think you're wrong, John. I think there's a real possibility that the individual who took Crissy, and the two girls in 2018, is still out there, waiting for Thursday night, and that some woman is going to suffer terribly if he's not stopped."

"Then stop him. Good luck."

He reached for the bottle of bourbon, but Beth knocked it out of his hand. In spite of being stunned, he made a quick save. Otherwise, the bottle would have crashed to the floor. He set it down hard on the table. "What the hell was that for?"

She looked equally as irate as he was. "How can you be so nonchalant?"

"Practice," he retorted. "It's another of my self-preservation tactics."

"Self-preservation. *Self.* That's the key word here, isn't it? The Mellin case messed up your life. But are you prepared to stand by and see another woman vanish off the face of the earth?"

"If that happens, it'll be a shame, but it won't be my problem."

Her chest seemed to cave in. She made a sobbing sound. "I don't think you act mean; I think you genuinely are."

He held up his index finger. "Don't shortchange loaning socks and fondness for my dog."

She gave a bitter laugh. "If your only form of defense is sarcasm, that's pathetic. I'll admit that after everything we went through this evening, and here, surrounded by your family memorabilia, I was beginning to think that maybe I'd misjudged you, that maybe you did have a sensitive side. But my first impression was spot on. Your arrogant disregard never fails to resurface.

"The bottom line is that you don't give a damn about anything. I saw it the minute you walked into that scuzzy bar, and again this morning after you dragged me from the airport.

"You ooze indifference. Nothing gets to you. That Mellin case opened you up and scooped you out. You're empty. Heartless, soulless, and unfeeling. You don't really *feel* anything, do you? *Do you?*"

Pushed to his limit, he moved in on her until just shy of touching, their faces close. "You think I'm unfeeling? Let me tell you something. I've done nothing but feel remorse and regret for over three years. Every morning I wake up with self-loathing for ignoring my instincts, for not telling Barker to go fuck himself and start looking for Crissy hours—*hours*—before we did.

"I told that conceited asshole that the neighbor kid, Billy, was a conspicuous suspect, a perfect scapegoat, too obvious and easy. I told him we needed to broaden our scope, widen our net, look at other people.

"But Barker wanted to be done with it. He wanted it quickly wrapped up to make himself look good. He assigned the ogre to interrogate Billy. He hammered that poor kid, confusing him, feeding him the answers that Barker wanted to hear. When I called them on it, Barker sneered at me. 'Don't tell me how to run my show, Bowie. Be a team player, or you'll never be a team leader.'

"So I fell into step and followed procedure, grumbling about it, yeah, but also not acting on my gut instinct that we were looking in the wrong place and at the wrong guy. Why did I capitulate, you ask? *Why?*" He inched closer to her. "Because I was vying for the same goddamn promotion as Barker.

"And because I wanted it, wanted it bad, wanted the pay increase, bad, I failed both Crissy and Billy Oliver. Trust me, Ms. Collins, I have enough *self*-disgust to last me for the rest of my life."

He ended on a near shout that awakened him to how he had borne down on her. His breathing was labored, heavy enough for the hot gusts to stir the pale strands of hair framing her face.

Forcibly, he released the tension in his muscles. He angled himself back. Her eyes, wide with shock, were the color of the bourbon he'd been drinking and just as intoxicating. He fixed on them and focused on bringing himself under control.

He didn't quite succeed, though. Strictly by willing it, he couldn't regain control over everything. He couldn't rule the fever infusing his blood, or where it was funneling, or the volume of it that filled him, swelled him, made him hard. He had no dominion over a desperate craving to draw her against his straining body and take her mouth with his.

Christ.

Speaking in a low rumble, he said, "Move away from me, Beth. Now. And don't ever accuse me again of being unfeeling. I'll show you different."

Chapter 11

Monday March 10

As he jogged along the pathway that encircled the park, he refused to acknowledge the occasional raindrops landing on his shoulders. Nevertheless, with every step, he cursed the whimsy of Mother Nature.

Never had it been so merciless as on the night of November 7, 2022. When said aloud, that date had an upbeat cadence, like that of a marching song in a victory parade. Which had been befitting. That night, on the occurrence of the last blood moon, he was to have had the penultimate spiritual experience.

However, Mother Nature had intervened with rain, fog, and impenetrable cloud cover. He hadn't gotten even a glimpse of that glorious red moon. He'd felt like a groom having waited lustfully for his wedding night, only to be blinded before getting to see his bride's nakedness.

Perhaps he should have regarded the inclement weather as an omen and called off his purpose. But it wasn't like a dental cleaning that could be rescheduled for the following week. No. The date of that total lunar eclipse had been ordained in the instant of the Big Bang.

He'd memorized the timetable, had known precisely when the eclipse would begin, at what time it would be in totality, when it would end. He hadn't been fool enough to write down all that information, or to circle the date in red on his calendar. But it had been etched on his mind. Underlined. Stars drawn around it.

During the weeks leading up to it, he'd willed each day, each hour, to go by faster, to move him closer to exaltation and acceptance. One act, and they amounted to one and the same.

In a perpetual daze of expectancy, he hadn't paid much attention to the weather forecast, although it had been inclement for days. Heavy rains had caused local flooding and all the inherent hazards. But it was Louisiana, after all. He had reasoned that the low pressure system responsible would pass soon enough.

On the afternoon of November seventh, he'd sipped a pre-dinner glass of wine with his wife while dinner was baking in the oven. A roast chicken, he remembered. He'd lent a sympathetic ear to his son's complaints about his algebra teacher's unfair grading curve and had encouraged him to apply himself and soon the solutions that were evading him would click.

But while in that nest of normalcy, anticipation had been fizzing inside him.

Dusk came early in November. By the time dinner was over and the kitchen cleaned, it had become evident to him that conditions outside were worsening, not improving.

That unforeseen handicap had given him pause. For an

hour or so, he'd wavered. But ultimately he had decided that he couldn't squander that blood moon. The next one wouldn't occur for twenty-seven months. He would go mad. Besides, he couldn't let all his preparations for this night go to waste.

So, banishing his apprehension, he'd given his wife the plausible excuse he'd devised months earlier and had left his house to cruise the streets until he'd spotted an available female within the required age range. When he found her, he'd taken her. That part had been remarkably easy.

Although why wouldn't it be? It was no accident that she'd been there when she was required. Her fate had been sealed just as his had been. Who would dream of questioning the orchestrators of Destiny?

The following day, he'd learned her name from the media coverage of her disappearance. Crissy Mellin.

He remembered the moment he'd pushed back the hood of her zip-up and had seen that her strawberry-blond hair was the same orangish shade as a blood moon. He'd taken that as a clear sign that his choice had been sanctioned. But he'd been wrong. Devastatingly, horrifically wrong. The experience hadn't been the thrill ride he'd counted on. Rather, it had been fraught with difficulties he hadn't made contingencies for, most of them brought about by Crissy herself.

She had fought him. *Fought* him. Fought him with all her might, stupid girl. What should have been bliss for both of them had turned ugly, awful, undignified, untenable.

He'd gotten through the ordeal unscathed, but he had been denied the exhilarating experience he'd yearned for. His disappointment had been crushing and demoralizing. Worse, it hadn't earned him the honor he coveted with his entire being.

The long, tedious wait for his next opportunity began. He'd had to behave normally, go about the mundane routines of an ordinary life, while he'd felt the restless fury of a Thoroughbred, born to run, who'd been hobbled and penned. But now, the opportunity was upon him! The night of March thirteenth–fourteenth. This Thursday. His excitement was superseded only by his determination to be more discriminating in his choice of sacrifice. She had to be a young woman who understood how special she was to have been selected, who would be compliant and accept with humility and gratitude her reason for being born.

To her eternal damnation, the significance of the rite had escaped Crissy Mellin.

By now, he'd made the loop around the park, completing his daily two-mile jog. He used the app on his watch to check the statistics of this morning's workout and was satisfied. Even though his mind had been preoccupied, his body had performed well.

He cooled down as he walked to where he'd parked his car. He was about to get in when he noticed that the windshield was wet. He looked skyward and despaired over feeling a heavy mist settling like a mourning veil over his face.

He was now convinced that had the heavens been visible that night in '22, had the ritual been consummated in the glow of the blood moon, things would have gone seamlessly. There would have been no call for violence.

He'd had more than eight hundred days to wonder why Mother Nature had jinxed him that night. He now had two days to worry if that meteorological mischief-maker would taint the ecstasy this time.

Chapter 12

Beth awoke to the sound of rain beating against the tin roof.

It seemed impossible that she had slept, but she must have been so drained physically and emotionally that her body had demanded a shutdown.

After John's anger-fueled account of the Mellin investigation, followed by the whispered dare he'd issued her, which had been fueled by something else entirely, he'd turned his back to her and brusquely motioned toward the bedroom. "Get some sleep."

She'd tried to think of something to say in response to his tirade, or to that teeming moment that had left her wishing he'd acted on the impulse she couldn't fail to recognize even though he hadn't even touched her.

But the atmosphere had seemed electrically charged. She'd feared that saying the wrong thing could have caused a spark that would reignite either his wrath or an agitation even more combustible.

Deciding that the safest course was to say nothing, she'd retreated to the bedroom and closed the door. Only then had she drawn a sufficient breath.

For minutes after, she'd stayed with her back to the door, listening to him moving around the main room. The sliver of light beneath her bedroom door had become progressively dimmer as lights were turned off. Then she'd heard his bedroom door closing, and that strip of light went dark.

She'd used the bathroom. With her finger and toothpaste she found in the medicine cabinet, she'd cleaned her teeth. Realizing that her shoes were in the other room beside the chair, she'd decided to leave them there. She'd also decided not to undress.

The two-bulb fixture in the ceiling was the only source of light, and when she'd clicked it off at the wall switch near the door, the room had gone completely black. She'd felt her way to the bed. Metal springs under the mattress squeaked when she slid under the covers.

Then she'd stared into the unrelieved darkness, wondering why she felt so dejected. But of course she knew why. She'd wanted that withheld kiss. She wanted it now.

She wondered why he appealed to her at all. She'd never been attracted to his type, which Max had termed a "he-man." That called to mind men in chaps or kilts or armor who rebelled against the rules of society and adhered to their own code of honor. But they were fictional heroes. In real life they didn't exist. Or so she'd thought until John Bowie had walked into that bar.

He'd looked at her with keen insight, as though he knew the first time they locked eyes that she'd had a chemical reaction to him, that she'd felt a frisson low and deep. That sizzle had both thrilled and frightened her. It still did.

She acknowledged that a large part of his appeal was his elusiveness. He wore an aura of aloneness like a second skin. He was the kind of man women wanted to tame, save, heal. The kind of man that broke women's hearts.

She lay thinking of all the reasons he was wrong for her, listening to light raindrops ping against the tin roof until she'd fallen into a dreamless sleep.

It was now daylight, but the bedroom was dim. Through the window she saw leaden gray clouds hovering low above the treetops. Last night's gentle rainfall had turned heavy and sullen. The room was chilly. She was grateful for the socks.

She flashed back to John's wry smile as he'd handed them to her and said they'd be too big.

Considering the volatile nature of their evening together, and the tuning-fork sexual note on which it had ended, she didn't know what to expect from her next face-to-face with him. There was sure to be awkwardness.

But delaying the inevitable only heightened her dread. Better to get it over with. She got up, used the bathroom and cleaned her teeth again, then went to the bedroom door and eased it open.

She almost stepped on Mutt before she saw him. He'd been lying on the threshold and immediately jumped to his feet. "Hey, boy." Tail wagging and quivering with gladness, he nuzzled her palm when she extended it to him.

She saw that John's bedroom door stood open, but there was no sign of him, and no lights were on. "Where's your master?" With Mutt at her side, she ventured into the main room, switching on lamps to alleviate the gloom as well as her mounting apprehension.

On the dining table was a scrawled note anchored down by his pistol.

Gone to get your things. Mutt's been fed, but he may want to go out again. P.S. All you have to do is point the gun and pull the trigger. Don't hesitate.

He'd written his departure time at the top of the sheet. He'd been gone for more than an hour. She looked down at the dog. "Did he say how long he planned to be gone?" Mutt gazed up at her with a moonstruck smile, tongue lolling.

A pot of coffee had been left on the hot plate. She filled a mug and added her fixin's. As she stood sipping it, she looked toward the open door to John's bedroom. "Promise not to tell," she said to Mutt as she walked over and peeped in.

The room had its fair share of clutter, but it was better organized than the other rooms. The clothes he'd been wearing yesterday had been folded and placed in the seat of a rocking chair, his dress shoes underneath it. He'd made the bed, and that was disappointing. She wouldn't have minded seeing the rumpled sheets he'd slept between, although it shamed her to admit it.

A low chest, painted matte black, served as a nightstand on the left side of the bed. On it were a digital clock and a framed photograph. The latter drew her like a magnet. She made her way over and bent down to get a better look.

In the picture was John, dressed only in swim trunks and a baseball cap turned backward. From beneath the cap, his hair curled around his ears and the back of his neck. He had the calves of a habitual runner. His pecs were lightly covered with a fan of hair. And he was ripped. Biceps, abs, everything was altogether yummy.

But the most startling thing in the photograph was his broad smile. She'd never seen that smile. She wouldn't have believed his stern features capable of producing one of such unmitigated happiness. She reasoned that it had a lot to do with the preteen girl beside him.

She was wearing a modest one-piece swimsuit. She was coltishly thin, all arms and legs, knees and elbows. Her smile revealed twin rows of braces. Her dark hair was in pigtails, although a few rebellious, curly sprigs had escaped the braids.

Her slender left arm was around John's waist. His right was draped over her shoulders. They stood ankle deep in a body of water that extended to the horizon, leaning into each other.

A day at the beach? Who was this girl? Who was this *man*?

Beth had never met the John Bowie in the picture, and that was a pity, because she thought she would like to know him.

Made despondent by the thought, she returned to her bedroom. "Stay," she told Mutt when he would have followed her in. He dropped down onto the threshold again. She commended him with a "Good boy" and a pat. She was about to close the door, then hesitated and left it open a crack. "Growl again if you hear anything suspicious."

In the bathroom, she undressed, showered, and shampooed. It felt wonderful, but she didn't linger. Loath to put on yesterday's clothes, which were mud-spattered and worse for wear, she considered the flannel robe that hung from a hook on the back of the door. It had seen better days, better *years*, but it smelled of dryer sheets. She pulled it on, then wrapped a towel around her head. Back in the bedroom, she saw that Mutt had nosed open the door just wide enough for him to squeeze through. He was curled up in the center of the bed, dozing. She said, "I'm not sure that's allowed."

"It's not and he knows it."

Startled, she turned. John, holding a shotgun at his side, used only the tip of his index finger to push open the door the rest of the way. She'd come around so quickly, the towel on her head came unwound. She caught it as it fell.

John took her in, the ugly bathrobe, the unruly wet hair.

She did the same with him, the black rain slicker, the unruly wet hair.

Arrested by the sight of each other, both stood stock-still.

Mutt leaped off the bed to give John an enthusiastic welcome back. He danced around John's wet pants legs until John acknowledged the greeting by scrubbing his knuckles across his head.

He did so absently, never taking his eyes off Beth. Nor she did look away from him. When she realized she was nervously twisting the damp towel between her hands, she forced herself to stop.

John finally broke the spell and ducked out of sight for a moment. When he reappeared, he no longer had the shotgun. "Everything all right here?"

"Yes. Fine."

"Sleep okay?"

"Like a baby."

"Good, good. There's coffee if—"

"I found it. Thank you."

"Was it still hot?"

She bobbed her head.

"Good." An awkward silence stretched out. Mutt jumped back onto the bed but John seemed not to notice.

She indicated the robe. "I found it in the bathroom."

"Aunt Gert's, I think." He drew a breath and let it out slowly. "You do a lot more for it than she did." His eyes scaled down all the way to her bare feet, and he kept his head down for a time, rubbing his forehead.

Beth held her breath.

When he raised his head, he hitched his thumb over his shoulder. "You'll have fresh clothes. I brought your suitcase. Purse. I guess your phone is in it?"

"Yes. Thanks." She glanced toward the window. "It's pouring."

"Like a son of a…gun."

"You went in the boat? The way we came? In this rain?"

"Nothing I haven't done dozens of times. I had a tarp to cover up your stuff." He turned away, but only long enough to pick up her suitcase and purse where he'd left them just outside her line of sight.

He carried them over to the bed. "Mutt." The dog looked at him with imploring eyes, then over at Beth as though begging her to intercede on his behalf, but John snapped his fingers and Mutt hopped off the bed. John set her roll-aboard and purse on it.

She said, "I look forward to being in fresh clothes."

"Yeah. I need to change, too. I'm still dripping rainwater." He went over to the door. With one hand on the jamb, he turned back. "Do you want breakfast?"

"Um—"

"Because I wasn't expecting to be here last night, so there's nothing fresh in the fridge. I could thaw out a loaf of bread and toast it."

"Oh, don't go to the trouble. I can do without."

He bobbed his chin. "When you're ready, we'll go. Just tell me where to drop you."

Her heart plummeted. The floor seemed to undulate beneath her like the first tremors of an earthquake. So this was how it was going to be: He wasn't going for it. How naïve of her to think that he might have slept on it and changed his mind. All along, he, and Max, had warned her what his decision would be.

She swallowed her disappointment and managed to say, "I suppose I'll go back to the hotel I checked out of yesterday."

He nodded and turned to leave.

She said, "We can't get there by boat."

"I keep a car here." He pointed through the window. "That way. A two- or three-minute walk." He glanced toward the suitcase on the bed. "Do you have a rain jacket with you?"

She gave him a smile that was supposed to look prideful and undaunted, but felt wobbly. "I'm a New Yorker."

By the time they set out for their walk through the woods, the rain had slackened to a drizzle. It had just as well have been raining in earnest. Every leaf on every tree they walked beneath dripped large splats of rainwater, each seeming to find its way down the back of her neck and into her jacket, which had been dishonestly advertised as weatherproof.

Her footwear was also inadequate. Her shoes hadn't completely dried overnight, and soon became even soggier and more uncomfortable. She was miserable in every way possible.

Fortunately, within the short time frame John had estimated, they reached their destination, which was a prefab metal storage building situated in a clearing carved out of the surrounding woods. It was nearly indiscernible because of its camouflage paint job.

"It blends right in," she remarked.

"My friend Mitch and I painted it ourselves. He's a vet. We copied the pattern off a pair of his fatigues."

The garage door had a padlock on each side. John unlocked them and raised the door. Inside was a compact car, facing out. As soon as John opened the passenger door, Mutt jumped in and settled on a blanket in the back seat. She climbed in. John drove the car out. After it cleared the garage door, he went back to secure the building.

The road that led away from the building barely qualified as such. It amounted to parallel, rutted furrows, worn into the forest floor by car tires. Eventually it spilled them onto a narrow state highway. They went five miles before reaching the first vestiges of civilization. It was disconcerting to realize just how remote the fishing camp was.

"Do you want to stop and grab something? Coffee? Donut?" John nodded toward a diner.

"No thank you."

They said nothing more until Beth saw that they were nearing their destination. "The next exit," she said.

"I see the sign. Is it nice?"

"Your standard cookie-cutter hotel."

He took the exit and pulled into a parking space near the entrance, cut the engine, and then sat staring through the windshield.

Beth endured the taut silence for almost half a minute before reaching for the door handle. "Thank you for the lift."

"Beth—"

"And for your hospitality last night. It was—"

"Will you wait a minute?"

She looked at him expectantly. "What?"

"What are you going to do?"

"Have breakfast." She checked her wristwatch. "If they're still serving."

He gave her a look that said, *Very funny.* "Are you flying out this afternoon?"

"Should I?"

"Yes, damn it. Barker's got to be convinced that you lost interest or that Brady came down hard on you and drew a line in the sand. Whatever he thinks, I'm afraid you won't be safe until you're away from here. "

"Possibly. But if something terrible befalls me, it won't be your problem, as you so eloquently phrased it last night."

"Bloody hell," he said under his breath. Then, "Something else I said, maybe with less eloquence, was that *I can't help you.* I won't."

She studied his features, the rigid jaw and shuttered eyes, and contrasted them to the smiling face in the picture on his nightstand. "Who's the girl in the picture?"

For an instant, the diamond-hard eyes flicked. But he recovered quickly. "What picture?"

"Really, John? You're going to pretend you don't know?

The only picture in that fishing camp that was taken within the last decade."

"You went snooping?"

"Yes."

He turned his head aside and watched raindrops turn into rivulets that slid down the windshield. "My daughter."

Beth had assumed so. "When was it taken?"

"Within the last decade."

She disregarded the droll comeback. "Her mother got custody?"

He gave her a sharp look, but it didn't express anger. He stared at her with total detachment and a silent command to back off. She would have preferred it if he'd lost his temper.

"It's none of my business," she said. "I didn't mean to open old wounds."

He went back to staring through the windshield. For the longest time he didn't say anything. She vacillated between opening the car door or staying to see what he would say or do until he ordered her out.

She was reaching for the handle again when he made an amused sound. He turned and gave her a crooked smile that had more sadness behind it than humor. "Beth, since I met you, all you've done is open old wounds. Even so," he said around a weighty exhale, "if I don't do this, I'll regret it forever."

Taking her completely off guard, he leaned across the console, curved his right hand around the back of her neck, and pulled her toward him. Beneath the inviting heat of his lips, hers seemed to melt. They became pliant against the undemanding pressure he applied and parted at the first brush of his tongue.

Her mouth yielded to its first tentative and seeking thrusts. Met with no resistance, it became bolder and then, when he tilted his head for a more secure fit, his tongue went deep, and its give-and-take became skillfully evocative.

He placed his left hand on her rib cage between her waist and the underside of her breast, his fingers pressing, lightly squeezing. She wished the lining of her jacket weren't so thick. Better yet, that she wasn't wearing a jacket. Or wearing anything. She wished to feel his hand caressing her bare skin, her breast.

His withdrawal was gradual but unquestionable. When she realized he was ending the kiss, she actually leaned forward in an effort to sustain it, but he was already beyond reach.

He resettled himself in the driver's seat. "Make sure you're on that flight." He held her gaze for a beat, then got out of the car, went around, and retrieved her suitcase from the back seat.

Her cheeks, which moments ago had been aflame with arousal, were now burning with humiliation. By the time he pulled open the passenger door, she had collected herself enough to take the handle of her roll-aboard from him.

"Goodbye, John. Take care of yourself." Mutt whined at her from behind the back seat window. "You, too, Mutt."

Then she turned away and walked toward the hotel entrance. After the automatic doors had closed behind her, she turned to get one last look.

But he was already driving away.

Chapter 13

When John and the ogre rounded a blind corner at the same time, they came to within an inch of running smack into each other.

It hadn't been an accident. John had gotten there first and had seen the other man coming down the hallway toward him. He'd backed out of sight and waited until just the right moment to step around the corner and almost cause a collision.

"Hey, Frank, how's it goin'?"

John's friendly tone and amiable smile took the other man aback. "Uh, you know, typical morning. Another day, another dollar."

"Tell me," John said. "I'm up to my eyeballs in paperwork." Making a point of leaning sideways in order to see around the man's massive body, John looked down the hallway in the direction of Tom Barker's office. "Is Barker in?"

Frank's initial discomposure had worn off. Between

pads of flesh, his porcine eyes turned into slits of suspicion. "Why?"

"Nothing major. Just something I've been wanting to talk to him about."

"Run it past me. Maybe I can help."

John brightened. "Maybe. Do you know anything about transmissions?"

The slitted eyes blinked several times. "Transmissions?"

"Yeah, I overheard the boss telling somebody—can't remember now who—that he had a transmission guy who's top-notch. Even better," he said with a wink, "he gives cops a discount on repairs or replacement. My gears have been grinding lately, and I thought—"

"That's a pile of bullshit, Bowie."

John frowned with puzzlement. "Really? Which part? The boss doesn't have a guy? Or he has a guy, but the guy doesn't give discounts?"

The ogre gave him a baleful look. "I've got work to do." He sidestepped John but deliberately rammed into his left shoulder on his way past, snarling in an undertone, "I'm on to you."

"Goes both ways," John said as he flicked a piece of colored paper at the ogre's face. It hit him square in his broad forehead, bounced off, and fell to the floor.

The ogre looked down and saw that it was a gum wrapper, wadded into a ball, rain-soaked and muddy, but recognizable as the brand he habitually chewed.

He raised his oversize head. The two men stared eye-to-eye with full understanding of each other's malice. The ogre was the first to break away and resume his progress down the hallway.

Earlier, when John had returned to his house to retrieve Beth's things, he'd given the dwelling, the shed, and the property a thorough inspection. He'd even searched his SUV for a tracking device.

He'd found the gum wrapper near the entrance to the cul-de-sac. He figured the ogre had left his car on the shoulder of the main road while he'd explored the dead-end lane on foot.

After the torturous farewell scene with Beth in the hotel parking lot, he'd driven all the way back to the fishing camp, returned the compact car to the camouflaged garage, secured the cabin, and then had paddled the boat back to his house, where he'd dragged it into its hiding place.

Taking those precautionary steps had been time-consuming, but he'd felt they were necessary. He would have to be extra vigilant now that the ogre had discovered where he lived. He was even reluctant to leave Mutt alone in the house. Before locking him in, he'd told him, "If anyone poses a threat to you, tear his throat out."

At least he'd made the ogre aware that he was aware.

Now, as he entered the CAP unit, he greeted fellow detectives with a raised hand or a terse hello but didn't stop to chat with anyone. When he reached his desk, he booted up his computer and checked his email inbox, but only tackled the time-sensitive ones.

Or tried to tackle them. He would be in the middle of composing a reply when he'd realize that his hands had come to rest motionless on the keyboard. Sentences were left unfinished because his mind continued to revert to those last few minutes with Beth.

When they'd parted, the disappointment and accusation in her eyes had submersed him in guilt. Recalling those same eyes, dazed and lambent after their kiss, filled him with lust.

Re-filled him with lust. Because he'd been bedeviled ever since he'd slid into the booth in that bar and looked into her face. He'd wanted her before he'd learned that she wasn't just some restless barfly hoping for an afternoon delight, but rather a smart and ambitious woman…who had the potential to make his life hell on earth again.

In that most unromantic of settings, he'd wanted her right then. He'd wanted to see what kind of hair was tucked under the ball cap. He'd wanted to see under her white t-shirt. He'd wanted to see her under him, naked and tangled up.

He still wanted that. But being around her also had awakened him to the hollowness inside him. The Mellin case and its aftermath *had* scooped him out. She'd been right about that, and he'd purposefully kept himself empty. But now, because of her, an alien yearning was seeping into that vacancy. He denounced it. He couldn't give it a foothold. He must not.

"Not gonna happen." He spoke in a whisper so the coworker nearest him wouldn't overhear, but he felt he had to say it aloud in order to affirm it, to make it substantive and permanent.

And anyway, she'd made plain her contempt. Because he'd refused to get involved, she thought he was a self-preserving coward. Well, he would just have to live with her low opinion, because his refusal was final.

"So get over it, John."

He propped his elbow on the edge of his desk and cupped his hand over his mouth. He stared at the words on his monitor, which he didn't remember typing and could make no sense of now. He watched the cursor blink.

But his focus on it didn't prevent him from hearing Beth's impassioned voice. *"...the individual who took Crissy... still out there...waiting for Thursday night..."*

"Shhhhhit!"

Before he could talk himself out of it, he discreetly reached beneath his desk and into his boot, where he'd had a thin pocket sewn into the shaft. He slid a thumb drive from it.

After Barker was appointed head of the CAP unit, John had surreptitiously transferred the entire Mellin case file onto two thumb drives. He kept one in his boot. In the event that a cold case investigation into Mellin ever ensued and, coincidentally, John and the file were to suddenly disappear from the department, Mitch had the second thumb drive.

He inserted his into a port and began searching for a name and a telephone number in Galveston. It took him a frustrating twenty minutes to find that information; then he placed the call from one of his burner phones.

"Detective Morris, please," he said to the person who answered. When asked to identify himself, he did. "I'm working a case here, and I believe Morris might be able to provide me with some background on a suspect." He was asked to hold.

Moments later, a female voice said, "Gayle Morris."

As John introduced himself, he realized that his palms

were damp, his mouth dry. "I'm calling about a missing person case you had in May of 2022. Larissa Whitmore."

He heard her sigh. "You don't forget those."

"No, you don't. Were her remains ever recovered?"

"Negative. Not a trace."

"What's Patrick Dobbs's status?"

"He was convicted of statutory rape, now serving his sentence. He's filed an appeal."

"On what grounds?"

"He claims that the whole time he and Larissa were together, she used a fake ID that put her age at twenty-one. It fooled bartenders as well as him. He didn't know she was a minor."

"That argument didn't come out at his trial?"

"It did, and it was supported by several witnesses. But the prosecutor shot it down. He and Larissa were stoned, all over each other, sex was a sure thing. Therefore, the prosecutor argued, it would have been in the accused's best interest *not* to question her age. The jury thought so, too."

John fiddled with a stray paperclip as he pondered the blowback that might come from taking this conversation further. To hell with it. "Detective, please don't think I'm a loony tune."

She chuckled. "Can't promise."

John liked her. "Did you or anyone working on that case consider a tie-in with the blood moon that night?"

"Of course. Dobbs took Larissa out in his boat to look at it."

"We had a young woman over here named Crissy Mellin. She disappeared on the night of the next blood moon, which was in November."

"Yes, I know. When we learned about it, I assigned somebody to see if there was any correlation between your case and Larissa Whitmore, and also to two previous cases."

"In 2018? Jackson, Mississippi, and Shreveport?"

"Yes. But nothing came of our inquiries. Dobbs wasn't near either of those cities on the nights of the 2018 abductions. In fact, when one of them occurred, he was in Croatia on a humanitarian mission, teaching English to schoolkids."

"So you never found any link?"

"None. What about your case? If I recall, your suspect hanged himself while in custody."

"That's right. Billy Oliver."

"Didn't he confess?"

"He signed a confession and claimed to have disposed of her body where it would never be found. You'll be able to hear all about it on TV." He told her about the upcoming episode of *Crisis Point.*

"I'll be sure to watch. Are you in it?"

"No. But I was on the Mellin investigation team. Until recently, I didn't know anything about the blood moon aspect. Zilch. I guess nobody thought it was relevant because you couldn't even see the moon the night Crissy went missing.

"But this upcoming program has got me thinking back on that case. Four missing girls, four blood moons, four remains never discovered. It seems too bizarre a coincidence for our team to have overlooked the moon angle."

She said, "That's why I tipped you."

John's fingers went numb. He dropped the paperclip. "You tipped us?"

"Yes. As soon as I heard about your presumed abduction and realized the moon had been red that night just like when Larissa Whitmore disappeared. You were leaning hard on...Oliver, was it? But at that point he was classified as a person of interest. Jackson and Shreveport had never even gotten that far. Neither had nailed down a suspect, so, I thought until you had indisputable evidence on that young man, you'd probably want to check out those two cold cases, see if you could find a connection to yours. We talked about it at length."

John bent his head over his keyboard and pinched the bridge of his nose. "Detective Morris, do you remember who in our department you talked to about it? At length."

John burst through the office door with such impetus, it crashed against the inside wall, cracking the pane of glass stenciled with Tom Barker's name.

He was sitting behind his desk, feet propped up on the corner of it, lazily swiveling back and forth in the leather chair, talking on his cell phone. He gaped as John crossed the room in three strides. In the process of rounding the desk, he knocked Barker's feet to the floor, then yanked the cell phone out of his hand and hurled it against a file cabinet.

"What the—"

"You son of a bitch." John grabbed a fistful of his shirt and hauled him out of the chair. He drove his other fist into Barker's nose and relished the sound of cartilage crunching and seeing blood spurt from his nostrils.

Barker screamed.

John shoved him back into the chair with such force it rolled backward and slammed into the wall. The impact dislodged a brass plaque of commendation and sent it to the floor, barely missing Barker's head as it fell.

John leaned over him. "You knew. You knew about those missing persons cases, their tie-in to the blood moon. Jackson, Shreveport, Galveston. You knew, but you didn't follow up because you were too fucking intent on wrapping up Mellin and getting your promotion."

He thrust his index finger toward Barker's swelling nose. "I'm going to bring you down. For Billy Oliver. For Crissy Mellin. And for my own goddamn gratification."

He withdrew his hand and stood up straight. "And if you send your gorilla to my house again, I'm gonna shoot him in his bloated gut. Not so he'll die, but so he'll wish he was dead. You'll lose your muscle, and without him, you're a limp dick."

Barker glared at John from above the hand he'd placed over his smashed nose. "I'm gonna have you charged with assault."

"Do it! I can't wait to have my day in court. But in the end, I think it's going to be you on trial, not me."

"I want your badge and your service revolver on my desk. Now," he shouted, although it was nasally. "You're over, Bowie. Out! Fired!"

John threw his head back and laughed. He tossed his badge wallet onto the desk. He took his service revolver from its holster, removed the clip, and laid both on the desk. "Thank you. I can draw unemployment." Leaning over the man again, he said with quiet intensity, "Now I've got no procedural boundaries, no job to lose, and that ought to make your asshole pucker."

He straightened up, turned, and walked out of the office. Personnel who had congregated outside the door to watch the unfolding drama parted for him when he didn't break stride.

As he passed the ogre, he paused and smiled at the man. "What I said about shooting you in the gut? I was kidding." Leaning closer in, he said, "You mess with me again, I'll blow your fucking head off."

Chapter 14

Beth answered her phone.

"What room are you in?"

"Why?"

"I'm in the lobby. What room are you in?"

Beth considered hanging up on him. "You sound like you're in a state."

"I am. I'm unemployed. Now, for the love of God, what room—"

"Three oh seven."

John clicked off.

She was in a state herself. She was furious at him for his refusal to help her, and even angrier over his kissing her like that, then, seeming that it had had no effect on him, sending her on her way.

Contending with both those disappointments, she hadn't yet decided whether to stay or return to New York. Her roll-aboard stood unopened near the door where she'd left it when she'd come in. She stepped around it now to answer his knock. He came inside and squeezed past her and the suitcase. Neither said hello.

She shut the door. "What do you mean you're unemployed?"

"Just that."

"You got fired?"

"Yep."

"Barker?"

"The one and only."

"I'm sorry."

"Don't be. I've never been better." He squatted in front of the mini bar, took out a small bottle of bourbon, uncapped it, and raised it in a toast. "Cheers." He drank half of it in one swallow.

"What happened?"

At some point he'd changed into office clothes, but he still had his rain slicker. He tossed it onto the bed, threw himself into the easy chair, and jerked at the knot of his necktie.

"It's not what happened, past tense, that concerns me. It's what will happen in the future. In the immediate future, I'm getting you out of here. If Barker put someone on my tail before he went to the hospital, they'll assume we're up here…" He glanced toward the bed and saluted it with the bottle of bourbon.

"He went to the hospital?"

"The ER. He doesn't look so good, and I'm sure he's in a lot of pain."

She didn't know what to make of any of this, but especially not his wholehearted belly laugh. Up till now, his laughs had been limited to chuffs, his humor always wry and cynical. This laugh came from deep down and sounded too wicked to have been caused only by the whiskey, which he finished in a gulp. He tossed the empty into the wastebasket, where it landed with a clatter.

Then she noticed that the knuckles of his right hand were blood-smeared. "What have you done, John?"

He sobered instantly. "What you wanted me to do all along. Bridges are burned. I'm committed to conducting the investigation that should have been."

Before she could express her gladness to hear that, there was a knock on the door. "That'll be Mitch. I called and gave him the room number." He got up quickly and went to the door. "Hey, thanks, buddy."

"I owed you a favor, remember? We're square now." He walked in and, looking past John, said to Beth, "Hi."

She recognized him immediately. "You were in the bar."

He gave her a thumbs-up.

His friendly smile was framed by a grubby mustache. She looked from him to John. "This is your friend Mitch?"

John gave a shrug that said yes.

"*Him?* He's your former partner who wouldn't betray you under pain of death?"

"Wait," the other man said as he held up a hand and turned to John. "Under pain of death?" He stroked his mustache. "I dunno know about that."

John made a dismissive sound and asked, "Did that piece of shit pickup with the bullet holes belong to you?"

"No, but I've got another piece of shit that does. It's right outside. Y'all ready?"

"Hold on!" Beth exclaimed. The two men turned toward her. "What…I…Slow down and tell me what is going on."

"We don't have time to go into it now," John said.

"Time to go into what?"

He looked at her with frustration and impatience. "Beth, we don't—"

She interrupted him. "'I can't help you. I won't.' That's what you said—repeatedly—before you sent me packing. Now you bust in here, acting like your hair is on fire, and…" She ran out of breath. "Time to go into *what*?"

His friend folded his arms across his chest and leaned back against the wall as he'd done in the bar. "She's entitled to an explanation. Take a minute. If we pick up a tail, I'll lose him. No problem."

John gave him a perturbed look, then came back to Beth. "I called Galveston PD and spoke with a Detective Gayle Morris who was lead investigator on the Larissa Whitmore case."

He related what the detective had told him. "Those are the highlights. Bottom line, Barker knew all three of those women were abducted on nights with blood moons, same as Crissy. He sat on that information."

Beth looked over at Mitch, who said, "We knew about the Galveston case, and it seemed a dead end. Never heard anything about the two from 2018, so nobody followed up."

John said, "If Gayle Morris reached out when she learned about Crissy, I'm sure the departments in Jackson and Shreveport did, too. They would've been seeking a connection because both were still without a suspect. But if they contacted Barker, he didn't act on it. He wanted to button up the Mellin case and get his promotion."

Beth took a deep breath, blew it out, and asked, "What happens next?"

He took a step toward her. "I busted his face up, but that's nothing. What happens from here is going to be implosive. God knows how it'll turn out, but it's not gonna be pretty. I'll catch the backlash, and that's fine. I kinda look forward to it.

"But, trust me, you want no part of it. Fly back to New York today. Convince the new producer to delay the broadcast of that episode. Warn him that if he airs it as scheduled, and the believed facts of the story turn out to be wrong, his show will lose all credibility, and his tenure will be the shortest in the history of the network. Mitch will drive you to New Orleans and put you on that four o'clock flight."

"No way in hell."

He looked down at the floor and swore viciously.

"Told ya," Mitch muttered.

John shot him another dirty look.

"Listen," Beth said to John, "I started all this when I contacted you. I'm not going to abandon you with a problem that originated with me."

"You didn't originate it. Barker did. And now he knows there's going to be hell to pay."

"I'm seeing this through."

"It could cost you."

"Or cost another victim her life."

He scrubbed his face with his hands, then tried to stare her down. He looked over at Mitch, who merely shrugged. Then he came back to her. "All right. Never say I didn't try."

"Noted. Now, back to the immediate future."

"We get out of sight. We relocate to the fishing camp and start digging through all my files as well as yours. All your research notes, every idea, theory, prediction you've ever entertained about there being a serial criminal with a moon fetish. If he exists, we've got less than forty-eight hours to identify and find him."

She opened her mouth to speak, but he beat her to it. "Before you say yes, you need to understand that I'm untethered, unofficial, a free agent."

"Which means what, exactly?"

Mitch said, "Means the shit's about to hit the fan."

On the elevator ride down, John explained to her Mitch's work for the DEA. "It was sheer happenstance that we were in that bar at the same time."

"What was your fistfight over?"

"Nothing. It was all for show. It made Mitch look like a badass to those creeps he's trying to nail."

"And John needed to blow off steam," Mitch said.

She looked at John. "I had surrendered and left. You should have been relieved. Why did you need to blow off steam?"

Mitch snickered, but before he could respond, the elevator stopped on the ground floor. "I'll bring the truck around and meet y'all at the exit on the north side. It'll be a quick stop. Be ready to roll."

"Security camera?" John asked.

"Partially obscured by a canopy."

"What about your license plate?"

"Fogged out."

"Good. Let's do it."

Mitch flipped up the hood of his sweatshirt and loped toward the lobby. John and Beth went in the opposite direction. They didn't encounter anyone as they made their way past empty conference rooms and a small workout facility.

When they reached the specified door, John reached over and pulled up the hood of Beth's jacket, then did the same with his slicker. Seconds later, Mitch arrived in a pickup truck that truly was a p.o.s.

He made quick work of stowing her roll-aboard in the bed of the truck and covering it with a tarp while John helped her into the cab, where there were only two seats. "Sorry," he said. "You'll have to sit on the console."

"What about a seat belt?"

Mitch answered her question as he climbed in, engaged the gears, and took off. "Drug dealers don't believe in them. Just hold on tight to John. You won't mind, will you, John?"

"Just drive, Mitch."

"What about your car?" Beth asked John.

He told her he was leaving it there at the hotel. "If I was being tailed from the department, which I suspect, he'll have a long sit-in."

Eye on the rearview mirror, Mitch drove out of the parking lot. "Where to first?"

"My house. I've got to get Mutt. I can't leave the boat behind, either. We may need it later. Mutt and I will go by water and meet you two at the cabin."

Beth said, "Why can't I stay with you?"

"We'll need provisions. Mitch will drive you." He rattled off a list of food staples. "Don't forget dog food." He took two prepaid credit cards from his wallet and gave them to her. "Each has two hundred dollars on it." Looking down at her feet, he said, "Buy yourself some socks, and a pair of stouter shoes, and anything else you can think of that you might need."

"You make it sound like we're preparing for a siege."

In all earnestness, he said, "I hope it doesn't come to that."

Tom's wife's main concern was that the facial disfigurement would be permanent.

When she'd arrived in the ER and saw his misshapen nose and the eggplant-colored bruises that rimmed his bloodshot eyes, she'd burst into tears. When he'd looked in the mirror, he'd almost started crying himself. Not just over his appearance, but over the unfairness of life.

John Bowie's black eye had made him look rakish, dashing, dangerous, and sexy. It had contributed to his swagger. Peering over the wad of bandages holding his nose in place, Tom could barely see to walk, much less swagger. He was uglier than the ogre.

"The surgeon will fix it," he'd told his weeping wife. Her boo-hooing had driven him to distraction until an injection for pain had finally kicked in and made him loopy enough to ignore her.

It was suggested by one of the ER doctors that he consider going to New Orleans for the surgery, but he hadn't wanted to expend the time or effort. He'd entrusted himself to the local plastic surgeon.

He was at home now, and in bed. The anesthesia had worn off, but he had pills within reach on the nightstand. His wife fussed over him, but, behind her murmurs of sympathy, he sensed her misgiving that the defacement was temporary.

When his kids came into the bedroom, they were uncharacteristically subdued at the sight of him. They said all the expected sweet, nice things, but once they'd filed out into the hallway, he'd heard them gasping with laughter.

What ate at him was the probability that others also viewed him as a laughingstock. Subordinates who'd watched from the open doorway of his office as Bowie had unleashed his wrath were probably laughing up their sleeves and secretly high-fiving Bowie.

"Honey?"

"Go away."

"It's Frank Gray."

"Tell him I'll call him back."

"He's at the front door."

Tom pried open his swollen eyes. "Send him in."

The ogre tramped into the bedroom, took one look at Tom, and bellowed, "Christ on a cross."

"Mr. Gray, please, your language," Mrs. Barker whispered. "The children."

"Sorry."

"Get out," Tom said to her. "Close the door." She did as ordered.

Frank sat down in a rocking chair. Its joints groaned in

protest. Smacking his chewing gum, he ran his ham-sized hands over the smooth arms of the chair. "Nice finish. Is it an antique?"

Never minding the children, Tom spat out a string of obscenities. "Antique? Who knows? Who cares? I want to know what's happening!"

"Nothing. Bowie's still there at the hotel. Has been all afternoon."

"With her?"

"Duh. You owe my surveillance guy twenty bucks. He had to bribe the desk clerk. She hasn't checked out. But even for fifty, he wouldn't give out her room number."

"You're sure your guy followed the right car?"

"Hell yeah, I'm sure. He saw Bowie entering the lobby. Satisfied?"

"All right. I meant no offense. I feel like crap, is all."

The ogre rocked back in the chair and planted his large feet on the floor to keep himself reclined. "You know, Tom, Bowie isn't without admirers in our division. In fact, throughout the whole department. They don't let on, because they don't want to cross you and be subjected to the treatment he is. But they're there."

"You think I don't know that? Are you trying to make a point here, Frank? If so, get to it."

"Fine. I think Bowie added members to his cheering section today. Other detectives have asked for you to assign him to help them with tough cases. You've denied those requests and have kept him doing housecleaning and other chickenshit chores. He's been wasted. In trying to bring him low, you're the one who looks bad."

In so many words, Bowie had said the same thing during their standoff yesterday morning. Hearing it again from an ally made him want to grind his teeth. But that made his nose throb. "Are you joining Bowie's rah-rahs, Frank? Is that what this visit is about?"

"No, hell no. I despise the asshole. Just think of me as a little birdie in your ear whispering a warning. After today, when practically everyone who answers to you heard Bowie's ugly accusations, the tide may turn. There may be more rumblings in the ranks."

"I can squelch rumblings."

"Sure, sure. But if the men upstairs in the carpeted offices get wind of them, and word leaks into city hall, etcetera, somebody may start examining your methods with the thoroughness of a proctologist. In which case, you'll need all the friends you can get." He let that settle, then smiled. "I came to tell you, you can count on me. I'll always be at your back, on your side, Tom."

"I know that. Don't think I don't—"

"Unless..." The ogre moved his feet, and the chair rocked forward so far that he was leaning over Tom. "Unless the heat around you gets too hot. And you start thinking—See, Tom, I know how your mind works.

"And you start thinking that you need a fall guy, someone to blame for your..." His meaty hand drew a spiral in the air. "Malpractice, mishandling...mismanagement... mis..." The hand stopped spiraling and landed like an anvil on Tom's thigh. "Let's call a spade a spade. Your misdeeds."

Tom swallowed hard. The ogre smacked his chewing gum, then lifted his hand away from Tom's leg and hauled himself out of the rocking chair. "Have a good night."

Inside his pajamas, Tom had broken a cold sweat. He stopped the ogre at the door. “Listen, Frank, you have my loyalty, too. I would never throw you under the bus.”

Frank grinned. “Tom, where your future is concerned, *I’m* the bus.”

Chapter 15

When John opened the door of the cabin, Mutt scurried past him to be the first one inside to join the party.

Beth and Mitch were in the kitchen. She was laughing at something he was saying while he juggled oranges. Apparently they'd taken a break from putting away groceries. Still on the dining table were canned goods, boxes of brand-name food, a pallet of bottled water, a packet of Mutt's treats, and sacks yet to be emptied.

The whole scene pissed John off. He slammed the door.

Both turned at the sound. Beth's laughter ended abruptly. Mitch dropped one of the oranges. After a moment of silence that seemed to reverberate, Mitch bent down to pick up the orange, and Beth welcomed an ecstatic Mutt with a scratch behind his ears.

As John stalked in, he removed his slicker and threw it into the chair with the ugly throw. "An army led by Tom Barker could have marched up here, and you wouldn't have heard it." Addressing Mitch, he said, "You should have had your weapon ready for whoever came through the door. You're damn lucky it was me."

Beth stared in shock over his tone. Mitch looked amused, which further infuriated him.

"I heard you coming," Mitch said. "I knew it was you. And my gun is within arm's reach." He pointed to the shelf where John had placed his own pistol last night.

He blinked to clear his eyes of a red haze of anger. For the time being, that's how he was going to label the surge of emotion, and blood pressure, he'd felt when he'd walked in on such a lighthearted domestic scene.

"Was everything at your house all right?" Beth asked.

"If anybody's been there since I left it this morning, I couldn't tell it. How'd you two do?"

"I made certain no one followed us," Mitch said. "I left my pickup at the camo garage. Took us two trips to cart all this stuff here." He motioned toward the crowded dining table.

John walked over to it. In addition to the grocery sacks, white plastic bags had been piled in a chair. He flipped back the handles of one. Inside were articles of women's clothing.

"I'll pay you back what I spent on the credit card," Beth said. "I didn't bring that many changes of clothes with me, and most of them were—"

"It's fine."

"I took the liberty to create us a workspace." Her laptop had been placed next to his. "I'm ready to begin whenever you are, but I need to call Max first."

"Sure. But better if you don't make any more calls on your own phone."

"I figured that. Mitch removed the battery for me."

John could hardly feel sour toward Mitch for taking that precaution. He walked over to the drawer of phones, got one out, and passed it to Beth. She thanked him and headed toward the bedroom.

Mitch said, "Hey, I've got to be pushing off, so I'll say goodbye now."

She smiled and extended her right hand to him. "Thank you for the ride, for getting me here safely, for everything."

"You bet."

"Angela sounds lovely. Good luck with the baby."

"Thanks. Take care of yourself."

"You too." To John she said, "I won't be long." She went into the bedroom and closed the door behind her.

A rare and awkward silence extended between the two friends; then Mitch gestured toward the refrigerator. "I got you a six-pack."

John look toward the appliance. "Thanks for the thought, but from here forward I need to keep a clear head."

Mitch waited for a count of five, then said, "Look, John—"

"Don't say it."

"What?"

"What you were going to say."

"Oh, so you're a mind reader now?"

John pulled in a deep breath. "Okay, what were you going to say?"

"Do you know what you're doing?"

John gave his friend a forbidding look. Mitch remained impassive. Then John lowered his head and massaged his forehead with his middle finger and thumb. "I know, I know. I shouldn't have dragged her into this."

Mitch gave a short laugh. "I think it's the other way around. You wouldn't have touched that case again if it weren't for her."

"Not true."

"Bro, come on. You should've seen your face when you walked in just now. I feared for my life. You wanted to clobber me with a club and drag her off by the hair to your cave, there to dwell."

John lowered his hand from his face and looked at Mitch with exasperation. "What the hell?"

"You know what I'm saying." Appearing hesitant, Mitch stroked his mustache several times before continuing. "She's great. Awesome. But is she why you're going out on this very skinny and unstable limb? Are you…? Are you doing it just to…"

"Get her into bed? If that's what you think, then you're insulting her and me."

"Sorry. But I'm your friend, so I had to ask. You're raining down hell on yourself, John. Again. I just want you to be doing it for the right reason."

"I want to see justice done."

"I get it. But you almost didn't survive that case."

"No 'almost' to it, Mitch. I didn't survive it. I'm still struggling to survive it. I didn't do right by that girl, and I drag around that guilt like a ball and chain. And what about Billy Oliver?"

"Nothing that went down was your fault."

"Feels like it."

"Only to you."

"I'm the one that counts. If I can get answers to the questions I should have asked back then, if I can save another woman from the same fate, then maybe, *maybe* I can live with myself."

Mitch chinned toward the bedroom door. "What if she's wrong and there is no moonstruck bogeyman lying in wait?"

"Then the only thing this hell-raining has cost me is a work situation I despised. You said yourself that I should have walked out a long time ago. You asked me why I stayed. Well, this is why."

Mitch still looked doubtful. John said, "Let me ask you a question. What if it turned out that Beth's prediction was right, and another woman was taken, and I had done nothing to try to prevent it?"

Mitch sighed. "Damn. Why'd you do that? Valor leaves me no argument." He snuffled, then took his pistol from the shelf. As he slid it into a holster hidden inside his threadbare jeans, he looked toward the closed bedroom door. "You have my permission." John took umbrage, but before he could say anything, Mitch raised his hands in surrender. "Just sayin'."

John mumbled an obscene insult, but they walked together to the door, where Mitch turned to him. "Call me if you need me."

"Thanks, but I don't want to rain down hell on you, too."

Mitch poked him in the chest. "Call me." Then he turned and jogged down the front steps.

"Mitch."

Mitch stopped and looked back, and for several seconds

the two communicated only with their eyes. Then Mitch said, "You, too, buddy."

And without anything more, he left.

Beth gave Max a thorough and candid account of the day. This time she didn't omit or sugarcoat anything. She summed up by telling him without apology that she was hiding away with John Bowie in a fishing camp in a swamp.

"Jesus," Max said. "That's a thing?"

"It's a thing. This one has been in his family for generations. It's like a museum with very unique exhibits."

"None I'd pay to see."

She laughed. "No, you wouldn't," she said, noticing a length of twine attached to the wall at both ends. Dangling from it was a row of aged Christmas cards. "Before, I lied by omission because I didn't want to upset you. I know this isn't what you want to hear. I know you don't approve, and that you'll—"

She was interrupted by a gurgling sound that alarmed her. "Are you strangling?"

The alarming sound continued. She came up on her knees on the bed. "Max? *Max!*" Then she realized that he wasn't choking. "You're laughing?"

"Well, it's funny."

"Funny? You scared me half to death. What are you laughing at?"

"How long have you worked with me?"

"What?"

"Answer me."

"Five years."

"Right. For five years you've sat in on meetings, listened in on telephone conversations, seen me at my worst, which is actually when I'm at my best."

"Yes, and so?"

"How could you not see my manipulation for what it was?"

She dropped back onto her bottom, making the bed springs squeal.

He was still laughing a phlegmy laugh. "You've seen me do it to unsuspecting people a thousand times. From postmen to producers to politicians. But when I used it on you, you were blind to it."

She sagged against the pillows on the bed, too dismayed to speak.

"You came into my office with your cheeks flushed, asked for a minute and then spent thirty advancing the possibility that something was wormy about that Mellin investigation. Ineptitude, or a cover-up, or whatever.

"You insisted the case, ergo our story that documented it, warranted another look. And why? The main reason why? Because of a blood moon, a phenomenon shrouded in mystery and superstitious bullshit." He paused for a beat. "I was riveted."

"*What?*"

"It's juicy. It's blood-tingling. But even if the spooky moon stuff doesn't amount to anything, I can smell the stink of corruption in that PD all the way up here. The more I warned you not to meddle in it, the more hell-bent you became to fly down there and talk to Bowie. "

"You bastard."

"Would you rather me not have needled you into it?" He waited, then said, "I didn't think so."

"Why didn't you intercede with Brady? Wouldn't that have been simpler? You could have advised him to postpone the broadcast until—"

"Because that suck-up wouldn't have agreed to anything I suggested. And even if he had agreed to hold off until we'd done more investigating, he'd have sent someone else down there to do it. One of his flunkies, not you. You discovered the tantalizing hook that everyone else had missed; you deserved to be the one to pursue it."

"All right. So, knowing that, why didn't you just say, 'Here's your ticket, Beth, be on the next flight?'"

"I had to test your conviction. If it was only a fanciful idea that had fired your imagination, I had to know it. I had to save you from committing professional suicide."

"And protect your own butt in the process."

"You're damn right. I'm nothing if not self-serving. I've never pretended to be otherwise. But the more I pushed you, the harder you pushed back. In the end, you were willing to risk your job and reputation on this theory that the next blood moon is going to spell doomsday for some young woman."

"What if nothing happens and I'm proven wrong?"

"What's the harm? You may eat some crow, but only in front of me, and I won't tell. We'll sell Brady on the lie about your vacation with old friends, and he'll be none the wiser. Not that he's all that wise to start with," he added under his breath.

"You're not taking John Bowie into account," she said softly. "Whether I'm right or wrong, he's already suffered severe consequences because of my meddling."

"True. By busting his boss's nose, he's probably screwed his future in that police department, but if he has as much grit as you've implied, he'll land on his feet."

"I hope you're right."

After a thoughtful moment, he said, "I should have paid more attention to his disgruntlement back when we started considering that case as an episode."

"Is this another manipulation?"

"No. I swear on my next cigarette. I think I missed an opportunity. If I'd contacted Bowie myself, and handled him right, he—"

"Handled him right? We could have sold tickets to see you try."

He barked a laugh, coughed, and spat. "Well, if I'd gotten him to open up, we'd have had another story with a different ending."

So would John, she thought. Perhaps a happier one.

Max took a few gravelly breaths. "Just how mad at me are you?"

"I want to be, but how can I be? Your maneuvering got me here. I'm mad at myself for not seeing through your bluff."

"Cut yourself some slack. I'm an unprincipled, cagey son of a bitch with decades of conning to my credit." Then in all seriousness, he said, "You've got the makings of a great story here. Tom Barker, asshole extraordinaire, whose malfeasances need to be exposed. Bowie, the dour, reluctant hero with integrity. Plus a blood moon and the spookiness that conjures. Jesus, gives me goose bumps just thinking about it."

"The blood moon or the story?"

"The Emmy. Get it for me, Beth."

Chapter 16

John heard the bedroom door opening behind him. He turned in his chair at the folding table, now serving as their shared desk. "How'd it go?"

As she was walking over, Beth absently gathered her hair into a ponytail and secured it with a stretchy band. She sat down in the chair beside him. "It was interesting."

"That's an interesting adjective."

"He knocked me for a loop." She recounted her conversation with Max Longren and ended on a self-deprecating laugh. "I've witnessed important, powerful people conclude a meeting with him, naïvely unaware of how craftily they'd been manipulated. I can't believe he used his reverse psychology on me, and that I fell for it."

"Are you mad at him?"

"He asked me that."

"And?"

"Last night he told me to pack up and return to New

York ASAP, like he was issuing me an order. It made me even more determined to stay and see this through."

"Is that a good thing, or bad?"

"It's a wait-and-see."

She'd said it casually, almost flippantly, but, in the following moments, the statement changed tenor and took on importance. They were sitting shoulder to shoulder, but their heads were turned to each other. *Close* to each other.

The cluttered room seemed to grow smaller. Every creature in the swamp seemed to have stopped its industry and was now suspended in motionless, breathless expectancy. From his blanket on the floor, Mutt whined as though sensing a sudden change in the atmosphere that had lifted the hairs of his coat.

John watched Beth's eyes drift over his facial features as though she were taking stock and cataloguing them one by one. In a husky voice, she said, "Your name came up."

He raised his eyebrows, letting them speak for him.

"Max said that he regrets missing his opportunity with you."

"To do what?"

"Talk about your disgruntlement over the investigation. He believes he might have gotten you to open up."

"He's delusional."

"Essentially, that's what I told him." She smiled, but it was a small one and so brief that it had barely been there before her lips went lax.

John didn't smile at all. He was looking at her mouth and thinking about how warmly she had responded to his kiss this morning, wondering if she would be as receptive, or even more so, if he kissed her now.

Looking closely into his eyes, she said softly, "John?"

Optimistically, he leaned in. "Hmm?"

"We have work to do."

He sat back and sighed, "Yeah."

She motioned toward his computer. "Any progress so far?"

"While I was at my house this afternoon, I called the police departments in Galveston, Jackson, and Shreveport. I hoped to gain their confidence before Barker had a chance to alert them to my dismissal and tell them that I'm an ex-cop who's making up fairy tales.

"I started with Detective Morris in Galveston, since I'd already talked to her, and she seemed to have formed a favorable opinion of me. Of course that will change if I wind up in jail."

"*Jail?*"

"Barker might file charges, Beth. Avoiding arrest was one reason I wanted to hustle us out of Dodge this morning. Anyhow, unaware of all that, Morris didn't hesitate to give me the names of the lead detectives for the cases in Jackson and Shreveport.

"The guy in Jackson, Roberts, seemed like a decent guy, devoted cop, said he hated that their young woman is still categorized as missing. No real leads, no remains, no closure. And, by the way, he disapproved of your show's exploitation of Crissy Mellin's case."

"It's not meant to be exploitative. Rather, empathetic."

"I can't debate that until after I've seen it."

"I have the final version on my laptop."

"Can I take a look?"

"Whenever you want."

"Later. In the meantime, Roberts agreed to send me his case file. But he warned me not to get too excited. Boiled down, the young woman had no enemies with a reason to kill her, no lovers or ex-lovers.

"Their one person of interest was the short-order cook at the Waffle House where she worked. He had a crush on her, but she didn't return his romantic interest, which seemed like a motive. But he'd been working an all-nighter and was still on his shift when she was reported missing by her roommate. Her bicycle was found on the side of the road roughly midway between the restaurant and her apartment."

"What about regulars who would have known her? Or any customer who happened in and liked what he saw?"

"All checked out. Police had seven days' worth of security camera video. Using car tag numbers and credit card receipts, they were able to track down and question all the people who went in and out of the restaurant that week. Nothing came of any of those interviews."

"Her bicycle?"

"No sign of a struggle around it. Investigators theorize that she stopped when she was approached by whoever snatched her. If she had any sense of potential danger, it came too late."

"What about Shreveport?"

"A detective nicknamed Cougar. Talks in a growl, but he was cooperative. The girl there took her dog out to do his business, no sign of a struggle, no one in her apartment complex even heard her dog bark.

"CCTV cameras videoed her on the playground, but

she walked into a darkened area behind one of the buildings. When her dog was next seen on camera, he was dragging his leash. That leads me to believe that the perp knew her routine, knew where the cameras were and how to avoid them."

"Someone who lived in the complex?"

"They looked at everybody. Even got search warrants for a couple of the men who looked iffy. Never found one single scrap of evidence, even circumstantial. They're still monitoring them, but so far neither has raised a red flag."

"They'll be watching them Thursday night?"

"Cougar assured me they would. The departments in Galveston and Jackson will also be on high alert, but Galveston has Dobbs in prison, Jackson and Shreveport never had a suspect, and ours committed suicide. All to say, it still appears that there's absolutely no connection among these four disappearances."

"Except for the moon."

He grimaced. He'd dreaded having to tell her the reactions of his fellow detectives. "None think it was a factor, Beth, except that Dobbs used the moon to get Larissa on his boat and away from shore.

"Cougar was especially doubtful. He admitted that he'd been soft on that angle since he first heard about it from Gayle Morris. Three and a half years had passed between his case and Morris's. He said, and I agree, that serial killers usually don't go that long without being triggered.

"I grant you that the blood moons are an intriguing element, but even full moons drive people to do crazy shit. Ask any law enforcement officer or anyone who works in a hospital emergency room. People dance naked in public fountains, pregnant women go into labor. You get what I mean.

"Anyway, those three detectives listened politely and attentively, they didn't brush me off, but if I'd been them, I probably would have. They'll be even more leery of me if they find out that I no longer have a badge. Most telling, they haven't sent me their case files, and I think those are essential to our progress."

"I believe they will," she said with heart.

John wasn't as convinced. "Barker might have got to them, halted any help they might have provided."

"I'm remaining optimistic. What do we do in the meantime?"

"When you came out, I was reading through the notes I took on my last interview with Carla Mellin. It ended antagonistically. I was trying to figure out the best way to approach her now. I don't think just appearing at her door will get me far."

"She no longer lives at that door."

"What? You're sure?"

She told him about her encounter at Carla's former address. "After he slammed the door in my face, I canvassed other neighbors, which was an exercise in futility. After failing to reach you, and coming away empty-handed there, I took it as a sign to go back to New York."

"Damn it." John stacked his hands on top of his head and reared back to look up at the stamped tin ceiling. "Can't anything be easy? I was hoping to start with Carla."

"Me too. I thought you might have heard from her during these intervening years."

"No. There was no love lost between her and those of us who worked the case."

"That hostility comes across in her interview. She said the police failed her, failed Crissy."

"Can't argue that."

"In the episode, Carla is identified as a 'working single mom.' There was no mention of Crissy's father."

"Deceased. He was a rover. Once when he was away, Carla was notified by authorities in Missouri that he'd been in a fatal car-train accident. Best day of her life, she told me.

"She used to work for a credit union. I called it earlier this afternoon and was told that she quit soon after Crissy's disappearance. No one there has heard from her since."

"Does she have any relatives we can contact?"

"A sister. I have her contact info somewhere in here," he said, pointing toward the thumb drive in his laptop. "She may be willing to help. Or, just as likely, she'll tell me to go to hell." He turned in his chair, angling himself to address Beth more easily. "We need to enlist some help."

"Mitch?"

"He'd be willing, but he has time constraints. Besides, I wouldn't want to jeopardize his concentration. One slip while he's working, and he's dead. I'll only ask for his help if it becomes absolutely necessary, and even then he might not be available."

"So who?"

"There are a handful of people within the department that I trust. I propose getting them to do the grunt work like looking up addresses and phone numbers."

"You're sure they're trustworthy?"

"As sure as I can be. They're not Barker fans, and have made it known, which has cost them promotions."

"Call them. I trust your judgment."

"All are on the day shift. I'll start calling them when it's over. I don't want them doing this anywhere inside the department."

He turned to his computer and opened a document. "I've made a list of key people we should talk to. Look it over. You may want to add to it. While you're doing that, I'm going to take Mutt out, walk around the property."

At the mention of his name and the word *walk*, Mutt awoke, shook himself, and headed for the door. John lifted the shotgun off the wall-mounted rack. He made sure it was still loaded, and pocketed two more shells he took from an old cigar box shelved in a bookcase.

Beth asked, "Is the shotgun necessary?"

"For my peace of mind, yes." He nodded down at his pistol, which he'd left on the table next to his computer. "Point, pull the trigger." He waited for her nod, which she gave him with obvious reluctance. He then followed Mutt's lead out the door.

He made a loop, checking both the camouflaged garage and the hiding place where he kept the boat. Then he propped himself against a tree trunk and began making calls, opening each one with, "This is Bowie. I'm sure you know what happened today."

Everyone to whom he spoke was happy to assist. He explained the basic research he needed done, stressing that it had to be done covertly, using a personal computer. He gave each the number of a burner phone. "If I change phones, I'll notify you. In the meantime, this is the only way you can reach me, but get back to me as soon as you have something, even if it's the middle of the night. This is acutely time-sensitive."

Each cautioned him not to underestimate Tom Barker's treachery.

When he returned to the cabin, Beth was in the kitchen, butcher knife in hand. "How was your walk?"

"I'm glad we got it in when we did. It's going to rain again." He joined her in the kitchen and, as he filled Mutt's food and water bowls, saw that she was chopping fresh vegetables. "What are you making?"

She replied with a question. "Omelets okay?"

"Fine. Need help?"

"No thanks." She lifted a bottle of beer from the countertop. "I helped myself. Want one?"

"Would love it, but I'm abstaining. I told Mitch I needed to keep my head clear."

"I added a couple of names to your list of people we should contact."

He sat down at the makeshift desk, woke up his computer, and read her additions. Noticing one in particular, he said, "Gracie Oliver died."

Gracie, Billy's grandmother, had reared him by herself. His mother had never named his father, possibly because she didn't know. She died of a drug overdose when Billy was still in diapers. Without hesitation or complaint, Gracie had taken him in. She nurtured and loved him, and her affection was reciprocated.

When Crissy went missing, John and Mitch had questioned Gracie several times about her grandson's relationship with their neighbor. John remembered her anxiously twisting an embroidered linen handkerchief and saying over and over, *They're friends, Mr. Bowie. My boy wouldn't do that girl no harm.* John had been inclined to believe her. Tom Barker hadn't.

Beth abandoned her chopping and moved up behind his chair. "I hadn't heard that she died. When?"

"A few months back. She was in a nursing home. Mitch's wife saw a notice of it in the parish's online newsletter. She called to let me know."

Last night, Beth had accused him of being a man without feelings, one who didn't give a damn. What she didn't know, nor would even suspect, was that his emotions used to run hot. None of them, from rage to remorse, had had a moderate temperature setting.

That had changed the night he'd had to tell Gracie Oliver that her adored grandson Billy had hanged himself in his jail cell.

Straight from the gruesome scene and Barker's repulsive, insensitive remark, he and Mitch had gone together to Gracie's house, hoping to reach her before the media reported it. He couldn't bear the thought of her seeing Barker on TV boastfully making the announcement.

When John broke it to her as gently as he could, she'd collapsed. He and Mitch had waited until friends from her church were notified. They'd arrived in numbers, soon filling the modest mobile home to mourn with her. He and Mitch then had extended her their pathetic, useless condolences and had said their goodbyes.

John had barely made it out the door without suffocating. He'd stormed from her house ready to murder Tom Barker for having said they should celebrate Billy's suicide. If it hadn't been for Mitch, literally wrestling with him to hold him back and shaking him until he'd calmed down, he might have acted on the impulse.

That was the night his life had begun to unravel.

It was also the night he had assumed the indifference immediately evident to Beth. That night, as Mitch had driven him away from Gracie Oliver's house, he'd put his emotions in deep freeze and had donned a fuck-you attitude as impenetrable as a suit of armor. He wore it still to prevent him from ever again feeling too deeply, personally, hurtfully, destructively.

He now stirred himself out of the reverie and made himself focus on the business at hand by reading over the names Beth had added to their list of people to contact. "Who's Victor Wallace?"

She had returned to the kitchen to continue preparing dinner. "Just before I left New York, I came across an online article he'd written. He teaches sociology at a community college in Orleans parish, but his syllabus includes extra credit lectures on the occult, fantasy, goth. Like that. I thought I might contact him to see if he had anything to say about the superstitions relating to blood moons."

Another name she'd added had caught his eye. It was that of the deputy sheriff who'd discovered Billy hanging from the water pipe in his jail cell. "Isabel Sanchez," he read aloud.

"Do you know her?"

"Yes. She was traumatized by what happened on her watch. Blamed herself for letting it happen. She got counseling, but couldn't cope with the guilt over it and ultimately resigned from the SO."

"She declined our request to give an interview for the show, but I thought I would add her, see what you thought."

Without even having to ponder it, he said, "I think we should leave her alone."

He checked his inbox for the dozenth time. None of the emails he was hoping for had come in. He got up and went into the kitchen, where Beth was adjusting the flame beneath the skillet on the ancient propane-fueled stove.

Her ponytail had slipped and hung lopsidedly against her nape. The incandescent bulb in the fixture overhead made her eyes shine like polished topaz in a jeweler's case. Her lower lip caught that shine, too. The light also cast half-moon shadows of her breasts onto her midriff.

"Everything to your liking?"

He jerked his eyes up to hers. "Huh?"

She used the tip of the butcher knife to point out the ingredients she'd chopped and separated into mounds. "See anything you don't like?"

Huskily, he replied, "No. I like it all."

Chapter 17

A few minutes later they were seated across from each other at the dining table. As John picked up his fork, she said, "It's not your grandma's gumbo."

He took a bite of the omelet and nodded with appreciation. "It's good." He reached for the bottle of Tabasco in the center of the table and sprinkled his omelet liberally. "No offense."

"None taken," she said, laughing. "In Louisiana, isn't it considered one of the five basic food groups?"

He took another few bites, told Mutt he knew better than to beg, and ordered him to go lie down. As Mutt slunk away, he said to Beth, "It really is tasty. I wouldn't have pegged you for a cook."

"I can cook an omelet and make a passable spaghetti Bolognese. Cooking for one isn't very motivating."

"You don't have anyone to cook for?"

"Not currently."

"Divorce?"

"I've never been married. Only one of what I would call a relationship."

"How serious?"

"We lived together for a while. A *short* while."

"What happened?"

She pushed a bite of omelet around her plate, picking up stray chunks of tomato and bell pepper. "Soon after he moved in, we discovered we had some irreconcilable differences."

"He never put the seat down?"

She smiled, then said, "I expected monogamy. He didn't quite grasp the concept."

In the faithfulness department, he was no one to judge another man. Then again, his first affair had been in retribution for his ex's second. At that point, there hadn't been much of a marriage to salvage. Nevertheless, Roslyn's betrayal had hurt.

He said, "If the guy knew how important that was to you, and he cheated anyway, you're better off without him."

She pointed the tines of her fork at him. "Exactly the conclusion I reached minutes before kicking him out."

"No one since?"

"No one notable."

"You've got plenty of time." He paused, then asked, "How old are you, anyway?"

"Thirty-three."

"Damn." He lowered his chin to his chest and said under his breath, "I knew it."

"What?"

He sighed. "You're too old for me."

She laughed. He laughed. When it subsided, he decided to venture into territory he thought might be restricted. "I was an only child. You?"

The humor in her expression evolved into desolation. She looked down at the tabletop and followed the wood grain with the tip of her index finger. "I had a sister two years younger."

He noticed she used the past tense. He waited. If she said no more, he wouldn't push.

After an audible swallow, she said, "I think Dad must've been disappointed that one of us wasn't a boy. But, unlike me, who was studious, actually somewhat of a bookworm, Adele turned out to be an incredible athlete, which dad could better relate to."

"What sport?"

"Tennis. By middle school, she was playing at a level well beyond her age. Her potential was evident. She truly was amazing." She looked across at him as though to make her point. "I was proud of her."

Then she lowered her head again. This time she tinkered with her unused spoon. "Our family life revolved around her lessons and practices, tournaments and elite training camps. My parents' focus was on her continuing to excel and eventually go pro."

"Did she?"

"No. She died of a brain tumor. Only three months after it was discovered. She was sixteen. I was a senior in high school." She looked up at him again and took a swift breath. "It was a rough year."

"I'm sorry."

She gave an obligatory nod. "My parents were shattered, especially my dad, who had put so much stock in her future. When I left home to attend LSU, it was like an escape from the shrine to Adele that our house had become. Paradoxically, their grief was a living thing that consumed them.

"A week before I graduated from university, they were found by a concerned neighbor, dead in their bed, lying side by side. Two gunshots. The pistol was in my father's hand. They called it a murder-suicide. But I believe they'd made a pact. They had nothing to live for."

"They had you."

She gave a rueful shrug. "As I said." Their eyes held until she suddenly pushed back her chair and carried her plate to the sink. "I have dessert. A pint of ice cream, a pint of sorbet. I barely got them here before—"

She broke off when his computer chimed. He almost knocked his chair to the floor as he got up and rushed over. He didn't even sit down before accessing his email. "Yes!" He smiled over at Beth. "Roberts and Cougar both came through."

The next few hours were spent reading through the documents, notes, and interview transcripts that had been sent to him. But plowing through the material had yielded nothing that the detectives hadn't already told him. His initial excitement had fizzled, then died.

For the past half hour, he'd been slouched in his easy chair, staring into near distance, sullen and incommunicative.

He'd declined ice cream when she'd offered to dish it up. When Mutt wandered over to him seeking a pat, John had rubbed him behind the ears, but had paid little attention. Mutt had given up and gone to lie down at Beth's feet.

She'd been browsing through a boring report filed by the detective in Shreveport when she bravely broke an extended, broody silence. "They really do have precious little."

John grumbled, "Nothing precious about it."

"We can discount the Whitmore case," she said. The file from Gayle Morris in Galveston had popped up in John's email shortly after he'd received the other two. "Detective Morris is thorough, but that case isn't relevant."

"Larissa Whitmore's body was never found."

"But the culprit is in prison."

"Dobbs seems too conspicuous."

"Like Billy Oliver."

"Exactly like that. If Dobbs threw that girl overboard, it doesn't make sense to me that he then curled up in his bunk and went to sleep. Billy is dead, Dobbs is locked away. Both dispatched. What are the odds?"

"You think they're scapegoats?"

"I don't know what to think." He pulled himself out of the chair and began pacing. "For the moment, let's not discount the Whitmore case."

"Why?"

"Geography. You yourself said the abductions were regional."

"You said they weren't."

"I was being a jerk, wishing you would go away. But afterward, I looked at a map. The four cities are located within an area bordered by two parallel interstates running east to west, and another two running parallel north and south."

"You're including Galveston?"

"It's just a jog off Interstate 45. It's not a perfect square, but if our perp lives somewhere inside that area, those cities would make convenient hunting grounds. In advance of the blood moon, he set up shop."

"A place to do his dirty work? He couldn't have owned or leased any kind of structure without leaving a paper trail."

He spread his arms out from his sides, indicating the cabin. "I have."

"But he may not be as smart as you."

"Or he's a lot smarter. You, too, because you raised a good point. So, okay, let's assume that he chose these cities because he's well acquainted with them, knows the highways and byways. On the night of the blood moon, he drives into town, cruises the streets until he spies a vulnerable target. A young woman walking her dog. One riding her bicycle."

"Crissy was leaving a convenience store."

"He could easily have grabbed them and been gone in under a minute."

"I doubt any of those women willingly went with him. How did he subdue them?"

Beth was playing devil's advocate, but rather than become irritated with her, John seemed to welcome the dialogue. Speaking his thoughts aloud had energized him. Brow furrowed, fingers linked over his nape, elbows extended, he walked a tight circle.

"There are all kinds of ways to subdue the victim," he said.

"Right now, let's focus on once she's in his clutches. What next? Does he do the deed then and there and dispose of her immediately? Or does he transport her to a place he's prepared?"

"I would say the latter."

"So would I. He's not impulsive. This is one patient son of a bitch. He waits for blood moons to get his thrill. My guess is that he takes them somewhere. Like a trophy." He flipped his hand toward the head of the fearsome razorback on the wall.

"He has a lair," he continued. "But not one in each city. No, this is someplace near his home where he can go on a regular basis. He goes to gloat and savor his successes. If we find him and his den, God knows what else we'll find."

He stopped moving and looked down at her. "Proving yourself right might involve some horrific stuff, Beth. You need to reconcile yourself to that. If we catch him, you need to be prepared for anything, and it could still be beyond your worst imagining. We may find three bodies. Possibly Larissa Whitmore, too."

"She was in the Gulf of Mexico, on a boat, with Dobbs."

"Even he doesn't dispute that."

"It could have been an accident of which he was unaware, as he claims."

"Or, some other dude did it." He frowned with concentration and started pacing again. "May fifteenth, right? College exams were done, the boardwalk and Pleasure Pier on Galveston were crowded with people ready to kick off summer. Whoever he is, he would have blended in. He spotted Larissa in a bar. She was getting soused on tequila and high on weed."

"Making out with Dobbs."

"A problem for our guy. Definitely. But he's got until what? What was the time frame of the eclipse that night?"

She checked her notes. "In Central time zone, coast of Texas, nine-twenty-eight to eleven-eleven P.M."

"Okay. Unrushed and unnoticed, he could have stalked her all day. Then…then…Shit. How would he have gotten her off that boat?"

"He could've been on the boat with them."

"A threesome? Dobbs would've said so. And how would the culprit have gotten back to shore?"

"Of course," she said, looking chagrined. "What was I thinking?"

He pressed the heel of his hand against his forehead. "Don't beat yourself up. My brain is fried, too."

"Want to take a break?"

"No time," he said with a stubborn shake of his head. "I've walked a mile here, but I'm back to where I started. Is his choice random? Or does he stalk them and know where they're likely to be on the night he takes them?" He looked at his computer, which had gone to sleep. "Pull up their pictures again, please."

Earlier he had composed the equivalent of a bulletin board, filling his screen with close-up photos of the four young women, two on top, two on bottom. "Give them a good look, Beth, and tell me what they have in common."

She studied them individually, then leaned back and looked at them collectively. "John, I don't see anything."

"That's right."

She turned around to him.

"Whatever it is that draws him isn't a physical trait. Not long blond hair, or blue eyes, or a particular body type."

"So he does pick at random."

"Or they have a common trait that isn't visible."

"Like what?"

He chuffed. "Well, let's see." He began ticking off on his fingers. "Good singing voices, strict religious affiliations, or atheism. Same birthday. Cheerleading. All were mean girls, all made the honor roll."

"You're saying that it could be anything."

"Anything." He stared into the monitor, the cold light highlighting his eyes and, behind them, his stark desperation to gain insight.

"Those other detectives have compared notes on their victims' characteristics but haven't connected one pair of dots. They believe that these women had the rotten luck to be in the wrong place at the wrong time, and that the only thing they have in common is that they were abducted on the night of a blood moon."

He turned away, but had taken only a few steps when he stopped, then came back around abruptly. He said softly, "That's it, Beth."

"What?"

Speaking rapidly, he said, "Nowadays, there's a lot of interest in the occult, fantasy, wizardry, all that. Especially among young people. E-games, Halloween costumes. Hell, the whole Goth thing. Maybe it's the *victims* who are fixated on the blood moon, not the perp."

Beth experienced a tingle of optimism. "I think you could be on to something."

"I think so, too." He socked his fist into his palm. "Let's say our perp is a religious zealot who thinks that all things mystical or supernatural are evil and that anyone who buys into it is—"

"A disciple of Satan."

"Yes. A handmaiden of the devil. He's been called to set them straight. He's been sanctioned to kill them in order to—"

"Punish them."

"Or to purify and save them."

"What about Crissy Mellin?" Beth asked. "Was she interested in anything like that?"

"I never knew to ask, but we'll ask Carla if and when we get to talk to her." He'd been riffling through their notepads and pens, empty water bottles, the detritus of their hours of work at the computers. "Where's my phone?"

"End table. Who're you calling?"

"Morris in Galveston. She's the one who tipped the blood moon aspect to Barker and the other two detectives." He pulled up his recent calls and clicked on her number. After several rings, the detective answered amid a lot of background racket.

"Gayle, it's John Bowie. Bad time for you to talk?"

"Bath time. One tub, three brothers. Hold on while I relinquish refereeing to my husband."

While they waited, John put the call on speaker so Beth could listen in.

Once back, the detective started by asking if he had received the file she'd emailed. "I did. Thank you."

"Anything new turn up?"

"Nothing new, but I've been thinking of the perp as the one with an obsession for blood moons. But what if it's the women who have the obsession? He targets them because of it."

"I'm listening."

"You said you found nothing suggesting that Dobbs was into mysticism, the occult, astrology, any of that."

"Nothing."

"What about Larissa herself? Did she have any interests in that arena? A zodiac tattoo? Anything like that?"

"I got no indication of it. I asked her parents and friends about her interests, hobbies. Nothing like that was mentioned. The posters in her bedroom were of hunky men in G-strings and idols like Beyoncé. Nothing witchy or out there. I don't think Larissa was that cerebral. Sorry, John."

He looked at Beth, his disappointment plain. "It was a long shot."

"A good idea, though."

"I thought so. I envisioned each of the women caught unaware, abducted while moongazing."

"Doubtful they would have been doing that in Jackson or Shreveport."

"Why's that?"

"Our blood moon here in '22 was seen against a night sky. But the ones in 2018 weren't that awe-inspiring in this region. The one in January occurred around eight o'clock in the morning. And because of the Earth's positioning, it was only a partial eclipse.

"Shreveport's in July of '18 was also partial. It, too, occurred in daylight. On other parts of the globe, those blood moons were brilliant. In the southern US, not so much."

Chapter 18

Beth woke up. Noticing light beneath the bedroom door, she got out of bed and pulled on Aunt Gert's robe. After securing it with the tie belt, she tentatively opened the door. The only light on in the main room was the wall sconce with the Mardi Gras beads.

John's back was to her. He sat at the dining table, fully clothed, elbows on the table, head in his hands.

Detective Morris's explanation hadn't been what he'd wanted or expected to hear, but he'd politely thanked her for the clarification and apologized for imposing on her. Then he'd ended the call and, with exaggerated control, as though his phone were made of hand-blown glass, he set it on the table.

Beth had extended her hand toward him, but he jerked his arm out of her reach. "John, it's in my notes."

"I didn't see it."

"It's—"

"Not now."

Jaw rigid, eyes implacable, he'd gone over to the door, yanked his rain jacket off the coat tree, and walked out without another word. Mutt had trotted after him, his tail almost getting caught in the door as it had swung shut.

Now Mutt was curled up on his blanket. As she emerged from the bedroom, he opened his eyes and looked at her but didn't stir as she walked barefoot across the room to the dining table. "John?"

He lowered his hands from his head and sat up straighter, rolling his head around his shoulders. "Hey. What are you doing awake?"

"Why are you up? Have you slept at all?" When he didn't respond, she asked, "How long did you stay outside?"

"Until your light went out and I thought you'd be asleep."

On the table were a bowl of melted ice cream and a bottle of bourbon. The drinking glass beside it was empty. "Which came first? The ice cream or the whiskey?"

"I made a float."

She pulled out the chair adjacent to his and sat down. "You told Mitch you were abstaining."

"From beer. I didn't say anything about bourbon." He dug his fingers into his eye sockets. "I only had a splash."

She thought it might have been more than a splash, but he looked beleaguered not drunk. "The times of those 2018 eclipses were in my notes."

"I heard how both of them that year were particularly significant. The super blue…and so on. I missed the tidbit about their timing locally. And hearing it hit me at a bad time, just as I was trying to piece together something that sort of made sense.

"Of course I know an eclipse of any kind doesn't look the same all over the world. But the picture I'd seen of a blood moon on TV the other night, the vibrant one that the weatherman was going on about, is the image I've held on to.

"It hadn't occurred to me that not all would be that clear and total. It should have, but it didn't. No wonder the detectives in Jackson and Shreveport were lukewarm on me. I was making a big deal out of nothing."

"It's not 'nothing.' Just because the moon isn't visible doesn't mean it isn't there. Those were still blood moons."

He looked at her fully for the first time and gave her his wry, humorless grin. "Brilliant me. I deduced that on my own while I was outside. I looked up at the sky to curse the moon, but, even though it's almost full, I could only detect it by a slightly lighter patch of clouds. I still cursed it. And it felt *good*," he added with emphasis.

"That's when it hit me. Those four young women might not have known there was a spectacular moon, but *he* did. Even if he couldn't see it, the blood moon was feeding his twisted compulsion."

"That's right."

"I sent Roberts and Cougar emails to that effect. Maybe it'll shake something loose for them." He reached for the bottle of bourbon, but only to recap it. "The good news is that I wrapped my mind around all that. The bad news is that it doesn't do us any good. It doesn't clue us to who or where he is, waiting for Thursday to roll around."

Beth would have been devastated, but not surprised, if he'd called the whole thing off then and there. But when she hesitantly asked what was on their agenda for tomorrow, he said, "Carla Mellin, if I hear back from the officer trying to track her down."

"Do you think she'll see us?"

"If we ask first, no."

"We just show up?"

"It's not courteous, but we don't have time to dick around. Better not to give her a choice."

"We can't force her to talk to us."

"I'm a cop."

"Not since this morning."

"Yeah, but she doesn't know that."

She smiled and looked at the kitchen clock. "It's a few hours before dawn. You should use them to sleep." She stood up. "What time should I be ready?"

He pushed his chair back, grabbed the tie belt of the robe, and reeled her in between his spread knees. She was taken off guard but didn't stop him when he pulled the knot at her waist free, bent his head and worked it inside the robe until it rested against her midriff. "I'm ready now."

"John…"

"Do you have any idea what hell it's been to keep my hands off you?" He slipped them inside the robe and settled them on her hips.

"If memory serves, this morning, after kissing me quite thoroughly, it was you who couldn't leave fast enough."

"For your own good, Beth."

"It didn't feel like that."

"Believe me, it was one of the hardest things I've ever had to do." He nuzzled the side of her breast. "God knows I wanted to stay and kiss you again, and not stop there."

Filtered through her tissue-thin tank top, his breath was humid and hot.

She placed her hands on his head, lightly. But then his mouth was opening and closing over her nipple, and his hair became enmeshed in her fingers as she clutched at it.

He raised his head and looked up at her. The light from the sconce shone directly into his eyes, making them look mercurial and fervid. His scruff was rough against her forearms, exposed now that the wide sleeves of the robe had fallen back.

He turned his head and touched his tongue to the pulse point on the inside of her wrist, then murmured against it, "We're going to sleep together."

His fingers began flexing and contracting against her hips, drawing her closer. "It's only a matter of time. It's been only a matter of time since I asked you if that seat was taken. You knew it. I knew it."

He lowered his head again and pressed kisses into her middle, working his way down even as he tilted her hips upward and closer, until he reached the strip of exposed skin between the bottom of her top and the elastic waistband of her sleep shorts. He lightly nipped her with his teeth, then swept his tongue across the love bites.

A yearning sigh ghosted through her lips.

"Like that?"

"Um-huh."

She felt his smile against her skin as he slipped his finger into the waistband and gave it a downward tug.

Then his cell phone rang. They froze. He swore as he removed his hand. The elastic snapped into place against her belly. She stumbled backward, tripping over the tie belt that dangled from its loops.

"I've got to get it," he said hoarsely. "It's probably my guy with info on Carla."

"Of course." She fumbled her attempts to retie the robe's belt.

He picked up the phone and, without taking his eyes off the wet spot his mouth had left on her tank top over the tip of her breast, clicked on his phone. "Bowie."

It wasn't his guy. It wasn't any guy.

A young and tremulous female voice said, "Dad?"

Chapter 19

Tuesday, March 11

They skipped," the ogre said. "Don't know where to."

"Excuse me?"

"Evaded us."

He didn't elaborate. He didn't need to. Those two words were enough to further sour his boss's disposition, which could already curdle cream. Against the advice of his doctor to take it easy for several days, Tom had phoned Frank early, waking him up and summoning him into his office.

"Within half an hour," he'd said before hanging up.

On the drive in, Frank had checked with the man who'd been on night watch at the hotel where Bowie and the woman were cozied up. His man had reported that Bowie's car hadn't gone anywhere and that there'd been no sign of him.

"The woman?"

"Nope. Neither of them."

Hearing that had made Frank uneasy. Bowie had last been seen entering the hotel almost twenty-four hours ago. Even during a sexathon, they had to come up for air sometime.

Frank ordered his man to confirm that they were still in the hotel.

"Desk clerk says she hasn't checked out."

"That doesn't mean shit. Set off the fire alarm. Bribe a maid to let you into her room. Only as a last resort, play the cop card. Barker wants to keep this quiet for now. Whatever you do, be quick about it."

Fifteen minutes later the guy called him back. He'd given one of the hotel's housekeepers a sob story about his sister, Beth, who often went on drinking binges. She confirmed that Ms. Collins was still checked in. Then he'd talked her into letting him into room 307 to check on his sister's well-being.

He'd told Frank that the Do Not Disturb sign was hanging on the doorknob. The bed was still made. Towels hadn't been used. One empty bourbon bottle from the mini bar was in the trash can.

And Frank had thought, *Oh fuck*, knowing he had to break this news to Tom Barker.

Now he had, and Tom was thumping his desktop with his fist in a steady rhythm of fury. "He's made fools of all of us."

"He's slick."

"Bullheaded son of a bitch. He can't be enjoying this ducking and hiding any more than we are."

Frank said nothing but thought, *He's got the girl.*

"That goddamn Mellin case. Why won't he just let it go?"

Since it was a rhetorical question, Frank didn't respond to it, either. Instead he said, "What do you want me to do, boss?"

"Go back to his house and—"

"I've already sent somebody. It'll take him a while to find the place, and when he does, I doubt he'll find Bowie there."

"He couldn't have gotten away from that hotel unseen unless he'd had help." He glanced past the ogre into the squad room beyond the door. The window in it now had a jagged crack created by Bowie. "Nobody out there would dare to cross me."

Frank shifted in his seat. "Probably not, but I told you yesterday that—"

"Bowie has a cheering section. I'm aware. But cheering from the sidelines and playing the game are two different things."

"I guess it boils down to if they like him more than they fear you."

Tom scowled. "They fear me, all right."

The ogre didn't comment.

"What about Mitch Haskell?" Tom asked. "Are they still thick?"

"Dunno."

"Find out."

"That's not gonna be easy. Isn't he working undercover for the feds?"

"Find out. Also, have someone check the security cameras at the hotel, especially the rear exits."

Frank sighed. "Look, boss, if they were caught on camera, it'll probably show them climbing into an Uber car."

"If that's the case, identify that car and driver and find out when and where they were dropped off."

"Which is exactly what Bowie would expect us to do. He'd no longer be where they were dropped." Frank took a breath. "What I think? I think we sit back and let Bowie do all the hiding and ducking while we wait for him to show his head."

Tom scrutinized him without saying anything until it became uncomfortable.

Belligerently, Frank said, "What?"

"It's sounding to me like you're scared of him, Frank."

He didn't like that. Not at all. Especially because there was a speck of truth to it. Physically, he could pound Bowie to mush. But Bowie was smarter than him, and he had a cold way of smiling while he was threatening to blow your head off that made you think that he would do it, and that he'd enjoy it.

Tom was still eyeing him with a faint smirk.

"Scared of Bowie?" he scoffed. "That'll be the day."

"Kinda sounds like that," Tom said.

The two stared each other down, and Frank was pleased when Tom was the first to relax and break eye contact. He said, "Before you got here, I went to see the superintendent. It took only one look at me to get his authorization. He was queasy about the negative publicity it will no doubt generate, but he said he'll put a spin on it. Something to the effect that when he spots a bad apple, he gets rid of it so it won't spoil the whole barrel."

"Authorization for what?"

"A warrant for the arrest of John Preston Bowie. Assault and battery and assorted lesser offenses against a police officer. That's the official mandate." He leaned forward across his desk and lowered his voice. "But what I really want to happen, Frank, is for you to locate the son of a bitch but not to bother with bringing him in. Got it?"

Loud and clear. "What about her?"

"Two can be disposed of in a swamp as easily as one."

Frank grunted understanding and heaved himself up.

As he headed for the door, Tom said, "I don't believe I need to remind you how much is riding on your success or failure."

The ogre turned and flashed his grotesque grin. "Mainly your ass, Tom. Mainly your ass."

Last night, immediately upon hearing his daughter's tearful voice, John had covered the speaker, apologized to Beth, and told her it was a call he had to take. He'd bade her a quick good night and then had retreated into his bedroom and closed the door.

Now as she came into the main room, he was in the kitchen making coffee. "Good morning."

He told her good morning, then, "I have to go see my daughter." Before she had time to respond, he continued in a clipped voice. "The officer I charged with getting an address for Carla Mellin came through. So we'll drive into town together. We'll go see her after my talk with Molly."

"Okay." She didn't remark on that being the first time he'd called his daughter by name.

Obviously distressed, he ran his fingers through his hair. "I'm meeting her at a coffee shop within walking distance of her school. She's upset. I hope you understand that it's not a good time to be making introductions. It shouldn't take long."

"I don't mind waiting in the car."

"Thanks. Her first class is at nine, so…" He motioned toward the wall clock, and Beth got the message.

"Give me ten minutes."

During the drive into Auclair, he said little. That now familiar dent stayed between his eyebrows, indicating to her that whatever was going on with his daughter was troubling him greatly.

Fearing he might get prickly if he thought she was prying, she asked mildly, "How old is Molly?"

He stirred as though he'd been completely lost in thought. "Sixteen. In that picture you saw of us on the beach, we were celebrating her twelfth birthday. That was before the bottom fell out."

"Of…?"

"Everything."

Beth let the conversation die there. For the rest of the drive, he kept his eyes on the road, and neither said anything until he pulled into the coffee shop's parking lot. "That's her."

The girl was standing outside the entrance scanning the parking lot for arrivals. She'd filled out since the picture on John's nightstand had been taken, but she was still lanky. Her dark hair curled wildly. Rather adorably, in Beth's opinion. She was dressed in wide-legged jeans, a long-sleeved t-shirt, and the clunky sneakers her generation loved. A backpack was hanging from her narrow shoulders

"You're sure you'll be okay?" John asked.

"I'll be fine. Go."

As he walked toward his daughter, she gave him a tentative smile and said meekly, "Hi, Dad."

He pulled her into a tight hug, rocking slightly. They held on to each other for a long time. When he released her, she glanced back at the car.

"Is that the car from the fishing camp?"

"Yes."

"Who's that with you?"

"Nobody."

"Somebody."

"I'll tell you inside."

They went in and were led by a waitress to a booth. They scooted in facing each other. Molly ordered a smoothie. He ordered a black coffee. He asked about her classes, friends, general parental stuff to which he got general, monosyllabic, adolescent replies.

"How's the art project coming?"

"Okay."

She'd replied with a desultory okay to all his inquiries, when it was evident that everything was definitely not okay.

Their order arrived. She drew the straw toward her mouth and took a long sip, studying him over the tall glass. When she leaned back, she said, "Did you have a black eye?"

"Thanks to Mitch."

"Uncle Mitch?" she exclaimed, showing some animation for the first time. She even laughed. "Why were you two fighting?"

"Just horsing around. He got a bruised belly out of it."

"When's their baby coming?"

"A few more months. They found out it's a boy."

"Cool. Have they named him?"

"I forgot to ask."

She rolled her eyes at what seemed an unforgivable omission, then looked out the window toward his car. "Do you have a girlfriend?"

"No. She's, uh, work-related." He told her about Beth's affiliation with *Crisis Point.* "You remember when they were down here filming? The episode airs next week."

"Then what's she doing here now?"

"Part of her job is to make sure everything is accurate. She's double-checking a few key elements of the story ahead of the broadcast."

His daughter eyed him with a shrewdness that defied her youth. "Why's she asking you?"

"Because I've refused to talk about it before now. She wanted to know why."

"I want to know why she's dredging it all up again. You were a mess."

"I'll grant you that. I hate that it's being dredged up, but, in all honesty, it needed to be." She was about to say something more, but he held up his hand. "Listen a minute. I can't go into the nitty-gritty, but the situation could become complicated."

"For you?"

"Yes. Beth's probing—"

"Her name is Beth?"

"Beth Collins. Her probing has yanked the tail of a tiger. Some people inside the PD aren't too happy with me for talking to her." He didn't want to tell her yet that he'd been fired and add to her upset. Nor did he want to frighten her, but she needed to be cautioned.

"Till things settle down, stay aware of your surroundings. Tell me if you see anybody lurking around, or anything that's out of the ordinary. Okay?"

"Okay," she said with apprehension.

He reached over and patted her hand. "I'm on top of it, but just pay attention to what's going on around you. If something feels off, heed that instinct. Got it?" She nodded. "Good. Now let's talk about you. What's going on?"

"Nothing. I'm okay."

"That's why you called me in the wee hours, bawling your eyes out? Because you're okay? Because there's nothing the matter?"

"Nothing new." Tears filled her eyes, and she said in a stage whisper, "I hate her!"

"Molly—"

"Dad, you don't know."

"I do know."

"Then why do I have to live with her?"

"Because the judge said so."

"She is such a bitch. How did you stand to be married to her? She's silly and selfish and shallow. She has this new boyfriend. He's gross." She shuddered.

John's blood pressure spiked. "He doesn't fool with you, does he?"

"No."

"You swore you would tell me if any of her boyfriends ever—"

"None have and he doesn't. If anything, he pretends I'm not there."

He relaxed. "What's gross about him?"

"He comes and goes. Moves in, moves out. When he's not there, she whines. When he is there, they fight. She accuses him of having another woman, and he probably does. I have to listen to all of it."

John rubbed the bridge of his nose. "I know, sweetheart. I hate it for you. I hate it for me. But you can't change the situation, and neither can I. We just have to cope until you're of age."

"She doesn't like me living with her any more than I like being there. Maybe if you asked her again to let me live with you, she—"

"She would never agree. You know that. It has nothing to do with you. She's spiting me. And I can't afford to fight her in court. Besides, by the time we filed all the paperwork and got a court date, you'll be eighteen."

"I don't think I can wait that long, Dad. I really don't."

"We made a deal."

"I know."

"We exchanged promises."

She nodded, looking so forlorn, he hesitated to continue, but knew he must.

"If you break your promise to me, Molly, the deal's off. And I mean it. If you put me through that again, there'll be no negotiation, no compromise, no 'I'm sorry, Dad, I'll never do it again.' Understand me?" Her lips was trembling, but she nodded. "Let me hear you say it."

"I understand."

"You uphold your end of the bargain, and I swear to you, I'll uphold mine." He reached for her hand and squeezed it. "I love you."

"I love you, too. I just wish—"

"I know what you wish. I wish it, too. But even when we're not under the same roof, I'm always there for you. Call me anytime, even in the wee hours."

"To bawl my eyes out?"

"Especially for that. I don't mind." He gave her hand another squeeze, then looked at his watch. "It's ten to nine. Time to hustle. And I want a private showing of that art project when you're finished."

"You'll have one."

When they got outside, they hugged again; then she motioned toward the car. "Can I meet her?"

"Now's not really a good time. You've got class, we've got an appointment."

"Does she live in New York?"

"Yes."

"Sweet. Is she young or old?"

"Younger than older."

"Is she cool?"

"Define cool."

"Is she hot?"

"First cool, now hot. Why are you asking all these questions?"

She grinned. "Because you got all weird when you were talking about her."

"All weird?"

She laughed. "Gonna be late. Bye." She bussed him on the cheek and jogged off, turning once to wave as she rounded the corner of the building.

He walked over to the car and got in.

Beth said, "She's adorable."

"Thanks."

"Everything all right?"

"For the time being."

Beth didn't fish for information, but he felt she was owed an explanation. "Teenage angst, but she's got some legitimate grievances. She's a great kid who deserved better parents. Roslyn didn't fool anybody about her affairs, especially Molly. She's abnormally intuitive."

"I wonder where she gets that."

He shot her a look, and she smiled cheekily.

Then he returned his eyes to the road and continued. "The divorce followed close on the heels of the Mellin case. The split was contentious, a real shit show. I was a wreck. Drinking too much. Angry all the time.

"Molly felt betrayed by her mother and wanted to stay with me, but the judge wouldn't grant even joint custody. She had to go with her mother. Then, a few months into the new normal, Molly ran away."

"Oh God, John."

"Yeah. She was fourteen. Barely. Didn't show up for school, didn't come home that afternoon. Roslyn called and accused me of harboring her, enticing her by spoiling her.

"Of course, I went crazy with worry. Mitch and I cruised the streets all night looking for her. The next morning, the manager of a twenty-four-hour gas station found her sleeping on the floor of the ladies' room. He talked her into giving him my phone number."

"You must've been frantic."

"Pulling my hair out. Then about a year ago, she did it again. That time she was gone for three days before she called me, crying, asked if I would come get her. She'd been walking the streets by day, going to a mission at night. She got frightened by some of the people who wandered in there."

Beth murmured a sorrowful sound.

"That's when she and I made a pact. She's very artistic. From the time she could hold a crayon, drawing, painting was all she ever wanted to do. After I picked her up at that mission, and scolded her severely, I told her that if she would stop endangering herself like that, and stick it out with her mom, I would send her to an art conservatory in Manhattan." He named it.

"I know of it. It's renowned."

"And expensive as hell. I'm still not sure how I'll swing it—especially now that I'm unemployed—but that's my deal with her. Last night she was so upset, I was half afraid she wouldn't show up this morning. My heart clutched when I saw her. The good cop wanted to hold on to her and not let go. As bad cop, I emphasized that our deal is off if she runs away again."

"I don't think she will."

"At least she'll think twice. She wants that bright lights, big city school."

"She also doesn't want to disappoint you."

"You think?"

"Yes, John. Based on what you've told me, you're her person. When she's falling apart, she turns to you for restoration. That should make you feel good."

"It does." He paused before adding, "Even if her timing last night was lousy." He cast her a meaningful look.

She smiled shyly. "It was rather lousy."

"Probably for the best, though," he said, returning his eyes to the road. "I may have had more than a splash of bourbon in my float."

"Oh. So you were looking at me through whiskey goggles."

"You looked damned good. Felt even better." He braked for a traffic light and turned his head toward her. "Only a distress call from my daughter could have made me stop."

"Not true. *I* could have stopped you."

"Would you have?"

"Not in a million," she whispered.

His cock didn't get the message that now wasn't the time to act on the invitation behind the sultry look she was giving him. "Fair warning, Beth. I won't forget you said that." He reached across the console and placed his hand high on her thigh. "In the meantime, thanks for putting up with the Bowie family drama."

"You're welcome." She spoke softly, and they continued looking at each other until the light turned green.

When they were moving again, she said, "While waiting for you I made some calls. One was to my landlord to ask if the leaky faucet in my bathroom had been seen to. I also called Victor Wallace, the sociology professor. I obtained his number through the college office. The words *Crisis Point* are as good as 'open sesame.'"

"Or 'police officer.'" She smiled, and he asked, "Was the professor open to talking to you?"

She laughed. "Yes. He wanted to know if our interview would be on TV. I had to let him down gently. He was on his way to class and couldn't talk then. We scheduled a Zoom for later this afternoon."

"Progress," he said.

"Then why are you frowning?"

"It's happening too damn slow."

Just then, a phone rang. He had a collection of burners in a ziplock bag in the floorboard. He fished around in it until he found the one ringing. It was one of the police officers working with him in secret. He answered quickly. "I'm here."

"Barker issued a warrant for your arrest. He and the ogre also had a closed-door meeting. Ogre left it licking his chops. Watch your back."

"Thanks. Don't use this number again. I'll call you on another."

He disconnected and said to Beth, "Never a dull moment."

Chapter 20

He drove down the road that was so familiar to him now he knew where to swerve to avoid the deeper potholes. Inside this natural tunnel formed by trees whose branches meshed above the road, there was only dusky light. The heavens stubbornly refused to clear.

But there would be no rain or clouds on Thursday night. He was certain of it. Everything would be perfect this time.

Crissy Mellin, her burnished-gold hair notwithstanding, hadn't been right. It was as simple as that. He felt nothing except a powerful disdain for the young woman who had ruined the ceremony for him.

He did, however, experience an occasional twinge of remorse over the young man the police had blamed for her abduction. News of his suicide had been upsetting to him.

Why, though, should it have disturbed him? He'd had nothing to do with it. The police had made a terrible mistake, but Fate had also had a hand in it. As unfortunate as the circumstances had been, Billy Oliver was predestined to die in that jail cell.

Nevertheless, it was a mystery to him why Oliver had confessed to a crime he didn't commit. He'd been shocked to learn that. The *why* of it was befuddling. But if there were an explanation, it wouldn't be a mystery, would it?

Having now reached his destination, he shook off his reflective mood and resolved to think only forward. No more dwelling on what had been, but what would be. His heart kicked up its pace as he got out of his car.

The padlock he'd installed was much too fancy for the building, but it was advertised as the best. He punched in the code, heard the reassuring clink of metal within the mechanism, and pushed open the door. The hinges were well lubricated and didn't squeak at all.

He switched on the light, a ceiling fixture enclosed in a wire cage, like the ones used in gymnasiums. Unattractive but serviceable, it filled the open space with glaring light. He'd learned from last time that he required more wattage than he'd had. Brighter light didn't create as pleasing an ambiance for such a sacred ritual, but it was more practical, and this time he had to think less aesthetically and more practically.

He regretted that the setting wasn't more like a temple with a row of fluted columns along each side and an altar draped in embroidered silk. His altar was a handmade workbench constructed of unvarnished wood. He'd bought it at a junkyard, paying in cash to a man tossing chicken feed into a henhouse.

He fantasized walls covered in opalescent tiles rather

than corrugated tin that was pocked with dents. To help alleviate the ugliness, he'd thought about taping up posters with celestial themes, but purchasing anything even marginally connected to the ritual was risky. The smallest thing could get him caught. The walls remained unadorned.

Nor were they soundproofed, which was a concern, although there was very little chance of being discovered by making noise. There was no one within at least a mile of here.

He'd stumbled upon the building purely by chance one day when he was out for a drive and took a wrong turn. It was set well back from a narrow dirt road that was traveled only by someone who was lost, as he'd been.

The track leading from the road to the building was overgrown. Weeds and underbrush grew halfway up the exterior walls. A thick, leafy vine, hanging from a live oak tree, draped the side of the building most visible from the road, providing a natural camouflage.

After discovering the structure, he'd returned to it often. Eventually he'd determined that it was ideal for his purpose. Clearly it hadn't been used for years. A place didn't become this derelict unless it had been abandoned by an owner with no plan to return. He'd simply claimed it, and no one had ever challenged him.

The interior was fifteen by twenty feet. In one corner was a deep utility sink. A mop and containers of bleach and other industrial-strength cleaning agents were within easy reach, as was a box of latex gloves. One couldn't have too many.

Since the debacle in '22, he'd upgraded the plastic

sheeting with which he'd lined the concrete floor. The material he was using this time was much thicker but still pliable, and pliability was important. Handling dead weight could be cumbersome.

Above the workbench cum altar were two shelves he'd attached to the wall with stout brackets and screws. The lower shelf was lined with a spotless white cloth. On the cloth lay a collection of surgical instruments, lined up evenly and in the order of their length, shortest to longest. He'd sterilized them numerous times, but he would do so again before Thursday, probably more than once.

The upper shelf was empty. The space was reserved for something special. He would place it there ceremonially and reverently. That would be the final step. Then everything would be ready.

Nothing would go awry this time.

Only two more days! His chest became tight with excitement when he thought about it.

Chapter 21

The middle-class neighborhood into which Carla Mellin had relocated was a tract development at least fifty years old. Some of the houses had been updated; most needed to be.

Carla's was one of the latter. The house wasn't terribly unkempt, but it signaled desolation, as though the bitter unhappiness of its resident had seeped through its walls from the inside out.

The officer who'd done the research for John had told him that Carla was currently staffing the admissions desk at a twenty-four-hour medical emergency care center. Her shift was from four o'clock in the afternoon until midnight.

It was early to be calling on someone who probably slept late because of her work hours, but he and Beth were never going to have a welcome mat rolled out for them, and this was their best chance of finding her at home.

He turned off the car. "Well, here goes nothing."

"Maybe I should go first. Alone. She'll be caught completely off guard. I'll be less—"

"Mean-looking."

She smiled. "Intimidating."

He gestured her toward the house and wished her good luck.

As she made her way up the walk, he took a phone from the plastic bag and called Mitch. As soon as his friend answered, John said, "Guess who."

"A fugitive from justice."

"So you've heard?"

"Deduced. You're on the lam? Someone from the PD called my office, said the matter was urgent, left a number for me to call back. I haven't yet. What do you want me to tell them?"

"To fuck off."

"Happy to oblige."

He imagined Mitch's grin through the dreadful mustache, but in all seriousness, he said, "The warrant's for assault. I think that's a formality. Barker's unleashed the ogre. Be careful."

"Same goes, bro."

"Later."

During the rushed exchange, John had watched what was playing out at Carla's front door. It seemed an age between the time Beth had rung the doorbell and it was answered.

Carla opened the door only a quarter of the way. Through the crack, she scowled at Beth. He could tell the instant Beth introduced herself. Carla's reaction was swift and hostile. She was about to close the door in Beth's face, but whatever Beth said caused her to hesitate.

She listened, then looked beyond Beth toward the car. Beth said more, Carla said something back, then closed the door. Beth returned to the car, and when she got in she was slightly out of breath.

"No soap?" he said.

"She's agreed to see us, but I think I woke her up. She wasn't dressed. We're to give her a few minutes. She'll let us know."

"That's better than I expected."

"Yes, but I warn you, she's spoiling for a fight. With me because of the show. With you because of what she called the botched investigation."

"She has every right."

"It's not you she resents as much as Tom Barker. She asked if you still worked for 'that jackass.'"

"Did you relieve her of that worry?"

"No. I left that for you to tell, if you choose to."

"Word of the arrest warrant is out. I called to give Mitch a heads-up that they would undoubtedly try to contact him, looking for me. They already had."

"John, you can't get arrested."

"The hell of it is, I can. Let's hope I'm able to avoid it." He hitched his chin toward the house. "She's waving us in."

When they reached the front door, Carla greeted them by saying, "I didn't get to bed until two o'clock this morning, and I have to be back at work by noon."

John said, "I thought your shift was from four to twelve."

"They changed it. As of today, it's noon to eight P.M." Then she turned her back to them and started down a dim hallway.

She had dressed in an '80s era track suit, terry cloth scuffs on her feet. She hadn't bothered to groom herself at all. The aroma of fresh coffee filled the house. She had a mug of it, but they weren't offered any as she led them into a small living room and ungraciously pointed them toward a sofa. She sat down in a recliner but kept it upright.

John began. "I apologize for getting you up early."

"Well, I'm up, you're here, what do you want?"

"We wouldn't have bothered you at all if we didn't think it was important."

"Have you found Crissy?"

"No."

"Then I don't know what you have to say that would be of any interest to me."

To hell with this. He didn't have time to spar with her. "There's a possibility that Crissy's abductor is going to strike again, tomorrow night, if he's not identified and stopped in time." He paused and blandly added, "If that's of any interest to you."

She divided a look between them, landing back on John. "Where'd you get that notion?"

"From Ms. Collins. I'll let her explain."

Beth scooted forward on the sofa cushion in order to shorten the distance between them and try to establish a rapport. "Ms. Mellin, do you know what a blood moon is?"

Carla looked at John as though asking him if she'd heard right, then went back to Beth. "It turns orangey. What about it?"

"There was a blood moon the night Crissy was taken."

"There was? News to me."

"There was cloud cover here, and the eclipse occurred in the wee hours."

Beth spent the next several minutes explaining why the phenomenon might be significant. John interjected only a few comments. Carla said nothing but listened intently, especially when Beth began telling her about the other women who had vanished just as Crissy had.

Beth finished by saying, "Louisiana lies in the swath of the US where tomorrow night's blood moon will be a total eclipse, and, weather permitting, the viewing should be ideal."

Carla looked at John. "You've talked to your counterparts in those other cities?" He nodded. "What were their reactions to your prediction?"

"Skeptical."

"Doesn't surprise me. This moon business sounds real far-fetched."

"When Beth first bounced it off me, I thought so, too," he said, having decided that complete transparency would be the best tack to take. "Those detectives haven't dismissed the eclipses out of hand, but they lean toward them being coincidental. Also, no one has isolated a common trait among the four victims, which is rule of thumb for serial criminals.

"An even bigger snag for those who've worked those cases is that Galveston has their culprit in prison, as he was when Crissy was taken. Ours is dead by suicide. That cancels them out as possible suspects in Jackson and Shreveport."

"Billy wasn't your culprit," she said flatly. "I kept telling that buffoon Barker he wasn't. That poor boy wasn't clever enough to pull off something like that, even if he'd wanted to, and he wouldn't have wanted to. He and Crissy were friends, and friends for him were hard to come by. Gracie had homeschooled him, which was good in some ways, but it had made him socially awkward."

"We were aware of all that," John said. "I'm not defending Barker's stubborn belief that Billy was guilty, believe me. I'm simply pointing out facts that we, as investigators, couldn't discount.

"Billy's grandmother took him out of school in the middle of second grade because of behavioral issues. In his public school records there were numerous reports of aggression against teachers and classmates, general unruliness. He may not have misbehaved around you and Crissy, but—"

"No, he didn't. Know why? Because we treated him kindly, didn't make fun of him, call him a dummy. All those incidents were his reaction to being bullied. They failed to put *that* in their damn reports."

Patiently, John continued. "There was another red flag. We discovered a number of pornography websites bookmarked on Billy's computer. Some of it very graphic."

"He had the typical urges of boys that age," Carla said. "Didn't you like looking at pictures of naked women when you were sixteen?"

"Still do."

Beth cut him a sharp glance.

Carla harrumphed, but he could tell that because he wasn't patronizing her, he was gaining ground.

He said, "He lived next door to you. That proximity was another factor we couldn't ignore. I was in their house on several occasions that week. You could see Crissy's bedroom window from Billy's. Did she ever indicate to you that he made her uncomfortable? That he might be watching her? Anything like that?"

"Never. Not once. If he'd been creepy, would she have taken him places with her? Walmart, grocery shopping, a movie sometimes. Little outings like that."

Gracie Oliver had told John the same thing. *Billy idolizes that girl because she befriends him and treats him with dignity.*

In his and Mitch's interview with Billy, he told them that Crissy had invited him to walk with her to the convenience store that night. He'd blubbered, "It was raining, so I didn't go. Why didn't I go? If I'd only gone…"

Carla was saying, "If Billy had been of a mind to, he could've done something bad to Chrissy at any time. He never laid a hand on her. I'll stand by that till the day I die. Billy didn't harm anybody." Her lip quivered. "Except himself. And poor old Gracie had to hear all those awful things said about him even after he was gone."

John never would have expected a demonstration of such a tender emotion from this hard-shell woman. He looked at Beth and saw that she was equally surprised.

She said, "We don't believe it was Billy, either, Carla. We believe the guilty person has gotten away with it, which will give him confidence to do it again. We're running out of time to even identify him."

"Well, I don't know what you expect me to do about it." She glanced at a wall clock. "And I can't sit here any longer jawing about it. If I'm not on time, it'll piss off the person I'm relieving."

When she made a move to get up, Beth raised her hand to stay her and pressed on. "For the moment, let's assume the same individual took all four girls. Let's assume that the eclipses were significant to him, that he was adhering to a superstition, or observing a religious ritual. Was Crissy acquainted with anyone who had a fascination or preoccupation with anything like that?"

"Most of her friends go to mass."

Beth fought to contain a smile. "What I had in mind was a ritual that's a little more untraditional."

"Stargazing? Moon cycles? How about voodoo? Now, there's a preoccupation."

John said, "Carla, please. I know this sounds off the wall, but—"

"Sounds plumb crazy. I've got better things to do than listen." She stood up.

A second later, Beth was also on her feet. "What about zodiac signs?"

"What about them?"

"Did Crissy read her horoscope?"

"Lots of people do."

"So she did? Was she obsessive about it? Did she plan around it? Had she had someone prepare her natal chart?"

"What the hell is that?"

"It shows the position of the sun, moon, planets at the exact moment of a person's birth. Some believe it's a forecaster of—"

Carla waved her hand in front of her face as though swatting at a housefly. "I never heard of such, and if Crissy had a chart like that, I didn't know about it. Frankly, Ms.

Collins, this all sounds like hocus-pocus you cooked up for your TV show. Which, by the way, I didn't want any part of, and resented my tragedy being turned into entertainment for couch potatoes.

"The only reason I consented to giving that interview was to get you people off my back. I wouldn't watch that program if you tied me to a chair and propped my eyelids open with toothpicks. And *you*." She turned to John. "You had your chance to find the person who took my girl. But you didn't."

"That's right," he bit back. "I was pressured to stop looking, and I did. It was a self-serving decision that I'll regret forever."

"Well, you're more than three years too late for regrets, aren't you?"

"Too late for Crissy, yes. Too late for Billy. I don't want to be too late for someone else."

"I don't give a rat's ass if you get absolution or not, Mr. Bowie." She sneered, "You all were so proud of yourselves, waving around that false confession."

"I wasn't proud of it, Carla. I think Billy was bullied into writing that confession by the men who interrogated him."

Her eyes narrowed with malicious satisfaction. "Billy didn't write that confession at all, you fool. He couldn't have. He was dyslexic." She snickered, adding, "Surprise!"

Chapter 22

With dismay, Beth said, "Billy couldn't read and write?"

"Enough to get by," Carla said, "but he would freeze up when he was stressed. Whenever his frustration reached a boiling point, he'd act out."

John was so angry with the woman, he was on the brink of acting out.

"Why wasn't Billy placed in special classes?" Beth asked.

"They didn't figure out the problem until he was around ten. By then Gracie had been homeschooling him for several years. She read up on dyslexia and learned ways of helping him."

"She dealt with it on her own?"

"Tutors cost money she didn't have, and she didn't want to put Billy back in school and have him made fun of."

Turning to John, she said, "Under the pressure you police were applying, he sure as hell couldn't have written anything like that confession. His letters would've been all jumbled up."

John unclenched his jaw. "This confounds me. Absolutely confounds me. Why in God's name weren't we told?"

"Gracie did tell."

"She didn't tell Mitch Haskell and me. We thought hearing about the suicide was enough for one night, so we didn't mention the note to her."

"Well, Barker came along behind you and told her. She insisted that Billy didn't write it, couldn't have. You know what Barker did? He laughed at her and said, 'Nice try, lady.'

"He accused her of making up the dyslexia only to clear Billy's name. She had no way of proving he was dyslexic because he'd never been officially diagnosed, and it wasn't in his school records."

"Why didn't you tell me, someone, *anyone*, Carla?"

"Gracie begged me not to. After being humiliated by Barker, she caved in. She was grieving. Besides, a woman of her generation 'knew her place.' It wasn't in her nature to fight back. Not like me. I fight back, and I fight dirty."

"Real dirty, Carla. Real dirty."

"Damn right, Detective. You're stuck with an unsolved crime that you're trying to pin on a villain that's into moon worship."

She snorted with contempt, then turned to Beth. "Your *true* crime TV show is about to air a program that's pure fiction. That presents you with a problem, too, doesn't it? For the next few days, you two are gonna be awful busy. Now, get out of my house."

She left the room, went to the front door and pulled

it open, then slammed it behind them as they crossed the threshold.

Without a word being spoken between them, they got into the car. John drove to a municipal recreational complex where he parked facing a sodden soccer field dotted with puddles of rainwater.

Staring out across it, he said, "When we were talking to Carla about Billy's difficulties in school, why didn't she tell us then? Why did she let us go on about the moon, etcetera, then smugly play the dyslexia like a winning ace?"

"She wanted to hit us hard with it."

"Which is probably the only reason she allowed us inside."

"Maybe," Beth said, "but I think she wanted us to know about Billy so we would keep looking for the real culprit."

"Then why didn't she just come right out and say so?"

"Not her way."

"You've got that right." His desolation obvious, he stared through the rain-streaked windshield. "Doesn't matter how she told us. What am I going to do with this new information? Somebody wrote that confession and made certain it would be found on Billy."

"Tom Barker."

"He wouldn't have done it himself."

"If he orchestrated it, he's as good as guilty of doing it."

"Absolutely, but if I go barging into headquarters hurling accusations, he'll have me arrested on the spot for reconfiguring his nose."

"Skip him, then. Go to the top of the food chain."

"The superintendent?" He grimaced. "That would be

dicey. He was pissed over my bad-mouthing during that investigation, and Barker has further soured him on me."

"What about someone in the DA's office?"

"First thing they'd ask is, 'Where's your evidence?' I don't have any. All I have is a picture of the confession. The real one, if it hasn't mysteriously disappeared, might have some forensic evidence on it, but it's locked up in the evidence room, and I can't even get into the building.

"The dyslexia is hearsay, told to me by a woman whose bitterness against the PD is well documented. Nothing Carla told us can be corroborated. To a prosecutor it would look like my allegations are payback for Barker's firing me."

"Then what do you intend to do?"

"Keep going at it but stay off Barker's radar for as long as I can. Even now he'll have hounds like the ogre trying to sniff me out." He paused, then added, "I'm afraid Carla could catch some blowback."

"From Barker?"

"Up till now, he's considered her an outspoken pest, but if he finds out she knows about Billy's dyslexia and the fraudulent confession, she'll be elevated to a threat."

"What could he do to her?"

"When he's backed against a wall, and his position is at stake? I hazard to think what he'd do. She's a scorpion with a nasty sting, but who could blame her? Her daughter disappeared without a trace.

"I know what it feels like to have a child missing for just a few days. Even a few hours is more torture than any parent should have to endure. Carla is far from my favorite person, but I don't want to cause her any more hardship."

This coming from the man Beth had accused of having no feelings for anyone or anything. She wished she could take back those harsh words. She wished she could advise him, but she didn't see a way out of his conundrum, either.

Besides, as Carla had cited, she had a problem of her own. "I can't sit on this and let that program be aired next week. I need to consult with Max on how we should approach Winston Brady with the bad news that the episode will have to be revised or scrapped altogether. Either way, Brady isn't going to be happy. He'll probably want to shoot the messenger. *Moi*."

"Make your call. I'm going to get some air." He opened his car door.

"It's raining."

"I won't melt. Honk if you need me." He got out, flipped up his hood, and started walking across the soccer field unmindful of the puddles.

She got Max's voice mail and left a message, telling him that she was all right but that there'd been a rather startling development. "It's a game changer, so call me back as soon as you can." She also sent him a text to that effect.

On the far side of the field, John was walking along the sideline, a phone to his ear. Raising the hood on her rain jacket, she got out and jogged across the field. He saw her coming and ended his call. When she got close, he asked, "What did Longren say?"

"I couldn't reach him and tried not to sound too frantic on his voice mail. I considered calling Richard, but I don't trust him not to raise a hue and cry throughout the production office." She gestured at his phone. "Who were you talking to?"

"Nobody's answering. I left messages for Roberts and Cougar, telling them about Billy."

"What do you think they will take from that?"

"If they're smart, the same thing I take from it. If Billy is ruled out as the perp here—and I think that's safe to say—it's an even greater likelihood that we're all looking for the same unidentified suspect. For the hell of it, I also called Gayle Morris in Galveston and left her the same message."

Beth fell into step with him as he resumed pacing. "What are you thinking?"

"I've been running through the list of people Barker could have either bribed or coerced to write that confession and plant it on Billy to be easily found."

"What were you doing in the jail that night?"

"Barker and the ogre were coming down so hard on Billy I'd asked his court-appointed attorney if I could interview him again in the jail and out of their hearing. He didn't object so long as he was present. He and I had just arrived at the jail when all hell broke loose."

"When Isabel Sanchez discovered Billy. Could she have been bribed to plant the confession?"

John frowned. "I'd hate to think it of her. I figured it was the trauma of finding Billy that had caused her anxiety and led to her resignation from the SO, but maybe it was guilt.

"Whatever the cause, her meltdown was genuine. I didn't plan on bothering her, but this has gotten too big. Barker and crew need to be made to account. With all that's at stake, I can't continue being Mr. Nice Guy. I have to get her to talk about what went down in the jail that night."

Now motivated, they started back across the field toward the car.

Beth looked up at him from beneath her hood. "Remind me of when you were Mr. Nice Guy?"

"Every time I've entertained dirty thoughts about you but didn't act on them." He slanted a look down at her. "I'm practically a saint."

They got into the car. He started the engine but didn't engage the gears. "The thing about sainthood," he said, "is that it's not at all what it's cracked up to be." He reached across the console and curved his hand around her nape. Before she had time to even anticipate what was coming, his mouth was on hers. It was more than a kiss; it was a fusion. For half a minute, they greedily indulged themselves.

He ended it by sweeping his tongue across her damp lower lip, then pressed his forehead against hers. His breath fell hot and fast on her face. "I had to have a taste." Then he released her, settled back into his seat, and put the car in reverse.

John had former deputy Sanchez in his contacts, although he didn't know if the phone number was still good. He feared she wouldn't answer from an unidentified caller, but after the fifth ring, a wavering woman's voice said hello.

"Isabel? It's John Bowie."

She didn't say anything.

"Can you hear me?"

"Yes."

"It's been a while." She didn't respond to that, either. "How are you getting along?"

"I'm all right."

Her shaky tone said otherwise. He had second thoughts about continuing, but he reminded himself of his purpose. "I know you've had it rough, and I don't want to impose, but I wondered if I could come see you."

That goosed her. "Come see me? No! Absolutely not."

"Please. If it wasn't important, I wouldn't ask. I promise I won't take up much of your time. I just want to—"

"I can't…I can't talk to you." Her voice cracked; he heard her sniff. "Please understand. My husband, my kids. I've got them to think about. Sorry, John, I have to go now."

"Wait!" *What about her husband and kids?* Then he got it. "Were you cautioned not to talk to me? Have you been threatened?"

She didn't reply, but her unsteady breathing was answer enough.

He looked across at Beth, whose expression told him she shared his concern. "Isabel, the last thing I want to do is put you and your family at risk. You and I don't have to meet face-to-face, but—"

"I'm hanging up now."

"—can you please just answer a few questions?"

"Please don't call me again."

"I'll make them yes or no questions."

"I have nothing to say about Billy Oliver." Before he could plead further, she clicked off. "Damn!"

"What in the world, John?" Beth said. "She sounded scared to death."

"She was."

"Of you?"

"Of talking to me. Somebody issued her a warning against it."

"You really think so?"

"Had to be." He palmed his phone and accessed another number. "I didn't even mention Billy Oliver. She did."

Beth digested that, then asked who he was calling now.

"Molly. The ogre and his men aren't screwing around. They're threatening family members now. I told Molly to be on alert. I need to underscore that."

From behind his desk, Tom Barker asked, "Was Sanchez at home alone?"

"Best I could tell," the ogre replied.

"How'd she react to seeing you at her door?"

"She started crying."

Tom laughed before remembering that it made his nose hurt like hell. "The first time your mother saw you, she must've cried, too."

Rather than take offense, Frank grinned. "It scared that Sanchez woman out of her wits when I asked how old her kids were now. Believe me, she's not gonna talk to Bowie."

"Bowie may contact Billy Oliver's lawyer. The old coot was there when it happened."

"I thought of that," Frank said. "We're in luck. The old coot has since died."

"What about Mitch Haskell?"

"He finally called me back. Said he hadn't seen Bowie for months. So long ago he couldn't remember exactly when it was. They had a falling-out over Bowie's binge drinking."

"Do you believe that?"

"I wouldn't, except that he said his wife had laid down the law for him to stay away from Bowie, or else no pussy. Between Bowie and the wife, the wife won."

Tom was still doubtful of Haskell, but he moved on. "Learn anything more about how they got out of the hotel?"

The ogre shook his head. "The security camera videos are only good for twelve hours before they're recorded over. We don't even have him entering the lobby."

"Fabulous." Tom picked up a pen on his desk and began fiddling with it. "Who else would Bowie try to contact?"

"That Mellin harpy. I sent one of my men to the trailer park where she'd lived. She's no longer there. He's trying to track her down."

"She can't be far. She gave *Crisis Point* an interview."

"They could have recorded the interview in Key West or freakin' Anchorage. Besides, she wouldn't give Bowie the time of day. She despises him for not finding her daughter."

"I guess." Making Tom more miserable than his throbbing nose was the thought of John Bowie getting the better of him. "You know what would help?"

"Bowie getting hit by a Mack truck?"

"If the Mellin girl's body was discovered."

Pensively the ogre asked, "Do you ever wonder who took her and what happened to her?"

"Not really, no. But I wish that one of these days somebody would step into a shallow grave, or get their fishing line tangled up on an arm or a leg and pull her out of a bayou. Once she'd been identified, we could point to her remains and say, 'So that's where Billy Oliver dumped her.' His granny is no longer with us to dispute his guilt."

"Everyone would shake their heads in sorrow," he went on wistfully. "Then that would be the last they ever thought of it. We could close the case for good, and the disillusioned former detective John Bowie, along with his worthless allegations against me, would be ridiculed."

Frank chuckled. "That's some daydream, Tom."

"It's my wet dream."

Chapter 23

John and Beth's return to the fishing camp sent Mutt into a frenzy of joy. "He's going to drive us nuts if he doesn't burn off some energy," John said.

He stayed outside to play fetch the stick. Beth sat down at her computer and emailed Professor Wallace an invitation for their Zoom, then called Max. To her disappointment, she got his voice mail. She left a second message, urging him to call her back.

Again, she considered calling Richard and asking him to track Max down, but she rejected the idea for the same reason as before: She didn't want to ring an alarm bell before conferring with Max on how to finesse Brady.

John and Mutt came inside. He filled Mutt's water bowl and took a bottle of water for himself from the fridge. He asked Beth, "Any luck?"

"In reaching Max, no. When he doesn't want to be found, he accidentally-on-purpose forgets where he left his phone. The Zoom with the professor is at five-fifteen. Will you sit in?"

"I'd like to hear what he has to say about the blood moon mystique."

"He was in a rush, so I didn't tell him specifically why I was reaching out, only that I was doing research for a *Crisis Point* episode."

While listening, John had also been checking his various phones for messages. "Gayle Morris texted five minutes ago. Said to call."

"Probably in response to what you told her about Billy."

He accessed her number. She answered right away. They exchanged cursory greetings; then John said, "I'm putting you on speaker so Beth can listen in. What did you think about Billy Oliver's faux confession?"

"John, if that was rigged, your department has raised the bar on police corruption."

"It's no longer my department, Gayle."

"Pardon?"

"Barker canned me yesterday. I apologize for not telling you sooner, but you deserve to know. You also need to know that I'm not shrugging this off and quietly slinking away. No hard feelings if you choose to hang up now."

She didn't say anything for a moment. Then, "How high up does it go? Does it start and stop with Barker?"

"To be determined."

"Have you taken it to Internal Affairs?"

"No, because I wouldn't know who among them to trust. Barker's got some enemies, but also people who kowtow to him, either out of fear or for favors."

"So what are you going to do?"

"Try to gather some evidence. So far, I don't have anyone to back me up. Only three of us were in Billy's cell within ninety seconds of Isabel Sanchez finding him. Myself, Billy's lawyer, now deceased, and Barker's number one heavy who everyone calls the ogre."

"And Sanchez? Have you taken her temperature on the matter?"

He told her about his attempt to talk to the deputy. "Somebody scared her into silence."

"God, I hate dirty cops."

"Me too."

Morris took a deep breath, then said, "For the time being, I don't know you're rogue, okay?"

"Got it. Thanks."

"Now that that's settled," she said, "the reason I called. I told you we hadn't found anything to indicate that Larissa Whitmore was into the occult, astrology, etcetera."

"Did you learn different?"

"From Patrick Dobbs."

John and Beth looked at each other with surprise. Beth asked, "How'd that come about?"

"As we know, Larissa was living loose, but her parents are devout Catholics. They would have considered anything like that taboo. If Larissa was even dabbling in something, she would have kept it secret from them."

Beth said, "But she would flaunt it to an older, more sophisticated young man she was trying to impress."

"Exactly my thought," Morris said. "I called Dobbs's attorney and got his permission to speak with his client by phone from the prison. His only stipulation was that he would listen in and caution Dobbs not to answer if what he said had the potential of jeopardizing his appeal."

"Okay," John said.

"I asked Dobbs if Larissa had talked to him about anything like the occult. No, he said, *but* she did have a tattoo on her rib cage beneath her left arm. She told him she got it there because it was beneath her bra strap and her parents wouldn't see it. But in her teeny-weeny bikini top, which he admitted to untying, there it was."

"Gayle, I'm dying here," John said. "What was the tattoo?"

"A red crescent moon."

"Luna," Beth exclaimed on a soft gasp.

"What? Who?" John said.

"The Roman goddess of the moon," Beth said. "She's symbolized by a crescent moon."

"She's right, John," Morris said over the phone. "I looked it up. If you're into all that, Luna is a big deal."

"Ah, most definitely," Professor Victor Wallace proclaimed when they finally got around to talking about Luna, which had taken much longer than John would have preferred.

Their introduction to him had amounted to him establishing himself as an expert on a number of subjects by talking about his book.

"Ms. Collins, the article you read online was an excerpt from it," he'd said, smiling at them on the monitor. "It focuses more on the occult and its influence on civilizations throughout history, but I touched on folklore, superstitions, the paranormal. All things mystical." He'd raised his hands to the sides of his head and waggled his fingers. "Including mankind's fascination with astrological phenomena."

"That's what we're most interested in," John had told him. "The mystique surrounding blood moons."

"A fascinating topic to be sure. One that's held people in thrall for millennia."

They hadn't told the professor why they were particularly interested in Luna, but Beth had eased the moon goddess's name into the conversation by quoting Gayle Morris. "If you're into all things lunar, I understand that Luna is a big deal."

Now, after his exclamation of affirmation, the professor continued. "It's said that a temple to Luna was built by the Romans in the sixth century B.C. But the old girl had been around for a long time before then. She's held up well and remains very popular. I referenced her in my book on pages..." He picked up a well-worn paperback and began shuffling through the pages.

He wasn't as musty as John had expected a professor to be, although his office looked like the set of an Indiana Jones movie. The bookcases behind him were weighted down with old-looking books and artifacts made of various materials.

John wasn't sure what most of them were depictions of, although one was easily identifiable as a penis, no doubt crafted by a wishful-thinking sculptor. Whether male or female was cause for speculation.

To him it looked like a lot of crap, but he figured the

razorback on the wall behind him wouldn't appeal to the professor.

"Here," he said. "Pages one sixty-two through sixty-four, in a chapter on festivals and observances of ancient Rome. Luna had one in her honor."

John was afraid he was going to launch into a lecture on Luna's festival; the man had a tendency to go off on irrelevant tangents. Beth must have sensed his impatience, because before the professor could get too wound up, she interrupted him by saying, "I looked up tattoos relating to Luna."

"Tattoos?"

"Yes. The one that seems most popular looks like this." She held up a drawing she'd done for him to see. She'd copied it from images on the internet and had had Gayle Morris confirm that it matched Larissa's tattoo as described by Patrick Dobbs.

The professor leaned in. "Yes, that's a common symbol for Luna. And sometimes the crescent has another crescent sitting atop it. I always thought it looked like a pair of horns." He smiled. "I said that once in a lecture, and one or two devotees in the audience booed me."

John perked up. "You give lectures on this topic?"

"And related topics, yes."

"Where do you conduct them? Who attends them?"

"I give them wherever I'm invited. Usually on campuses, and typically in relation to studies in sociology or humanities. My audience is largely comprised of students, but many people attend simply because they have a passionate interest in all things mystical, past and present."

"There are that many people with a passion for it?"

"I think more than we know, Mr. Bowie. Many afficionados stay closeted because their particular interest might be regarded as satanic. For instance, I did a lecture at a well-known university with an enrollment above twenty thousand. Only sixty people attended.

"But in the weeks following it, I sold more than two hundred downloads of the recording of my talk. I know there are online clubs, chat rooms, things like that, and most of the people in them use a name that's nothing like their real one. They're funny or tongue-in-cheek."

He winked. "I know because I sometimes lurk. I want to know what the current rage is so I can tailor my lectures accordingly. What's popular this month? Is it dragons? Ghosts? Witchcraft or werewolves? Interests wax and wane like the moon."

He tilted his head, looking curiously into his camera. "Speaking of, may I ask why you're interested in all this? Specifically in blood moons? Ms. Collins, you told me you were doing research for your television show."

"*Crisis Point* has produced an episode documenting the disappearance of a young woman." She gave him an expurgated version of Crissy Mellin's story.

"I remember when that happened," he said. "The New Orleans TV stations covered every aspect of it. You've made a TV show out of it?"

"Yes. But since it was produced, I've learned that there were previous disappearances in this general region of the country, all of which occurred on the night of a blood moon. It seemed too much of a coincidence."

"I would agree. And you, Mr. Bowie? What's your connection?"

It was one thing to confide his expulsion from the PD with a fellow cop like Morris, but he didn't want the professor delving into it. He skirted the question. "Going back to your lectures. Do people just show up or do they register beforehand?"

"They register. I take walk-ins if there's room. Which there usually is," he said with chagrin. "But I still ask that they sign in so I can add them to my mailing list."

"You have a mailing list? Could you share it with us?"

"Of course. I have Ms. Collins's email. I'll send it as soon as we conclude."

John felt a bump of optimism. One never knew when there was going to be a break in a case. The discovery of a minute detail that had previously gone unnoticed would be the wished-for golden key.

"How are the names on your mailing list categorized?" he asked.

"Alphabetically."

"Great. That's great." He didn't want to wait for the list to be emailed. "Can you access it now?"

"Well..." He began rearranging stacks of papers on his desk and riffling through loose sheets. "I have a printout somewhere." Then, "Here."

"Would you please check for these names, see if they're on there?" The professor slid on a pair of reading glasses. John started with Crissy and then worked backward to the first girl who'd disappeared in Jackson, Mississippi.

The professor checked for all the names, but shook his

head after each. "No," he said, dousing John's momentary optimism.

"That would have been too easy," John said, and gave Beth a rueful smile, then noticed that his phone was vibrating on the table. "Sorry. I'm getting a call." He looked at the readout. "Molly," he said to Beth. Then to the professor, "Thank you for your time and insight. If you could please send us that list…?"

"Right away."

"And if it's not too much to ask, send us links to those chat rooms."

"No trouble at all."

"Much obliged, Professor." As John headed toward his bedroom, he answered his phone. "Hey."

"Hi."

"You made it home okay?"

"Yes. And joy! *He's* here."

"Are they fighting?"

"No. But Mom is pissed with me because I didn't go to the table for dinner. I brought my plate to my room."

"Well, I'm glad you're in. You didn't notice anyone following you?"

"No, Dad. And I looked."

Her annoyed tone annoyed him. "Molly, don't blow off this heads-up. I didn't issue it for the fun of it. Don't take it lightly."

"I don't. I promise. I'm sorry. I'm just grumpy."

"Hang in there."

"I miss Mutt. How is he?"

"I wore him out this afternoon."

"Fetching tennis balls?"

"Sticks. Right now he's sacked."

"How's Ms. Collins?"

"Listen, don't go out again tonight. All right? I'll check in with you in the morning."

"She's there with you, isn't she?" Then in singsong voice, "I know she is."

"Good night," he said singsong. "Sleep tight. "

Smiling, he hung up and rejoined Beth in the main room. She asked how Molly was.

"Hating life. Roslyn's boyfriend is there. A familiar refrain." He sat down in the chair beside her. "What did you think of the professor?"

"Well, he came through with his mailing list. I just opened up the attachment in his email."

"How many names are on it?"

"Looks like several hundred."

"Several *hundred*? Jesus. Even eliminating the women, that's a lot of men to check out. We could put fifty people on it immediately, and it could still take weeks. And who's to say our perp ever attended one of Wallace's lectures? I wouldn't if you paid me. And I need the money." He got up and rounded his chair. "But what else have we got? Nothing."

"He also sent links to the chat rooms. Maybe we start by searching for names that are on more than one. And names that show up routinely. That would narrow it down."

Wearily, he said, "I'll get some of my people on that. I'll also send the links to Gayle, Roberts, and Cougar, and encourage them to put people on the hunt. But manpower is scarce, and these are cold cases, and I'm no longer a cop. Beth, I'm afraid—"

"Don't say it."

He didn't speak it aloud, but each acknowledged that time was running out. She broke the gloomy silence by asking, "Have we eaten today?"

He gave a soft laugh. "Now that I think about it…"

"Lasagna?"

"You know how to make lasagna?"

"I know how to take it from the freezer and turn on the oven."

"Fine."

He sat down at his computer and accessed his file on the Mellin case. Once the frozen entree was in the oven, Beth sat down beside him. "How can I help?"

He explained, "I copied notes taken by every detective and patrol officer who'd interviewed anyone about Crissy. As I find a name, you consult Wallace's list."

They'd been at it for about twenty minutes when one of John's phones rang. He looked at the readout, snatched up the phone, and put it to his ear. He was looking at Beth in wonderment as he answered. "Isabel?"

Chapter 24

John said, "Thank you for calling me back."

Deputy Sanchez's voice was breathy and faint. "When my husband got home from work, I couldn't hide how upset I was. I told him what had happened today. He wanted to go straight to the police." She laughed shakily. "I told him that's the last thing we should do. He insisted that I call you. He's here with me."

John put his phone on speaker but indicated to Beth that she shouldn't make her presence known. Introducing her now and explaining why she was in Auclair might rattle Isabel. He didn't want to give her any cause to hang up.

He said, "Who got to you, Isabel?"

She didn't pretend not to understand the question. "Frank Gray."

"That doesn't surprise me."

"You know how intimidating that man can be before he says a word. When I opened the door, I recoiled at the sight of him."

"Why did you even open your door?"

"He said it would be a bad judgment call not to."

"So he began with a veiled threat."

"Yes, but after I complied, he turned casual and chatty. He asked how I'd been. Did I miss my old job and all my cronies in the sheriff's office? Then, as though in passing, he asked me about my children. What grades were they in, did they like sports, music, what? That made my blood run cold. I knew he was leading up to something.

"Then he asked if I'd heard that you'd been fired. I told him no. How would I have heard? I hadn't had contact with you in years. He said that was good, because you had threatened retribution against Tom Barker and that any friend of yours was an enemy of Barker's and, by extension, of the entire PD. He advised me to play it smart and not to talk to you. An *or else* was implied. Then he left. Not long after that, you called. I was still shaking."

"Did he say what not to talk to me about? Was it Billy Oliver?"

She began to cry. In the background, her husband could be heard speaking softly, lending encouragement.

John kept his voice soft. He didn't want her to feel pressured. "Isabel, did you know that Billy was dyslexic?"

"Dyslexic? No."

"I learned that today from Carla Mellin. The odds that Billy wrote that confession are practically nil."

"He couldn't have written it if he'd been Shakespeare," she said. "He didn't have anything to write with."

"That came up when we were investigating his suicide," John said. "How the hell did Billy get access to pencil and paper? The only explanation offered was that he'd sneaked them past all of you guards."

"John, he didn't. I and all the other deputies in the rotation were being scrupulous. Billy was so distraught over his missing friend, and being accused of taking her, we were afraid he would harm himself. Anytime he was returned to his cell after being out, we made sure he wasn't bringing anything in."

"Why wasn't he on suicide watch?"

"We suggested it, then requested it, but it was never implemented."

"Christ," John said under his breath. Beth was shaking her head in disbelief.

"But it started before that," Isabel said.

"What started?" John asked.

"The irregularities."

"Give me a 'for instance.'"

"The camera that monitored several cells, including Billy's, wasn't working. I reported it. A day went by. Nobody came to check it. I reported it again and suggested that Billy be moved to another cell until it was repaired.

"One of the building maintenance men finally appeared. He looked at it, did some tinkering, told me that it needed a part, which he couldn't get until the next day. That was the night Billy hanged himself."

"Talk me through what happened that night, Isabel. Take your time."

Again he heard her husband speaking softly, but urging her. She said, "After his evening meal, Billy was taken out to be interrogated."

"By the ogre?"

"He said he was fetching him for Tom Barker. Billy was gone for hours. When he was returned, he wasn't even crying. His eyes were vacant. It was like his soul had been sucked out of him." She paused for several seconds. "I escorted him to his cell and locked him in. Shortly after, I went to check on him. That's when I found him. You know the rest. You were there almost immediately."

"That poor kid didn't stand a chance against Barker and the ogre. They did a real number on him."

"The interrogation sessions were recorded, weren't they?" Isabel asked.

"Yes, and I've seen them," John said. "In all of them, it's obvious that the ogre bullied the kid, terrified him until he finally broke and gave them answers he knew they wanted."

"Just to make it stop," she said.

"Yes." John picked up from where he'd left off. "After days of talking to Carla, Gracie Oliver, and Billy himself, Mitch Haskell and I were almost certain he was incapable of pulling off an abduction that flawless. When we told Barker that, he called us softies and turned Billy over to the ogre."

He paused, then asked softly, "Isabel, when he was returned from that final interrogation, did you pat him down before returning him to his cell?"

"That's the one time I didn't. He was so pathetic." With that, the dam burst. She began weeping in wracking sobs that were difficult to listen to. Beth looked anguished. John let Isabel cry uninterrupted and, even after the weeping subsided, gave her time to compose herself.

Finally, she said in a frail voice, "I didn't pat him down

because I felt sorry for him and didn't want to contribute to his humiliation."

"I understand," John said. "His soul *had* been sucked out of him, Isabel. He couldn't even read the suicide note that was planted on him. I think we all know who did it."

With repugnance, she said, "The ogre."

"Who coincidentally was the one who found the note on Billy after I'd cut him down."

"I don't remember that. I was hysterical."

"The ogre got to that cell in record time. Almost knocked the attorney down in his rush."

"Like he had been standing by, expecting a crisis."

"Yes, just like that." John felt like shit for resurrecting the turmoil she had been through. "Forgive me, Isabel."

"For what?"

"Did the ogre tell you how this started?"

"No."

"I busted Barker's nose all to hell." She actually laughed, but John added, "His heavy was dispatched to your house today because of me."

"Lord, John, don't apologize. Telling you the truth has done more for me than years of counseling. Fear kept me bottled up about those two. I needed this catharsis. So I don't blame you. I thank you."

"I swear to you that I'm gonna get the sons of bitches."

"How?"

He huffed a dry laugh. "I have no idea. But, listen, it might get hairy for anybody even remotely connected, so stay vigilant."

"Actually we're leaving town for a few days."

"Good idea. But if the ogre and Barker are ever brought up on charges, I could use your backing. Would you be willing to tell a prosecutor everything you've told me?"

"With pleasure."

After hearing Isabel's account of Billy Oliver's last few hours, neither John nor Beth had much of an appetite, but when the lasagna was ready, they sat down at the table and went through the motions of eating.

With half his portion still left, he pushed his plate aside, propped his elbows on the table, and pushed all ten fingers into his hair, holding his head between his palms. "I've got the same problem I had this morning after learning about Billy's dyslexia. Who do I go to with this information about what led to his suicide?

"If I confront Barker and the ogre, they'll know it was Isabel who talked, and that could mean serious repercussions for her. In addition to concern about Carla, now I've got the safety of Isabel's family to worry about, too. I should wear one of those international signs around my neck, warning anybody I approach that I'm a biohazard."

"You can't take all this on by yourself, John. You've got to bring someone else onboard."

"Who do you suggest?"

"The police superintendent."

"I don't trust him."

"Then the FBI."

He scoffed. "The feds wouldn't put much stock in anything I have to say. I'm a hot-headed burnout who assaulted his superior, and I'm on the hunt for an unidentified suspect who gets off on all things mystical." He imitated the professor's finger waggling. "I'm sure that would inspire the feds' confidence."

He tilted his chair back on two legs and looked up at the ceiling. "What a damn mess. Barker will go to any lengths to protect his hide. He's without scruple. And the ogre is cutthroat, literally. I don't see a way out that doesn't put other people in jeopardy."

She looked down into her plate of lasagna, which didn't look anything like the picture on the box. Slowly, softly, she said, "If you had it to do over again, would you stop me from boarding that flight back to New York?"

The front legs of his chair hit the floor. "No. No. That's not—"

"Or going farther back, would you decide to stay in bed and forgo meeting me in the bar?"

"Beth, I regret my inability to nail this fucking case shut and get justice for the people who deserve it. I don't regret that meeting."

Even more slowly, more softly, she said, "I think you do, John. I think *I* do because I dragged you into this damn mess." She picked up her phone and pushed back her chair. "I'm going to try Max one more time before it gets any later."

He didn't say or do anything to stop her from leaving the room. That was telling. He'd denied having regrets, but how could he not wish he'd stuck to his guns and refused to get involved. He'd told her the Crissy Mellin case had had an H-bomb effect on his life. It hadn't been going great guns when she'd appeared on the scene, but since her intrusion, his situation had become a thousand times worse. That pained her.

In the bedroom, she sat down on the bed and took a moment to lay aside her personal dilemma and to organize her thoughts about the *Crisis Point* episode. If she got through to Max, there was much to catch him up on. She decided to start by giving him bullet points, so he would have the whole picture immediately, then go back and provide details as he asked for them.

She tapped in his number. As soon as he answered, she didn't even give him time to speak before demanding, "Why haven't you called me back?"

"Beth?"

"*Richard?*"

"Whose number is this?"

"None of your business. What are you doing with Max's phone?"

Chapter 25

"You're a butthole. A horse's ass."

Mutt went on sniffing around the base of a tree, unmindful of John's litany of self-incrimination.

After cleaning the kitchen, he'd decided to take Mutt out for the last time of the night, and also to take a look around. In light of today's events, he was even surer that he would have a bull's-eye on his back if Barker and the ogre ever located him.

He made a circuit, checked the garage and the boat's hiding place. "The ogre would sink my boat, but they could have other people searching the swamp. Think anyone could find us?" The dog looked up at him, then sat down to scratch his ear with his back paw. "Right. Why worry?"

While listing all the people whose safety he was worried about, he hadn't had time to tell Beth that she topped that list. Stupidly, he'd babbled about all the ways his life had become more complicated since she'd entered it. He hadn't meant it that way but had realized too late how it would sound to her. He knew he'd hurt her.

"Let's go back, see what she's doing."

Mutt stopped scratching, and they headed back toward the cabin. When they got there, her bedroom door was still closed.

Every man since Adam knew that was never a good sign.

John bolted the door and replaced the shotgun in the rack. In the kitchen, he filled Mutt's water bowl and considered taking a good belt of bourbon. He even took the bottle from the cabinet before rejecting the idea and replacing it. He washed his hands. After drying them, he hung up the towel with excessive care. He acknowledged that all these activities were cowardly postponements of the inevitable.

He went to the bedroom door and tapped it lightly with his knuckle. "Beth?"

No response. He tried again with another tap and a repetition of her name. Still nothing. A spike of fear shot up from his belly and into his chest. "Are you all right?"

She pulled the door open. Instantly obvious was that she had been crying for some time. "No, I'm not all right. Max died."

She turned her back on him and walked over to the bed where she lay down in the fetal position and pulled the quilt up to her waist. She folded one arm beneath her head and stared blankly at nothing.

For a moment, he was at a loss for words, but then asked, "Why didn't you come tell me?"

"There was no reason to."

That stab hurt. But he couldn't just turn around and

leave her like this. He went in, but stopped midway between the door and the bed. "I know how much he meant to you. I'm very sorry."

She moved her head in a small nod.

"What happened?"

"I called. Richard answered. I asked what he was doing with Max's phone. He told me." Before she got through that last sentence, she choked up.

"Did his heart fail? Was he in the hospital?"

She exhaled a soft laugh. "No, he was at his desk. He'd come in this morning at his usual time. He complained to Richard that he couldn't make coffee worth a crap. He admonished him to learn how to brew it correctly by watching how I made it. That was, if I ever came back from Louisiana." As she said that, her eyes made brief contact with his.

"Sometime later, Richard found him slumped over his desk, where he would have wanted to be when he drew his last breath. He told me he'd rather be dead than attend the retirement party being planned for him." She smiled wanly. "He got his wish."

Mutt wandered in and bumped past John's legs as he walked over to the bed. John called him back.

"No, it's okay." Mutt rested his chin on the side of the bed. With her free hand, Beth stroked his head. "Richard tried to notify me, of course, but as you know, I'm not using my own phone. He didn't recognize the number of the burner, figured my calls were spam, and didn't even listen to the voice mails I'd left. He hasn't had a spare moment since..."

She stopped to swallow and blot fresh tears using the

corner of the pillowcase. "He told me it was like a tsunami had come through the network building. When I called that last time, he answered out of irritation, not knowing it was me. He said his day had been manic, his nerves were frayed."

John didn't give a shit about Richard's manic day or his nerves. Dozens of questions were flitting through his mind. Would he be driving her to the airport in the morning? Or would she want to go tonight? When would she come back? *Would* she come back? Where did this leave everything? Where did this leave *them*?

He knew these were selfish concerns, but also justified. The floor had dropped out from beneath him, too.

"Do you know the funeral arrangements yet?"

"There won't be a funeral. Max had mandated that. He told me once that he didn't want a media circus, where nearly everyone in attendance would be celebrating not mourning. Even his son. Max wasn't religious. He had stipulated to his lawyer to have him cremated and be done with it. No farewells, sad or otherwise." She began to cry in earnest.

"Beth." John started toward the bed, but she held out her hand.

"Please, just..." She motioned toward the door.

"Can I bring you something?"

"No thank you. Close the door on your way out."

"I can't leave you like this."

"I'm telling you to."

"Come on. Let me—"

"No. I want to be alone. Please go." She turned onto her other side, away from even the sight of him.

He stayed where he was for a full minute. She didn't move.

He had to say Mutt's name twice before he dejectedly obeyed and followed him from the bedroom.

Being shunned by Beth left him more dejected than he'd already been, but he forced himself to resume going through Crissy Mellin's case file. He'd practically memorized everything in it and soon realized that he wasn't concentrating. His mind kept derailing.

In frustration, he closed out that file and pulled up the photographs of the four women. Even though he'd stared at the compilation for hours, he now tried to see it with new eyes and from a different perspective.

After about half an hour, he felt a familiar tickling sensation in his gut. He trusted it, because historically it had heralded the spark of a new idea. He thought it through once, then a second time, then reached for his phone and called Mitch, who answered, saying, "You still alive?"

"For the time being. I wanted to catch you up."

"Talk fast. Any minute I'm expecting a call to action."

John began with Carla Mellin's revelation. "Billy Oliver was dyslexic. Those bastards wrote the confession and planted it on him." He went on to summarize what Isabel Sanchez had related. "Ogre's veiled threats included her kids."

"That fucker needs to die."

"I second the motion."

"How's Beth holding up through all this?"

"Well, then there's that." He told him about Max Longren. "He was her mentor. A father figure, I think, although she hasn't put it like that."

"Is she going back to New York?"

"She's not talking. We've got a lot to sort through on this blood moon stuff, but she's torn up. I just don't know."

"Anything I can do to help?"

"Maybe. What do you know about the dark web?"

"I know it can be scary as shit for a variety of reasons."

"Do you know any feds who specialize in surveilling it?"

"A handful." He chuckled. "They're scary as shit, too. Why are you asking?"

He told him about Victor Wallace. "He told us there were clubs, websites, chat rooms frequented by people who are into paranormal stuff like that. All things mystical."

"That covers a lot of different factions beyond moon gazing."

"I know, but we got more info on that today." He told him about Larissa Whitmore's tattoo. "This goddess's name is Luna. She's symbolized by a crescent moon."

"That's one hell of a coincidence," Mitch said.

"Too much of one. I think Patrick Dobbs is paying the penalty for some other man's crime."

"I'd lay money on it."

"Okay, so where I'm going with all this…I got to thinking that if there are chat rooms on the internet, there must be equivalents on the dark web. The thing is, we saw no evidence that Crissy had anything like that on her computer, did we?"

"No."

"I've got the detectives in the other cities checking to see if their women did, but if so, I think they would've remembered it as soon as I told them about the blood moon." He stopped there, hesitant to divulge what was, at this stage, only a nebulous idea.

Mitch said, "Bro, I can hear you thinking loud and clear. Lay it on me, because at any second I'll have to run."

"You may laugh."

"May, but may not."

John shared his new insight. Mitch didn't laugh. In fact, when John finished, Mitch said, "I like it. I like it a lot, John. Keep— Ah, shit. Gettin' the call. Gotta run. I'll have some of the dark web moles look into it. Be safe."

And like that, Mitch was gone, but John was glad he'd had time to run this new brainstorm past him. He valued Mitch's opinion and was gratified that he hadn't laughed outright or tried to rationalize the idea to death.

He wanted to run it past Beth. He looked behind him toward the bedroom, from which he hadn't heard a sound since she'd ordered him out. If she was crying, she was doing so silently, which was worse than if she'd been wailing. He hoped she'd been able to fall asleep.

In any case, he wasn't going to be talking to her tonight. Which was just as well, because his brain felt like he had climbed Everest twice in one day without supplemental oxygen.

He began closing his files and was about to leave their computer table when Beth's laptop chirped, signaling a new email. He didn't intend to snoop but saw that it was from Victor Wallace.

The message read: *I've discovered something that might be helpful to you. I'll wait up for ten minutes. If you don't call, then possibly tomorrow.* He'd included his phone number.

John was bone tired. He closed his eyes and tried to talk himself out of it. But he called. When the professor answered, he said, "It's John Bowie. Ms. Collins is unavailable."

"I realize it's late. This can wait until tomorrow."

"No, now that I've got you, what have you got for me? Us," he said, casting another look over his shoulder toward the bedroom.

"I've noticed something that had escaped me while we were checking the missing women's names against my mailing list."

If there was a *voilà!* in that statement, John was too tired for it to register. "Okay."

"It's regarding their names themselves."

"What about them?"

"They all have double letters in them. Anna, Allison, Larissa, and Crissy. Crissy's last name Mellin also has double letters. Had you never noticed?"

No, he hadn't. Anna was the missing girl in Jackson, Allison in Shreveport. He'd never even heard of them until two days ago. Was that the common trait he'd been hoping to discover?

He asked, "Why would the double letters be meaningful?"

"They may not be at all except to a numerologist. They would certainly arouse his interest."

"A numerologist?"

"How much do you know about numerology?"

"Zero."

"Ha! Good one," he said, and gave a short laugh. "Although zero rarely factors in. Only the numerals one through nine."

John ground his palm against his forehead and wished he'd rethought making this call this late at night when he was already close to brain-dead. "Give me a numerology breakdown for dummies."

"I'm no expert, either, but basically, it's a method of divination based on an alphanumeric system. The most widely used numerical chart is the Pythagorean."

John was already lost. "What's the chart for?"

"The chart pairs each letter of the alphabet with a number between one and nine. Each number represents certain character traits. By using the letters and their corresponding numerals in your name and/or birthday, you calculate your five core numbers. Each of your core numbers applies to a vital aspect of life. Profession, relationships, and so on. Therefore, those who put stock in the system use their core numbers as road maps for their life path, guidelines to influence decisions, major or minor."

"Like a zodiac sign."

"Um, similar, yes. The two aren't mutually exclusive."

"So why would double letters in a person's name be arousing?"

"Just as you'd suppose. The letter's numerical correspondent, and the trait it signifies, is twice as strong in that individual's makeup." He paused, then said, "Of course, many people think it's mumbo-jumbo. But your perpetrator might not. I thought I should at least bring it to your attention."

"Thank you. I'll get Beth's read on it in the morning. If questions arise, can we call you?"

"Feel free to. Good night, Mr. Bowie."

"Thanks again."

John turned out lights as he made his way into his bedroom. He took a quick shower and got into bed. It felt good to be lying down, but his brain was slow to unwind. He must have fallen asleep eventually, because he awoke to a soft, cool hand pressing his shoulder. "John?" He turned from his side onto his back. Beth was standing at the bedside. He levered himself up on his elbows.

She removed her hand from his shoulder and stood looking down at him with uncertainty. "I was rude to you earlier. You were trying to be helpful, but I was just so upset that I…" She pulled her lower lip through her teeth.

"You told me your parents worry about you. You worry over Molly. No one ever worried about me. Even though I was their firstborn, to my parents I was an afterthought, if they thought of me at all. The wrong daughter died. I'm not telling you this so you'll pity me, but so you'll understand what Max meant to me.

"He wasn't a father by any stretch. Not even to his own flesh-and-blood son. But he cared about me enough to correct me, chide me, commend me. He wanted to see me do well. He was my…my Yoda. My lodestar.

"I'll survive his death. But I'll mourn it." She wiped her eyes with her fists. "I'm sorry I woke you. I just wanted to apologize for turning you away." She gestured behind her toward the door. "Thank you for listening. I'll just—"

"Hush." He reached out and captured her hand.

He threw off the covers and pulled her down beside him, gathering her close. If she realized he was naked, she didn't comment or resist. Rather, she snuggled against him. He tucked her head beneath his chin and stroked her back. Her breath stuttered against his chest. She made small, choppy sounds as she brought her emotions under control.

"Shh, shh." He rubbed his chin back and forth against the crown of her head, then kissed it and kept his lips there against her hair. She quieted, and, for a time, all they did was lie together, breathing in unison, their hearts beating against each other's, while his hand continued to move up and down her back consolingly.

Then she tilted her head back against his biceps and looked at him. She reached up and lightly brushed her fingers across his lips.

He exhaled through his mouth and against her fingertips, and looked at her with what he hoped didn't look like pleading, although it was. "Beth?"

"Yes," she whispered. "Yes."

Thank Christ.

He rolled her onto her back, pushed his knee between hers, used his hips to secure hers to the bed, and slid his fingers up through her hair to hold her head in place while he kissed her.

He was sick to death of talking and thinking and talking some more. He allowed his mind to go blank and let carnal appetite take over. God, he'd been hungry for her, and now couldn't get enough.

Her mouth was sweet and hot and delicious and giving, but greedy in its own right. Her dainty tongue flirted with his, and he permitted the play. For a time. Then he claimed her mouth again in a purely male manner, and that elicited a needy sound from her.

He let up a little to kiss the corner of her lips, dabbing that alluring spot with the tip of his tongue. He kissed her brow, her cheek, which was damp from tears. He kissed along her jawline to the soft skin beneath her ear. He kissed her neck and the triangular hollow at the base of her throat, where he paused to catch his breath.

Then he did a one-handed pushup and with his other pulled her tank top over her head. To help get it off, she raised her arms. When she lowered them, one languidly came to rest on his shoulder. The other she laid across her forehead and closed her eyes, making of her body an offering, and he seized on it.

He caressed her breasts. Their smooth slopes, the plumper undersides, their beguiling crests. He lowered his mouth to one. Against his tongue, the texture was velvety, but its firm assertion told him that Beth wanted this, wanted him. So he worried it with his tongue, tugged it into his mouth, fanned it with his breath, then did the same with the other.

This was the fulfillment of a fantasy. He indulged, hoping that he wouldn't wake up and discover that he was dreaming. But if he was, it was a graphic dream. Beth's breathing was now being interrupted by her soft gasps. The hand she'd propped on her forehead flexed and contracted into a fist. She grew restless, her hips now trying to move beneath the pressure of his, to create friction between his erection and her cleft.

He raised his head from her breasts. Beth opened her eyes, lowered her arm from her forehead and used it to encircle his neck. She pulled him to her and lifted her head just high enough for their lips to meet. As they kissed, he slid his hand down into the waistband of her sleep shorts. He petted her, stroked, sought, found her wet. He gathered moisture, then drew his finger up and across the spot that caused a reaction like an electric shock through her whole body.

Her sleep shorts went the way of her tank top.

Their legs slid against each other as they readjusted, hers separating, his opening them wider. Then, with intent, he pushed into her. When he was fully buried, he lowered his head and kissed her, open-mouthed but with tenderness.

As he began to move inside her, passion intensified. The kiss didn't end; it escalated into an exchange of thrashing breaths. John never wanted it to end. At the same time, his thrusts grew more urgent in a rush toward the finish.

Beth was already there. Her fingers dug into his butt cheeks, her back bowed, she cried out.

He plunged in deep, she clenched around him, and he came. And came. And came.

When completely spent, he settled on her, enfolding her beneath him. He pressed his face into her neck and breathed in the fragrance that was uniquely hers. Tension drained from her slowly. Her legs relaxed but continued hugging his thighs, only less tightly than moments before. Her fingertips trailed along his back and lower, past his waist. Far past his waist. Her leisurely exploration delayed him going soft inside her.

They stayed like that for a long time.

When he finally separated them, he drew her close and pulled the covers up over them. She nuzzled his chest, breathed his name, and fell instantly, peacefully, to sleep.

Chapter 26

Wednesday, March 12

John came awake and was immediately and keenly aware that he and Beth hadn't changed positions since they'd fallen asleep. Her head was still on his chest, her hand on his pec, her knees tucked into his lap.

He turned his head and looked at the clock on the bedside table. It was damn early, but past time to plunge back into cold reality.

He tugged on a strand of her hair. "Beth?"

"Hmm?"

"We have to get up."

"I don't want to." She snuggled closer to him.

His dick was giving him fits. "This isn't going to work. We can't lie here naked without something happening, and we don't have time for it. There's a lot to be dealt with today."

"I don't want to," she repeated on a moan. But she

turned away from him, worked her way over to the side of the bed, and placed her feet on the floor. He reached across and stroked her back, which she arched and stretched while she sat there clearing the cobwebs.

Once fully awake, she looked at him over her shoulder and smiled shyly. "Good morning."

"Good morning."

The look she gave him would have melted an iceberg in ten seconds; then she left the bed and picked up her two articles of clothing where they'd landed when he'd sent them sailing.

As she opened the door, he said, "Mind letting Mutt out on your way through the main room?"

"I'm naked."

He chuckled, "I don't think he'll mind."

She went out. He heard her greeting Mutt with an admonishment not to get any fresh ideas, and that caused John to smile.

And the sappiness of that smile brought him up short. *God in heaven, what am I doing?* He vigorously dry-scrubbed his face, got up, and went into the bathroom. When he looked at himself in the mirror above the sink, gone was the goofy smile.

In its place was grim resignation. The man reflected in the mirror knew that one potent bout of hot sex wasn't going to change the circumstances.

This isn't going to work, he'd said to Beth, talking about their cuddling under the covers.

But he could have been referring to their future. Or their lack of one. Her life was a thousand miles away. His was a train wreck, and the wreckage was piling up. And he was too old for her, anyway.

When this was over, however it ended, she would go back to New York, and he would go back to being his old self, the master of not giving a damn.

Resuming a fragmented life with no Beth in it? It was a bleak prospect, and he realized why, and the realization caused him to lean weakly against the sink.

"Bowie, you dumb shit, how did you let this happen to you?"

The epiphany left him feeling depressed. He joined Mutt outside and tossed him a few sticks, but his heart wasn't in it. Mutt sensed it and lagged before he did. Back inside, he filled Mutt's food bowl. While his dog chowed down, he made coffee, then called Molly.

Trying to sound upbeat, he wished her a good morning.

She sounded no bouncier than he. "Hi, Dad."

"Did I wake you up?"

"No. I got up early to work on my art project. It's due next week."

"You haven't told me what it is."

"It's a surprise. You'll get your private showing after I get my grade."

He could tell she was in the doldrums and guessed they had nothing to do with her art project. "How are things on the home front?"

"They suck. I heard *him* leaving a while ago, so at least he won't spoil breakfast. But Mom and I had a knock-down, drag-out fight last night. She barged into my room still angry with me for not eating dinner with them. She called me a spoiled little shit, said, 'Who do you think you are?' and asked when I was going to grow up. I told her I would as soon as she did."

"I'm sorry, sweetheart."

"I know. It is what it is."

"Only for now. Not forever. When things get bad, remember that. And, listen, don't forget to keep your wits about you." He reemphasized everything he'd warned her of yesterday. "If you sense that something's off, anything out of the ordinary, call me immediately."

"I promise."

"If you can't reach me, call Mitch."

"Cross my heart."

"In fact, call me when school lets out."

"Seriously, Dad?"

"Just to check in. Okay?"

"*Okay!* Jeez."

That sounded like a spoiled little shit, but he let it go and told her goodbye. By then the coffee was ready. Beth reappeared looking restored and dressed similarly to how she'd been when they'd met in the bar.

The jeans and white t-shirt stirred him now even more than they had then, because now he knew what she looked like out of them. That made it difficult to cool his jets, as he'd resolved to do only fifteen minutes earlier.

He passed her a mug of coffee. She inhaled the aroma. "Ahhh. Thanks."

"I didn't really get to tell you last night how sorry I am about Longren."

"Your actions spoke louder than words," she said softly.

Damn. That *look.* Did she practice it?

When he didn't say anything, she glanced around the room. "I think that being here, in a totally different environment and having distance from the reality of his death, has blunted the pain somewhat."

"Which leads me to the inevitable question, Beth. Are you going back, or staying on?"

"Staying on here? You mean past Thursday?" She put her hand to her cheek. "Oh God. That's tomorrow."

"Right."

"Well, of course I'm staying on. Even if I were missing an elaborate funeral, Max would be furious if I went back for it. He practically ordered me to stay and see this through, with or without the moon aspect. The last assignment he gave me was to get the story, get...get his Emmy."

John was more relieved than he let on. "Okay then, there's a lot to talk about that you don't know yet."

They ate a quick breakfast of cereal and fresh fruit, then sat at their computers, where he informed her of his conversation with Victor Wallace.

"I wasn't snooping into your emails, I swear. It just popped up as I was shutting down. I saw his name."

"What did he want?"

He reached for a notepad and pen. After writing down all the names, and bringing her attention to the double letters, he told her what the professor had hypothesized. "He confessed to being no expert, but he gave me a crash course."

Gauging his expression, she said, "You don't seem to give it much credence."

"Do you?"

"Not personally, but devotees would. I had a friend in college who added a silent letter to her name only because it would change her core number to one she thought was more advantageous."

"People take it that seriously?"

"Yes. People all over the world."

"Okay. I'm not ready to dismiss anything. I'll pass this along to the others, too. Maybe numerology will be a bingo for one of them."

"What else?" she asked. "You said there was a lot to talk about."

"This is kind of off the wall, but here goes. Last night, a new thought occurred to me. I massaged it for a while, and eventually developed a theory around it, which I ran past Mitch."

"And?"

"Well, he didn't laugh at it. At least not out loud. He was working and had to end the call on the run, so I'm not sure he fully digested it."

"John, *what*?"

"All of us—you, me, the other detectives—have been looking for a common trait among the victims. Can't find one. Nothing. Nada. So, what if it's not the victims who have a common trait. What if it's the perps?"

"Perps plural?"

"Perps plural."

"How did you arrive at that?"

"The geography was always a hangup for me. I'm not sure why, it just didn't feel right. If a serial killer is territorial, he usually strikes like a smash-and-grab thief. It's opportunistic. He sees, he wants, he takes. In and out. Done and done. The victim's body is usually discovered sooner, and, more often than not, it's found close to where she—or he—was last seen."

"*Crisis Point* has documented many kidnap-murder cases," Beth said, "and they bear out what you just said."

John pointed to his monitor where the photos of the four girls were on the screen. "These four cases don't follow that pattern. None of the bodies have been discovered. Percentage-wise, you'd think that at least one would have been." He braced his hands on his knees and leaned forward. "Just for the hell of it, let's assume it's more than one perp."

"Three copycats since the Jackson case?"

"Possibly."

"Possibly," she said, "but I can tell by your expression that you're thinking *no*."

He dipped his head and looked at the floor for a moment before speaking directly to her. "Understand that this is strictly conjecture on my part, and it will be a hard sell."

She leaned toward him, focused and interested.

"Think about those chat rooms the professor told us about. People who have a shared fascination in the occult, assembling on the internet to swap ideas, information, personal experiences."

She nodded.

"Now think about such assemblies taking place on the dark web. What if there's an underground, super secret, super sick club on the *deep* dark web. And our perps are members."

Chapter 27

Members of a dark web chat room who have an obsession with blood moons," Beth said in a hushed voice. She extended her arm for John to see. "That gave me goose bumps."

"I had a gut reaction when I thought of it. That's why I think it has validity."

"And you think their assemblies are all conducted online?"

"I do. Whether creeps or clergymen, they'd be too cautious to have ceremonial gatherings, especially if they were in costumes and masks and performing rituals that involved tattooing, bloodletting, or sacrifices. It's not like a book or knitting club."

"We did a *Crisis Point* episode on a group that was selling human organs on the dark web. Max surmised they changed their handles more often than their socks in order to protect their anonymity, not only from law enforcement agencies, but from each other."

"Right. And to join some that are into really dark shit, you have to have skin in the game."

"What do you mean?"

"You have do something with a high risk factor. Something, which, if found out, would spell your ruin. Fear of exposure would keep you honest, keep you from ratting out anyone else. Without making that kind of commitment, you don't get in."

Beth frowned in thought. "So Crissy and the others were…?"

"I don't know, but let's say they were the initiation. They were the ticket in for the wannabe aiming to be allowed into the really exclusive group. He would post pictures to prove he did it. He'd post links to news stories about his dastardly deed. He'd have proved himself worthy of being accepted."

Beth tented her hands and used them to cover her mouth. "I hate to say this, to even think it, but it sounds so ghastly and bizarre, it could be true."

"I don't know," he sighed. "A secret society is merely a guess, and I could be dead wrong. There could be one clever psycho who took all four women and set up Patrick Dobbs and Billy Oliver as fall guys for two of those abductions.

"Or maybe there is a society, and it does meet like a book club. They get drunk on vino and chant amorous praises to Luna. They play rock-paper-scissors to see who does the honors on the next blood moon, and they don't know beans about the dark web." He frowned and shook his head in self-deprecation. "Saying it out loud sounds ridiculous."

"You said Mitch didn't dismiss it out of hand."

"He told me he'd get some moles to nose around on the

dark web and will let me know if they turn up anything. In the meantime, I'll pass all this along to my counterparts in Galveston, Jackson, and Shreveport. But I'll be surprised if they don't suspect me of taking hallucinogens. And they'd be right to. At this point it's all fabrication."

"Truth is stranger than fiction," Beth said. "Some of the cases we've documented on *Crisis Point* prove that. Seemingly normal people are capable of doing anything." She pressed his shoulder as she stood.

"Call the other detectives, John. If they're skeptical, challenge them to come up with a better theory." She started for the bedroom. "While you're doing that, I need to call New York."

The burner phone Tom Barker used exclusively to communicate with the ogre vibrated on his desk. He snatched it up. "Tell me something good."

"No sign of him."

"Beth Collins?"

"Has also pulled a vanishing act."

"Mitch Haskell?"

"Spotted the tail I put on him. Slipped it by crossing a lane of traffic, bumping across the median, and making a U-turn onto a busy highway."

"Fire whoever was following him."

"Hell, no. He's one of my best men. Haskell was just luckier."

"Luckier, hell. He was smarter. Call him. Threaten him with something."

"I tried that. When I called the cell number I had sneaked, I got a recording in Haskell's voice saying, 'Hi, this is Domino's. Leave your order and then fuck off.' His office says he's on assignment and could be for several days. They asked us to please stop calling, that he'll contact us at his earliest opportunity."

"Bullshit."

"That's what I said."

Tom mouthed a stream of obscenities. "Frank, nothing you've told me is good."

"I saved the best for last. I followed Bowie's kid to school."

Tom's heart cartwheeled. "Tell me."

"His ex got the house in the divorce. I arrived there in time to see her boyfriend leaving. About an hour later, she drove the girl to school."

"What's the girl like?"

"Lots of dark, curly hair. Tall. Too skinny for my taste. I'm parked down the street but have a clear view of where her mother dropped her. Awaiting your instructions, boss. Feel better?"

Not all that much. His nose was still swollen, discolored, and sore as hell. This morning his wife had had the gall to ask if it was ever going to look normal again and suggested that another visit to the plastic surgeon might be in order.

"You still there?" Frank asked.

"I'm thinking."

"Well," the ogre said, smacking his chewing gum, "while you're at it, give this some thought. If you so much as touch that kid of his, Bowie will kill you."

"She's been a pain in his ass for years. He's had to use vacation days to search for her when she's run off. She's given him nothing but grief."

"She may not be the apple of his eye, but he would come after you with one of his namesake knifes and gut you on principle. You'd be better off at the mercy of Rambo."

Even knowing that scenario wasn't too far-fetched, Tom resented it. "Thank you for that warning, Frank," he said dryly. "I'll keep it in mind as I deliberate. Stay where you are. If and when the girl leaves the school, follow."

"Then what?"

"TBD. I'll get back to you with a plan."

"Did you emphasize how urgent it is that I speak with him?" Beth was pacing at the foot of the iron bed, trying to stem her agitation and not sound crazed. Executive producer Winston Brady's assistant was unmoveable.

"I conveyed that, Ms. Collins, but Mr. Brady is also dealing with urgent matters today. I'm sure that as soon as his schedule permits, he'll get in touch with you. Have a nice day." She hung up.

She hung up! If ever Beth had speculated on what her status at *Crisis Point* would be if Max were no longer there, she had her answer.

"Pompous jackass," she muttered in regard to Brady. She called the direct line to what was still officially her office, even if not for long. Richard answered, "Ms. Collins's office."

"This is Ms. Collins."

"Beth! Oh my God! You were so overwrought when I told you about Mr. Longren, I worried about you for the rest of the night. How are you? You were taking it so hard."

"I still am. However, right now, I'm livid. Brady refused to take my call."

"When?"

"Just now. Even though I told his assistant how urgent it was that I speak with him, she didn't budge from 'He's unavailable.'"

"Honestly, Beth, I am not surprised that he had no time for you. The man is positively frenzied. As long as Mr. Longren was alive, he was still the figurehead producer of the network's most highly rated show. Now everyone is anxious and paranoid over how his sudden absence will affect their positions here, and that includes Brady."

"He should be anxious. Up till now, anything that went wrong, he could blame on that doddering old tyrant, Max Longren," she said bitterly. "His safety net is no longer there."

"Too true. I swear, his lips must be chapped from kissing so many behinds. The network execs, as well as the show's sponsors, are pressing him for a guarantee that losing Longren won't negatively impact the quality of *Crisis Point*."

"That's exactly why I'm desperate to talk to him," Beth exclaimed. "He must, *must* cancel the broadcast of that Mellin episode."

Richard sputtered. "That's what you wanted to tell him? Then God bless his harpy of an assistant for not connecting you."

"Explain, please."

"Brady is maniacally pushing everyone to finish a video obituary for Mr. Longren, which will be tacked onto the end of that episode. Two sponsors have devoted their commercial time to it. As we speak, his long and illustrious career is being edited down to one hundred twenty seconds."

Beth stopped pacing and dropped down onto the bed. "You cannot be serious."

"Would I make that up?"

"Max would be horrified. He didn't even want a funeral. Why is Brady doing this?"

"I suppose he wants to make himself look good."

"Well, if that's his goal, he's going to fail miserably. Airing that episode will ruin him. The network execs and sponsors will hang him in effigy in Times Square."

"Because of the tribute?"

"Because of the Mellin story itself."

"What's the matter with it?"

"Vital aspects of it are just plain untrue."

"How do you know?"

Just in time, she stopped herself from naming John as her source. "The misrepresentations of the truth about that case that I'd come to suspect have been corroborated by individuals close to it. Trust me when I tell you that the story we produced is far from factual, and if it's broadcast as is, Brady will never work again in this industry. He wanted top billing in the credits. Well, he's got it. But he'll rue the day. First, he'll be a laughingstock, and then he'll be a leper."

Richard didn't respond. Today of all days, she didn't have the patience to deal with one of his sullen spells. "What, Richard? Talk to me."

He cleared his throat. "I've, uh, heard through the grapevine that not only is Brady dedicating that episode to Mr. Longren, he's giving him credit as executive producer. He had done the heavy lifting on it and would have signed off on it if he hadn't suffered that medical emergency. Brady thought it only fair to give him top billing."

"Oh my God," she groaned. "This is a disaster. That episode is a falsehood. If it's credited to Max, his reputation will be shredded. Posthumously, yes, but his legacy will be permanently tarnished."

Unseeing, she stared at the Christmas cards dangling from the string tacked to the opposite wall, tapping her forehead with her thumb knuckle in the hope of dislodging from her mind a way to prevent this catastrophe. There was only one.

"Richard, I can't let this happen. You have got to convince Brady to talk to me."

"*Me?*" he screeched. "I hold no sway over Winston Brady. He probably doesn't even know I exist."

"Tell him it's an emergency."

"I—"

"Better yet, tell him his career is on the line. That should get his attention."

"Beth—"

"Swear that I'm doing him an enormous favor for which he'll thank me later."

"Beth!"

"Plead, bargain, lie, whatever it takes. And don't tarry. Go to his office right now."

"*Beth!*"

"*What?*"

"Something that hasn't occurred to you is that…that if the episode airs, and if it's as untrue as you say, your reputation will be shredded, too. Brady generously added your name to the credits as associate producer."

"Are you free?" John asked as soon as Gayle Morris answered.

"Not for long."

He'd saved her for last after having spoken with Roberts and Cougar. The result of those conversations was mixed. From the start, Cougar had been lukewarm at best on the moon having anything to do with their young woman's disappearance.

The new information John gave him on numerology and his speculation about a secret society on the dark web had made the other investigator even more leery. But he'd grudgingly agreed to look back through his files and see if they might have overlooked a weirdo who had a thing going with a moon goddess.

John really couldn't blame the guy for his sarcasm.

Roberts in Jackson was a bit more receptive. After listening to John's spiel, he told him he remembered a guy they'd questioned because he'd been acquainted with their victim and had a prior arrest for exposing himself. "During questioning, he admitted to routinely visiting porn sites on the dark web. 'Routinely' turned out to be three times a day."

"You cleared him?"

"His wife provided him with an alibi for the night Anna

was taken. But in light of what you've told me, I'll follow up on him and get back to you when and if I have something."

"Might be wise to have someone watching him tomorrow night."

"For sure."

John had thanked him and, now, he was lucky enough to find Gayle Morris with a few free minutes. "I'm short on time, too, but I wanted to bounce this off of you. It comes with a warning. It's going to sound crazy and like I'm losing it, or am already around the bend."

"I wish I still smoked," she sighed. "Go ahead."

"Numerology."

"Oh, hell, that's dense."

"Very, and I'm skimming the surface." He told her about Victor Wallace and gave her a rudimentary lesson on how the system worked. "All four girls have double letters in their names. The professor said that would arouse a numerologist's interest."

"You think that's the common thread we've been looking for?"

"I don't rule it out. Neither does Beth."

"But?"

"But maybe we've been looking for the common thread in the wrong place." He then advanced his theory.

When he finished, she whooshed. "Wow. Four crimes, four culprits, but one motive whose underpinnings are Roman mythology and mysticism."

"Does it have legs?"

"Shaky ones, John. Like earthquake shaky."

"I admire your candor."

"It's waaaay out there."

"I know. I also know it's asking a lot, but could you go back to Larissa's family one more time? Ask about her friends, a relative, anybody in her realm who was into numerology or the paranormal of any stripe. Anyone who might, just might, surf the dark web in search of like-minded people. That person may not be guilty of anything, but he or she could play on the same playground as the men who are, and could point us toward it."

"John, I'd help, but I'm working a case where either parent could've drowned their two-month-old baby girl in her little pink bathtub. They're lying to cover for each other, and there's a mistress in the mix. I have a lot on my plate."

"I get it."

"Larissa Whitmore's disappearance is a cold case."

"I understand the pecking order, Gayle. I *do.* But just for a nanosecond pretend that Patrick Dobbs didn't pitch Larissa into the Gulf. Some other dude did."

"I'm inclined to agree. But my boss, and his boss, and the prosecutor believe Dobbs was the dude. If I got all of them in a room and started talking about a secret society of men with hard-ons for Luna, an ancient Roman moon goddess, who are stealing girls with double letters in their names, possibly for human sacrifices, and conducting their meetings on the dark web, they would probably demote me to meter maid."

She sighed again. "I want to help you, John, truly I do. But you know the politics of police departments. Sometimes you gotta go with the flow. I've got three boys to educate."

"I get that, too," he said, thinking of the art school Molly had her heart set on. But he also thought about the one time he'd gone with the flow, and look how that had turned out. Here they were, still after Crissy Mellin's abductor.

"Thanks, Gayle. You've been patient with me, and I appreciate your time and attention. Let's hope this whole blood moon thing is nothing more than an inexplicable coincidence."

"Goes without saying."

They ended the call by wishing each other good luck. He hadn't heard Beth as she'd moved up behind his chair, but he sensed her there and turned around. He took one look at her face and said, "What's wrong?"

"It's dreadful."

She recounted her conversation with Richard, and finished by saying, "It'll be devastating to Max's legacy, and death to my career."

"So do what you've advised me to do. Skip the chain of command. Go to the person up one rung from Brady and tell him or her of the pending disaster."

"It's too late for that."

"You've got a week to set things straight."

She huffed a humorless laugh. "Actually, I don't. That was the second news bulletin Richard had for me. It seems that after Max's body was taken away, the paperwork he'd been working on was cleared off his desk and somehow—Richard doesn't know how—it got to Brady.

"In his hen scratching fashion, Max had written down notes on the possible connection between November 2022's blood moon and Crissy Mellin's disappearance. He'd expanded on everything he and I had talked about.

Someone—Richard doesn't know who—brought to Brady's attention that tomorrow night there will be the first blood moon since that one.

"Brady thought it would be an ideal tie-in, a great 'gimmick' for the narrator to mention that at the top of the program. So, rather than waiting to air the episode next week as scheduled, they've moved it to tomorrow night. To coincide with the blood moon."

Chapter 28

Upon John's recommendation, Beth retreated to the bedroom to call one of the network executives who had been as close a friend as Max had had. She was told that he was out. Although she impressed on his assistant how important it was that he call her back, Beth had little confidence in the woman's smoothly spoken promise to pass along the request.

Then, as much as Max would hate it, and hate her for even thinking of it, she called the production company for which his son worked and asked for him. Being Max's only blood relative, he would wield more influence over the network than she. She hoped to convince him to intervene.

She identified herself to his assistant and was put on hold. When the assistant returned, she said, "He's unavailable, Ms. Collins, but he did ask me to give you a message. He extends you his condolences, but wants to hear none you might wish to extend him."

That renunciation discouraged her from reaching out to any of Max's ex-wives. She hadn't heard back from Richard, but it was doubtful he would have the courage to approach Winston Brady on her behalf. Asking anyone else affiliated with the show to take up her banner would be pointless. She knew how these things worked. Whenever there was a shake-up in personnel, even a close ally would suddenly become a competitor.

She returned to the main room and sat down beside John, who was scrolling through what she now recognized as Crissy Mellin's case file. "Looking for anything in particular?"

"I just checked Billy Oliver's autopsy report to see if a tattoo had been noted. None was."

"Did you ever ask Carla if Crissy had one?"

"Yes. She said no. It's in my notes of the first interview Mitch and I had with her when she provided us a detailed physical description of Crissy."

"Some people frown on ink, so she might not have wanted you to know about Crissy's. I'll call her and ask again."

"Better idea," he said. "Let's ask her in person. We need to bring her up to date on several things."

Beth checked her watch. "She'll be at work."

"Good. She has to let us in and can't kick us out."

When they walked through the entrance of the emergency clinic, Carla looked up from her computer monitor and scowled when she saw them. "If you're here for a booster shot, we're currently out. If you're sick, there's an hour and a half wait. Fill out this form." She slapped one onto the counter and set a pen beside it. "If you're here for any other reason, you'd had just as well turn around and leave."

John said, "We only need a minute."

"Too bad. I don't have a minute, and if I did I wouldn't spend it talking to you. I've said all I'm going to."

John looked around the waiting room. Several people were watching them, one a young mother trying to pacify a squalling infant who was making a hell of a racket. "Is there an empty room where we can talk?"

"I'm *busy.*"

A coworker, who'd had her back to them when they came in, was now looking curiously over her shoulder. "I'll cover for you, Carla."

John smiled and thanked her, then said to Crissy's mother, "She'll cover for you, Carla."

She growled with aggravation. "Go through that door." It opened off the lobby into a hallway. She led them into an empty examination room where she assumed a hostile stance and crossed her arms over her chest. "All right, you've got me for one minute."

Beth said, "We thought you'd like to hear what Isabel Sanchez told us about the night Billy hanged himself."

Between the two of them they summarized what the former deputy had told them. Beth said, "She was never convinced that Billy had written that note after he was returned to his cell. She's almost certain, as we are, that it had already been planted on him. She's been too afraid of reprisal to point fingers at the men responsible."

"With reason," John said. "Yesterday one of Tom Barker's heavies showed up at her house and subtly threatened her children if she talked to me."

"Well, that's something, I guess," Carla said. "Her story helps exonerate Billy, but only helps. It doesn't change anything."

"It changes the content of the *Crisis Point* episode. A large portion of it is patently untrue." Beth explained to her the consequences that would result from the broadcast being moved up by a week. "I haven't made any headway toward getting it cancelled."

"I'm not the least bit concerned about the ruination of your TV show," Carla said. "Wasn't it that Max Longren's idea to do the story on Crissy in the first place?" Ruefully Beth admitted that it was. "Then why should I care if his legacy is blackened?"

John said, "You should care because this information from Deputy Sanchez not only helps to exonerate Billy, but it also shines a spotlight on Tom Barker's corruption. His ambition undermined the investigation and got in the way of our catching whoever took Crissy. That's why we're here, Carla. The guy is still out there, and tomorrow night there's another blood moon."

"Not that nonsense again."

John didn't acknowledge her eye roll. "Might be nonsense to you and me, but he takes it seriously. Ever heard of Luna?"

For a moment, she gave him a blank stare, then said, "Of course."

"Really?" Beth said. "In what context?"

"Luna, as in *luna*-tic."

John and Beth exchanged a look, but he was undaunted by the woman's sarcasm. "Good one, Carla."

"I thought so. Y'all have a nice day." She made to go past him, but he sidestepped to block her path.

"You've had more than your minute, Mr. Bowie."

"Was Crissy into numerology?"

"What the hell?" She looked at Beth with scorn before coming back to him. "She read her horoscope. Big deal."

"Did she ever refer to the double letters in both her first and last names? Did Billy? He also had double letters."

"Why are you wasting my time with this crap?"

John took off the white gloves. "Because, Carla, it might help find the person who took Crissy and in all probability killed her." She flinched as though he'd slapped her, but he pressed on. "Isn't getting justice for your daughter worth a few minutes of your precious time?"

She backed away from him. "That was unnecessary and cruel."

He stepped forward and got right into her face. "What was done to Crissy was cruel. It was cruel to you, too, and the culprit got away with it. Now, talk to me, damn it."

She pursed her lips into a stubborn moue.

In an attempt to defuse the animosity on both sides, Beth said, "Please, Carla. Answer our questions."

She didn't respond, but she didn't walk out. John backed down. With exaggerated patience and politeness, he asked again, "Did Crissy have any interest in numerology, or any acquaintances who did?"

"I never even heard her say that word. Now, there, I've

answered your question. That desk gets busy. I need to get back."

"One more question."

"I—"

"One more," John said. "Did Crissy have a tattoo?"

"You asked me that the morning after she disappeared. I gave you and that other detective a physical description of her."

"I know I asked you then. This morning I went back to my notes and that's what I'd written down. No tattoos. But I'm wondering, Beth is wondering, if Crissy might have had one you didn't know about."

Beth said, "The reason we're asking is that the girl who disappeared a few months before Crissy had a tattoo she'd kept hidden from her parents. No one knew about it until yesterday when the young man accused of her disappearance told about it. It was under her arm, covered by her bra. It was a red crescent moon, the goddess Luna's symbol."

Carla snorted. "Back to Luna." She divided a disparaging look between them. "Crissy would never have gotten a tattoo."

"Perhaps without your knowledge."

"Nope."

"Maybe peer pressure—" Beth began, only to be cut off.

"No. Wouldn't have mattered if I approved it or not, whether it was hidden or in the center of her forehead, under no circumstances would she have gotten a tattoo, because of the needle. She had a needle phobia like none other. She'd scream like a banshee. Whenever she had to get a shot, I practically had to hog-tie her."

She looked each of them in the eye, hard, then said, "Call me if you ever catch the bastard who took my girl. I want to see him shackled, in handcuffs, and an iron collar around his neck. Otherwise, leave me the hell alone."

After leaving Carla, her strong admonishment still ringing in their ears, John suggested they pick up a late lunch of carryout and find a place to park and eat. "That warrant hasn't gone away, so I don't want to risk going into a restaurant."

"I'm not really hungry," Beth said absently as she checked her borrowed phone for messages.

"Well, my breakfast has worn off. Besides, it'll give us a chance to figure out where we go from here. Any luck?" He chinned toward the phone in her hand.

"No. I wish to heaven Richard would grow a pair and storm into Brady's office, demanding that he talk to me."

"How likely is that?"

"As likely as Carla having us over for afternoon tea."

At a drive-through he got a loaded burger for himself and a salad for Beth, then drove around a sleepy neighborhood to a municipal park. He pulled into the crushed shell lot, turned off the car, and dug into their lunch.

Around his first bite, he said, "I don't get Carla's hostility toward us."

Beth was squeezing dressing over her salad. "She still holds you—and everyone on the police force—responsible for failing to find Crissy."

"Of course, but I've owned up to all the foul-ups. I've

apologized for my part in letting her down, and now I'm trying to make amends by getting justice for Crissy and Billy. None of that has made a dent with Carla. In fact she's thornier now than—"

One of his phones rang. He checked the readout. It was Morris, whom he hadn't expected. He answered and put it on speaker. "Hi, Gayle."

"You bastard."

"Sorry?"

"You laid a guilt trip on me. I skipped lunch so I could talk to the Whitmores and just wrapped up a conference call with them. I told them about the numerology stuff and asked if Larissa or any of her acquaintances were into the paranormal of any stripe, as you phrased it.

"They reminded me that I'd already asked them that. I apologized but told them to stretch. Was anyone in Larissa's sphere a little 'off'? After a moment's thought, her dad said, 'That tree trimmer.' They'd hired him to do some work in their yard, and he was good, so neighbors also retained his services."

"Which kept him in proximity to Larissa for a length of time."

"You got it. The two of them talked, flirted, and hung out for a week or two. But then Larissa tried to close it down. She told her folks that he was into some 'weird stuff.' This coming from a reputed party girl."

"Indicating that the 'stuff' must have been really weird," John said. "Do you think he influenced the crescent moon tattoo?"

"I asked. They didn't know, because they didn't even know about the tattoo. But it's possible."

"Did you get his name? Is he still around?"

"Yes to the first, and he lives in Beaumont. He has two priors. Both for stalking, which resulted in restraining orders. He was never even looked at because we had Dobbs naked and stoned and Larissa's DNA all over him and his boat. Which brings me to the best part."

John said, "The stalker has a boat."

"Yes, sir. I'm going to get Beaumont PD to keep an eye on him, but not to spook him until I can get the log books from every marina along at least one hundred miles of coastline, Texas and Louisiana. Let's see if his boat launched from one of them on May sixteenth of '22.

"And before you ask," she continued, "I already checked your date in November. This guy was serving thirty days in jail for harassing one of his stalking victims. He's not Crissy's abductor. But I think you're on to something, John. It's multiple perps. They're the common factor, not the women."

"Gayle, I can't thank you enough."

"Don't thank me. If this is the guy who took Larissa, we completely dropped the ball and made a suspected murderer out of Patrick Dobbs. I'll keep you updated, but right now I gotta run and get busy. You asshole, you just doubled my workload."

She hung up before he could form a comeback.

He clicked off and looked across at Beth. "What do we do with this?" she asked.

"First off, call Roberts in Jackson, report this, and urge him to take another, closer look at the dark web guy who gets his jollies exposing himself."

John quickly demolished his burger. While Beth was

finishing her salad, he called Roberts and fortunately caught him at his desk. John related what he'd learned from Gayle Morris, and, as he'd anticipated, the information was galvanizing. "I'm on it," the detective said.

"Go back to the wife, too. Words like aiding and abetting, complicity, and conspiracy may alter her memory of that night."

"Will do. Thanks, Bowie."

He clicked off. Beth stuffed the last of their trash into the sack. "Now what?"

He gave her a slow and suggestive grin. "Want to get a room?"

She looked at him with surprise and answered with smoky eyes and a sexy smile. "Yes."

"And rid each other of clothing?"

"Definitely. As quickly as possible."

"God, don't I wish," he groaned. "Another time."

He slid his pistol from its holster. "But we have a tail, and I recognize the car by the hail damage on the hood. It belongs to one of the men the ogre uses. So kiss me. Good. Make it look like the kind of kiss that counts. I'll take it from there."

Chapter 29

Frank, who are these incompetents? Mitch Haskell shook the tail you had on him, now Bowie has given his the slip. Where did you scrape up these imbeciles?"

The only reason Barker didn't bellow the questions was because it seemed that everyone who worked in the CAP unit was currently trying to look busy mere feet beyond his office door. "Where did Bowie shake him?"

"He told me that Bowie and the Collins woman were in a municipal park, in a car—not his truck—making out."

"Making out?"

"Like teenagers, he said. Anyhow, all of a sudden the car started up and shot outta there before my man could get his Big Gulp back into the cup holder."

"So they just sped away?"

"Basically. He went after them, but never spotted them again. He'd gotten the license plate, though. I ran it. The car is registered to a Charlie Lamont. So either Bowie stole that car, or borrowed it, or…you know."

"Actually, Frank, no I don't know. There's precious little I know because a troop of Cub Scouts could track better than your so-called tough guys."

"Okay, so Bowie gave him the slip. He has to go back to his house sometime. I've got a man still posted out there."

"Is he any sharper than these other two? Please, God."

"One of my best. I put him there because when Bowie does show up, and an altercation ensues, this guy takes no prisoners. That goes for women, too. He's merciless. Okay? You can relax on that score."

Tom heard the familiar wet, smacking noise in his ear and thought of the ogre's disgusting maw.

"But here's the juicy part," the ogre was saying. "Well, it's the juicy part except for them making out in the car like teenagers. Guess where my man picked them up?"

"I don't want to guess."

"The doc-in-a-box where Carla Mellin works."

Tom dropped the Bic pen he'd been fiddling with. "How did that come about?"

"Because I'm smart, that's how. I sent him there to engage the charming Ms. Mellin in conversation, tell her he looked forward to seeing her on the TV show about her daughter, or some such bullshit, then to advise her that that should put an end to it once and for all, that she ought to put it behind her and not talk about the investigation, or Billy Oliver, or anything regarding it anymore. By the way, Isabel Sanchez took my advice to heart. They've cleared out."

That was good news, but Sanchez was more biddable than the Mellin woman, who took bitchery to a new level. "How did the charming Ms. Mellin react?"

"He never got a chance to talk to her. He went into the clinic complaining of a phony intestinal issue. Another woman checked him in as a patient, but Mellin was working the desk, too. He was seated in the lobby, waiting for an opportunity to approach her when in walked Bowie with Beth Collins. He couldn't believe it."

"Bowie didn't recognize him?"

"Naw. He's not employed by the PD. He's one of the time-and-a-half 'overtime hours' you pay me for."

"So what happened?"

"He told me that Mellin looked none too happy to see them, but the three of them spent ten minutes—he timed it—in the back. Then Bowie and the woman left. He beat it outside and managed to follow them. They picked up fast food and drove to the park."

"Did they meet anyone there?"

"No. That's it. You know the rest."

Tom settled back in his chair and swiveled it in a tight arc. "Why would Bowie go see Carla Mellin?"

"Gee, I can't think," the ogre said. "Could it be because the one thing the two of them have in common is the disappearance of her daughter and all that came after? Just a wild guess."

"Don't talk to me like that, Frank."

"It was a joke."

"Not funny."

"Okay. Sorry."

Tom seriously doubted that, but he let it go. He picked up the pen again and thumbed the clip, making it click. "The car Bowie was driving. What was the home address on the registration?"

"His pre-divorce house. Clever son of a bitch."

It galled Tom every time the ogre said something even partially complimentary of Bowie. "You've been to his place," he said. "You said it was far out."

"The other side of nowhere. The boondocks."

"Has he had time to get back there?"

"Not quite. Anyhow, he isn't there. I checked in with my man on-site right before calling you."

"Where are you now?"

"Where I told you I would be. Still parked down the block from the high school. Been here all day. I'm developing piles."

"No sign of Bowie's daughter?"

Some smacking, a labored sigh. "Boss, you trust me, right? So I've got to be honest with you. I've got a bad feeling about this."

"How's that?"

"Has it escaped your notice that Bowie seems to beat us at every turn? It's like…like for the last three years he's been preparing for the day when all this between the two of you would come to a boil."

It seemed like that to Tom also, but he would cut out his own tongue before admitting it. He said, "You're sounding scared of him again, Frank."

"I don't want to step on a booby trap, is all."

"What time does her school let out?"

"Boss—"

"Goddamn it! Stop whining and tell me what time her school gets out!"

"I swear I don't know."

"When it does, be there."

"Sure. And do what?"

"Do I really have to spell it out, Frank?"

The ogre remained silent.

"*Frank!* Do I really need to spell it out?"

"No."

"Good. I'll be waiting to hear from you when it's done." He disconnected.

The ogre held his phone in his meaty palm and closed his fingers around it, thinking what a good idea it had been to start recording, days ago, all his conversations with Lieutenant Tom Barker.

Once John was convinced that they'd left behind the man with the hail-damaged car and weren't being followed by anyone else, he told Beth that she could relax. Since they'd raced out of the park, she'd been keeping an eye on the passenger-side mirror and frequently turning her head to look out the back window.

"We're okay now," he said.

"Are you sure?"

"I'm sure."

"Then why do you still have your pistol?" She looked down to where he held it in his right hand resting on this thigh.

"Because I could be wrong."

"That's becoming a familiar and unsettling refrain," she

said, but she settled more comfortably in her seat. "How did you know he was there? When did you spot him?"

"He was in the waiting room of the emergency care clinic."

She looked across at him, her jaw slack. "You didn't let on at all."

"Tried not to."

"Why didn't he arrest you on sight?"

"Because he's not a cop, and he doesn't know that I know him. He's one of the ogre's retainers. I've tried to identify as many of them as I can. This guy mostly does surveillance."

"Has he ever killed anyone?"

"I doubt it. The ogre wouldn't use him for that. He knows he's not that bright. Actually, if an assassin were assigned to me, I'd prefer a smarter, more competent and efficient one. It would be over before I knew it."

She hugged her elbows. "Don't talk like that." Then, almost to herself, she added, "I can't believe I'm actually having a conversation about the efficiency levels of hit men."

"Beth." He waited until she turned and looked at him. "I told you that first night when we got to the fishing camp that you were out of your element, that you weren't used to a man like me."

They looked at each other somberly. He wanted to reach across the console and press her arm or squeeze her knee, but the .45 in his hand was in direct contradiction to any reassurances he could offer.

Returning his eyes to the road, he said, "He wasn't at the clinic for us. When we came in, he gave away his astonishment. It's a guess, but I think he was probably sent there to intimidate Carla the way the ogre did Isabel Sanchez. To warn her of repercussions if she talked to us.

"She's always been outspoken and critical about how badly Billy was treated, how Barker botched the investigation. You can bet he's already heard that we had a private conversation with her. That's gonna make him even more nervous."

"And perhaps desperate?"

He didn't answer. He didn't have to. The pistol was answer enough.

They reached the camp without further incident and returned the car, which John realized was now compromised, to the garage. Mutt was thrilled to see them, of course. John stayed outside with him for several minutes of play.

When he came back indoors, Beth was talking into a phone. "Richard, you know how crucial it is that Brady be made to understand. Please see what you can do. Goodbye." Looking upset, she disconnected, then tossed the phone onto the table.

John said, "He's not persuaded?"

"He's not even answering. He's ghosted me. I was leaving a voice mail."

"Lily-livered SOB."

"Yes, but I get it, John. Jobs in our industry are coveted. He's afraid of losing his in the shake-up that's bound to happen."

He checked his watch. "School's out, and Molly hasn't

called." He had pestered her until she'd grudgingly promised, but after being followed today, he would continue to pester her.

He tapped in her number, and she answered immediately. He said, "You were supposed to call me."

"It's been three whole minutes since the bell, Dad. I was about to."

"Where are you?"

"Outside waiting on the bus."

"Lots of other people around?"

"Yes. I'm surrounded. But..."

"What?"

"Don't freak out."

"Because you said that, I'm already freaked out. What?"

"When I got off the bus this morning, I looked around like you told me to and noticed a car parked down the street. It's still there."

Seven hours later. He ran his hand over his head but tried to keep his voice calm. Tried to keep *himself* calm. "Can you tell if anyone's inside?"

"No, the windshield is reflecting. It's probably nothing."

"Probably, but I want you to go back into the building, call an Uber using that credit card I gave you, and—"

"Daaaad."

"Listen to me," he said sternly. "This isn't open to negotiation. I'd come and get you myself, but I'm an hour's drive away, and I don't want you staying there that long.

"Have the Uber pick you up at a door on the opposite side of the building, out of sight of the car, and don't go outside until Uber gets there. Have the driver take you straight home, and keep looking out the back window, see if that car is tailing you. Okay?"

"Can I come to you instead?"

"Molly—"

"Please, Dad."

"Sweetheart, I've told you how rocky things are now. That's why I have you taking all these precautions. I want to keep you safe."

"I won't be safe at home. Mom and I might fight each other to the *death*." Her voice cracked and she added brokenly, "Hold on just a minute."

John looked over at Beth, who was wearing a frown of worry. "Something's going on with her," he said.

"Is there anything we can do?"

"I don't know yet." He held up a finger when Molly said, "All right, I came back inside the school. I was about to lose it in front of everybody."

"What's going on? What's the to-the-death fight with Roslyn about? Because you didn't sit at the dinner table last night?"

With misery in her tone, she said, "I didn't want to tell you this morning."

"Tell me what?"

"They're getting *married*." On the last word, she began to cry. "She's marrying that stupid loser. They were going to break it to me last night. That's why she went mental when I didn't eat with them. Tonight we're going out to dinner so I can get to know my new stepdad better.

"I'd rather *die*. I don't want to know him better. I don't want to know him at all. Mom said that tonight's celebration dinner is a command appearance, and that I had better be pleasant, if I knew what was good for me."

She sobbed. "Dad, please, please, please let me come to you. I'll do anything. I promise. Just don't make me go back home. I can't stand it. I really can't."

There was a lot of adolescent drama behind that plea. Nevertheless, it wrenched his heart and made him gut-sick that his daughter was so unhappy. It also made him furious at Roslyn for being a dictator rather than using a more diplomatic approach to announce her upcoming nuptials.

He tamped down his anger at his ex and spoke softly and earnestly to his daughter. "Molly, ordinarily I would say yes and to hell with what Roslyn thought about your staying with me for a while. But my situation could turn dangerous. I don't know that it will come to that, but there's a chance it will, and I won't put you at risk.

"Give me a few days to smooth things over, and then I'll have a face-to-face with your mother and see if we can work out an arrangement that allows you to spend a couple of days a week with me. She may be more agreeable to it now that she's getting married. It would give her more privacy with her groom."

"Oh, gawd, don't make me hurl."

"Can you hold out for a few days while I try and clear up some matters?"

"Do these matters have to do with the program about the Mellin case and Beth Collins?"

He considered lying, then said, "Yes."

He looked over at Beth, who was losing her valiant battle with the network. For all he knew, in a few days' time, matters would be much worse than they were now, but he had to give his daughter some explanation for why he couldn't shelter her right now.

"Remember I told you that Beth's job is to make sure that everything is accurate and factual?"

"Some of that program isn't?"

"Since coming down here, she's discovered that a lot of it isn't. Until she green-lights the episode, the network should postpone it. Instead, it's been bumped up a week. She's been unable to persuade the powers-that-be to hold off. All to say that by poking into the Mellin case again, Beth and I have ruffled feathers. Angry people are coming at us from all sides."

"You're worried about me, but what about you? Are you safe?"

"I'm staying at the cabin, and I can take care of myself."

"What about Beth?"

"She…she's made of stern stuff, but, yeah, I'm worried about her safety, too. So you can understand why you're better off with your mom until this blows over. All right?"

After a long silence, she mumbled, "All right."

"The best you can do for me is to go home. Go to dinner with them and be pleasant. That'll get Roslyn off your back."

"It won't be easy."

"Life's not easy, sweetheart. Nothing about it is easy. Now, got the credit card?"

"Yes."

"Summon the car. Be sure and take a picture of the driver's ID and text it to me."

"Daaad."

"Just do it. And don't forget to keep checking behind you. Also, text me as soon as you get home and are inside the house. Keep watchful. Promise me."

"I promise."

"Molly, the only reason I'm turning you down about coming to me is because I love you so much."

"I know, Dad. I know. I love you, too."

Chapter 30

Carla had been in a high snit ever since her unwelcome visitors had left the clinic. She'd snapped at patients as they'd filled out admission forms, asking the inevitable dozens of questions. She'd been short with coworkers, even the one who'd covered the desk for her while she was fending off Detective Bowie's bothersome questions.

Now, on her way home from work, she had been stopped at a railroad crossing for a freight train that had to be the longest in railroad history. As she watched the cars roll past at a snail's pace, she cursed that damned TV show. Its broadcast tomorrow night was going to resurrect the rabid curiosity over Crissy's disappearance that had lingered like a stench for months following it.

The crime itself, along with her outspokenness against the police department's failure to solve it, had given her a celebrity status she'd neither anticipated nor desired. After several months of dodging reporters and curious stares, she'd changed jobs and moved away from the mobile home park where memorials left for Crissy had turned into a soggy, unsightly trash heap. Her goal had been to escape the public eye, fade into obscurity, and eventually attain anonymity.

Now that *Crisis Point* episode would stir it all up, and she would become an object of curiosity and speculation again. She could kick herself for agreeing to give an interview. But she had, and she couldn't undo it.

Even Beth Collins, who was one of their own, had said her attempts to halt its airing had been in vain. Of course, her concern was the episode's inaccuracy and how it was going to ruin careers and trash reputations.

Well, good. Carla didn't give a fig. Let it besmear Max Longren's legacy. Let it—

She slammed on the brakes at that thought. She rewound and replayed what had just occurred to her, and by the time the caboose rattled across her field of vision, she had concocted a plan for retribution that would serve them all right.

As soon as she crossed the railroad tracks, she pulled onto the shoulder of the road and reached for her phone.

An inch of bourbon was in the glass John carried over to the table where Beth sat leaning forward from the seat of her chair, staring into the monitor of her laptop. He set the glass down on the table. "Take a sip."

"What are we drinking to?"

"Molly's getting home safely."

"All well?"

"Except for having to go to dinner with the stupid loser. If the word *stepdad* is spoken, she can't promise not to gag."

Beth smiled at that and took a sip of whiskey. "Hmm, nice. Thanks."

She handed the whiskey back to him, and he used the glass to motion toward her monitor. The audio had been muted, so he couldn't hear what the suave narrator of *Crisis Point* was saying. "Is that the episode? I haven't gotten around to watching it yet."

"We just came out of the first commercial break. Tom Barker is about to be introduced."

"This ought to be good." John sat down in the chair beside her.

She turned up the audio, and they sat through two minutes of Barker's self-congratulations. "Nauseating," she said. "Had enough?"

"More than enough."

She paused the video. "There's so much wrong with this, John, and I don't know what else to do to try to keep it off the air."

"I'm at a loss, too. About your problem. About mine. We've got all this new information, but so far it's done us no good. We're no closer to identifying the unsub than when we started."

"Maybe everyone is right and I'm wrong," she said. "There is no bogeyman with a Luna fetish waiting for tomorrow night's moon. Not that I'm wishing there is, but—"

"*If* there is, we will have missed him."

"I can't bear to think that."

"Me neither."

"We've only alerted three law enforcement departments to the blood moon angle. How many are there?"

"Departments? Agencies?" John chuffed. "Hundreds if you stay within Mississippi and Louisiana. Add Texas, and you've got thousands. And we don't even know that he's regional."

"Could we issue a bulletin of some kind that would go to those agencies?"

"Official channels are closed to me now. And even if they weren't, who would we tell them to be on the lookout for?" He raised his eyebrows. "He could be a pip-squeak or a pro wrestler. A family man or a hermit who lives in a cave and dances in body paint around his campfire.

"We've got nothing, Beth. Not even solid reputations to give us some believability." He pointed to her. "You're being given credit for producing a true crime episode that you now claim isn't true." He pointed to his own chest. "I'm a cop, known for the chip on his shoulder, who's been fired and has an arrest warrant out for him. A bulletin from us would be immediately tossed."

She rubbed her temples with the fingers of both hands, then pushed them up into her hair. "Then what do we do?"

"Well, whatever else I do, I'm going after Barker. If I'm going to jail anyway, I first want to do him as much damage as possible."

"Earlier today, you dismissed taking all this to the DA. Maybe you should reconsider."

"Okay," he said. "I'll play the prosecutor. You be me."

She nodded and sat up straighter. "Lieutenant Barker and Frank Gray caused Billy Oliver's death."

"How do you know this?"

"I just do."

"Did they tie up the bedsheet?"

"No, but—"

"He hanged himself, Detective Bowie. You were there. You saw. You cut him down."

Beth wet her lips. "Isabel Sanchez has agreed to testify to what took place before that. Her account is compelling."

"But speculative. In a court of law, under cross-examination, her testimony wouldn't hold water."

"What about the note?" Beth said. "It could have forensic evidence that would prove who wrote it."

"What if it proved that Billy wrote it?"

"He would have been under duress."

"Most confessions are written under duress." John held his hands out at his sides. "It would go something like that."

On the muted monitor, Barker was waxing eloquent, actually grinning into the camera. John said, "And even if, by divine intervention, the two of them were convicted and given life without parole for Billy, we still don't know who took Crissy and what he did with her."

"You're way too hard on yourself, John. How could I have ever thought that you don't give a damn?"

"When I walked into that bar, I didn't. You had me pegged." He looked into her eyes, saw the anxiety there. "A better question would be how I could have dragged you into this."

Before she could respond, her burner phone rang. She looked down and gasped, "Oh my God, it's Brady." She answered quickly. "Winston? Thank you for calling me. Hold on a sec. Don't hang up." She pressed the phone against her chest. "This is going to take a lot of explaining. I'll go into the bedroom."

"Go!"

She scampered into the bedroom and shut the door. He finished the whiskey in one stinging gulp, then carried the glass into the kitchen, where Mutt joined him, looking hopeful. "Sorry, buddy. I didn't realize it was past your suppertime."

He was filling the food bowl when the phone he used for Mitch jingled. Clumsily, he set the bowl on the floor, spilling half the contents, before he rushed over to grab the phone. "I'm here."

"You sound out of breath. Did I catch you postcoital?"

I wish. "I spilled a bowl of dog food. What's going on?"

"I was tailed this morning. Lost the asshole, but it put me on guard. I packed Angela up and sent her to Lafayette to stay with her parents until I give her the all-clear."

"I'm relieved to hear it. Beth and I were followed today, too. It's also possible that Barker had someone watching Molly."

"Jesus."

"That's unconfirmed, but I don't put anything past him." He gave Mitch a capsulated rundown of their day, which included the contentious encounter with Carla Mellin. "She's still a viper."

"Are y'all okay?"

"For the present. Beth and I are back at the camp. Molly is with her mom and soon-to-be stepdad."

"Excuse me?"

"You heard right. Roslyn is getting married. To hear Molly tell it, they deserve each other."

"Poor kid." Mitch sighed. "Well, my news is better than yours. The dark web moles came through with some familiar handles."

"They did?"

"Even better, they know who they belong to, and some are regional. Regional-ish. The boys isolated those for you. I'll text them. Understand that your guy may be a whole lot deeper than the people behind these names."

"But this is a starting point. Thank you, Mitch. The moles, too. I'll buy them all a beer soon. If I'm not in jail."

"John." Mitch paused strategically. "You mind my asking how you're figuring all this is gonna play out?"

"Beth and I have been discussing possible outcomes. None positive."

"'Fraid of that. How is she?"

"Feeling the strain, but she hasn't caved."

"And the two of you…?"

"None of your goddamn business."

"Oh, that's a definite yes." He chuckled, but then sobered. "I have the next two days off. Angela's gone. If you get in a bind, I'm a call away."

"Thanks, but I hate to involve you any further."

"I was involved from the start. Barker screwed me over, too, don't forget. You're not the only one who feels rotten about that fuckin' travesty of an investigation."

They said their goodbyes. Seconds later, John received a text with a long list of social media handles. He saw immediately that most related in some clever or quirky way to a faction of the paranormal.

He texted a copy of the list to his counterparts in the other three cities and gave them a brief explanation of what they were. He didn't disclose how he'd obtained them.

Mutt, who'd cleaned not only his bowl but also the floor,

ambled over to be let out. John was closing the door behind him when one of his phones rang. It was the detective in Jackson. "Did you get my text?" John asked.

"Just now. I had my phone in my hand to call you. The guy we looked at years ago?"

"The wagger with the alibi?"

"I went to see him today. He acted squishy, you know?"

"I know squishy."

"He got even squishier when I asked if he had any tattoos."

John's heart became a drumbeat, and it lasted for the next several minutes while the detective talked. John was signing off with him when he heard the bedroom door opening. He turned and gave Beth a smile and a thumbs-up.

The other detective was saying, "At first I thought you were a little nuts and that this blood moon stuff was horseshit. Thanks, Bowie. You've made our cold case hot."

"Send me everything you have on the guy and keep me posted. I'll do the same." He ended the call, dropped the phone, and pumped the air above his head with his fist. "That was Roberts. Their person of interest has a red crescent moon tattoo on his shoulder. They have him in custody."

He picked up his phone again and began composing a text message to Morris and Cougar while continuing to bring Beth up to date. "And that's not all. Mitch and dark web moles came through." He told her that news. "What I thought we'd do is—"

It wasn't until then that he realized she wasn't reacting with the enthusiasm these developments warranted.

"Sorry," he said. "What about Brady? How'd he react when you told him he's about to commit career suicide?"

"He fired me."

John looked at her, aghast. "He *fired* you?"

She dropped down into the chair in front of her laptop. "On the spot. Effective immediately. Although he is being gracious enough to leave Max's and my names in the credits."

"You can't be serious."

"Brady certainly was. Richard has been appointed to clean all personal belongings out of my office and send them to my apartment unless I specify another address."

John dragged his hand down his face. "I don't even know him, and I want to use a pair of pliers to rip off his balls."

"If you knew him, you'd want to even more."

"How could he discount all the debunked facts in that episode?"

"He didn't even give me a chance to tell him about them! I didn't get a word in edgewise. He didn't hear anything I said because he was too preoccupied with giving me the heave-ho. Of course, because I'm a member of the old regime, he's been waiting for a valid excuse to usher me out. Carla Mellin gave him one, and it's a dilly."

"Carla?"

She took a deep breath and let it out slowly. "She called him this afternoon, and got put through because of her 'moving contribution to the episode.' Which I know is hogwash. Half the questions put to her, she refused to answer.

"Today, however, she was apparently more talkative. Brady advised me not to bother asking for a letter of recommendation, because even my late, great mentor wouldn't have endorsed a *lunatic*."

John cursed. "She used that line?"

"She did, with elaboration. In short, she told him that I'm trying to sabotage tomorrow night's program because of my belief in the supernatural powers of a blood moon. I've been to see her twice, both times harassing her with questions about the occult, numerology, astrology, tattoos symbolic of Roman goddesses, and the like. I've tried to draw a connection between the mystic world and her daughter's disappearance, which is not only untrue but insulting.

"And my partner in all this madness? None other than John Bowie, the bungling detective. With whom, she suspects, I'm being intimate." She glanced up at him self-consciously before continuing.

"Initially you had blamed the corruption within the PD for your failure to find her daughter. Now I have brainwashed you into believing this mysticism nonsense." She pulled at a loose thread on the sleeve of her t-shirt. "The funny thing—"

"This is character assassination, Beth. There's nothing funny about it."

"The funny thing," she repeated with emphasis, "is that when it's laid out like that, everything Carla told him is true. I can't defend myself or I'll appear even more deranged than she described."

"But why did she do it?"

"Why else? Retribution. She resented that we turned her tragedy into 'entertainment for couch potatoes,' remember?"

He tugged at his lower lip. "I don't know. Her animosity,

especially toward you, still seems excessive. Why doesn't she turn some of it onto Tom Barker? She's got more reason to hate him than anyone affiliated with *Crisis Point*."

"She gets her vengeance on him in her interview. When you watch it, you'll see. She questions both his competence and integrity. Not straight out, but she plants seeds of doubt, and dislike for him, in viewers' minds."

"Has he seen the episode yet?"

"I doubt it. Episodes are kept under wraps before they air. I have the Mellin one only because I was working on it."

"When Barker does see it, he may go after her."

"In what way?"

"Hell if I know and hazard to guess." He straddled his chair backward to face her and reached across to caress her cheek. Softly, he asked, "Any chance in hell of Brady cancelling the episode?"

"No. When he paused to take a breath, I tried to impress upon him how disastrous it was going to be if he aired it tomorrow night. He laughed and suggested I burn some incense to the moon goddess to ward off evil spirits." She laughed lightly. "That's not a bad idea. It certainly couldn't hurt. Do you have any incense around?"

Her knew her attempted humor was part of the brave front she was putting up. "Are you going to be all right?"

"Yes."

He looked at her doubtfully.

She said, "Honestly, I'm fine. With or without Carla's interference, it would have happened eventually." She took a deep breath. "You were about to tell me what you thought we should do next."

"Right. Professor Wallace. We could send him that list of handles, see if he recognizes any from the sites he's lurked on."

"Maybe if one has popped up on several different sites, he would have noticed and remembered."

"That was my thinking. Why don't you call and explain? If he agrees, I'll text him the list. But if he asks how we came by it, tell him it's classified."

"Is it?"

"It is as far as I'm concerned."

Beth placed the call, and the professor answered immediately.

Feeling optimistic that he would agree to help, John forwarded the list to him immediately. No sooner had he sent that text than a call came in on another of his phones.

His ex's name was in the readout. "Christ. She's all I need." He answered with, "I hear that congratulations are in order."

"Don't play cute with me, John. I want you to bring Molly home. *Now.*"

Chapter 31

"What are you talking about, Roslyn?"

Beth was on the phone with the professor. When she heard John address his ex-wife, she turned her head and looked at him inquisitively. He gave a shrug and an impatient shake of his head.

Roslyn was saying, "Like you don't know."

"I don't know," he said with heat. "The last I heard, she was going to dinner with you and your intended."

"She wasn't ready in time, and I didn't want to lose the reservation. We had champagne chilling. I wasn't going to let her inconsideration spoil our celebration. She said for us to go ahead, that she would drive herself when she was ready. Of course I refused to allow that since—"

"Since she has only her learner's permit," he said, impatiently finishing for her. "Are you telling me that she didn't make it to the restaurant?"

"No, I'm telling you that she called an Uber, using a credit card that you gave her without my knowledge."

"I don't need your permission to give my daughter a credit card, Roslyn. She doesn't abuse it. It's to use in case of an emergency."

"Like running to you."

He could feel anxiety like a fist taking hold of his lungs and beginning to squeeze. "Did she get to the restaurant or not?"

"Oh, she did. Acting like the queen of Sheba. She was horrid. Absolutely horrid. She ruined the whole evening for us. She was snotty and sullen. I wanted to slap her. When they brought out the cake—"

"Jesus," he whispered.

"—she threw her napkin in an expensive plate of food she hadn't touched, and stalked out."

"You haven't seen her since?"

"I was going to let her have it as soon as we got home, but she isn't here. I know she ran to you, John, because—"

"Did she take your car?"

"No. That's the first thing I checked. It's still in the garage. But she's resourceful, and now she has that secret credit card—"

"She's not with me. I haven't heard from her since she texted me that she'd gotten home from school. I'm hanging up."

Beth had concluded her call and was looking at him with concern.

"Molly is unaccounted for." His throat was so constricted he could barely speak the words. With butter fingers, he called Molly's cell. After the tenth ring, it went to voice mail. "Molly, your mother called me looking for you. If you're on your way to me, fine. Good. Don't worry about her rants. I'll handle her. Just call me to let me know you're all right. If you can't get here, I'll come pick you up.

"Look, I know you're upset. But remember our pact. We'll work things out with your mother, I swear. Even if we have to go to court. Call me back. I love you."

He clicked off, threw the phone down onto the table, and raked his fingers through his hair. Beth said, "You're afraid she ran away again?"

"No. I'm afraid she didn't."

"This is Barker. Who's this?"

"Your worst nightmare."

"Well, hello, Bowie."

"Have you got my daughter?"

Tom looked across at the ogre, who was wedged into his chair on the other side of Tom's desk and, as usual, was opening a fresh stick of chewing gum. Tom put his phone on speaker. "What makes you think so?"

Bowie, speaking softly, said, "If you have laid a finger on her, I'm going to choke you, slowly, with your own intestines."

Tom waited a moment to reply, then drawled, "Frank here warned me of that, didn't you, Frank? He warned that you would gut me on principle."

"Where is she?"

"Given her history of running away, I thought you'd have kept better track of her."

"Put her on the phone. On FaceTime."

Barker *tsk*ed. "You know I won't let you see her, John. Or even talk to her. Not unless I get something in return."

"Like what? Exoneration?"

"For what?"

"Billy Oliver's death."

He laughed. "Your memory is rusty. That boy hanged himself. Everybody knows that."

"Put Molly on the phone. *Now*, damn you!"

"John, if you're negotiating a hostage release, you've got to come to the table thinking reasonably, not making demands."

"What do you want?"

"You."

Bowie's heavy, frantic breathing soughed through the speaker. Music to Tom's ears. He said, "I'll let your kid go in exchange for bringing you in. See how simple? We make a swap. How fair is that?"

"You'll turn her over?"

"You're thinking more clearly already."

"To who?" John asked.

"Pardon?"

"Who will you turn her over to? And if you say the ogre, you've got no deal."

"How bad do you want your kid to be let go?"

"How bad do you want me in cuffs?"

Tom looked over at Frank to get his opinion. The blob just sat there, observing while chewing his gum like a cow with cud, offering no advice whatsoever.

Then Tom had a flash of brilliant inspiration. "Beth Collins. Bring her along. I'll hand the girl over to her."

"Negative."

"You don't trust her with your daughter?"

"I don't trust you with Beth. No deal."

"Look, Bowie, you're being awfully high-handed. If you want your kid—"

"If you want me, I choose who Molly gets entrusted to. Take it or leave it. If you leave it, I'm calling the feds, and alleging kidnapping."

"It would never stick."

"But it would be bad publicity the night before your big television debut."

Again, Tom silently consulted the ogre, who said in a low voice, "I'd prefer the babe, but..." He shrugged his massive shoulders. "Whatever."

Tom gave him a dirty look and went back to Bowie. "All right. Who're you bringing?"

"You'll see. Where does this exchange take place?"

"Nowhere too public. I'd rather keep this just between us."

"I'm sure you would. In fact, I counted on it."

"How about your place? Frank tells me it's out in the boonies. What say we meet there in two hours?"

"See you there."

"Hold on, hotshot. I'm not finished negotiating the terms."

"What else?"

"If you resist arrest, I won't be responsible for what happens to either you or your girl. No tricks. And you had better be as meek as a fucking lamb. Frank's a bit testy after sitting in his car all day outside the high school, said it gave him hemorrhoids. If I were you, I wouldn't test his mood."

"I'll be there. But if I see that Molly's been hurt—"

"She hasn't been."

"—or if she gets hurt—"

"She can blame her daddy. Her future is entirely up to you."

Barker hung up and smiled smugly. "In two hours, Frank."

The ogre shook his large head, looking troubled. He'd even stopped chewing. "Boss, you sure about this?"

"Don't ask me that again."

Beth had been able to follow John's conversation with Barker. After its abrupt end, John immediately called Mitch, who answered on the first ring. John said, "How soon can you get here?"

"To the fishing camp? Half an hour."

"Make it twenty. Barker and the ogre have Molly."

"Leaving now."

As John disconnected, Beth said, "John, you and Mitch can't go meet them. Just the two of you?"

"You heard Barker. He wants to keep it between us. You know why? Because he has every intention of killing me."

"All the more reason for you to call the police."

"They are the police."

"Then the FBI, like you threatened."

"That was a bluff. By the time they got into play, Molly could be dead."

"*You* could be dead."

"We can't argue about this, Beth."

He sidestepped her to walk over to the wall where the shotgun hung on the gun rack. He took it down and scooped a handful of shells from the cigar box and dropped them into the pocket of his black rain jacket, which was hanging on one of the hooks inside the front door. He propped the shotgun against it.

From the top drawer of a bureau, he took several clips

for his .45 and placed them in the other side pocket. A knife was stored in another drawer. He took it out of its scabbard, tested its razor-thin blade against the pad of his thumb, then bent down and slid it into his boot.

"You carry a knife in your boot?" she asked.

"It fits in a scabbard. When we were partners, Mitch had them made for us."

"Why?"

"Because you can't trust the bad guys."

Watching him preparing like a soldier for battle, Beth wrung her hands. "Molly must be terrified. How did he get to her?"

"Maybe when she came home alone from the restaurant. Somewhere between the Uber car and the house. Or maybe she was snatched when she left the restaurant, before the Uber car arrived."

He stopped in the middle of the room and dug his thumb and middle finger into his eye sockets. "God, when I think about that cretin touching her." Then he lowered his hand and gave his head a hard shake. "I can't think about that now. I'll go crazy."

"Should you notify Roslyn?"

"Should, but I'm not going to until I have Molly back and can report to Roslyn that she's okay."

As soon as the words left his mouth, he and Beth looked at each other. Beth figured that he was thinking the same thing she was: Molly may not be okay. She didn't dare say it. However, her apprehension must have been visible.

His eyes became as sharp and steely as the knife inside his boot. "We're all coming back. Molly and me and Mitch."

She squared her shoulders. "And me. I'm going with you."

"Out of the question."

"Think about it, John. Whatever's happened while she's been with them will have been traumatizing. Having another woman there—"

"I get your point, but it's not going to happen."

"John—"

"That's the end of it," he said, slicing his hands. His features had turned as hard and uncompromising as they'd been in the bar when he'd first learned that she represented *Crisis Point.*

Then his head dropped forward. "I didn't mean to snap at you. I'm worried on your account, too. I hate leaving you here alone, but I'm leaving you armed, and with a secret. Come in here."

He led her into his bedroom and opened the closet door. He knelt and moved aside several pairs of footwear, then pried up a section of the hardwood floor. Beneath it was a cavity about four feet square and six feet deep, disturbingly resembling a grave.

"It's dark and musty, but I think Mutt will warn you if he hears someone approaching. Get in here. Keep this with you." He reached underneath the nightstand and produced a pistol that had been secured to the underside.

"When did you do all this?" she asked.

"I began preparing for this day soon after the Mellin case. I knew it was coming."

"You just didn't know that I would bring it."

"Beth, no. You didn't cause this. It's been waiting to happen."

He wanted to say something profound and meaningful that would cover the broad range of sentiments rattling around inside him like dice in a cup. But he wasn't a poet, so he kept it simple. "I wish I hadn't limited myself to only once with you."

"If I have any say in the matter, you haven't."

Each second counted. Nevertheless, he held her gaze for a precious few, then checked the pistol he'd retrieved and set it on the nightstand. "It's loaded and the safety is off, so be careful handling it. But keep it within your reach."

"Point and pull the trigger."

"Several times."

While waiting for Mitch, John worked out a plan. He kept it to himself, not sharing it with Beth because she had become increasingly fearful for both him and Molly, and it showed.

He was only slightly better at concealing the fear gnawing at him. He knew the cruelty the ogre was capable of and the delight he derived from it. It made him ill to think of the ogre anywhere near Molly. He pulsed with a craving to dispatch Frank Gray without fuss or muss.

He wanted to deal with Tom Barker on a more personal level. He'd masterminded this sadistic plot, using Molly as a pawn, hitting John where he knew he was most vulnerable. Barker he wanted to kill with his bare hands.

He knew, though, to keep those murderous impulses under control for now. Police training had taught him that mistakes were made when one allowed raw emotion to dictate decisions and actions. To keep them from overtaking him, he focused on readying himself mentally.

When Mitch arrived, he gave Beth a quick hello hug, but he had also been trained in special ops. John recognized the coiled tension just beneath the surface. Because he didn't want Beth to overhear the plan he'd outlined, he drew Mitch aside on the pretext of checking weapons.

Mitch, accustomed to absorbing stratagems under pressure, took it all in without question or comment, then said, "Let's do it."

He turned away, but John hooked his elbow and pulled him back. "You don't have to do this."

"Fuck you. Of course I do."

"If we pull this off, I'll owe you big-time."

"You sure as hell will. How about being godfather to my son?"

John swallowed thickly. "That'd be…thanks. But one more thing before we go. If it comes down to a choice of getting me out or Molly, it's her. Got that? You're soon to be a father. You understand."

Mitch nodded. "I don't count on having to make a choice, but I understand." He slapped John on the back and said, "See you outside." He waved to Beth on his way through the door, then melded into the darkness beyond the cabin.

John pulled on his jacket and double-checked the ammunition he'd placed in its pockets, then went over to Mutt and scratched the top of his head. "Look sharp, buddy."

Beth was standing near the door, actually trembling. John walked over and placed his palm against the side of her neck, curling his fingers around her nape. "I'm coming back."

"Make it a promise."

He pulled her up and toward him. It wasn't a long kiss, but he made a solemn vow of it.

Chapter 32

John steered into the cul-de-sac and took his foot off the accelerator, reducing his speed to a crawl. Since it was well after eleven o'clock, most of the houses were dark.

"All quiet," Mitch said.

"But they're here," John said, noting the car parked alongside his SUV in front of the bungalow.

He drove the length of the lane and rolled to a stop in the darkest spot beneath the low branches of one of the oldest and most stalwart oak trees. He parked facing its trunk, cut the engine, and killed the headlights.

From the driver's-seat window, he had an unobstructed view of the bungalow's cheerless facade. Which meant that whoever was inside could also see him broadside. He stayed as he was, motionless except for his right hand, which curled around the pistol in his lap, and his eyes, which skittered across the front windows of the house, looking for movement.

All the blinds had been closed, but in the slits between

louvers there was faint light. The end table lamp, most likely, he thought. The overhead light would have been brighter.

Where was Molly? Was she bound? Gagged? Unconscious? Injured? Would they use her as a human shield?

The questions revolved inside his head like a carousel spinning out of control. His heart was thudding. His ears buzzed with anxiety. His entire being felt supercharged by adrenaline. Each tick of his watch seemed louder than the one before it.

He looked over at Mitch, who turned his head and looked back at him. They'd already said what needed to be said, and now Mitch tipped his head in a silent but cogent communication.

John turned back to the driver's window and stared at the house as he tucked his pistol into the waistband of his jeans at the small of his back. Then he lifted the handle and pushed the door open.

He had taken the precaution of dimming the interior car lights as far down as they would go, so he wouldn't be such an easy target for the ogre, if not to kill, at least to maim and render useless.

But even without the lights, he was definitely vulnerable as he got out and stepped away from the car with his hands raised. With one shot, he could be dead in less than a second.

But he didn't think that Barker would have him killed right away. Barker wanted to see him humbled and pleading, suffering as the ogre did his worst before finishing him off. Barker would want to stage a memorable scene in this live drama with himself cast in the lead role. At least, that was what John was banking on.

Curtain up, he thought as he called out, "Barker!"

The front door opened a crack. Through it, Barker chortled, "Glad you could make it, John. Hope you don't mind that Frank and me made ourselves at home."

That cocky opening line could have been scripted. Barker was playing it exactly as John had expected. "Send Molly out."

"Who'd you bring with you?"

"Haskell."

"Figures." Then, "Get out of the car, Mr. DEA. Real slow."

John angled his head back and said, "No, Mitch. Not until they send Molly out."

Barker said, "She stays with us until you surrender yourself."

John raised his hands higher. "I already have."

"Do you think I'm stupid?"

"Is that a rhetorical question?"

"You wouldn't come unarmed."

"I wouldn't risk Molly's safety."

"Right, right. Let's see under your jacket. Easy like. And, uh, regarding Molly's safety, Frank's got the bore of his pistol tucked up tight under her chin. If you or your crony so much as fart, her head is red mist."

John wanted to barge toward the house, leap over the front steps, grab Barker by the throat, and squeeze until his eyeballs burst. His desire to do that was so extreme, he actually swayed forward and back.

Barker laughed. "I can tell you're just itching to do something valorous, but what good would it do you? You and the girl would be dead. Neither of you would be around to bask in the glow of your heroism." He sighed. "So what would be the point, huh?"

"How do I know you haven't already killed her?"

"You don't trust me?" Barker asked in a mocking voice.

"Let me see her."

"She's alive."

"I want a guarantee."

"The only guarantee you're getting from me is that if you're trying to buy time, drag this out with all this chatter, we'll end it now. Frank kills her, I kill you. What's it going to be?"

"I'm not going to do anything that would jeopardize Molly's life. Mitch's either."

"See how easy that was?" Barker said. "We understand each other; we're all playing by the same rules. Now, lift your jacket."

"What?"

"I'm not going to ask again."

John raised his jacket, revealing nothing except his belt buckle.

"Now the back." When John hesitated, Barker said in a measured and malicious tone. "Turn around and lift your jacket."

Reluctantly, John did as told.

Barker laughed. "See? Told you so. You wouldn't come unarmed. Pinch the hilt between your thumb and finger, take the gun out slowly, and toss it. Don't cheat on the distance, either. Keep in mind that Frank has a twitchy trigger finger, and, to tell the truth, that girl's whimpering is getting on my nerves."

Swearing, John did as asked. He tossed the pistol far out of his reach.

"Now," Barker said, "if you and your sidekick continue to behave, we can make this swap peaceably. He leaves with the girl. I arrest you."

"That's bullshit, Barker," John said. "You're not going to arrest me. There's no way in hell you're going to let me leave here alive. But I want to see Molly driving away with Mitch."

"Aww, that's touching. You're a saint. I don't know that I would sacrifice myself for one of my kids."

"I know you wouldn't," John said. "But you and I struck a deal. Molly for me."

"You're not exactly in a position to bargain, are you?"

"Those were your terms, Barker. That's what I agreed to."

Barker took his time answering, and John could hear a mumbled exchange between him and the ogre; then he said, "Okay. We'll let her go when you get to the porch."

John nodded. Motioning, he said, "Come on, Mitch."

"No, he waits in the car," Barker said.

"You told him to get out."

"I changed my mind."

John taunted, "You're scared of him."

"He waits in the car!" Barker said, sounding like he was unraveling.

"All right, all right, but what about Molly?" John asked.

"What about her?"

"She'll need help."

"Help? No, she won't. She can walk out on her own. Or,

she'll be able to unless Haskell shows off his derring-do. If he tries to rush to your rescue, Frank will kill the girl, and I'll stop Haskell with this." He poked a rifle barrel through the crack in the door. "Phttt, phttt, phttt. You get the picture. Your former partner is bye-bye."

John hesitated, then looked over his shoulder and said, "It's tempting, I know, but do what he says, Mitch. Stay in the car. I'm trusting you to get Molly out safely."

Then he came back around and started walking toward the house. Barker instructed him to stack his hands on the top of his head, and he did. He climbed the steps in a measured, deliberate tread, his gaze never wavering from the opening between the door and its jamb. It was too narrow for him to see into the room. He didn't know the ogre's position. He couldn't see Molly.

When he reached the edge of the porch, Barker ordered him to stop. "Where's Molly?"

"In the bedroom."

"Get her."

"She's—"

"*Get her!*" John yelled.

At that moment, a terrible racket erupted from behind the house, followed by a shout. "John! Back here!"

Barker whipped his head around. "What the fuck, Frank? Go see!"

The ogre barreled across the room, through the kitchen, out the back door, and began to aimlessly fire his pistol into the darkness.

In the nanosecond that Barker was distracted, John kicked the front door open. It slammed into Barker, propelling him backward several stumbling steps. With the ferocity of an avenging angel, John kicked him in the crotch, the steel-reinforced toe of his boot solidly connecting with Barker's scrotum.

He screamed, fell to his knees, and dropped the rifle to clutch himself in agony. John picked up the rifle and swung the stock of it against the side of Barker's head.

He toppled to the floor, out cold.

"Molly!" John rushed toward the bedroom.

Mitch had opened the passenger door of the car at the same moment John had opened the one on the driver's side. Then, as fluid and soundless as mercury, he had slid out while John was diverting the men inside the house by presenting himself, hands raised.

Because of the risk of being seen visiting a cop's house, Mitch had always parked a distance away and had come and gone through the surrounding woods in the dark to reach John's house. He knew his way around.

Tonight, while John had kept Barker and the ogre distracted, he had moved through the woods like a wraith, disturbing nothing, not making a sound on his way to the shed behind the house.

He'd held a low-wattage flashlight in his mouth and dialed in the combination on the well-oiled padlock. As soon as it opened, he'd switched off the light. Inside the shed, the darkness had been stygian, but John had told him where he would find the items he needed.

His eyes had soon adjusted well enough to make out

shapes. What he couldn't detect by sight, he'd located by feel, following the directions John had given him. With the timer in his head counting down the seconds, he'd worked quickly and within ninety seconds had found everything he required.

He'd carried it all outside and set to work. He moved rapidly but efficiently, his ears constantly attuned to what was going on in front of the house. Task finished, he'd hunkered at the base of a live oak, John's shotgun across his lap.

When he heard Barker order John to stack his hands on the top of his head and had visualized John walking toward the porch, he'd crossed himself, murmured a Hail Mary, and waited for John's signal.

It had been a short wait.

"Get her!" John yelled.

Now! Mitch began banging the hand spade against the empty metal pail and shouted, "John! Back here!"

Within seconds, the ogre burst out the back door, rapidly firing at a target he hadn't yet identified and couldn't see.

Nor did he see the trip wire.

Mitch had stretched it taut between two trees twenty feet beyond the back steps. The ogre fell like a block of lead, landing face-first on the ground. He lost his grip on the pistol. It landed yards away.

Before Frank recovered his wind or his wits, Mitch was on him, grabbing his hands and pulling them behind his back, securing them with a zip tie, all within a matter of seconds.

Mitch snapped up the shotgun, aimed it at Frank's head, and ground his booted foot against the back of his thick neck. "My choice whether I break it or not."

"Fuck you," Frank grunted.

For once, his size worked against him. His breaths were gusting from his mouth. He spat out a wad of chewing gum. He couldn't throw Mitch off, though he tried.

Mitch said conversationally, "Or I may save myself the trouble and just use the shotgun." He tapped the double barrel against the ogre's head. He stopped struggling.

"Mitch!" John came running from the back of the house. "Is she okay?"

"She's not here."

Mitch swiveled his head toward John. "What?"

"Molly isn't in the house, not in their car."

"What about Barker?"

"Unconscious and disarmed."

John, looking diabolical, kicked the ogre in the vicinity of his kidney. Then he went down on one knee, bent over him, drew the knife from his boot, and placed the tip of it in the man's ear. "Is my daughter dead? Did you kill her?"

"No," Frank sputtered into the dirt. "I swear. No!"

"You've got two seconds, *two*, to tell me where she is, or I sink this knife into your brain."

"Fuck you, Bowie. You're so smart, you find her."

Mitch increased the pressure on his neck. "It's as meaty as a ham, John, but I can make his neck bones snap like twigs. Just give me the word."

"Thanks, but I've got this." Calmly, quietly, John whispered to Frank, "You want to live? Tell me where she is. Two seconds."

The ogre remained silent.

"Okay." As he tickled the ogre's ear canal with the sharp tip of the knife, he began his countdown. "Two."

"I—"

"One."

The ogre, the terror, the bully screamed, "Wait! I'll tell you, I'll tell you, I'll tell you."

Mitch and John looked at each other; John bobbed his chin. Mitch let up on the man's neck but worked his boot beneath the ogre's shoulder and pushed him onto his back. He was drooling. His eyes were wild with fear. They darted between the barrels of the shotgun, the wicked knife, and John and Mitch, both of whom were glaring down at him with evangelical intent.

He blubbered. He sobbed. "After school let out, she gave me the slip. Barker went apeshit. Ranting and raving. He called me in to account. You," he said, meeting John's fierce gaze, "you called, accusing Barker of taking her. He…he—with me sitting right there—pretended that we had her. It was a hoax. A…a…a ruse. To…to…you know, to draw you out."

As though John had officially assigned Mutt to guard her, he trailed Beth from window to window, chair to chair, bedroom to bedroom to kitchen as she roamed the cabin, too keyed up to light anywhere.

Her anguish over the severance from the TV show paled in significance to the unthinkable torment John was experiencing now. She also was sick at the thought of Molly being at the hands of the ogre and Tom Barker. She didn't hazard to speculate what it would do to John if his daughter was harmed, or what he would do to the men who'd harmed her.

She hadn't been fooled by his and Mitch's need for privacy to check their guns. They'd been devising a plan. While she was slightly resentful that she hadn't been included, she was also relieved that she didn't know the details. Knowing what they intended to do might have made this waiting worse. As it was, worry was eating her alive.

Restless and needing something to distract her, she wandered over to the table and sat down in front of her computer. The professor had agreed to look over their list of social media handles, but she hadn't heard back from him yet. She doubted she would until tomorrow.

Suddenly she was struck cold with the realization that it was already tomorrow. Yes, there on her computer screen: *12:02 March 13.*

She and John had been fed so much information in the last two days. It was such a small amount of time to digest it all. What had they missed? What had they missed? What? *What?*

Had the professor referenced in passing something that they hadn't picked up on, hadn't yet explored? She recalled him saying of the trends "waxing and waning." Alliteratively, "witchcraft and werewolves."

Wolves howled at the moon.

She woke up her laptop and opened it to that virtual meeting with the professor, which, fortunately, she'd recorded. As he explained the nature of his lectures, her attention lapsed and her gaze wandered from him to the overstocked shelves behind him.

In addition to the interesting and unusual artifacts on display, he had an extensive library. Had he read and absorbed everything in those books? Is that how he could give knowledgeable lectures on such a variety of subjects and yet stay within the realm of the supernatural?

She paused the video in order to examine the book titles and noticed that, although the shelves appeared messy and haphazardly arranged, the books were actually grouped by subject matter.

She saw only three books on werewolves, but one entire shelf was given over to books on witchcraft and its dozens of subdivisions. Two shelves were lined with books about the moon and related astrological subjects, both scientific and mythological. Fact side by side with myth.

There was a section on numerology, which she found curious. He'd told John he wasn't an expert, but she supposed that having a collection of books on the subject didn't make him one.

Still...the professor didn't come across to her as being that modest. Indeed, he enjoyed expounding on a topic.

She got up suddenly and stumbled over Mutt in her haste to get to her bedroom. She took her suitcase out of the closet where she'd stowed it and placed it on the bed. The zipper stuck several times in her rush to open it.

She tossed aside her hair dryer, a bag of toiletries, and a pair of sneakers, then plowed both hands through folded articles of clothing until she reached the bottom, where she'd placed Professor Victor Wallace's book.

His article had piqued her interest, so she'd ordered his book. It had been delivered mere hours before she'd left for her flight from LaGuardia to New Orleans. She'd read the first two chapters on the plane but had found it tedious reading and hadn't opened it since.

Now she sat down on the bed and flipped through the opening pages until she reached the table of contents. She ran her index finger down the chapter titles.

Numerology. Chapter seven.

She slammed the book shut as though it were a Pandora's box from which she wanted nothing sinister to escape. She held it flat against her chest, against her thumping heart.

The professor took such pride in his work; why had he qualified his knowledge of numerology as inexpert when he'd written a chapter on it? Why hadn't he suggested that John read that chapter if he sought a better understanding of the system?

On weak knees, she returned to the main room. The freeze frame of him in his office was still on her monitor. Leaning into it so closely her nose almost touched the screen, she surveyed the shelves of his bookcase.

Though she was desperate to dispel the thought that was pounding in her brain, she forced herself to be thorough, to read every book title she could distinguish, to look at each object, to go slowly and not be in so much of a hurry that she might miss something. It was maddening to wonder what the professor himself was blocking from her view.

Then it leaped out at her, so unmistakably identifiable it stopped her heart.

That instant, her phone rang. She nearly jumped out of her skin, panicked at the thought that it was the professor calling her back.

But then she recognized the number in the readout and answered with shaky hands. "John?"

"Beth, is Molly there at the cabin?"

"Here? No. What—"

"Barker didn't have her. Never had her. It was a ploy he knew would get me there."

Beth tried to unscramble her brain and make sense of what he was telling her. "Then where is she?"

"That's just it. I don't know. Mitch is on the phone with Roslyn. She hasn't had contact with her since she left the restaurant alone. I'm thinking…Jesus, Beth, I think she's run away again."

"Oh, John. Where are you now?"

"Mitch and I are on our way back to the cabin. His truck's in the camo garage. He's volunteered to scout around the places where Molly went before. As soon as I hang up from you, I'll start calling around, ask those few police officers I trust to help in the search."

"What about Barker, the ogre?"

"I'll tell you when I get there. Shit, Roslyn is demanding to talk to me and won't take no for an answer. I'll be there soon. We're only a few miles away."

"All right, but hurry. There's something you need to see."

"About Molly?"

"No, the professor."

"Wallace? He found someone on the list of handles?"

"No." She took a quick breath. "He has a do-it-yourself tattoo kit on his bookshelf."

Chapter 33

Thursday, March 13

Mutt sensed John's return before Beth did. She joined the dog at the door and had it already opened as John came up the steps. "Is there news?" Even as she asked, his expression told her there hadn't been.

"Her phone goes straight to voice mail," he said. "Obviously she's turned it off, and she's smart enough to take the battery out so we can't trace it. She did that the last time."

He replaced the shotgun in the rack, then removed his jacket and hung it on the peg. His features were taut. The cleft between his eyebrows was as deep as she had ever seen it. She wasn't sure he had even noticed that she had brought him a cup of coffee until he took it from her. Absently he thanked her.

"First I called the restaurant," he said. "It had closed for the night, but the manager was still there. I played the cop card, told him the young woman I was after was last seen leaving the restaurant and asked if the parking valets were still around. They'd all left, but he said he would call the captain, ask if any remembered her leaving, and would let me know. Still waiting on that.

"I've got one of my buddies in the department checking with Uber to see if a car picked her up at the restaurant. I gave patrol officers who aren't Barker loyalists a description of her—Roslyn told me what she was wearing—and asked them to be on the lookout. Sheriff's deputies, too.

"I've called every medical facility I know of, the one where Carla Mellin works included. Molly hasn't shown up in any ER, thank God. I left my contact info with them in case she does."

"How is Roslyn dealing with it?"

"In her usual way. She's in orbit. She's accusing Molly of pulling this stunt to spite her for getting engaged, and she's probably right about that. Of course, Roslyn is also blaming me for encouraging this kind of irresponsible behavior. Her ranting is counterproductive, but, must say, I understand her anger, because I'm angry, too. In fact, I'm mad as hell.

"Molly has put me through this twice before and swore she never would again. I won't let her off without paying some consequences, but priority one is to find her and bring her home. And by home I mean wherever I am. I should have picked her up today when she begged me to. If I'd done that, she wouldn't have done this."

In a soft voice, Beth told him that he shouldn't blame himself, but she knew that the banal words fell on deaf ears.

"The not knowing is pure hell. The only positive thing about this situation is that Barker and the ogre don't have her."

"I want to hear about that encounter," Beth said, "but the important thing is that you seem unhurt. Mitch, too, I assume."

"We got away without a scratch."

"Barker and the ogre?"

"Temporarily out of commission."

"That's good enough for now. You can tell me the rest later. In fact, everything can wait until you hear from Molly." She didn't realize that she'd been twisting her hands together until he looked down at them.

"Her timing couldn't be worse, could it?" he said. "What about the professor?"

"You don't need the distraction, God knows. But if I sat on this, I think you'd hate me for it." Without further delay, she motioned him toward their computer table. The video was paused on the professor at his desk and the overloaded bookshelves behind him. "Here," she said, pointing. "You have to get close to see."

He sat down and leaned toward the monitor. "Son of a bitch."

"Could he possibly be our man?"

"A home tattoo kit for a guy who wears argyle sweaters?" John said.

Beth saw that he was referring to a framed picture on one of the bookshelves. She'd noticed it before. It was of the professor, posing with a woman and a boy, presumably his son.

She said, "Doesn't quite fit, does it?"

"No. Yet the kit is in plain sight. Like he was toying with us."

"There's something else." She picked up the copy of the professor's book and opened it to the page she'd marked with a Post-it. "He wrote eight pages about numerology and has a collection of books on it. Why did he downplay his knowledge of it?"

In thought, John scratched his chin with his thumbnail. "It's not a smoking gun, but it's starting to make sense. He circulates in that community."

"Do you still think there's an underground society of some sort, or did he commit all four abductions?"

"I don't know, but his location is central enough for him to have. He travels around for his lectures. He would see young women on campuses." He contemplated it, then said, "He's looking good to me, Beth. If we had some pretext to have him watched tomorrow, we—"

"It is tomorrow, John. That's why I didn't want to postpone telling you about this. It's past midnight. It's March thirteenth."

"Christ. Remember what I said about the moon always being there even—"

"If it's not visible."

"You were talking to him when Roslyn called to tell me Molly wasn't at home. Where did you leave it with him?"

"He was flattered that we'd asked for his help again and said he would get right on it."

"Some of those handles we sent could belong to him. He'd get a grin out of that." He motioned for her to rewind the video. "Let's listen to our chat with new ears."

Beth, accustomed to watching videos and looking for contradictions, glitches, or nuances, paused it several times to comment on a hand gesture or a shift in the professor's facial expression, but saw nothing that indicated he was a serial criminal.

"He seems perfectly benign," she said. "He looks, acts, and sounds exactly like what he is."

"Serial criminals usually do. That's why they can commit numerous crimes before they get caught. They're the last person anyone would suspect."

They were almost at the end of the video when a phone jingled.

John reacted like he'd been snake bit and jerked it from his pocket. "This is Bowie." He listened.

Beth could hear a male voice but couldn't understand what he was saying. She could tell, though, that whatever it was, it wasn't what John had hoped to hear.

"I appreciate the follow-up. Thank you," he said, and disconnected. "The restaurant manager. One of the valets remembered Molly because she seemed upset when she came out of the restaurant and was rude to him when he asked if she was waiting on a car. She struck off down the sidewalk alone."

He stood up and started pecking in a number on the phone. "I've got to let everybody know that was where she was last seen." He made a call, talked in the shorthand of police officers, and ended it by saying, "Can you alert everybody to that, please? Be sure to include Mitch. Thanks."

He went to the door, lifted his jacket off the peg, and put it on. "At least I have a starting place."

"We," she said. "*We* have a starting place. I'm going with you this time. No argument. Leave Molly a note, telling her we're out looking for her. Tell her to call you and then to stay put till we can get back."

He must've thought that was a reasonable course of action. He sat down again and began to scrawl on a legal tablet. "Let Mutt out, please. And fill his bowls. We don't know how long we'll be gone."

She did that, then went into the bedroom and got her jacket. When she returned to the main room, John was in the kitchen pouring coffee from the carafe into a thermos.

She let Mutt back in, and he sensed their urgency. He kept in stride with her as she went over to the table to turn off her laptop. She noticed that there were less than two minutes left to run. She reached out to stop its play when her hand froze in midair.

She nudged Mutt aside and sat down on the edge of the chair seat. She backed up ten seconds of the video and replayed it, then quickly paused it and reversed it again. Her heart in her throat, she croaked, "John?"

He was moving quickly around the room, turning off lights. "Yeah?" He came over.

"Listen. Listen closely."

She restarted the video where she'd stopped it. The professor was talking. Distantly, a phone rang. A chair was heard scraping back across the floor, then John's whisper, coming through the professor's monitor, was barely there but loud enough to be heard. "Molly."

The professor's eyebrows lifted.

Beth paused the video there. "Molly called you, remember? You got up to answer and told me who it was so I would know why you were leaving the virtual meeting." She pointed to the monitor. "Look at his reaction when you said her name."

"And a few hours later, he talked to me about names with double letters."

The two of them looked at each other with dawning horror.

Molly woke up with the worst headache ever. For a time that's all she could concentrate on; then gradually she became aware that the surface beneath her was hard and cold and that she was uncomfortable all over.

Fearing that any movement at all would sharpen the splinters of pain piercing her brain, she lay perfectly still, wondering why she felt so bad. The flu was going around at school. Had she caught it?

But then memory came drifting through the dense fog of her mind, and she remembered.

She had left the restaurant, furious at her mother, nauseated by the whole "new happy family" scene. She hadn't had a plan other than to get away from that stupid cake with the sparklers flaring from it, and the people at other tables clapping and calling out well wishes. She'd had to escape the whole farce.

As she'd exited, she batted away the valet who'd approached her about retrieving her car. She'd seen that the nearest corner was half a block away. Fuming and upset, she'd walked toward it, wanting to get out of sight of the restaurant quickly, thinking that possibly either her mother or the loser would chase after her, demanding that she return to the celebration.

She'd rounded the corner and hadn't gone far when a

car pulled up to the curb and idled. The driver's window slid down. "Excuse me, miss. I think you forgot this when you left the restaurant." He opened the car door and stepped out, extending a purse toward her.

"Nope. I have mine," she said, patting the small bag hanging from her shoulder.

"Oh, well, someone else's then. My mistake." And then he'd swung the purse at the side of her head. Her last thought had been, *What just happened?*

Something terrible had happened, she realized now. A woman's worst nightmare had happened. Like Crissy Mellin and others who'd disappeared without a trace.

That couldn't happen to her, though. No! Not to her!

But, oh God, if it had, it would positively kill her dad.

Spurred by that thought, she opened her eyes. She was dizzy, making it difficult to bring the wavering shape bending over her into focus and keep it still. But finally she did. She recognized the man who had smiled at her through the open car window. He was smiling now.

"Ah, good. You're awake. I was afraid you wouldn't come to before I have to leave, and I had hoped for a chance to get to know you, Molly."

He knew her name? As muzzy as she was, she knew she'd never met him. She tried to sit up and only then realized that her hands and feet were bound.

"Don't strain," he said, placing his hand on her shoulder. "You can't get loose, and you could hurt yourself trying."

She wanted to yell at him that she was already hurt. The purse he'd struck her with must've been packed with iron, and she wondered if the blow had in fact cracked her skull.

He was leaning down close to her, blocking most of her field of vision, but what she could see beyond his head and shoulders was a high ceiling supporting metal walls. It was an ugly enclosure. A garage? A boathouse?

She shuddered beneath his caressing touch on her shoulder. She detested his smarmy smile. He was looking at her like they were friends. Or lovers. That thought made her want to throw up. Shrinking from him, she asked, "Who are you?"

"Your liberator."

She didn't know what that was supposed to mean exactly, only that it sounded scary. "Get your hand off me." Her voice warbled. She wished for more strength behind it. "My father will kill you."

"I'm sure he'd want to. The volatility of his personality is obvious."

She didn't know the definition of that *v* word, but, if he knew her dad at all, he never would have done this to her. "If you value your life," she whispered, "you'll take me home."

"You'll be going home, Molly. To Luna."

That sounded freaking crazy. She became even more frightened and decided to say nothing more. She got the impression that he wanted to engage with her. She would deny him that. She was expert at shutting people out. She did it to her mother all the time. She closed her eyes.

She sensed him standing up. His footsteps squeaked on the floor, which made no sense to her, so she reopened her eyes to slits. Plastic. The floor was lined with thick black plastic like heavy-duty trash bags were made of.

He was going to kill her, wasn't he?

Turning her head slightly, she saw him standing at a crude workbench, his back to her. He'd pulled on latex gloves. It took her a while to figure out that he was using tongs to pick up stainless steel instruments and dipping them one by one into a shallow basin and swishing them around in some sort of solution.

Sterilizing. That's what he was doing; he was sterilizing those utensils, which looked like they belonged in an operating room. After their dunking, each was lined up with its fellows on a white towel.

Unable to hold it back, she screamed in terror.

Startled, he turned around and said sharply, "Stop that, Molly. It won't do you any good. Nobody can hear you."

"Go to hell," she sobbed, sagging weakly.

Her outburst had launched rockets of pain inside her head. Her stomach heaved. Bile surged into her throat, but, by an act of will, she kept from spewing it. She knew she must have a serious concussion, and struggling could jostle her brain and make it worse. So she lay still, in misery and fear.

He finished with the instruments, making small adjustments to their alignment on the towel, then peeled off the gloves and dropped them into an oil drum, also lined with plastic. He rolled down his shirtsleeves and buttoned both buttons on each cuff.

"Now. The final step." He walked over to a hook, which had been screwed into the wall, and reached into a plastic shopping bag hanging there along with a sport coat.

He took a box from the bag, walked it over to the workbench, and opened it. He studied the contents as though taking inventory, then turned to her and smiled. "Want to see?"

He carried the open box over to her. She gasped when she saw what was inside: stoppered bottles of red ink, a bottle labeled as an antiseptic, a tube of salve, and needles of various sizes in sterilized sleeves.

She found it difficult to breathe, and it hurt her chest to try. This freak was going to tattoo her!

"I ordered several stencils," he said in a conversational tone that mocked her horror. He pulled a folded sheet of paper from his pocket and held it out to her. It was the outline of a crescent moon. "I hope you like it."

His smile made her want to gag.

He returned to the workbench, removed the sealed lid from a rectangular storage container, and took out several cotton balls. He pulled on another pair of latex gloves before soaking several of the cotton balls with the antiseptic solution from the tattoo kit. He returned to her with them.

"Now, let's see." With his free hand, he took hold of her arm. She tried to pull it from his grasp but was helpless to do so. "Molly, Molly, this part won't hurt. I'm only going to begin the cleansing process."

He stroked the inside of her arm. "This looks like a good spot, don't you think?" With his index finger, he drew a circle midway up her forearm.

"Go to hell, you creep," she shouted, and again struggled to free herself.

He looked up and winked at her. "I don't mind a little feistiness."

"You're psycho. Sick. *Sick!* And you're going to die, you

know. My dad is going to kill you." She managed to raise her knees and bump them against his arm. One of the cotton balls fell from his hand onto the floor.

As he stared down at it with something akin to disgust, his demeanor changed. Speaking softly and with an undertone of menace, he said, "Now you're really testing my patience, Molly. I'm your liberator. You should mind your manners with me."

He made the warning emphatic by gripping her arm tighter. He then swabbed her forearm from her wrist to the crook of her elbow with one of the wet cotton balls.

She despised his touch but couldn't physically overcome him, and she was fearful that if she persisted in insulting him he would suspend his cleansing process and go to work on her with the surgical instruments. Until she could think more clearly and devise a means of escape, she determined that her best defense would be to keep her expression impassive and her reactions to a minimum.

He muttered to himself what sounded like a chant about cleansing, purity, perfection, Luna, Luna, Luna. She didn't know how long that would have continued if his wristwatch hadn't dinged an alarm.

It startled both of them. He froze for several seconds, then seemed to come to himself. He looked at his watch and said, "Oh. I was hoping to get the outline done tonight, but time has gotten away." He looked into her eyes. "I hate to leave you, but practical matters dictate. I have to be back home in time to drive my son to school. Today he has an algebra test he's been fretting about. He's studied hard for it, but he'll appreciate a last-minute pep talk."

He disposed of the used cotton balls, replaced the lid on the storage box, and closed the tattoo kit. He placed it on the shelf above the one with the surgical instruments, scooting it this way and that, until it was perfectly centered, and the front of it was flush with the edge of the shelf.

"There." He stepped back and admired it for several seconds before coming back around to her. "When I return, we'll start on your tattoo. I'll make several passes throughout the day. It may hurt a little, but I'll be as gentle as possible." He was so caught up in his own dreamy thoughts, he didn't seem to notice that she was no longer reacting.

"By tonight," he said, "your tattoo should be perfect. Everything will be perfect. Everything *must* be perfect." He gave her another of those sickeningly sweet smiles. "Perfect for your blood moon."

The empty shopping bag now hung limp on the hook. He retrieved it, took down his jacket and pulled it on. He unbolted the door. As he went out, he looked back at her.

"Remember, Molly, the goal is perfection. Please don't spoil it. Don't be the disappointment Crissy was."

Chapter 34

"Mitch? Me."

"Heard from her?"

"No, and it's worse. Beth and I don't think she ran away."

He began explaining about the professor, talking so rapidly his words stumbled over one another. "Later, I'll fill you in on why we suspect he's our perp, and if we're wrong I'll do penance and beg his forgiveness, but it feels right. Eerily right."

"I trust your gut."

"Problem is, we don't have cause to question him about anything. I've got some peeps in the department who are checking security cameras in the area of the restaurant.

"They've got Molly leaving it and disappearing around a corner at the end of the block. That's the last time she was seen. There was a car on the street, but it was drizzling, the video is blurry. They're trying to get a good angle on the license plate, but so far no luck.

"Meanwhile somebody's got my girl somewhere, and if it is this professor, it's doubtful he took her to his residence, because he's got a wife and son. Until he's ruled out, I need to keep track of him."

Mitch said, "You need my stingray."

"You read my mind. Is it handy?"

"I'm sitting on it. It's under the false floorboard of my pickup. Do you have his cell number?"

"Yes. Beth will call him. She's worked out a script that we think will prod him to make a move. *If* it's him. If not, then I don't know."

"Text me the numbers, his and hers. I'll set up and text you when I'm ready." Mitch clicked off.

Beth said, "How does that work?"

"When it's on, the device acts like a cell tower. Law enforcement use it to obtain a phone's IMSI. Every phone has one unique to it, and it's chock-full of information on the user. Once the stingray has the IMSI programmed into it, they can then locate and track the user, run surveillance, see who he connects with, so on."

"The user is unaware of this?"

"That's the idea. Its critics have invasion of privacy issues."

"Is it legal for Mitch to use it unofficially?"

"I don't dare ask, but I really don't give a damn." He drummed his fingers on the table. "Come on, Mitch. You said you were sitting on it."

Beth reached out and squeezed his thigh. "Take a breath. We'll find her."

Looking at her with anguish, he covered the back of her

hand with his and rubbed it. "I hate like hell that I've subjected you to all this. But, God, I'm glad you're here."

Just then Mitch's text came through: *Good to go.*

"You're on." John handed her the phone she had used for prior calls to Professor Wallace.

"Will Mitch be listening in?"

"Yes."

"Maybe you should call."

He shook his head. "You were the one who last spoke to him. You asked the favor, you're following up."

She took a deep breath, crossed her fingers, and placed the call. He answered on the third ring. "Professor, hi, it's Beth Collins. It's terribly early. Did I wake you up?"

"No worry. I had to get up soon anyway. Forgive me, but you sound on edge. Are you all right?"

"I'm in a time squeeze. I wondered if you'd had a chance to look over that list of social media handles we sent. I apologize for pressuring you about it, but I believe we're on to something."

"Oh?"

"Yes. That list, along with another lead, were sent to the detective in Jackson, Mississippi. It turns out that one of those handles is frequently used by a suspect that police had questioned about Anna's disappearance. He provided an alibi and was dismissed. But because of this new information, he's now in custody."

"Do they have evidence of his involvement?"

"They're working on it. He's very much into the paranormal, but he's no dabbler. His interest is obsessive and sinister. He goes to sites on the deep, dark web, the kind where they post photos of bondage and torture, ritualistic bloodletting, and there's lots of chatter about human sacrifices."

"Good lord."

"Yes, it's gruesome. It seems that poor girl might have fallen victim to someone who took his idol worship of Luna to the extreme. The blood moon is tonight, so there's a sense of urgency."

"But if this suspect is in custody, then—"

"That's the other thing. John Bowie believes that there's more than one individual who committed those abductions. That Crissy Mellin was taken by someone other than the man in Jackson."

"How did he arrive at that?"

"He's conjectured that there are like-minded members of a secret society who connect on the dark web."

"Who take their idol worship of Luna to the extreme."

"It's only a theory, of course," she said, intentionally making her tone defensive. "But the young women have nothing in common. He believes it's the men abducting them who do. Which is why that list of handles has become vitally important, and why I felt I should check back with you right away."

"Yes, I see now, and I hate to disappoint. I did give the list a once-over as soon as I received it." He chuckled. "On that first pass, one of the handles did leap out at me. It's one I use."

She laughed lightly. "Oh, well, you did tell us that you lurk occasionally."

"I didn't recognize any of the other names at a glance," he said. "After dinner, I watched a movie with my wife and son. It got late, and I went to bed. All to say, I haven't returned to it, but, in light of what you've told me, I'll do so immediately." He paused, then said, "It might help if I knew the source of this list."

John gave a stern shake of his head. "I'm sorry, Professor, even I don't know. John said it was classified."

"Ah, the intrigue makes it even more enticing. I look forward to studying it in more detail."

"Thank you so much. If one of those handles strikes you as even slightly familiar or curious in some way, please notify me."

"Certainly. But before you go, Ms. Collins, you mentioned that you'd sent the police in Jackson another lead. What was that?"

John signaled for her to tell him, but she thought it would be effective to hedge. "That's an active investigation now. I'm not sure I'm supposed to divulge any information."

John gave her a thumbs-up.

"Of course, of course," the professor said. "I was just curious. And possibly, if I knew what it was, I could provide some helpful insight. It is my field, after all."

"Well..." She paused as though still indecisive, and then said, "Remember we told you about the missing girl in Galveston having a red crescent moon tattoo?"

"Larissa...something?"

"Yes. The suspect they have in custody in Jackson has the same tattoo." She let that settle, then said quickly, "I apologize for rushing off, but I've got other calls to make. If you find something, please let me know immediately. Goodbye for now."

She disconnected, then slumped with relief.

John said, "You were brilliant. Let's go."

They bade Mutt a quick goodbye and started for the camo garage, thrashing through the woods. John's phone rang. He didn't stop but answered on speaker.

Mitch said, "She deserves an Oscar. Y'all heading out?"

"Yes," John said. "Where are we going?"

"From the fishing camp, head northeast. He's southwest of New Orleans, actually between you and the city proper."

"That's where the college is located. He must live near the campus."

"On Cypress Street. I'll head that way," Mitch said. "If he leaves his house, I'll know it and can track him."

Beth asked, "Will I have to keep calling him?"

"No. The stingray will ping whether or not his phone is in use. I'll track you both and let you know if you're closing in on him or getting farther away."

John said, "Thanks, Mitch."

"You bet. And, John, forget doing penance. That's your guy, and he needs to get got."

After he disconnected, Beth said, "He sounded so certain."

"He is. The professor was playing you. From the start, he's been laughing up his sleeve at us for contacting him and asking his help to catch the bad guy."

"But he called you about the numerology."

"A game. Maybe there is something to the double letters in the girls' names, but he might have fed us that as a red herring. It's obvious to me now that there's been a wink-wink behind every word out of his mouth. He's a trickster, a textbook sociopath."

"I think so, too. But I shudder to think how this will end if we're wrong about him."

"I shudder to think how it will end if we're right."

Tom Barker stepped out of the shower and wrapped a towel around his waist. He took a swig of vodka from the glass he'd left on the rim of the sink. He was using the guest room bath in order to prevent his wife from waking up and asking questions about the new goose egg on the side of his head and why he kept tenderly cupping his genitals. He hadn't arrived at any answers that didn't stretch plausibility to the limit.

He'd silenced his cell phone, but he heard the buzz of its vibration against the tiled countertop. At this hour of the morning, he should sound as though the call had woken him up, shouldn't he?

"This is Barker," he snarled, "and whoever this is, it had better be about something important."

The caller identified himself as Officer Clarkson. He was a rookie, none too bright, Barker's favorite kind.

"Were you asleep, sir?"

"Was. Not anymore. Why are you calling?"

"It's about John Bowie."

Tom plopped down onto the toilet lid, having forgotten the residual pain in his nether region. He sucked in air through his clenched teeth. Even though fresh from the shower, a sheen of sweat broke out on his torso.

With a dismissive inflection, he said, "Bowie? I fired him. He's out."

"That's why I thought you ought to know that something's up with him."

"What kind of something?"

"The unit is full of his followers. You know, the people who still admire him and say he got a rotten deal."

"Who says that?"

"A lot of people. Anyway, it's like they've been mobilized, and they're all in a flurry. On phones, on their computers, huddled and talking among themselves."

The glass of vodka clinked against Tom's teeth as he took a quick hit from it. Had the son of a bitch rallied his followers after the scene at his house? Trying to sound blasé, but actually holding his breath, he said, "You don't know what all the excitement is about?"

"I overheard the name Molly."

Hmm. She actually had *skipped.* "His daughter. She's run off before. She must have again. He's probably called in some people to help him look for her. Has an official missing person been filed?"

"Not yet."

"Then the faithful followers had better be flurrying on their own time and not on the PD's nickel."

"I think they are. Off duty, I mean. I'm sorry to have woken you up. I just thought you'd like to know, you and Bowie having a history over that Crissy Mellin case, and all."

"One for the history books."

"Um-huh. Which is why it's funny that they're whispering about that, too."

"The Mellin case? What about it? The upcoming TV show?"

"Uh, not exactly, sir. I overheard one of them saying that Bowie was right all along."

Professor Wallace carefully set his phone on his desk and absently tapped his fingers on the polished wood as he mentally replayed his conversation with Beth Collins, a wonderfully charming young woman. It really was unfortunate that her mission was on a collision course with his.

Hers was doomed to failure.

Yet one had to admire her perseverance and dedication to her quest. She had other calls to make? *To whom?* he wondered. Why the rush? Why were those calls so important that she had to cut short her conversation with him?

He picked up his phone again, accessed his text messages, and looked at the list of social media user names she and Bowie had sent him. As he scrolled down the list, he saw that it included several of his handles, not just one. How long would it take them to discover that?

No matter. He'd been open with them about visiting some of the darker websites. Visiting them occasionally did not a kidnapper make.

Indeed, most of the people who frequented those sites were oddballs and outcasts who'd resorted to an online community because they didn't fit in anywhere else. Oh, they talked the talk in order to cultivate and impress virtual friends, but they wouldn't have the courage to actually offer up a human sacrifice.

Which was why the inner circle was so elite.

How clever of John Bowie to have hypothesized that such an exclusive coterie existed.

Again, no matter. None who had achieved membership into Luna's inner circle had been caught, except for the man in Jackson. Victor wondered what his circumstance was, what his real name was, which handle belonged to him, and what mistake the fool had made to get himself caught all these years after he'd sacrificed the girl named Anna.

Thank goodness he'd been more careful. Crissy Mellin's disappearance remained a mystery to all and sundry. She didn't quite count, though, because she hadn't been purified. Therefore, he had been denied entrance through that sacred portal into the inner sanctum.

One ho-hum evening, while doing some research in preparation for a lecture on astrology, he'd done some exploration on the dark web. He was immediately attracted to one of the websites. So much so, he returned the following night, and the night after.

It was like entering a realm rich in fantasy, engorged with possibilities for success, power, sexual pleasure. It was a world apart from the stuffy life of a professor at a university of meager renown. At the heart of this wonderland, the source of all its suggested blessings, was the moon goddess Luna.

Almost nightly, he would linger on the site. He skimmed the milder posts, but he absorbed the edgier, more graphic ones: writings, photographs, sketches, paintings. Whether excellent or terrible, they were enflaming. They enticed him with their promises of deeper and darker material. Of *more.*

But soon he discerned that getting "more" was by invitation only.

He began posting, mostly complimenting another's

contribution, then adding something elaborative. He must have impressed, because after three months, he received a private invitation to join another group and was sent a link. He then had to undergo a stringent application process. It was a joyous day when he received a notice that he'd been approved. He was given access and was elated to be welcomed by members whose real names he would never know.

He knew nothing about the higher level, the inner sanctum, until about a year later when he received another private invitation. He was told such invitations were extended twice every third year to coincide with blood moons.

He came to learn that only those who received the invitation even knew there was a higher level reserved for the elite. Anonymity was absolute. Membership to the inner sanctum was extended only to those who the established members believed were devout enough to carry out the initiation ritual. If one was invited, and balked at what was required of him to prove his loyalty, the website was shut down, then reopened under a different name.

He had not balked. Quite the contrary. He'd received his instructions with delight, with zealous enthusiasm. He would be doing this for Luna, who would reward him with recognition and respect from the academic community.

Those dreams of global acknowledgment had been dashed when he'd failed with Crissy. But Luna had been benevolent. He'd been granted another chance.

He wouldn't fail this time.

Molly was perfect. Not because of her name, although the double letter gambit had been an amusement. No, it was because he had a tangential acquaintance with her. To reduce the chances of getting caught, he'd been advised by those who'd gone before to choose a sacrifice at random, someone with whom he had no connection whatsoever.

But taking John Bowie's daughter had been a tantalizing temptation he couldn't resist. When he'd heard her name coming from Bowie's own lips, he'd wasted no time in gleaning all the information on the detective that was available on the internet.

Divorced from wife Roslyn in 2023. One daughter, Molly. His ex-wife still lived in the home they'd shared. Easy-peasy.

Yesterday, he'd canceled his last class and had been at that address in Auclair in time to see Molly when she'd arrived home…in an Uber car. That was curious. She'd had a backpack as though coming from school, but he supposed there were dozens of logical explanations for that mode of transportation. Perhaps she'd simply missed the school bus.

At seven P.M. a man had arrived at the home, walked jauntily to the front door, and let himself in. Shortly before eight o'clock, he and a woman, presumably ex-wife Roslyn, had left together in his car.

Molly was home alone. What could be more ideal?

But before he could formulate a plan, another Uber car had picked up Molly, dressed for dinner out as the couple had been. She'd been dropped at Auclair's finest restaurant, where he felt it safe to assume she was meeting her mother and the man. He'd had better sense than to go inside and check. Instead, he'd parked at the end of the block and waited. Would Molly come out alone, or with the pair?

That latter would complicate things and probably

would force him to wait until tomorrow to take her. He'd thought that perhaps that was a sign he should heed. Was he intended to be patient and wait until it was actually the thirteenth of the month?

The wait for Molly to emerge had seemed interminable. But then, shortly after eleven o'clock, she had exited the restaurant alone and on foot.

In his mind, he'd flipped a coin. *Heads, follow her but wait until after midnight. Tails, take her now.*

It wouldn't be official until the clock struck twelve.

Jumping the gun could jinx him.

But could he pass up such a golden opportunity?

Wait! Couldn't this, too, be a sign sent directly by Luna?

Was this a special favor he'd been granted for having waited over three years for a second chance?

He'd acted on it, and it had been the right decision. Under Luna's guidance, he'd driven around the block onto the dark street out of sight of the restaurant, where Molly was walking down the sidewalk, appearing saucy and defiant, unaware of her fate.

It had gone flawlessly.

Now he got up from his desk and went over to the window. It was still dark out, but he could tell that there was cloud cover. However, clear skies were predicted for tonight. Forecasters were saying that for those who stayed up late to see the blood moon in totality, the view of it would be glorious.

His gaze returned to his phone lying on his desk. In retrospect, maybe he shouldn't have been quite so cute with Ms. Collins by admitting that one of those names on that infernal list belonged to him. *Classified* had an ominous ring to it.

It was far too soon for him to panic and act rashly. But if he missed this second opportunity to be initiated, he might never be accepted. That would be untenable.

He'd planned not to return to Molly until after delivering his son to school. But perhaps he should reconsider his timetable. Maybe he should accelerate the process with Molly and consummate the ritual as soon as possible. What would be lost by getting on with it?

He didn't see a disadvantage. In fact, it would be even better. He could celebrate his grand achievement when the moon was full and red without the distraction of having to clean up. It would already be done.

His mind made up, and now in a hurry, he left his study and went into the bedroom. He shook his wife awake to tell her that something had come up and that she would have to be his son's chauffeur that morning. She mumbled compliance. He thanked her and kissed her cheek.

Then he jogged down the stairs and grabbed his jacket off the hall tree. In a flash, he was out the door.

Chapter 35

"He's moving," Mitch reported.

"Which direction?" John asked.

"West-southwest, toward us, which is good. But we conducted a raid in this vicinity a while back, and it was a nightmare. Rural. Lots of narrow roads branching off each other like freaking capillaries. Currently, though, I'm closing in on him on route thirty-four. If he stays on this road, he and I'll meet soon."

"How soon?" John asked.

"Maybe ten minutes."

"I've been driving ninety, so we can't be far behind you." John gave him the state highway intersection he and Beth had just gone through.

Mitch said, "Then you're almost to thirty-four. Start watching for it. It'll be on your right. Badly marked, sharp turn."

"Got it," Beth said. She held up one of their phones where she'd pulled up GPS.

"If I meet him, do you want me to intercept?" Mitch asked.

"Negative. I hope he's leading us to wherever he's got Molly. Hook a U and follow him, but at a distance."

"Don't worry. He won't know it, but I'll be on him like white on rice."

No sooner had Mitch disconnected than another of John's phones rang. It was one of the officers who'd been assisting him. "We got a plate number on the car near the restaurant, ran it, belongs to Dr. Victor Wallace. That's the guy, right?"

"That's the guy. You just handed us probable cause to approach. Good work. Thank everybody for me."

"Have you notified the sheriff's office?"

"I was just about to."

Beth shot him a quick look, a *Really?* implied in her expression.

"Good luck, Bowie," the cop was saying. "We're standing by if you need anything else."

"Thanks."

"Uh-oh," the officer said in a low voice.

"What?"

"Barker just came in, looking thunderous."

"Play dumb."

"Ten four."

As soon as they were disconnected, Beth said, "You're not really going to notify the sheriff's office, are you?"

"No. I don't want a wet-behind-the-ears deputy to show up, lights flashing. This needs to be a surprise to the professor. If he senses he's surrounded and has nothing to lose, he may—"

Beth pressed his knee. "Don't say it. Or even think it."

Tom stalked into the CAP unit, knowing his outrage only made his bruises more florid. It made the new goose egg on the side of his head throb. At the sight of him, people who'd been busy as bees stopped what they'd been doing. Everyone fell silent.

He walked to the center of the room, placed his hands on his hips, and pivoted in a circle, taking in every traitorous face. With deceptive calmness, he said, "I want to know. What. The. Fuck. Is going on?"

No one moved, no one said anything. Some even had the audacity to gaze back at him with defiance. "You think this little mutiny is going to intimidate me? Oh, no. All it's going to accomplish is to get anyone who's assisting Bowie fired. Now," he said, hiking up his waistband, "who's going to tell me what he's up to this time?"

No one moved or spoke.

He went over to the rookie who had called to alert him to what was taking place in *his* department. Because of *Bowie*. The man was like a plague. Pervasive. Tenacious. Crippling. "Where is he, Clarkson?"

The young officer's eyes darted guiltily around the room, where everyone was looking at him with hostility. "They're saying now that his daughter didn't run off, that she was kidnapped last night as she left the Chop House. Bowie is hot on the trail of the man he suspects of taking her." Stammering, he told him about the license plate and the man's name.

"Why wasn't I notified?"

The rookie said, "I don't think…I don't think Detective Bowie trusted you to handle it."

"There is no *Detective* Bowie," Tom shouted. "Is that understood? This kidnapping crap is just that. His kid ran off, like she's done before. Probably to escape him. Now, tell me where he is." Again, he was met with silence. "I demand it!" he roared.

Clarkson swallowed hard. "I haven't heard anyone say. I don't think anyone knows."

Tom surveyed the stonewalled faces. If they knew Bowie's whereabouts, they weren't saying, and, although it was humiliating to admit, he feared that his continued attempt to beat it out of them would be futile.

He straightened to his full height and addressed Clarkson. "Since Bowie lives outside the city's jurisdiction, call the sheriff's office, have them dispatch deputies to see if he's at home."

He stabbed the young cop in the chest with his index finger. "Remind them about the arrest warrant for assault. Also inform them that he's currently impersonating a police officer."

He headed toward his office but, after a few steps, stopped and turned. "Has Frank Gray come in?" The rookie shook his head. "Then see if you can get hold of him. He's not answering his phone."

Tom heard someone say under his breath, "Can't blame him."

Ignoring the snickers that followed, he slammed his office door. The original crack in the window sprouted an offshoot.

Since John was concentrating on driving, Beth answered an incoming call from Mitch. Without preamble, he said, "Our target just sped past me. I could tell he was coming right at me, so I'd pulled into the ditch, opened my hood, and was bent over it as he went by. The license plate was his."

"Any sign of Molly in his car?" John asked.

"No, but we have him in a hot box now. He's between us, still traveling on thirty-four. Where I am, it's so narrow it doesn't even have a stripe. Isolated area."

"Are you turning around?"

"Already have."

"Don't get too close."

"I'm following his pings, not his car, which is a gray Honda. Have you got to the turnoff yet?"

"Beth says we're close. But, damn it! Not close enough. If he stops at a place that looks dodgy, don't wait for me to go in."

"Roger that," Mitch said. "His kidnapping days will be history."

Just as they disconnected, Beth exclaimed, "There's the road!"

She braced herself as John turned the car sharply to the right, toward the east...and straight into a blinding sunrise.

"Damn!" Reflexively he turned his head away from the disk of eye-piercing light.

Otherwise, he might have missed it.

He slammed on the brakes and swerved to the side of the road.

Beth cried out, "*What?*"

"Tin roof. The sun hit it just right. There's no car there. Get Mitch."

She had him on the phone in under three seconds. John shouted, "Spotted a dodgy place. Gonna check it out. How far away is he from us?"

Mitch said, "About to close on you."

"Shit! Stay on the line." John put the car in park and chambered a bullet in his pistol. Talking to Beth, he said, "I want to be there when he arrives. Back up the car. Back onto the highway. Out of sight. Hurry. And call 911. Ask for sheriff and medical. Mitch?"

"Here."

"If he doesn't stop here, keep following him; we'll catch up. But this feels right."

"I have your back."

John got out of the car as Beth ran around the hood to the driver's side. She clambered in, put it in reverse, and stomped on the accelerator.

John ran along a weedy path up to the structure he'd seen thanks to one benevolent sunbeam that had found its way through a thick vine, making a beacon of a patch of tin.

The keypad lock on the door was too sophisticated to bother with; he'd never get it open in time. Instead, he ran along the far side of the building around to the rear, where he wouldn't be seen if Wallace arrived.

He knocked on the corrugated tin wall with the butt of his pistol. "Molly! Molly! It's Dad. Are you in there?"

It seemed that an entire lifetime slowly unspooled in the seconds between his shout and her feeble answer. "Dad?"

His knees went weak. His head thumped against the wall in relief. "I'm here. I'm here. I'm waiting on the son of a bitch who took you, and he's due to arrive any second, so listen up. First, did he hurt you? Are you injured?"

"He hit me in the head. I think I have a concussion."

"Okay, okay, Beth is calling 911. Are you tied up?"

"Yes. Hands and feet. How'd you find me?"

"Later, sweetheart. Listen. Are you sitting or lying?"

"Lying on the floor."

"Don't move. I'm going to try to surprise him when he opens the door. Did he have a weapon? What did he hit you with?"

"A purse."

A purse? "You didn't see a gun?"

"No."

"Okay, good. I'm gonna get you out of here. Just stay down on the floor, low as you can, don't—" He broke off, listened. "Molly, I hear his car coming. I can't talk anymore and don't you say anything else and give us away. Got it? Not another word."

She didn't answer, minding him without an argument for once in her life.

John's heart was in his throat as he heard the car come to a stop and the engine die. The car door closed. Footsteps led up to the bolted door. He knew he had to time this just right, to catch him between opening the door and shutting it behind himself. He couldn't spring either too soon or too late.

He was out of sight of the door as he crept along the side of the building toward the front. He got close enough to hear metal sliding against metal as the bolts were worked, then the swish of the door as it was pushed open.

"Hello, Molly. Ready for your big day?"

John rounded the corner and launched himself at the figure standing in the open doorway. He knocked him face-down to the floor and put the muzzle of his .45 against the back of his neck. "Don't move or you are dead."

"Detective Bowie," he said pleasantly. "Surely you wouldn't kill me in front of your daughter."

"I wouldn't count on that if I were you, Professor." Mitch came up beside them. "I've known John for a long time. He gets pissed easily. I have to talk him down all the time." He knelt and cuffed the man behind his back. "I'll take over here, bro. See to Molly. Ambulance is coming down the road."

John went over to where she was lying just as he'd instructed her to. He pulled her into a sitting position, then gathered her into his arms and hugged her against his chest. Due to the tightness in his throat, he managed to speak only her name, but he said it repeatedly.

"Stop rocking me, Dad," she whispered. "I may throw up on you."

He stopped the rocking motion, laughing softly. "I wouldn't care."

"Can you take these things off my hands?"

"Right away." He pulled the knife from his boot and cut the zip ties. The raw marks on her wrists made him see red. He looked around and saw that Wallace had already been hauled away. Which was fortunate. He might have killed him bare-handed.

As he was freeing Molly's feet, a pair of EMTs hurried

in. They began asking Molly questions. She said, "I'm thirsty, but I'm afraid if I drink, I'll throw up."

"We'll get an IV going. What's your favorite flavor?" the young man teased.

"I'm riding to the hospital with you, sweetheart," John said. He looked the female EMT straight in the eye, daring her to contradict him. She didn't. Maybe because she'd watched him slide his knife back into his boot. "Meet you at the ambulance," he said to Molly.

"Okay, Dad. Is Mom totally freaking out?"

"Totally. But so was I. I'll call her." He kissed her on the forehead, then reluctantly moved away so the EMTs could do their job.

He wandered over to a workbench and looked at the surgical instruments laid out as though a butler had aligned them using a yardstick. On a shelf above the array was the tattoo kit Beth had spied in the professor's bookcase.

His stomach roiled when he thought of the torture that psycho would have put Molly through, what Crissy Mellin and the others girls had been put through at the hands of these twisted, moon-gazing motherfuckers.

He looked over at Molly, where one of the EMTs was checking her eyes while the other was starting the IV. John steeled himself against an onslaught of unmanly emotion and stepped outside.

Mitch was talking to a detective from the sheriff's office, with whom they'd both worked on cases before. On his way over to them, he saw Beth arguing with two deputies who were trying to keep her outside the tape they were stringing around the building.

"I'm with *Crisis Point.* There's a camera crew on their way. Do you want to be seen on TV—" Then she caught sight of John. "I'm with him." When they turned their heads to see who she was pointing toward, she ducked beneath the tape, ran to him, and, when she reached him, clasped his hands and searched his eyes.

"She'll be all right," he said, "but we got here just in time."

She wilted against him, wrapping her arms around his waist. "Oh, John. Thank God."

"Yes, but also thank you. If you hadn't seen that damn tattoo kit in the video..."

"I got lucky."

"Lucky? I don't think it was luck. We'll talk about that later."

He noticed that the professor was being ungently packed into the back seat of a squad car. As it moved past Beth and him, he smiled at them beatifically through the car window.

Beth shuddered. "He makes my skin crawl."

A savage compulsion surged through John. He might very well have acted on it if Mitch and the SO's detective hadn't approached him and Beth just then.

The detective's name was Glen Derby. He and John shook hands. "Derby, this is Beth Collins. She's—"

"I know. Mitch filled me in. Ms. Collins," he said, brushing the brim of his hat. Then he said to John, "How's your daughter?"

"Shaken, but looks like she's gonna be okay."

"That's good. Glad you got here in time."

"Me too."

When John realized that the man was having a hard time looking him in the eye, he looked quizzically at Mitch. He raised his eyebrows, but if he had one of his usual quips at the ready, he didn't say it aloud. John said, "What's going on?"

Derby exhaled. "I hate to heap this on you, but…" He exhaled again. "That warrant for your arrest?"

"You're gonna serve it *now*?"

"No. This is something else."

"Okay."

"A couple of deputies went out to your place with the intention of serving the warrant. You weren't there. They looked around."

The gurney was being wheeled out of the building. "Get to it please, Derby. They're about to take my girl to the hospital, and I'm riding along."

"That shed out back of your house?"

John looked at Mitch, who was stroking that wretched mustache and looking uneasy. John went back to the detective. "What about it?"

"Those deputies found Frank Gray in there. Dead. GSW to the back of his head. Point-blank range. He'd been dead for a while."

John didn't gasp as Beth did, but he shared her shock. He looked at Mitch, who said, "Wait for it. It gets better."

Clearly uncomfortable, Derby shifted his weight and cleared his throat. "The deputies called it in. Crime scene unit arrived. They found a pistol in the brambles about twenty yards from the shed. Recently fired. They ran the serial number. It's your service weapon, John."

Chapter 36

John responded with a huff of disbelief. "My service weapon? Derby, just about everybody in the CAP unit saw me surrender that gun to Tom Barker."

"And several of them heard you tell the ogre that you were going to blow his head off. Which somebody did."

"Mitch knows I wasn't that somebody."

"Told him that," Mitch said. "Told him all about that escapade last night, how it was a bait-and-switch set up by Barker, and how it all went down."

John said to Derby, "We left the ogre locked inside that shed, stewing in his own juice. You said deputies discovered him. How did they open the shed?"

"They didn't have to. The door was ajar, padlock shot to pieces."

"Huh. It's my shed, right? My padlock? I know the combination to it. Why would I shoot it out?" He glanced over his shoulder. The gurney was being lifted into the ambulance.

Coming back around, he said, "The last time I saw that pistol, it was on Tom Barker's desk alongside my badge and ID. If you want to know how it got into the brambles behind my house, start by asking him.

"By the way, you know how many homicides I've worked, Derby? Some of them I've worked with you. Do you really think that I'd use a weapon registered to me to murder a man? And then be stupid enough to throw it into the bushes twenty yards from where I'd killed him?"

He began backing up. "I'm going to the hospital with my daughter now. If you want to talk about this some more, you can find me there."

"Don't make yourself hard to find, John."

"Wild horses couldn't drag me out of town while Molly is in the hospital. Put an ankle bracelet on me if you like."

Derby gave him a pained look.

"Okay then." He turned to Mitch and slapped him on the shoulder. "You came through again. Saying thank you isn't enough."

"So don't bother. I love Molly, too, you know."

"Dare I ask for one more favor?"

"See to that ugly dog?"

"Would you mind?"

"Is that beer I bought you still in the fridge?"

"Help yourself."

He smiled. "Later."

They fist bumped, then John took Beth's hand and together they walked quickly toward the ambulance. "You still have my car key?" he asked.

"Yes, I'll be right behind you."

The EMTs had the gurney in place and were ready to go. Before climbing in, John turned to her. "It could take a while. Don't feel like you have to be there."

"Don't be stupid."

She said it sternly, but her lips were smiling and her eyes were warm. He touched her cheek with his knuckle, and whispered, "Watch yourself."

She tilted her head to one side and looked at him with puzzlement.

The woman EMT leaned out. "Mr. Bowie?"

He held Beth's gaze a second longer before climbing into the ambulance. The doors were shut and the vehicle pulled away. He hadn't had time to finish what he'd been about to say to her.

He told himself that it was just as well.

"As I've said, Ms. Collins, Mr. Brady is *in a meeting.*" His lofty assistant had lost her patience with Beth. "As soon as it concludes, I'll give him a message."

"Which he will ignore."

"He can't just up and walk out of the boardroom in order to talk to you. He's heading the meeting."

"If he airs that episode tonight, his head will *roll.* And probably yours, too."

So it had gone for the hour and a half that Beth had been in the ER waiting room, calling Brady's office at fifteen-minute intervals and being given the same spiel. She'd also called Richard's cell number repeatedly, but it had gone directly to voice mail each time, and he hadn't responded to her appeals for him to call her back.

She hadn't seen John since he'd been driven away in the ambulance. The ER staff courteously but firmly declined to answer her inquiries about Molly's condition since she wasn't family.

Family had shown up in the form of a tall, slender, attractive brunette. Appearing high-strung and harried, she'd strutted up to the desk and introduced herself as Roslyn Bowie. She'd been immediately admitted through a pair of double doors operated from the other side.

Now Beth's agitation level was at its peak over both Brady's assistant's condescension and anxiety over John's daughter. What was taking so long? She'd worried herself into believing that Molly's injury was more serious than originally thought.

Continuing with the assistant where she'd left off, she said, "If I don't speak to your boss because of *your* refusal to put me through, he won't thank you later. In fact, you'll probably be fired within the hour."

During a lengthy pause, the woman reconsidered. "I'll connect you."

Beth's chest expanded with relief, but she thanked the assistant with cool curtness.

After a fifteen-second interval, Brady came on and began by saying, "Stop calling me. You no longer work here."

"You won't either if you air that show tonight."

"It'll be broadcast at ten o'clock eastern time."

"It falls short of telling the whole story, Winston. The police here have a suspect in custody who could be tied to Crissy Mellin's disappearance."

Rather than react with the astonishment Beth had expected, he chuckled. "After all this time, this suspect appeared out of the blue?"

"It may seem that way, but he's been waiting for another blood moon."

"Oh, please."

"He was arrested about two hours ago. He had an adolescent girl in an isolated, corrugated tin shed. She was bound. He was preparing for some kind of sick ritual involving surgical instruments and a home tattoo kit. It was to have been conducted tonight during the lunar eclipse."

"Isn't the timing of his arrest awfully convenient for you and your blood moon theory?"

"You think I'm making this up?"

"It did occur to me."

"In the interest of time, I'll overlook the insult to my integrity. I did, however, anticipate your skepticism. You can speak to a sheriff's office detective named Glen Derby. I've obtained his cell phone number for you. He'll verify everything I've told you."

He thought it over. "Why do you think this guy has any connection to Mellin's abduction?"

"He fits the profile."

"So do hundreds of other whack jobs. You don't know it's the same guy, do you?"

"No, not yet, but—"

"Is there evidence that links him to the Mellin case?"

"There hasn't been time to gather evidence. Give it a few days, a week. Withhold the episode while this suspect is being investigated."

"And miss the blood moon angle tonight? No way."

"Would it make a difference if I told you that the victim this time was John Bowie's daughter? There's a connection for you. Doesn't it sound as though—"

"Sounds like this guy is a copycat, who saw the fabulous irony in taking that burnout detective's kid. There may be a story there worth exploring for a future episode, but nothing you've told me changes my mind about the Mellin story. It only makes me question your objectivity and validates having fired you."

"*Crisis Point* is supposed to be a documentary. As is, this episode doesn't include the police malfeasances that prompted Billy Oliver to take his own life. Now you want to also omit that police have in custody an individual who, at the very least, is a person of interest."

"Hello?" he said, mocking. "None of that has been proven. You still haven't convinced me that our story is *wrong*. It airs tonight at ten," he said brusquely. "That's final. Now stop bugging my assistant. Go away."

When he clicked off, Beth growled at her phone, "I hope they boil you in oil."

"Whew. Harsh."

She looked up to find John standing in front of her. She surged to her feet.

"How is she?"

"She's going to be okay."

She flattened her hand on her chest. "Good to hear. It was taking so long, I got worried that it was more than a concussion."

"They took X-rays and did a CT scan. No cracks or

depressions in her skull, no brain bleeds. All good news, but every test…Well, you know how it goes in a hospital. Hurry up and wait."

"Are they releasing her?"

"No, they're keeping her here for at least twenty-four hours. Just as a precaution. They advised me to leave for a while so she'll settle and rest."

Hesitantly Beth said, "I saw Roslyn when she arrived."

"At first Molly was glad to see her, but it wasn't long before Roslyn switched from concerned mother mode to full-blown Roslyn. The staff is running her out, too."

"You look exhausted."

"Must say, I am." He took her elbow and turned her toward the exit. "Since Mitch has Mutt covered, I booked a room in a hotel nearby. Nothing fancy. A shower and bed. I'll sleep a few hours before coming back to check on Molly one more time before driving all the way out to the fishing camp."

Beth said. "I don't remember when I last slept."

"Me either."

On the way to the hotel, she briefed him on her conversation with Winston Brady. "He'll be sorry," John said. "Whatever the fallout, the jackass deserves it."

"Yes, but Max and I are still credited as the producers. There go our reputations down the drain, and there's nothing I can do about it unless Professor Wallace confesses between now and ten o'clock eastern."

He commiserated, then told her that while giving Roslyn time alone with Molly, he'd called Gayle Morris and the detectives in Shreveport and Jackson and brought them up to date.

"They were shocked by the news that Molly had been abducted, but excited that Wallace's capture, the dark web slant, gives them a new, strong lead."

He'd also spoken to Derby, who'd told him that they were looking hard at Tom Barker as a suspect in the execution-style murder of Frank Gray.

"Derby told me that Barker is schmoozing the SO. He laid it on thick what a loss the ogre's death was to the CAP unit as a whole, and to him in particular. He offered to help with the investigation in any way he could. Of course he also made a big deal of my gun being found within yards of the crime scene."

"Aren't you worried about that?"

"No, but I hate myself for missing that Barker had it in his possession. I thought I'd left him lying on my living room floor unarmed. He must've had that pistol hidden somewhere to use on an as-needed basis. In my house, in his car. I'm sure he's held on to it, waiting for an opportunity to frame me for something."

"Why would he kill his right-hand heavy?"

"The ogre swore to Mitch and me that he'd been roped into taking part in Barker's absurd scheme. He'd predicted that it wasn't going to work, but Barker was insistent they carry it out. When Barker found him in the shed, if the ogre dared to say, 'I told you so,' that would have made Barker livid.

"Ogre made the fatal mistake of turning his back on him. And to Barker the ogre's death worked to his advantage. He could frame me for it, and all his dirty secrets died with the ogre. Or so he thought."

"Oh?"

He grinned. "Before we left them, Mitch and I took both their phones. They're in the trunk of my car along with their weapons. As the ogre handed his over, he told us he'd been recording his conversations with Barker. Just in case he ever needed an out. To use as leverage in a plea deal, he said.

"Those chats should make for some interesting listening to Derby and the PD superintendent. But Derby doesn't plan to bring Barker in until they have something substantive, and then Derby wants to blindside him with it. I told him I thought that was a good tactic. Give Barker enough rope."

Before they arrived at the hotel, he checked in with Mitch, who told him that he and Mutt had gone fishing, and that Mutt had caught more than he had. He agreed to hang around until dark and see to Mutt's needs before he left.

As expected, the hotel wasn't luxurious, but with the drapery drawn, the room was conducive to sleeping and the shower held promise.

But the instant the door closed with a solid click behind them, John placed his hands on her shoulders, turned her around, and fastened his mouth to hers with heat, urgency, and possessiveness.

She acknowledged that his arousal was an outlet for all the emotions he'd experienced last night and had had to keep under strict control. She didn't care. She'd been containing herself, too.

Without breaking the kiss, they struggled out of their jackets and tossed them aside. He backed her into the wall, his hands going immediately to her breasts, his strong fingers kneading, palms grinding against the centers, which were already raised in anticipation.

Feeling that reaction from her, he made a darkly carnal sound and rapidly undid and discarded her top. Reaching around her, he unhooked her bra and pulled it off, then ducked his head and drew her nipple into his mouth.

Her head dropped back. Her back arched away from the wall, while, blindly, she fumbled with his belt buckle, then with the metal buttons of his fly. Finding him rigid, she stroked him through his underwear.

He groaned a swear word, his head came up, and his eyes seared hers. "Finally gonna have our afternoon rodeo?"

"Yes, please."

He unbuttoned his shirt far enough to pull it over his head, while she shimmied out of her jeans and kicked them away. He put his hands on her bottom and squeezed as he looked down and admired first her bare breasts, now marked by his scruff, and then lower at the triangle of lace at the juncture of her thighs.

He whispered another curse, as, in one swift movement, he shoved his jeans past his hips. He lifted her onto his thighs, moved aside the leg of her underpants, and thrust into her. The raw lustiness of that caused her to gasp. There'd been no hesitation, no qualification. At this moment in time, the coupling seemed essential to both of them.

They moved against each other as though competing to see which of them could take more, give more. Then he hitched her up higher onto him, made an imperative thrust, and abruptly stopped moving.

"Kiss me," he said hoarsely. "Now."

Their mouths connected hotly. Her hands sought purchase on his back. He stayed as he was, but rhythmically rocked against the top of her sex until her breath caught and then ceased altogether. Unparalleled pleasure spiraled up from that spot, overtaking her body, her entire being. Her contractions around him became stronger.

His entire body tensed; he gave a sharp cry. She felt his pulsing in the innermost part of her, like an extension of her heartbeat.

Eventually their breathing returned to some semblance of normal. He separated from her, but caught her against his chest as she sagged toward him.

Together, they sank to the floor and sat facing, limbs loose and entangled, hands languidly caressing, faces flushed and nuzzling.

After a time, he stood and pulled her up with him. She followed docilely as he led her into the bathroom, where he turned on the shower. They lathered themselves, then each other. She was washing his chest when she addressed the triangle below his Adam's apple. "You haven't asked, but I'm on the pill."

"I should have pulled out."

"I doubt I would have let you."

He placed his index finger beneath her chin and tipped her head up to meet his gaze. "I doubt I could have."

That began another round of kissing and caressing with soapy hands. No part of one escaped exploration by the other. They emptied the squeeze bottle of shower gel.

Finally the water ran cool. They got out and dried and returned to the bedroom. They got into bed and lay spooned. His sex was heavy and full against her bottom. He placed his arm across her waist and cupped her breast.

They were quiet, replete, drowsy.

On the brink of sleep, she said, "Are you asleep?"

"Um-huh."

She smiled. "I've been meaning to ask what you meant when you said to me, 'Watch yourself.'"

She knew that he was still awake and had heard. But he didn't respond.

Chapter 37

John had set an alarm for four-thirty. Before returning to the hospital, they stopped at a restaurant and stoked themselves on steak dinners with all the trimmings to make up for the meals they had missed.

Molly had been moved from the ER into a private room. John went in to see her alone, but returned ten minutes later. "She's doing better. Vision is improving. They're controlling the headache with medication, and she's still being hydrated with an IV."

"That all sounds positive," Beth said.

"She'd like to meet you."

"Now? Is this a good time? I mean, is she up to it?"

He gave a wry smile. "More than up to it, she's insistent."

He ushered her into the room. Molly was half-reclined on the bed, her hair a wreath of dark curls against the pillow. What Beth hadn't noticed from seeing her only at a distance was the sprinkling of freckles across her cheeks. "Hi," she said.

"Hello, Molly." She walked over to the bed and smiled down at her. "I'm Beth."

She grinned. "I've heard about you. You came down here from New York to see my dad."

"Well..." Beth glanced at John, who kept his expression a blank canvas. "I came hoping to interview him for research."

"Hmm."

Beth sensed Molly's women's intuition had kicked in, because she looked back and forth between them with a knowing smile. Then to Beth, she said, "I'm going to New York after high school."

"Your dad told me. To attend a very prestigious art school."

"Do you know it?"

"Oh, yes. I've never been inside, but I've passed it many times."

"Is it totally sick?"

"Sick?"

"That means good," John said.

Beth laughed and said to Molly, "Yes. Totally sick."

"My art teacher says I should apply for a scholarship."

"That's a strong vote of confidence in your talent."

For the next fifteen minutes they chatted. Molly was avidly curious about her life in the city. No sooner would Beth answer a question than she was asked another.

During a pause, Beth changed the tenor of their conversation. "You endured a terrifying experience last night, Molly. I'm sorry it went so far before we got to you."

"Dad told me that if it wasn't for you figuring out that

it was that professor, he probably would never have seen me again." Her lower lip trembled. John walked over and smoothed back one of her curls.

"Hey, stop thinking about what could have been. I do enough of that for both of us."

Although tears still threatened, she gave him a shaky smile, then said to Beth, "Anyway, thank you."

"I'm grateful we got there in time, although I don't think Professor Wallace stood a chance against your dad and Mitch."

Molly grinned at that, but it dissolved when her cell phone chirped, and she saw the text. "Ugh. Mom's on her way, and she's bringing the loser."

"Do you want me to head them off and send them away?"

"And start a war? Thanks, Dad, but no. I'll tell them my eyes are wonky and making me seasick. Something like that so they won't stay long."

Beth said, "I'll say goodbye now and give you two some time alone." She patted Molly's arm. "It was lovely to meet you. I only wish the circumstances had been different. Take care of yourself. Good luck with the scholarship application."

"Send good vibes," Molly said.

"I promise to." To John, she said, "I'll be downstairs in the main lobby. Take your time."

After that, he made several trips in and out of Molly's room, fetching an extra blanket, getting her a cup of ice cream, going back for a ginger ale when the ice cream didn't sit well. Recognizing these errands as delay tactics, he poured the ginger ale over a cup of ice, then sat down on the edge of the bed and took Molly's hand.

"For real, how are you doing?"

"Did the detective call you?"

"Derby? Yes. He'll be here at nine o'clock tomorrow morning."

"Do I have to talk to him about it?"

"Do you want to see the professor behind bars?"

Looking miserable, she said, "Of course."

"Then, yes, you must tell Derby everything. But he's a nice guy, and I'll be right here with you."

She turned her head toward the window where the blinds were only partially open. "When I start talking about it, I may lose it."

"Doesn't matter. They have Kleenex," he said, pointing to the box on the nightstand. "You don't have to be brave in front of me, Molly. I already know you're brave. It'll be rough, sure, but it'll also be good for you to talk about it. Don't keep it bottled up. I know what that does to a person. I know what it did to me. It eats you alive."

"That's what the hospital psychologist told me. She came by this afternoon."

"I was told she would. I think it would be a good idea if you continued to see a therapist for a while."

"That would probably be a good idea."

He'd expected her to protest and was heartened by her agreeing to it so readily. "We'll find someone you like and feel comfortable with."

Seeming relieved that the matter had been addressed

and settled, she gave him a sly look from beneath her lashes. "Beth is amazing."

"Yeah, she's smart. Gutsy. You should have seen her in action today. Laying it on thick with the professor. Shoving that car in gear and speeding off in reverse. Taking on the deputies who tried to keep her..." Realizing he was babbling, he stopped, looked at his watch, and overreacted when he saw the time. "I'd better get out of here before your mother and her intended arrive."

"See?"

"What?"

"I say Beth's name, and you get all weird."

"I don't get weird. I don't even know what that means."

She gave him an arch look. "Yes, you do."

Yes, he did, and, in spite of himself, he grinned. "Don't be a smart-ass." He leaned down and kissed her forehead. "You gonna be okay? Honestly. I'll spend the night here if you want me to."

"No, they put something in the IV bag to 'help me relax.' I'm already getting sleepy. Maybe I'll get lucky and conk out before my next visitors get here."

"Good idea. Play possum." He stood but kept her hand in his. "I'll be here early tomorrow morning. Between now and then call me for any reason. Swear."

She crossed her heart. "Swear. You're my go-to person, Dad."

He met Beth in the lobby. As they walked to his car, he recapped Molly's and his conversation.

"She's suffered a trauma," Beth said. "She'll need therapy, more than likely for a while, maybe forever. But you are her mainstay, John. You're her dragon slayer."

"She said I was her go-to."

"See? Told ya." After a moment, she added, "Don't underestimate the value of that. My father never faced down a dragon for me."

"His loss," he said, meaning it. "But after seeing how you responded to the emergency this morning, I don't think you need a dragon slayer. Only a damn fool would mess with you."

They got into the car, but he didn't start it. "Okay if we sit here for a minute? I want to call Derby, see how it's going with Wallace." He placed the call and put it on speaker.

Derby answered and after exchanging hellos, he said, "Regarding Barker, we're pressing to get the ballistics report back on the bullet recovered from Frank Gray. Lab is trying to lift fingerprints off your service weapon, but Barker was smart enough to make that difficult."

"And even if his are recovered, he could explain it by saying he picked it up after I placed it on his desk."

"Right. I think this is going to be a preponderance of evidence case. You and Mitch Haskell are material witnesses. So is everybody who saw you surrender that gun. I think Barker will be sunk; I've just got to figure out how to do it."

"What about Victor Wallace?"

"Oh, he's cute," the detective said. "Just ask him."

"He's playing you?"

"Exactly like you said he would."

"Has he said anything about Crissy Mellin?"

"He asked if he could watch *Crisis Point* tonight. We denied him that privilege. He speculated on where and how her body had been disposed of. He also ventured that Billy Oliver might not have been the guilty party. He asked us if we'd ever considered that someone else had abducted her."

"Did he bring all that up before or after you'd pressed him on it?"

"That's just it, John. Nobody had even mentioned Crissy Mellin to him."

"Another wink," Beth exclaimed. "He's flirting. Please, Detective, if he gives up anything, let me know immediately. I'm hoping to keep that episode from airing, so time is of the essence."

"I'll goad him. If anything comes of it, I'll be in touch."

"Thank you."

John disconnected, then propped his elbow on the steering wheel, cupped his hand over his mouth, and stared through the windshield.

"You've got that dent between your eyebrows," Beth said.

He turned his head and looked at her. "Dent? I don't have a dent."

She smiled over that, waited a moment, then looked down into her lap. "John, this is my deadline, not Derby's, not yours. You've got time to finagle Wallace. You don't have to be under pressure to do so tonight."

"What was it you said to me earlier?" He reached across and raised her chin with his fingertip. "Don't be stupid."

She whispered, "Thank you."

"You're welcome."

Then she said, "I broke your concentration. What were you thinking so hard about?"

"I was thinking that maybe Carla Mellin would be willing to have a face-to-face with Wallace, and that if she did, it would rattle him."

He gauged Beth's reaction and saw that she favored it. "She told us to stay away from her unless we'd caught the person who took Crissy from her. Of course, we don't know with absolute certainty, but—"

"It feels right. And the way he's—as you said—flirting with us about it? These guys, these sociopaths, never want to get caught, but deep down they want to boast." Suddenly energized, he looked at his watch. "Seven-forty. Carla's new shift, she'll be off at eight."

"Locally, the show airs in an hour and twenty minutes."

"Maybe we can talk her into leaving twenty minutes early." He had Carla's cell number in his contacts and made the call. It went straight to voice mail.

"Do you have the number of the clinic?" Beth asked.

Within seconds, he did. A man answered. John asked to speak with Carla.

"Today's her day off."

"Thanks." He disconnected.

Beth said, "We'll try her at home."

"It'll be harder than launching a beach assault," he said, but he started the car.

John broke every speed limit getting to Carla's house, which looked even more forlorn beneath a sky that was approaching full darkness. The full moon had risen, but wispy clouds threatened to keep it from being the vivid, spectacular blood moon that had been predicted.

They walked to her front door. Yellowish light filtered through window shades in a corner room, which John assumed was a bedroom. TV light flickered in the living room where they'd talked with Carla on their previous meeting. He pressed the doorbell, and as footsteps approached, he muttered, "Here goes nothing."

The porch light came on above them. As before, Carla opened the door only a crack and peered out at them. "Didn't your mamas teach you any manners? Like showing up at somebody's house without an invitation."

Beth said, "You did invite us, Carla. On the condition we had the person who took Crissy in custody. We believe we do. He's being questioned as we speak."

That took her by surprise. Mistrustfully, her eyes sawed back and forth between them.

"There's a lot to tell, Carla, and we're very, very short on time," Beth continued. "In little more than an hour from now the episode on Crissy is going to air. I'm still trying to halt it. I came to ask for your help."

"Help how? And why would I help at all? I told you I don't give a damn about your professional reputation or that of your TV show. Who is this person anyway?"

"His name is Victor Wallace. Last night, he abducted John's daughter, Molly."

Carla shifted her hostile gaze to John, who said, "We rescued Molly and captured him before he did more than terrify her and give her a concussion, but he had some grisly activities planned for her tonight that would have resulted in her death. I'm taking it real personally.

"We've got him for kidnapping Molly. I'd love to attach him to Crissy's abduction, too. As to why you would help? If we can nail Wallace for it, Billy Oliver would be vindicated."

She screwed her mouth up into a frown of indecision. "I'll think about it." She tried to close the door, but John planted his foot in the narrow opening to prevent it.

Beth said, "Once that program airs, Billy will be regarded as the deviant monster next door who, when caught, took the easy way out rather than receive the punishment he deserved. Is that the legacy you wish for him?"

"It could be retracted."

"But the seeds of doubt would have been sown. Too often retractions are overlooked because they're not as sensational as the first news flash. You know that."

Her lips pursed tighter; then she said, "What are you asking me to do, specifically?"

"Face Victor Wallace," John said. "Accuse him of robbing your daughter of a long life. Accuse him of robbing you of her. It may crack him."

"'May,'" she huffed. "I doubt it."

"For godsake, isn't it worth a try?"

Carla looked at John with scorn. "Who are you doing this for? Crissy, Billy, me, or *her*?" She hitched her chin toward Beth. "I'm not stupid, you know."

No, but you're meaner than hell. He forcibly tamped down his temper, which would get him nowhere with her. Candor had worked before. "You told the people Beth works with that you suspected she and I were sleeping together.

That was a crappy thing to do. But so what if we are? That has nothing to do with what happened to Crissy, or to my daughter.

"For terrorizing her, I want to put Victor Wallace away for a long, long time. I was able to stop him before he killed Molly, but I failed Crissy. For whatever he did to her, I want to put him away for *life*."

"That's your job, Mr. Detective. Not mine. I can't help you."

Before she could close the door on them, it was pulled open wider. "I can help." The young woman standing just beyond Carla's shoulder said, "I'll face him."

Chapter 38

Tom Barker assessed Victor Wallace through the one-way window. "So that's the professor I've been hearing so much about."

"That's him," Derby said.

Barker had invited himself to the sheriff's office and had talked his way back to the hallway of interrogation rooms where he could observe the suspect through a glass pane. Derby resented Barker's intrusion, but there was little he could do about it.

Their criminal cases often overlapped, so the two departments had reciprocity. Barker had a right, even a duty, to be here, but Derby was having a hard time being cordial to the man he believed had killed Frank Gray less than twenty-four hours earlier.

Derby had assigned Wallace to a pair of his best interrogators. He'd told them, "He looks and acts like Mr. Rogers. Don't be deceived. Bowie said he likes to talk. Let him."

So far, Wallace had remained unflappable. He didn't answer any questions except the most mundane. Instead he rambled on a number of subjects, often mentioning the popularity of his lectures and the increasing interest in his book.

Barker said now, "I was expecting someone more sinister."

"He's sinister, all right," Derby said. "He was going to slice and dice John Bowie's daughter."

"I heard you caught him red-handed with the girl. Why are you giving him the third degree?"

"The Crissy Mellin case."

Barker gave a start. "Crissy Mellin?"

"Bowie thinks chances are good the professor here was the perp and that he's been waiting three years to do it again, to coincide with the blood moon."

Tom's distorted features twitched with amusement; then he chuckled. "Just goes to show how far 'round the bend Bowie has gone since that case. To this day, he refuses to admit that the Oliver kid was guilty. I mean, Christ, the boy wrote a confession to killing her and disposing of her!

"And I was this close," he said, indicating an inch with his fingers, "to getting him to tell me where he had dumped her body. I told him if he gave that up, it might be a bargaining chip he could cash in at his sentencing, that it would be a demonstration of his remorse, and so on. I sent him back to his cell to think it over. You know what happened."

He affected sadness as he shook his head. "But Bowie had been trying to steer the investigation in the wrong direction. He absolutely would not acknowledge his error. His downfall started then, and it's continued on a greased slope. Now, three years later, he's completely irrational. Blood moon? Give me a break. That's crazy. He's surly and unreliable. Can't control his temper.

"You only have to look at my face to see how violent he can be. I've given him ample opportunities to turn himself around, but after this attack on me, he gave me no choice. I had to let him go. Not just for my own safety, but for the safety of anyone else in the department who crossed him. Like Frank Gray."

Lowering his voice, he moved closer to Derby. "Those two couldn't stand the sight of each other. Bowie had been fired. He had nothing to lose by killing his arch-enemy."

Derby held up his hand. "Tom, maybe you shouldn't say anything more without an attorney present."

"*Attorney?*"

"I know about the trap you set for Bowie last night."

He looked chagrined. "I'll admit that wasn't by the book, but Bowie had managed to avoid arrest for days. When he called, accusing me of abducting his daughter of all things, Frank hatched this plan to draw him out."

"It was the ogre's idea?"

"Yes. Frank was, well, I don't want to speak disrespectfully, but he stepped over the line sometimes. I was leery of this plot he hatched, but Frank was convinced that it would work as nothing else would. 'Bowie's nuts about that kid,' he said. So," Barker said with a shrug, "I went along. I regret that decision now. Frank's brilliant plan got him killed."

Looking thoughtful, Derby tugged on his earlobe. "I've known John for a long time. I can't see him shooting an unarmed man in the back of his head."

"You didn't see him last night. Whew! When he discovered that we didn't have his daughter, he went apeshit, knocked me out cold. I don't know what happened after that. I regained consciousness. Went looking for Frank. But Bowie's place is almost uninhabitable unless you're an alligator or a water fowl."

"You didn't check the shed?"

"Didn't even see it. It's dark as hell out there. I stumbled around, but finally gave up the search, thinking that maybe Bowie and Haskell had taken Frank with them when they cleared out. When I learned this morning how he'd been found, it made me sick."

"I know that feeling," Derby said dryly.

"Derby?"

He and Barker turned to see the subject of their conversation walking down the hallway toward them.

"Well, well, look who the cat dragged in."

Bowie ignored Barker and spoke directly to Derby. "I need to see you immediately. Alone. It's about him." He angled his head toward the interrogation room, where the professor seemed to be pontificating to the deputies. "Back here." He turned and walked away in the direction from which he'd come.

Without a word or backward glance at Barker, Derby followed Bowie's long strides. Barker hurried to catch up. Derby said, "He said alone, Tom."

"But you can't just let him—"

"For the present, I can. I'll get back to you."

When John pushed open the door to the empty office he'd temporarily commandeered, Beth was saying into her cell phone, "I hope you'll listen to this message, Richard. Brady is ignoring the voice mails I've left him. The Crissy Mellin story has taken a shocking twist. She's alive, and sitting not five feet from me. She's alive and well. It's seventeen minutes to air time. I advise you get that message to Brady."

As she clicked off, John met her gaze. She acknowledged his and Derby's entrance with a nod, but John knew the other man hadn't noticed. He was staring with stupefaction at the young woman with strawberry-blond hair. She and her mother were sitting side by side in metal folding chairs. Crissy was composed, Carla less so.

After the stunning discovery that Crissy was alive, John and Beth had hustled them into his car. The first thing he'd asked was, "Were you even kidnapped, Crissy?"

"Yes, Mr. Bowie."

Carla had declared, "It's not against the law to pretend you're dead. I looked it up."

His angry response had been to tell her to shut up. Looking across at Crissy, to whom Beth had yielded the passenger seat, he'd said, "I've lived in hell over you for three years. Three *years*. Why didn't you tell me? Tom Barker? *Somebody?*"

Before Crissy could say a word, Carla had pounced. "I had to protect my girl from that psycho, that's why. By the time she escaped, Billy Oliver was already dead. There was nothing we could do for him.

"But the real culprit was still out there. Her identity had been blasted all over the media. We were afraid he'd come after her. Keeping her hidden was the only way she would be safe."

John had experienced warring emotions. The girl was alive. She wasn't dead from tortures he'd had recurring nightmares about. But he'd had those nightmares because of their ruse, which had cost him dearly. He felt he had a right to be at least borderline outraged.

He'd taken out his anger on other motorists who didn't get out of his way fast enough. During that hair-raising drive from Carla's house to the sheriff's office, Crissy had talked him and Beth through her ordeal.

Now he'd summoned Derby to listen to it. He made quick work of the introductions, then said to Crissy, "Tell Mr. Derby what you told Beth and me."

In the first few minutes, she confirmed that she'd been abducted but had escaped five days later. Derby wanted to know, as John had, why she hadn't come forward as soon as she'd escaped. She explained her and Carla's reasoning, then said, "I understand why y'all would be mad at us for that, but I was so scared."

Derby accepted that explanation for now. "How did it happen?"

"Mom asked me to go to the convenience store. It had been raining all day, but it had stopped, so I decided to walk. Billy came out of his house to see where I was off to. I asked him to come along, but he didn't want to go because of the weather. We parted ways at his house. The last time I saw him, he was going inside."

She told them that after she'd picked up the few items at the store and was headed home, a car had pulled to a stop beside her. The driver had lowered his window and told her she'd left something behind on the counter.

"He got out of his car, and that's pretty much all I remember until I came to, lying on the floor in a building with corrugated tin walls. My hands and feet had zip ties around them."

John looked over at Derby. "Sound familiar?"

Looking grim, Derby signaled for Crissy to continue. She described the scene in which they'd discovered Molly in detail down to the plastic sheeting lining the floor and the workbench with its array of surgical instruments. "He sterilized them each time he came to bring me a bottle of water and something to eat. Usually an energy bar."

John interrupted. "He told Molly her great moment was going to be that night during the blood moon. But he kept you for days after the November seventh one. Why do you think that was?"

"I don't know, except that occasionally he would talk to himself, saying that everything had to be perfect. There were times when he seemed very frustrated, not so much with me, but with himself." She hesitated, then added, "I think he was trying to work up the courage to kill me."

"Did he try to conceal his identity, wear a mask?" Derby asked.

"No."

"And he wasn't someone you knew or recognized?"

"No."

Carla barked an angry sound. "Don't you think I would have told you if I'd known who he was?"

John broke in. "I seriously doubt you would have, Carla.

While officers, including Mitch Haskell and me, were still out beating the bushes for Crissy, you didn't tell us she was alive. Now I understand your reason, but your self-serving silence had a far-reaching and detrimental effect on a lot people."

She folded her arms over her middle and turned her head away from him.

A taut silence followed. Eventually Derby cleared his throat. "Crissy, while you were captive, did he molest you?"

"No. I was afraid he would, but he didn't. If anything, he treated me like…like something he cherished."

Derby asked her a series of other pertinent questions, then asked how she'd managed to escape. She told them that her captor arrived one night carrying two duffel bags, one in each hand.

"He'd never brought them before, so I knew then that that was the night he would kill me. Because his hands were full, he pushed the door closed with his heel. Then he came over to me, set the bags down, and untied my feet so I could go to the bathroom."

"Bathroom?" Derby asked.

"A bucket in the corner," she said. "It was humiliating. Anyway, I went over to it. He'd set the duffel bags down and had gone back to relock the door. I knew my life depended on seizing that moment when his back was turned. I grabbed the bucket, rushed over, and swung it as hard as I could at his head. I felt the jolt all the way up my arm. He lost his balance and fell, banging his head on the floor. I didn't wait to see if I'd knocked him out, or even killed him. I just pulled open the door and ran like hell.

"It was dark as pitch, no lights anywhere, raining lightly.

I was running blind and probably went in circles, but I didn't allow myself to stop. I didn't even see a road for the longest time, and then I kept it in sight but stayed off it. I was afraid he would come up behind me in his car.

"At dawn, I was able to orient myself and started making my way in the general direction of home. But during the day, I was afraid he'd be searching for me, so I hid behind a dumpster at the back of an office building and waited until it got dark again. It took me four days to walk the rest of the way home, but I stayed out of sight as much as I could."

John thought of a question he hadn't yet asked her. "Could you have found your way back to that building? It's immaterial now, but I just wonder."

"No, Mr. Bowie. I swear. That was another reason we didn't tell. I'd gotten so turned around, and it was far. I never could have shown you where he'd kept me."

"In the meantime, she'd have been an open target," Carla contributed.

When no one spoke, Crissy continued. "It was the middle of the night when I got to the trailer park. Our front door was locked. I knocked. When Mom opened the door and saw me, I looked such a fright, she screamed. I was still in the clothes I'd had on when I went to the convenience store, and I hadn't eaten. Whenever I spotted an outdoor faucet, and no one was around, I drank from it."

Looking straight at John, she said, "I know I should have let you know. I'm sorry for all the trouble I caused. But I've lived in constant fear of him coming after me, right up till I heard you and Ms. Collins tell my mom that you'd caught him."

Nobody said anything or moved until Derby stirred himself. "Do you think you can identify him, Miss Mellin?"

"Definitely. No question. He's as real to me tonight as he was when I hit him with that bucket."

Beth said softly, "Show him, Crissy."

The young woman extended her arm toward the detective and pushed up her sleeve to her elbow, revealing a red crescent moon tattoo on the inside of her forearm. She said, "He didn't leave me with just this memento. He tattooed memories of him on my brain that will be with me forever."

The five of them left the borrowed office and trooped down the hallway toward the interrogation room. Barker was pacing, and when he saw them, he said, "It's about damn time." Then he recognized Crissy and Carla Mellin. He gaped like a fish on dry land. "What...what the hell...?"

"It's rather obvious, isn't it, Tom?" John said. "I don't think you're going to enjoy your TV debut tonight."

"He's not," Beth said, beaming. She held up her phone so John could see the text. "Richard skipped over Brady and went straight to the top. Two minutes from now, TV audiences will be seeing a rerun of a *Crisis Point* episode, not the one on Crissy."

He would have liked to celebrate her victory with a hug, but their attention was drawn to the window, where Crissy was talking quietly with Derby. "That's him," they heard her say.

"You're sure?"

"Positive. Can we listen in?"

Derby signaled another deputy to open up a microphone inside the room.

"—really is a phenomenon that shouldn't be missed. It begins here at ten-fifty-seven P.M. Totality will be at one-fifty-eight A.M. Surely Derby wouldn't deny me seeing that. You could escort me up to the roof."

One of the deputies shifted in his chair. "How'd you lure Molly Bowie into your car, Victor?"

"It's Professor Wallace," he said loftily. "I'm going to file a formal complaint against this department over your maltreatment of me."

Crissy said, "His voice is exactly as I remember. Can I go in?"

"Honey," Carla said, "I don't think—"

"I want to confront him, Mom. He had all the power before. Not anymore."

Without further discussion, Derby reached around her and opened the door. "Victor, there's someone here to see you."

Crissy walked into the room.

The professor stared at her with disbelief and dismay, and then with fury. He stood up, his placid features becoming congested with malice. "You. You ruined it!" It was a high-pitched scream more than a shout. "Because of you, they wouldn't let me into the inner sanctum! I, a professor. I who is more intelligent than the rest of them put together. I who wrote the book on it!"

He continued the rant long after Crissy had calmly turned her back on him and walked out, leaving him in the charge of his interrogators who had to physically restrain him.

Chapter 39

The professor's outburst amounted to an admission of guilt, although unintentional. Crissy made arrangements with Derby to return in the morning to provide an official statement; then they were released to go.

Barker put up a monumental protest over John's freedom to simply walk out. His tirade turned nasty when he got in Derby's face and asked just what kind of operation he was running here.

"I'm glad you asked," Derby calmly replied. "This operation investigates homicides that take place in the parish. Since you were one of the last people to see the ogre alive, I was going to bring you in for questioning. Thanks for saving me the trouble. This way, Tom," he said, smiling as he and another deputy led him, sputtering invectives, into an interrogation room.

John had the satisfaction of witnessing that scene; then he and Beth left to drive Crissy and Carla home. On the way, the latter said little. Her aspect remained defensive.

As they got out of the car, Crissy thanked Beth for the

role she'd played in identifying Victor Wallace. "If it weren't for you…" She choked up and couldn't finish.

"I'm just glad you've been liberated," Beth said. "At long last."

She hung back while John walked the two women to their front door, where Crissy bade him good night and apologized again for bringing so much hardship on him. He said, "I'm grateful you're alive. That's what matters most." She smiled at him shyly before slipping inside.

He was left on the porch with Carla, whom he faced squarely. "I have something for you." He reached into his jacket pocket and took out the thumb drive, which he'd removed earlier from its secret holder in his boot.

He took her hand, laid it in her palm, and closed her fingers around it. "If you ever doubt how much I anguished over Crissy, Billy, Gracie, read through all that. It represents over three years of my life."

She pulled her hand from his. "Let me ask you something, Detective Bowie. Fearing for your daughter's life—"

"I was. Last night at this time."

"You were fortunate enough to catch that degenerate in time. I wasn't. We didn't know who he was or when he might reappear. In my position, how far would you have gone to protect your daughter?"

It was a sobering thought. He would ponder it. But on some other night. He was taking the rest of this one off.

"John, look! It's started." Beth took his hand and dragged him along behind her as she ran through the woods from the camo garage to the clearing in front of the fishing cabin. Earth's shadow had begun to appear on the moon. "It won't be total for a while yet."

Looking up, he said, "Wallace got his hoped-for clear night. Too bad the only thing he'll see overhead is the ceiling of his jail cell."

As soon as John opened the cabin door, Mutt leaped across the threshold, obviously having urgent business to attend to outside.

John called the nurses' station on Molly's ward and was told she'd been soundly sleeping and that her vitals were excellent. "If she wakes up, remind her that she can call me at any time and that I'll be there first thing in the morning for sure."

He then called Mitch and started by asking him, "Are you sitting down?"

He gave him a condensed version of everything that had transpired since they'd last seen each other.

When he finished, Mitch was practically speechless. "John, would you have ever thought it? That she was alive, I mean."

"Honestly, no. Hoped, but you know how these disappearances usually end. Remains are found, sometimes years later. I thought that's what would happen here."

"Me too." Mitch then asked how Molly was doing.

"She was a little weepy when I left her tonight, but she's as okay as she can be. It'll take some time and therapy."

"She's got you. That's the main thing."

"Thank you again for today, Mitch. Actually for all the days I was…not myself."

"No thanks necessary."

"No, they are. Thanks for always being there."

"Are you getting sloppy on me?"

"Hell, no. It's just that I owe you more than I can ever repay."

"Okay. Tell you what. We'll be square if you get me through the christening and after-party without me killing my mother-in-law."

"Tall order."

"Tell me." They laughed, then, after a short silence that spoke volumes, Mitch said, "Later, bro," and clicked off.

While he'd been on the phone, Beth had uncorked a bottle of wine. With it and two mismatched glasses in her hands, she said, "Do you mind watching?"

"After the buildup it's had, I wouldn't miss it."

He carried two of the game table chairs outside and set them up just beyond the steps. But they only used one of the chairs. He held Beth in his lap as they sipped at their wine—he didn't have the heart to tell her he wasn't a big fan of wine. However, it did seem suitable to the occasion.

Mutt lay at John's feet. They watched the eclipse through its totality when the moon turned into a bright orange disk like the one John had seen on TV. Shortly after, he whispered into Beth's hair, "I'd rather be looking at you."

Without any objection from her, he stood and carried her into the house. He ordered Mutt to his bed, then went into his bedroom and shut the door behind them.

They undressed quickly and got between the sheets. Facing each other, he gathered her closer and worked his knee between her thighs. "Gotta be said that this is more comfortable than up against the wall."

"Hmm," she hummed. "But that had merit. In fact, it was thrilling."

"Oh yeah?"

"Your spontaneity was rather...barbaric."

He arched an eyebrow and gave her a lazy grin. "That good, huh? How good?"

She rolled her eyes. "You're asking me to rate your performance?"

"Well, a guy likes to know how he did. His self-esteem hinges on it."

She laughed, then swept her lips across his soft chest hair as she ran her hand down his rib cage, over the ridge of his hip bone, and closed her fingers around his erection.

"You rated high," she said, speaking in rhythm with her stroking. "Waaay up there. If there were a chart, you'd be off it."

He swore under his breath. "Not too much, Beth. I'm about to burst."

"We haven't done anything yet."

"You haven't. While you were moon gazing, I was otherwise occupied."

"Doing what?"

"Reciting the alphabet over and over. Counting backward from one thousand. Twice. Wondering how soon I could be inside you again."

With bedroom eyes, she looked up into his face. "I've been wondering that myself." Withdrawing her hand from him, she raised it to her mouth and sucked a bead of moisture off her thumb.

Resorting to near-barbarism, he kicked off the covers

and drew her across him. She came up onto her knees, then sank down on him and began rocking her hips forward and back.

"No, no, no, no." He angled himself up, bringing them face-to-face, and bracketed her hips between his hands to hold her still. "Not yet."

Her eyes were closed. She moaned, "Oh God, John, why?"

"I don't want to skip the foreplay."

She opened her eyes, looking surprised, and whispered, "Really?"

"Both times have been incredible. Wild, spontaneous, barbaric. Impatient on my part."

"No less impatient on mine."

"I'm not complaining, God knows. But I want to exercise a little patience this time."

He made a caress of removing his hands from her hips. He brushed back tangled strands of hair, then cupped her face between his palms. Using his thumbs, he traced the arch of her eyebrows and stroked her cheekbones. He outlined her lips with the tip of his index finger. She tried to catch it between her teeth, but he snatched his hand away just in time.

To punish him for that, she rotated her hips as seductively as a belly dancer. He growled, "You're gonna pay for that."

"I hope so. *Soon*. Please."

"You're not enjoying this?"

"Immensely, but—"

"How about this?" He cupped a breast in each hand

and lifted them to his descending mouth. His tongue played upon her nipples, with ardor one moment, with teasing the next, until she was pleading with him to let her move.

His hands left her breasts and moved around to her lust-inspiring ass. He imbedded his fingers in the soft flesh, and held her grafted to him. Burying his face in the curve of her neck, he whispered, "I've wanted to do this since I set eyes on you. Just like this. Ride me, but slow. Slow."

She began to move as much as his strong clasp on her would allow, until he himself couldn't remain still any longer. He placed his hands on the tops of her thighs, ran them up and down several times from her knees to the smooth creases that channeled down to form that enticing vee.

His thumbs slid down those twin pathways, and when they reached the meeting place, he wedged his fingers into the notch where they were coupled and found the heart of her sex, exposed and aroused and inviting him to fondle. Which he did, every movement of his fingers leaving her increasingly restless.

She exhaled a sound close to a sob and then began chanting his name as she ground against his hand. She wrapped her arms around his head and held it firmly against her chest.

He angled his hips up with strong thrusts, now reaching, pressing into her to the point where the feel of that silky heat that gloved him was surpassed only by the intensity of its contractions.

He needed to come or he was going to die, but he wanted to experience her orgasm. At the first jolt of her climax, he threw off his iron control.

He knew he would die remembering that instant of joy.

When he woke up, he couldn't bring himself to move.

Last night, after catching his breath from the mind-blowing sex, he'd reclined and brought Beth down with him. She'd sprawled atop him as bonelessly as a rag doll. Except a lot sexier.

Lethargic himself, he'd kept his eyes closed and allowed himself to enjoy that kind of intimacy. The kind that was perilous to indulge in because it required too much, the kind that was in direct contrast to the I-don't-give-a-damn attitude he'd forged.

But because he'd been unshackled from his bitterness over the Mellin case, he'd been able to relax and savor the aftermath, take pleasure in the weight and feel of Beth's sweet body, the heat that had radiated from her skin, the brush of her hair against his throat, the soft breaths feathering his ear.

Still snugly connected, they had slept.

At some point, she'd sleepily moved to his side, they'd readjusted, and now lay spooned. He wanted to luxuriate in it but knew all the responsibilities of the day were waiting for him.

He pried open his eyes. The filmy, gray light of predawn made everything in the room indistinct. Shapes were undefined, colors were dulled, adding to his feeling that this bed was his and Beth's own desert island, apart from all else, either tangible or conceptual. For a few precious minutes, he remained as he was, watching as the light seeping through the window curtain inevitably became brighter.

He'd promised Molly he would be at the hospital early.

He moved Beth's hair aside and kissed the back of her neck. She murmured and shifted her legs, rubbing them against his. He whispered, "You're free to sleep in and spend the day with Mutt. But I don't know when you could expect me back.

"If Molly is released from the hospital, I want to see her home, not leave her to deal with Roslyn's theatrics alone. Also, Derby will need me when it comes to formally charging the professor. And Barker, I hope."

She reached over her shoulder and covered his mouth with her hand. "Say no more. I'm going with you."

They kissed, then reluctantly got up. "I'll use the other bathroom," she said. "All my stuff is in there."

John let Mutt out, then showered and dressed. By the time Mutt scratched on the front door, his bowls had been filled and were waiting for him in the kitchen, where John had started the coffee. He was pouring the first cup when he heard footsteps coming from the other bedroom.

"Impeccable timing." He turned to pass the coffee to Beth.

But when he saw her face, his motion was arrested. She was looking at him with a mix of apprehension and anxiety. His gaze shifted to the open door of her bedroom where her suitcase was straddling the threshold.

He gave it a long look, then, in a measured move, set the cup of coffee on the counter.

She swallowed hard and wet her lips. "The network wants me back."

He didn't say anything. He didn't move, just stared straight into her woeful eyes.

"I had…uh…There were several messages in various

forms left on my phone overnight. Brady's out. They want me to executive produce *Crisis Point.* They want me to begin with a retelling of Crissy Mellin's story. A comprehensive two-hour episode, over which I'm guaranteed full authority and autonomy."

Somehow, he managed to draw in enough breath to speak. "That's great. Congratulations."

She took a step toward him. "John—"

"When are you leaving?" He glanced at the telltale suitcase. "Immediately, I gather."

"John, it's for Max." She clasped her hands at her waist and made a begging gesture with them. "His final words to me were about the Emmy. He said, 'Get it for me, Beth.'" Tears filled her eyes. "I have no aspirations of accomplishing that, but I owe him this story. I owe it to myself. I can't turn down this opportunity."

"Of course not. Do you need a ride to the airport?"

"Actually, I'm not flying out of New Orleans. The network flew two crews down here to cover the eclipse in totality, which wasn't in New York. They came by private jet. They're regrouping at an FBO about an hour's drive from here. I'm to fly back with them."

"Private jet. Wow. You're getting perks already."

"John, please listen. Don't—"

"I'll drive you to the FBO."

"No. You need to stay with Molly. I thought I could ride to the hospital with you and hire a car from there."

Before his chest cracked opened from internal pressure, he turned his back to her and picked up the cup of coffee now grown cold. "Sounds like a plan."

Epilogue

Six months later

Two things were different. No one was playing pool, and the *MotorTrend* the bartender was thumbing through was a more recent edition.

"Beer, please."

"Brand?"

"I'm not particular."

The bartender uncapped a longneck. As he slid it toward John, he whispered, "Same booth as before. Maybe you'll have better luck this time."

Doubtful, John thought as he picked up the beer and turned toward the booth. He'd thought he'd prepared himself, but his first sight of Beth made his breath catch and his gut clench. He'd hoped that she might have grown a wart on her nose or had an outbreak of adult-onset acne.

No such luck.

Denying that desire was running rampant through him,

he walked over, slid into the booth across from her, and set the bottle of beer on the table.

After a strained silence, she said, "I see you got my message."

"I'm here."

"I purposefully didn't leave my name."

"You didn't before."

"I figured you would know by the meeting place…"

She let that trail off, and, when he failed to comment, she picked up her glass and took a sip from the straw. As she returned the glass to the table, she said, "Mitch invited me to the christening tomorrow."

Peachy. He would be put through this agony two days in a row. He was gonna kill Mitch the Matchmaker.

"They sent me a birth announcement," she said. "When I called to congratulate them, Mitch described baby Andrew as a rock star."

John hated himself for wanting to take a bite of her soft, pink smile. He grumbled, "He's obnoxious over that baby. Brags so much, you can hardly stand to be around him. At least he's shaved off that godawful mustache."

"His bragging must make it difficult for you two to work together every day."

How sly of her to slip that into the conversation. He didn't respond. Instead, he picked up his beer and took a drink.

"Congratulations, John."

"Thanks."

"You should have been heading the CAP unit all along. You've certainly assembled a great team. In addition to bringing Mitch back into the fold, I heard you also talked Isabel Sanchez into joining your ranks."

"Who's feeding you all this information?"

"I heard a lot of local gossip from the production crew. They were here for several weeks, talked to a lot of people who were integral to the restructured Crissy Mellin story."

"For several weeks they were a pain in the ass. They overflowed all the good cafes and caused traffic jams around the police station nearly every day."

"I obtained a permit."

He knew that, but didn't say so.

"I assigned one of our female contributors to interview Carla and Crissy together."

"Did Carla cooperate?"

"She still has a sting, but it's not as vicious. Crissy has..." She searched for a word and used her hands to express it. "Blossomed. It's miraculous."

He took another sip of beer.

"She told me that you call her at least once a week to see how she's getting along."

He shrugged one shoulder. "The least I could do."

Looking exasperated, she sat back against the booth, and for a minute neither of them spoke. Then she said, "You're determined to make this hard, aren't you?"

That angered him. First of all, it was she who was making it hard. It was so damn hard his eyes were probably crossed. Secondly: "Define 'this,' Beth. What is *this*?" Then something occurred to him that made him furious. "Don't tell me you lured me here again in the hope of getting an interview. Is that what you're after?"

She fired back. “If that’s what I was after, I wouldn’t have specifically ordered everyone working on the episode *not* to approach you.”

“Then why did you call and ask me to meet you here?”

“I didn’t want there to be an awkward scene at the christening tomorrow.”

“I wouldn’t have made a scene.”

She looked at him doubtfully, and she was right to. There might have been some monumental awkwardness if she’d walked into the church while he, as godfather, had a vital role to play. Questions to answer, pledges to make. Taken off guard by seeing her there, he probably would have flubbed it all and ruined the observance for Mitch and his family.

“And,” she continued around a unsteady breath, “I wanted to see you, talk to you, and not in the presence of Angela’s slew of kinfolk, which Mitch warned me would all be attending the after-party. John…” She extended her hand, but drew it back without making contact. “I wanted to catch up on you, on everything.”

“Seems to me you are caught up. I can’t think of anything to tell you that you haven’t already heard from your talkative sources.”

Miffed again, she said, “I know that Barker was indicted for murder, was considered a flight risk, denied bail, and is in jail awaiting trial, the date of which is TBD, but it’s not going to be speedy. Meanwhile, his wife has filed for divorce.

“Professor Victor Wallace is also incarcerated, awaiting sentencing on two counts of kidnapping, etcetera, etcetera. Prosecutors are pushing for at least twenty-five years for each count. His wife, oblivious to his hobby, has sold their home. She and her son have moved to Dallas to live with her parents."

"Worse than that, he's had to cancel all his scheduled lectures."

She didn't acknowledge his droll remark, but continued in the same vein she'd been using. "The two previously overlooked suspects in Galveston and Jackson are now awaiting trial. Patrick Dobbs has been granted an appeal. Cougar in Shreveport still hasn't isolated a suspect in the disappearance there, but he's more aggressively working on it.

"You and Mutt have moved closer to town. Molly loves your new house. Even more, she loves getting to spend half of each week there with you."

"Roslyn and I worked out an arrangement. I think the stepdad is happy about it, too."

"Molly has applied for the art school scholarship."

"Fingers crossed."

"She'll get it," Beth said with confidence. "Does Mutt like the new house?"

"He likes any place so long as there's food."

"And you." She paused, then asked, "Have I left out anything?"

"Will you get Max his Emmy?"

He could tell she hadn't expected that question. She said, "We're talking about you."

"Not anymore we're not. What's the status of that two-hour episode?"

"It's done. Finished. It will premier *Crisis Point*'s fall season next month. It remains to be seen about the Emmy, but my goal was to create a program that Max would be proud to have his name attached to. In that I believe I've succeeded.

"In any case, I did my best to tell the story cleanly, without exploitation, but with enough entertainment value and suspense to keep the viewing audience interested."

She paused before saying, "There was no way to tell the story without including you, but it's acknowledged that you had declined to be interviewed. And, just so you know, I left Molly's name out of it. She's identified only as a minor whose parents asked that she remain anonymous."

He was more relieved and touched than he let on. He said simply, "Thank you for that."

She gave a small nod.

"What's next on the *Crisis Point* lineup?"

"I don't know. Once the Mellin episode was finished, I resigned."

That hit him like a right hook he didn't see coming. He actually recoiled. "Resigned? You left the show?"

"Left the network."

"What are you doing now?"

She left him in suspense while she took another sip from the straw. "Remember I told you about the minutiae that make a good show a better one?"

"Small things that give it oomph."

"You do remember."

"I remember everything."

That halted her momentarily. When she continued, he could swear her voice was huskier. "I spent years editing pieces under Max's tutelage, and he was a master. I'm going to shop myself out as a freelance editor. With my credentials,

I should be able to support myself, especially with the lower cost of living down here."

His heart skipped several beats. "Down here?"

"Louisiana has become a big draw for production companies. There's a lot of work. Since I grew up here, I have a feel for the area, which will be valuable to site locators and cinematographers. No more frigid winters. Sweltering summers, yes, but then I like the heat. I'll be able to eat gumbo whenever I'm hungry for it, and work at home in my pajamas. Although I plan to rent a small office for appearance's sake.

"So, you see? There are a lot of advantages to relocating, but the main one is that I'll be near you." She lowered her voice to a whisper. "I love you, John Bowie like the knife."

A fever spread through his entire body. The tops of his ears turned hot. He could feel his pulse in his fingertips.

She scooted forward on the bench, bringing her right up against the edge of the table. "I had to leave you that day. If I hadn't, if I'd stayed without finishing what I had set out to do, I would always have regretted it.

"You would have sensed my regret, and felt guilty for keeping me from achieving my goal, and the guilt would have caused you to shut down." She smiled ruefully. "As you've done anyway."

He took a long drink of the tepid beer because his mouth had gone so dry. Returning the bottle to the table, he said, "I haven't shut down."

"No? Since you got here, you've addressed my chin, my shoulder, my earring, my breasts."

"Only because your hands were making circles in front of them to illustrate 'blossomed.'"

"The point is, you haven't looked directly at *me.*"

He did then. He looked at her fiercely. Leaning forward, bringing their faces close, he said, "I look at you directly all the fucking time. Daylight or dark, sunny or cloudy, on the job, on days off, in daydreams, in wet dreams, I'm seeing your face, and it's been maddening, infuriating as hell, and bloody damned torture."

Her eyes clouded with unshed tears. "Why didn't you come after me? Why didn't you at least call me or take my calls?"

"God knows I wanted to."

"Then…?"

"Because, Beth, from the very start, I didn't see how it—how *we*—could possibly work. You had your career. I had mine to salvage. You had to deal with losing Max. I had to focus on Molly and all that was going on with her even before the abduction. You lived in Manhattan, and I lived in a swamp. I didn't see any of that changing."

"But all that has changed," she argued. "All those blockades you itemized are resolving themselves, or have already been resolved. I'm here, and I'm staying."

"One blockade won't change." He pointed to his forehead. "This dent? It's evidence of the difference in our ages."

"Oh, for crying out loud. Nine years! Just turned."

"Who told you?"

"Molly."

"Man! The lines of communication have been hot, haven't they?"

"The age difference is a ridiculous excuse, and you know it. What's the real reason?"

He'd struggled with it since he'd been sitting here. Hell, he'd struggled with it six months ago in this same spot, looking at this person, and wanting her in every way. "The real reason," he said roughly, "is because it would kill me to have you, and not be able to keep you."

"Well then, we don't have a problem." She slid out of the booth and got in on his side, crowding him into the corner. "I'm yours to keep, John. And I love that dent." She tilted his head down and kissed it.

He couldn't take any more. He wrapped his arms around her and buried his face in her neck. He said, "I want you, Beth. I want you so bad."

"You have me."

"No, I mean right now." The kiss they shared was ravenous, but only left them hungrier for each other. Breathless when they broke, he whisked his lips across hers. "Let's get out of here. Get out of our clothes. I want to French kiss you."

"You just did."

He nuzzled her ear, whispering, "Not everywhere."

She angled her head back and looked at him through smoky, topaz eyes, then scrambled out of the booth and retrieved her handbag from the other side.

On their way out, the bartender gave them a thumbs-up. "Y'all have fun."

"Count on it," John said over his shoulder. He walked her over to the only car on the lot except for his SUV. He gave her a quick kiss. "Follow me and keep up because I'll be driving fast."

When he would have turned away, she grabbed him

by his shirtfront. "Remember when you told me to watch myself? You didn't finish. Watch myself, or *what*?"

"Or I might come to love you body and soul."

"Oh. I didn't get to hear that part."

He wound a strand of her hair around his finger and pulled her face closer to his.

"And look what happened."